HARBINGER
OF JUSTICE

Book One
of
The Shadowbinders Trilogy

Andrew Watson

Harbinger of Justice
Book One of the Shadowbinders Trilogy
Copyright 2023 by Andrew Watson
First Edition: June 2023
ISBN: 978-1-7393400-0-1 (Hardback)
ISBN: 978-1-7393400-1-8 (Paperback)

Cover Design by Felix Ortiz
Map by Joshua Hoskins
Edited by Sarah Chorn

To Mum and Dad

For listening to me talk about made up people and places and nodding politely

nds

Gailion

Asuriya

Karbari

Yonfar

Celabar

Dock
Town

TARRIS

Prologue

5 years ago.

The man with the too-dark shadow staggered down the corridor, waiting for the voice in his head to speak again. Kyan was going mad, he was sure of it. He could feel insanity scratching at the walls of his mind.

He continued onward, scraping across the sandstone palace walls, ducking as he passed under glaring torches. Voices echoed from further ahead. Kyan turned down the corridor on his right.

You should have let me take care of them, Kyan, the voice whispered in his mind. Kyan flinched but otherwise ignored it.

He didn't want *it* to emerge again.

He picked up his pace, mustering himself to a jog. More shouting from behind but he didn't turn to see if the guards had spotted him. His footsteps cracked on the stone floor, his breath filling the quiet with an uneven whistling. His mind was an incoherent whirl making it impossible to remember if this was the right way out of the palace or not. Kyan slowed at an intersection to gather his bearings when three guards to his right shouted.

Probably telling you to stop, the voice said, amused.

I really am going insane, Kyan thought. He turned left, sprinting past the flames that lit the palace corridor. The palace was labyrinthine by design so that intruders wouldn't be able to find what they were after, or the way out. One of the others had a map on entering, but they were dead now, the map discarded somewhere in that Duat-forsaken place. The place through the rend in reality. The place with the ever-storming sky.

So Kyan had to escape the palace without the map. Alone. Well, almost alone.

A group of guards cut him off as he ran to an intersection, their swords pointed at his chest. Kyan glanced behind but saw more guards so he couldn't double back.

"Stop right there!" one of them called.

"Please, just let me pass. I don't want it to hurt you," Kyan said.

"Get on your knees. You can't run from us," the guard said, stepping forward.

Kyan dropped to the ground as the three approached from the front and more from behind.

"I wasn't running from you. I was running *for* you," Kyan

whispered, then his shifting shadow *lurched*.

Kyan closed his eyes. He didn't want to see it again, but he heard everything. Guttural gurgling and tearing echoed around him. It wasn't the sound of people fighting. It wasn't even the sound of people being slaughtered. It was too... instant. They didn't have a chance to scream or cry out.

Soon, only the low rumble of the flames in the braziers could be heard. Kyan thought about keeping his eyes forced shut forever, but eventually, he opened them to see the mess of blood and pieces of bodies all around. Kyan had killed before. Death wasn't new to him, but the sight turned his stomach. He wasn't sure how many guards *it* had killed.

There were seven. Four were behind us, the now-satiated sounding voice said.

Kyan put a hand on the blood-slickened sandstone, it squelched as he pushed to his feet. Stepping carefully through the... mess, to avoid the larger chunks, Kyan kicked into a half-hearted jog again. He felt sick.

How had it come to this?

Because they don't care about us, Kyan. You are a weapon for the Empress, nothing more. She probably didn't think any of you would return from this mission.

"That's not true." Kyan panted as he came to an outside pathway. Here, the left-hand wall opened up with a railing and arches framing the glowing city of Yontar against the night sky.

Kyan peered over the edge, he must have been a hundred floors up, the wind lashing at him as he leant out. It was a straight drop to the gardens below. Too high to jump.

Oh, but it's true. You know I'm right. Perhaps at one point, the Empress cared, but not anymore, the voice said. It was true she had become colder. She didn't come to see the Seven anymore. Not even to give orders, instead using Akarai to inform them of their missions.

Has she ever commanded you to protect the people? To help the people? No. It was always, attack them, take out this rebel group, fight off these people.

"Enough!" Kyan roared, white knuckles tightening around the railing.

"There!" a guard shouted.

Kyan broke into a sprint. He kept the outer wall on his left as he ran in search for a way to get to the lower levels. The night air was cool with the breeze brushing against him. A guard slid to a halt in front of him from a passage on his right, but Kyan jumped onto the railing before launching himself over the stunned guard. She came to her wits too late and reached for him just as he passed beyond her grasp. Breathing hard, Kyan landed and kept sprinting, noting a set of stairs at the next bend. If he could reach them, he could descend and get out of the palace.

The clatter of guards sounded behind him, padding paws and booted feet clashing with the low growl burbling in the throats of the pursuing palace beasts. Kyan had spent too long lost in the corridors of The Thousand Floor Palace. He had half the palaces guards and now the palace beasts on his tail. Even if he made it to the steps, they would be atop of him in no time, but he had to try.

He almost made it when a pudgy smiling blue face rose from the crest of the stairwell.

A korhin.

It stood at twice the size of Kyan, and about three times his girth. Its blue skin glowed in the torchlight as if wet. It stood on two short legs, with a thick gut for a torso, and a small head with plate-like, circular ears. Its legs were so short that its great belly touched the ground making it a rather slow creature. But it had the strength of ten men in its oversized fists.

Skidding to a stop, the korhin's fist came crashing down forcing Kyan to roll to the side. The korhin's second fist followed. Kyan's back knocked against the railing. He had nowhere to go. A quick glance showed that his assessment of those behind him was correct with eight guards and three palace beasts of varying species speeding towards him. This was it, then.

No, the voice whispered.

Kyan's shadow jerked upward and *caught* the incoming fist. It was transfixing to see his shadow become a tangible thing. The korhin grunted in confusion before screwing up its face and forcing down harder.

I cannot hold it, Kyan. You need to jump, the voice said straining.

The korhin growled, pushing.

Kyan. Now.

Kyan spared another glance for the oncoming pursuers,

before picking himself up, and diving over the railing into the black above the expanding city.

Wind whistled past him, but he still heard the crack of the korhin's fist when it hit the spot he had been not a moment ago. The city below was expanding as he hurtled towards it, and Kyan knew he would die soon, but he wasn't worried. He should be. He knew he should be because he was about to die. But he wasn't. This shadow was almost certainly affecting his thoughts. He felt that *it* wasn't worried and that he shouldn't be either.

His shadow slid from his body and formed something not quite solid. It spread into the shape of a glider, the likeness the Nuians to the north used; a main centre pole with wing like protrusions on either side that catch and glide on wind streams. Kyan had seen illustrations of their gliders and how they used them to ride the wind.

The ethereal black glider caught the wind and, with a jerk, Kyan's momentum slowed and he glided across the buildings below.

Yontar sat in a large stretch of desert. Its great walls holding back the black sands and creatures that roamed them. Architecture in Yontar was like that across Tarris; an assortment of building types and sizes with little concern for cohesion. Some buildings were short and squat, whereas others towered with pointed or domed rooftops.

Kyan wove through the streets falling to the height of the higher buildings, then lower, until he eventually dropped into an empty dead-end street. Breathing hard, he pressed his hands onto his knees.

"What are you?" Kyan whispered as he spun trying to find where the black blur went.

In the past, your kind called us shades, the voice replied.

"Shades?" Kyan repeated. He did not recognise the term.

Yes.

"How did you know to turn into a Nuian glider?" Kyan asked.

Come now, Kyan. I thought you were meant to be smart, it said.

Kyan knew the answer but it was unnerving. "Because I thought about it when I was falling."

Exactly. Now, come. We are still too close to the palace, it said.

"You can… read my thoughts?"

I can see what you are thinking of at that moment. Quickly, Kyan. We cannot stay here.

Kyan looked around. It was right. They were far enough that the palace guards weren't an immediate concern but after the scene he made…

"The others. I need to meet up with the others," Kyan said. He was certain at least two others had survived of the Seven.

Don't be foolish. What do you owe them? They didn't come back for you. They left you to die, the shade said.

Even now, after such a short time, his memory of the dark place was blurry with its storming sky and black rocky landscape.

Those bat-like creatures had grabbed Kyan pulling him back. He could still feel where the claws had ripped gashes in his side. Two of his comrades had watched. One reached for

Kyan but the other shouted, "He's gone!"

They both ran into the light, leaving Kyan to die.

"Where then? What do I do now?" Kyan said.

We do what they will not.

1

A Ruse of a Kind

People bustled through Market Street in the early morning glare. Merchants set up stalls on either side of the narrow street, a tan tarp taut above them, throwing the market into the cool of shade. A throng of people perused the goods, and the scent of spices hung thick in the air along with the clamour of bartering. Nya couldn't pick out the spices by name yet, but the aroma made her stomach grumble. Then again, it always grumbled. It had been a meagre scavenge the day before. But today. Today they would eat like kings.

It was early, some of the stands still being set up in front of homes and shops. Nya watched as Lani laid out the last of his goods. The older man's back was arched with age, and his short goatee was neat and groomed tidily. Lani was a wealthy man, evident by his name. Most in Tarris had three letter names, but as you went up the social hierarchy you gained extra letters and longer names. A four-letter name put Lani as one of the wealthier among the stands, and it said business was good.

That's why Nya picked him as the target. She knew some gangs stole indiscriminately, but the idea of stealing from those who had as little as she did always struck Nya as wrong.

But Lani? He would be fine if some of his stock went missing.

Nya sat atop a barrel at the mouth of an alley, nails digging into the coarse wooden rim. She counted two city guards. They were at the other end of the busy street strolling lazily with the crowd, but she knew they would push their way through if there was any trouble.

A cart trundled onto Market Street, its wheels crackling across the dusty road. It was time. Nya made the signal. Jut, the boy who stood on a corner further up the street, nodded and disappeared down a side street.

Two mercenaries stalked alongside the cart. They wore nothing on their upper body, revealing taut muscular physiques. Their baggy white trousers were tied with golden waist bands that swayed around their middle. A headscarf covered their face, revealing a deep set of hard eyes that held the stoic intensity of statues of war.

Irdu mercenaries. Private guards that cost some coin to hire.

People bowed their heads, stepping aside for the cart. For it to have a set of Irdu mercenaries showed a wealth uncommon in this part of Yontar. The cart was open top and Nya could make out the pinkish red colouring of fruit. *It must be a shipment from one of the orchards*, Nya realised. It was no wonder they could afford the mercenaries. In the desert maintaining an orchard was expensive, making most fruits extremely valuable.

A squeal cut through the din of the crowds as someone was pushed out from a dark alley. People scattered as a boy tripped, skidding into the street on their back and sending up a plume of dust and sand. The man driving the cart pulled hard on the reins, stopping just short of the fallen boy.

Then, from the alley, another boy tackled the first as he tried to sit up. Shouts broke out as the two city guards tore through the crowd and descended on the fighting kids.

The two Irdu mercenaries didn't move to intervene, but they walked to the front of the cart, hands on the curved blades sitting upon their hips.

Nya hesitated a moment. Von was really in character. Blood poured from Jut's nose as the city guard pulled Von off him. Nya shook her head and ran for the back of the cart.

Luk was standing at the back, lips drawn to a line. He had matted black hair, but unlike others on the street, he kept it carefully brushed. Nya was sure Luk would even call it styled, but it was still dirty with sweat and dust, so she wasn't sure *styled* was the right word. But it was a damn sight better than most she knew.

"Oh, lighten up. Everything is going to plan," Nya said, grinning. She jumped onto the back of the cart and started climbing.

"For now," Luk said.

Everyone was so focused on the fight that they didn't notice the two of them as they clambered up the back of the cart. They hung from the edge and Nya's eyes widened at the mass of apples. Nya's mouth watered as she took in the sweet scent. She had never tried an apple before. Apples were particularly rare in Tarris, as keeping an orchard watered was difficult and apple trees weren't as resilient as some of the other local fruit trees.

Luk pulled a sack from his trousers and held it open as Nya tossed apples into it. The fourth had just landed in the sack when Luk squealed. He jerked downward, but Nya grabbed him before he fell more than a few inches. Looking past his shoulder, she saw one of the mercenaries had come round the back and grabbed his ankle. The sack of apples toppled from the cart and landed at the mercenary's feet with a thud.

The shrouded Irdu man jumped to grab her too, but Nya hopped onto the cart still gripping her friend. The mercenary cursed as she pulled at Luk.

Luk whined under the strain, though Nya was sure it was more from fear than pain. She yanked Luk harder, but the Irdu had a firm grip.

"Kick your legs!" Nya shouted to Luk, who was now looking down and whimpering at the Irdu mercenary, as if to guilt trip him into letting go.

Luk shook his legs in an uncoordinated flail. The mercenary grunted as a swing brought Luk's foot down onto the mercenary's nose with a hard *snap*. The Irdu fell back, clutching his bleeding nose as Nya heaved Luk atop the cart beside her.

"Thank you," Luk whispered.

"Over here!" the mercenary shouted pushing himself to his feet.

Suddenly, all the attention fell on them. Onlookers; from the people buying, to the merchants running the stalls, all stared at her and Luk perched on top of the cart. Fingers jabbed in their direction, and some called for guards.

"We need to move, now," Nya said.

She slid a knife from her pocket and cut a hole into the tarp that covered the street. Then gestured Luk to climb through. He was smaller than her, and she wasn't sure the tarp would hold her weight. Luk grabbed two apples then, with a boost from Nya, clambered through the tear. It pulled under his weight, but he managed to inch over to the domed sandstone rooftop of the surrounding buildings.

A hand wrapped around the edge of the cart.

Nya snatched up two apples too before squeezing through the hole. The tarp creaked under her weight as she crawled towards the roof. The Great Sun Eye bore down on her now she wasn't shaded by the tarp. The heat stole her breath and gave her a moment of disorientation as she acclimatised to the sudden change. Nya shook it off and continued towards Luk, who sat on the roof waving her on.

The crowds were shouting, muffled to an incoherent din through the tarp, when a ripping sound tore through

13

the bustle below. Nya looked up at Luk wide eyed just as the tarp under her gave way. She lurched. Luk grabbed her outstretched hand, and Nya swung, hitting the building. Luk held tight, groaning as he hauled her up until Nya could grab the lip of the roof.

Screams could be heard from the street as the tarp fell onto the people below. Nya couldn't help but laugh.

"Thanks," Nya said.

Two shapes ripped through the tarp and spun until they spotted Nya and Luk. The Irdu mercenaries pointed their curved blades and ran for the alley beside the building they were on.

Luk sighed.

"Come on. It's been a while since we've had a good chase," Nya said. "It keeps you sharp." Nya grabbed Luk's leg and shook it. Luk brushed her off.

"Yeah, yeah," Luk said, standing.

They ran. Important streets like Market Street were rare in this part of Yontar, most were narrow and winding. So jumping between buildings wasn't difficult. However, the height difference between buildings was a different story. The height of a person's home or business was a sign of their power and wealth. This meant some stood as tall as six or seven floors, while their neighbours may only have two.

Ova's fiery Sun Eye beat down on them from a crystalline blue sky as they hopped from one roof to another. "We need to find a way down!" Nya shouted as they skidded onto the next roof. Luk nodded. They were exposed on the roofs, so getting back into the twisting streets was their best chance at losing the mercenaries.

They dropped onto a two-story home, from there onto a storefront, then into an alley. Luk leaned back against the wall, panting hard as Nya peered around to see if they were still being followed.

The street branching from theirs lay in the bright white wash of the Sun's gaze and was empty aside from a stumbling man in rags.

"I think we—" Nya started as the two mercenaries bundled around the corner. "Run!"

They bolted into the street and ran with all that their legs would give them. But Nya felt the burning seeping through her muscles and knew Luk would be to. They had to get rid of the mercenaries and soon.

"Throw the apples!"

Luk hesitated but as soon as Nya launched hers, one clipping the side of a mercenary's face, Luk joined in and tossed his. Only one of the four apples landed, but the mercenaries stopped chasing them to scoop up their prize. Nya and Luk continued winding down some streets, taking turns at random to throw off the mercenaries in case they decided to teach them a lesson. Eventually, they dropped down a short stairwell that led to a door. Breathing hard, they lay flat and watched the corner they came from.

After it was clear they weren't being followed, they glanced at each other and burst out laughing. They held their stomachs and rolled about the stairs until it hurt.

"How did you know they would stop chasing us if we threw the apples?" Luk finally managed wiping a tear from his eye.

"They stayed by the cart during the fighting. So I just hoped they cared more about the stock than us," Nya replied.

Luk rolled onto his back, facing upward. He was younger than Nya. She had never asked his age, but she thought he was about thirteen or fourteen. Nya couldn't help thinking of him as a younger brother. And family was everything to Nya.

She lay beside him. The steps weren't particularly comfortable, but she had slept on worse.

"Do you ever think we are doing the wrong thing?" Luk asked.

"What do you mean?" Nya asked.

"Stealing. Maybe we should get a job working for a merchant or something?"

Nya sat up and faced him. "Do you think someone would hire a bunch of street kids?"

"Maybe. I don't know," Luk said.

"Trust me, they wouldn't. And even if they did, they wouldn't give us enough money to live on anyway, so why bother?" Nya asked, eyes glazing over to see unpleasant memories.

"You're probably right," Luk said, sitting up. "And why would we find a job like that when we are so good at doing this?"

Nya smiled at him. They were good.

The apples were never the target. Jut and Von fighting

brought the city guards forward and kept them busy. Then Nya and Luk stealing the apples caught the attention of the street vendors, who watched, enthralled by the chaos of someone trying to steal from the Irdu mercenaries. That left time for the real target to be hit.

Der, Yui, and Fro snuck out and filled their sacks with as much of Lani's goods as they could carry and escaped before anyone even thought about turning around. The tarp falling was an accident but had certainly helped, Nya thought.

A good ploy to remember.

"Come on," Nya said pushing up from the steps. "We better make sure Von hasn't eaten the entire haul already."

Nya hopped over the crumbling wall surrounding the courtyard to the abandoned temple. It was a derelict skeleton of a building, with holes covering it as if it were sick with a wasting disease. The roof had collapsed and spewed debris across the temple floor. Little still stood in the temple.

However, right at the back of the one large chamber stood a statue of Is-Iakan, who took the shape of a bird with wings even larger than its body, which it wrapped around itself. It was a Nuian deity and rarely seen in Tarris, which was probably why the temple had been left to decay. Whoever had tended to this place of worship had probably died and so few left offerings for deities that the temple was abandoned.

The statue was the only thing that hadn't been looted or destroyed when the roof fell in, as if in testament to the deity watching over it.

Nya and Luk slid through one of the holes in the walls to find the rest of the Sand Rats already gathered around a bundle of food. Jut sat holding his bleeding nose but was wearing a toothy grin, Von sat cross-armed with a scrunched brow, and Der, Yui, and Fro, sat laughing and rummaging through the goods.

They had met a couple years ago in the sand-piled dark corners that most avoided.

Nya had lived on the streets with the Sand Rats for a while before she managed to wrangle a tiny storeroom attic for three hours' work each morning helping a spice merchant set up and deliver his goods, when her mother's condition worsened.

But she stuck with her friends. And being the oldest, they looked to her. So she made a crew. There were lots of crews and gangs in Yontar. Most were violent and cruel, but they weren't like the rest. They called themselves the Sand Rats. A group forged with the ferocity of desperation. Yontar tried to stomp them out, but they refused to yield, as yielding meant death. And not just Nya's death, but her friends and mother's too.

"That was some performance, Von," Nya called as they made their way over the uneven, rocky floor. He humphed and turned away.

"I told him his sister kisses well," Jut said, with the blood from his nose running over his yellowing teeth.

"Well, that's one way to make the fighting look real," Luk said with a shrug.

Nya curled up beside Von and gave him a squeeze. "Don't worry about it, Von. Jut would crap himself and run if your sister, or any girl, approached him," Nya said.

The rest of the group erupted into laughter, even Von's tight-knit brow loosened. All the while, Jut tried to voice an unheard defence.

Nya looked over the haul. It was a good one. Lani had a lot stocked today, from fruits and seeds, to spices and coffee. They would sell the spices and coffee to allow them to buy more food, but altogether it looked like it would last them at least a week if they rationed it. It was the most they had ever stolen in a day.

Relief eased some of the tension in Nya's back. She wore a brave face for the Sand Rats but when she had so many looking to her for food and safety the times between meals became a stress that built and built.

Nya jumped to her feet then hopped onto the edge of the statue of Is-Iakan, holding on by his planted stone spear. The chattering faded as all eyes landed on her.

"We did well today, Sand Rats," Nya said, waving over her people with a hunk of bread. "It's our finest score yet!" The group whooped with hands thrown into the air. "And it's only the first of many. From now on, we eat like kings!" Nya gestured broadly with a flourish and the Sand Rats cheered again.

Finally, I don't have to worry about feeding Mother, Nya thought, running her eyes over the mass of food they acquired, *at least for a little while.*

She dropped back down and they started chanting. It was a common song among the poor in Tarris. The tale of Tok. A boy who stole a kingdom from a king by using the blood of a God. It was Nya's favourite.

Even Von joined in, although he made sure to always be as far from Jut as he could be. Nya let herself smile. Revelry was rare and fleeting nowadays, like the wind bringing a cool sea breeze to the dry heat of the desert dunes. Nya closed her eyes savouring that breeze before it inevitably dwindled and faded to memory.

"Hey!"

A voice sliced through the song like a blade. The Sand Rats stopped and turned towards the noise.

Over where the far wall used to be, standing amidst the rubble, was Uri and his two thun-brained cronies. Nya's stomach dropped.

She couldn't even have one day. One desert-damned day.

"I heard there was an incident over at Market Street this morn'," Uri said, making his way into their temple, his bulk rolling with each step. A tuft of hair stuck out near the back of his head like the point of a sand fox's tail.

"Some members of Black Sands were seen nearby," Nya shouted. "Probably them." They placed the goods in a crater near the statue, so it was unlikely Uri had seen them yet.

Uri continued forward, the other two following. They were lowly members of The Ghrobans, which translated from the old tongue as "ones unchained". Most Ghrobans either didn't believe in the Judging after death, or didn't care if they were bound for an afterlife of torment. This meant they were free to kill and steal without a care for the tainting of their soul.

"It could have been... Yes, it could have been," Uri said, his fat cheeks pulling his lips into what he would consider a smile. "But I heard it was a bunch of little rats."

Uri stopped at the boundary of where the Sand Rats had managed to clear of rubble and debris. If Uri came any closer, he would be able to see into the crater where their haul lay.

"We wouldn't do something like that," Nya said. She knew she had to be careful. The Ghrobans would beat them for even insinuating they were wrong.

"Ah, but I think you would," Uri said and took another step. Instinctively, Nya backed towards the crater, but Uri noticed the move.

"And what might you be hiding behind you?" Uri asked, lumbering into the middle of their temple. His eyes widened while his lips loosed like the slow unfurling of a dead man's fingers, drawing to a line.

"Grab them."

2

Across the Sands

Rai didn't like many things, but the Artonian ale the dock inn stocked was a treasure. He didn't often come to the docks on jobs anymore, so he always made sure to arrive early and wait at the inn.

The Sun Boat Inn was one of the more decrepit establishments, with peeling yellow paint on shutters that hung askew, sand covering the floor, and splintering wooden tabletops. Like most of the establishments along the docks, it was a large, open room, allowing the sea breeze to whistle through the open windows filling the inn with a briny scent.

It was different from the inns back in Celabar, with their segmented areas and booths. Tables were haphazardly laid out across the floor, with squat stools surrounding them. The bar was along the far wall, opposite the entrance, with an array of unlabelled bottles stacked on a carved mud brick shelf that didn't match the rest of the interior. Rai sat at the counter, tan cloak draped over the back of the only stool he trusted to take a person's weight.

But for all The Sun Boat Inn lacked in ornamentation, it made up for with Artonian ale. And that was all Rai cared about. That and it was quiet, with no one else at the bar. However, from the sounds of the floorboard creaks, and the amount of food the bartender had ready to be made, Rai guessed three guests were staying upstairs. Still, the quiet was lingering and was only scratched at by the scuffling above. Quiet had begun to mean a lot to Rai over the last few years. In the unrelenting places of the world, stillness was an undervalued commodity.

Rai let out a satisfied sigh as he placed the empty tankard on the counter. The bartender stepped over and refilled it without saying a word. He knew Rai well enough by now. Three mugs, no more, no less.

"Who you escorting up this time?" the gangly man asked.

"Some merchants," Rai responded. The bartender grunted, then went back to arranging bottles behind the bar. That was another reason Rai liked this place. The bartender knew when to shut up. A rare skill nowadays.

That was a dig at me wasn't it? Fax said in his mind. Rai ignored it.

The constant background shouting sounded from the docks outside, blasting over the calming swish of the ocean, and creak of boats. An ordered chaos that was easy to predict and track.

I like it here, Fax said. Rai scoffed. *What?*

"I thought you'd prefer darkened alleyways or black caves," Rai whispered so the barkeep wouldn't hear.

Ha ha, Fax said in mock laughter.

The door to the inn swung open, then back at whoever had pushed it with a *thud*. Doors in Tarris were on weighted hinges, ensuring they closed after people passed through to minimise the amount of sand that blew in from outside. Foreigners often found how quickly they swung shut baffling.

I think that's for you, Fax said, but Rai didn't spin around. The door opened again, slower this time, then timid footsteps lead to Rai.

"Rai is it?" the merchant said in a nasally voice. Rai turned to see a short man holding his nose, a trickle of blood reaching his lip.

The merchants Tarrisian was pretty good. He was over-emphasizing some sounds, but not bad for a foreigner.

"Yeah, that's me," Rai said.

The man cowered back a little upon Rai facing him. He had that effect on people when they first met him. Something had been off about Rai since that night. The night he travelled to the dark realm and returned as two. It took Rai many years to realise what. His shadow was darker. Which made sense, as it was holding a snarky shade named Fax. Not only was his trailing shadow darker but every shadow he cast was too, including the smaller nooks around his nose. These darker edges made him look sharper, more threatening. People who met him may not notice what it was that made him look more fearsome, but they knew *something* was off.

Rai patted the stool beside him. The merchant warily sat, nursing his cracked nose. The barkeep flipped another glass from beneath the bar for the merchant.

"Much appreciated," the merchant said, inspecting the ale in his mug.

"So, what's your name?" Rai said after a long swig.

"Grenin," he replied, taking a sip, then trying to mask his disgust. He placed the mug back on the bar.

"Do you have your stock disembarked and ready to go? It's a three-day trip to Celabar. And I'd like to set off as soon as possible," Rai said.

"Yes, it's all with my wife outside," Grenin said.

"Great," Rai said, then downed the rest of his drink and slid three coins over the bar before walking for the exit. The bartender nodded without looking up. Grenin stood to follow.

"Hey!" the barkeep shouted and gestured to his barely touched ale.

"Ah, of course, sorry, yes," Grenin said and pushed another coin across the bar, then ran to catch up with Rai.

Stepping outside, the oppressive heat of the Tarris midday Sun hit Rai like a physical force. The air became thick, and breathing felt as if he were inhaling a fume cloud, despite the clear sky above. Rai looked up at Ova's fiery Sun Eye that stole any semblance of anything cool. This is why he preferred to nap during the afternoon, he thought, shaking off the heat.

The inn fed out onto a long thoroughfare where merchant

shops, cafes, and inns, such as The Sun Boat Inn were cut into the cliff face. Dock Town had started as just this strip of buildings cut into the cliff but slowly grew and now most of the town sat atop the cliff and sprawled out further into the desert with every passing year.

Sailors and ship hands scurried up jetties and onto the thoroughfare laden with crates joining the flow of the crowds. Gulls flew overhead cawing endlessly and diving at any unattended goods.

Rai immediately felt eyes on him. It wasn't common for merchants to come to Tarris and do trade in person. Most trade was done here, at Dock Town, and the local merchants brought the goods further into Tarris. Being a foreigner and hiring an expensive escort like Rai was akin to walking through town jangling a coin purse. The faster they got onto the open dunes the better.

"Is that your wife?" Rai asked, somewhat rhetorically, given she was the only other foreigner on the docks.

"Yes, Larina," Grenin said. They pushed through the throng, to where his wife stood watching all the dock workers speed past. Behind her, six crates were piled high, all tightly sealed. At least they weren't stupid enough to leave them open as some previous clients of his had.

"Stand beside your crates and do not take your eyes off them. I'll go rent us an aya," Rai said, bowing to Larina.

"Aya?" Grenin asked.

"Did you think we were going to walk to Celabar with the crates on our backs?" Rai asked. Grenin and Larina shared a nervous laughter, assuming he was making a joke as Rai walked off.

They're attracting a lot of attention, Fax said.

"I know," Rai said, pointedly keeping his eyes forward despite feeling so many on him.

Rai made his way through the crowd where workers ran about with crates, some on their way to stalls along the thoroughfare, where loud salesmen shouted their wares. Others were loaded onto carts to be pulled up to Dock Town and then beyond. Rai preferred his quiet inn. Out here, everyone was shouting to the point little was distinguishable. And the *smell*. The stink of unwashed sailors and fish buried itself up Rai's nose. He let out a quivered exhale.

That bad, huh? Probably because it's a little hotter today. Makes me glad to not have a nose, Fax said.

Rai came off the thoroughfare and onto the dusty path leading to Dock Town, which was lined with yet-more stalls.

He didn't have to walk far to find Twin Dari, the aya trader Rai frequented. He currently had three aya with him, all strong and sturdy. The huge, tranquil creatures stood at about three meters tall and seven long. They had thick, tan fur drooping over their eyes, which were small black beads sitting atop a nose the size of Rai's head. Their broad mouths could fit several people inside. But thanks to their size and docile nature, Tarrisians used them as transport for people and cargo across the large stretches of desert in Tarris.

Rai leaned in and scratched one of Twin Dari's many cats around the chin. It didn't open its eyes but let out a soft purr.

"Ah, Rai the mercenary. It has been sometime since you have made the trek to Dock Town," Twin Dari said, coming out from behind his stand. He was bald with a patch of hair on his chin, clothed in a long, dark robe.

"It's a special case," Rai said, leaving the cat to sleep.

"Yes, I've heard. Your clients are the talk of Dock Town," Twin Dari said with a knowing smile that didn't reach his eyes.

Great. If Twin Dari was noting his clients, then everyone in Dock Town knew of them. He was hoping to move quickly and not garner too much attention.

"I need an aya," Rai said.

"Take your pick. These three are fresh and in their prime," Twin Dari said, leading Rai over to the aya. Two were drinking from an unclean trough, while the other napped in the shade of the overbearing cliff.

Over drinking was a sign of illness in aya and although he trusted Twin Dari, Rai didn't want to be stranded in a desert village with his clients. It was likely that the two aya drinking were healthy like Twin Dari said, but why risk it?

"That one," Rai said, pointing to the napping aya.

"Very well, twenty derans. A reduced rate for a loyal customer, of course," Twin Dari said. Rai dug into his belt pouch, bristling at what the twin must charge those he wasn't acquainted with.

Rai payed for the aya and gestured back to where their cargo was. Twin Dari clapped twice and six children burst from nowhere and darted back towards the docks, aya in tow.

Rai set off after them, bowing thanks to Twin Dari.

The workers jumped into action, setting up a wooden platform atop the aya's back. Using a rope mechanism, they then loaded the merchant's boxes onto the platform. The workers moved with incredible efficiency as they clambered up the aya, clutching its fur, throwing rope and boxes to one another. Their work never ceased to amaze Rai.

"Wait, excuse me, that is—" Grenin said, trying to stop the children throwing his crates.

"It's okay. They are loading it onto the aya," Rai said as he approached.

"That thing is incredible," Larina said, watching the creature. The aya moved with a slow sureness, unperturbed by Twin Dari's workers bustling around it.

"An aya you say?" Grenin asked, watching as workers clambered onto the fixed platform and stacked the boxes in the centre.

"Yes. Not the fastest way to Celabar, but they are steady and strong, and will get us there in relative comfort," Rai said.

Larina ran a hand through the thick fur on the aya's leg. Aya always had thicker fur around their legs. "Is it yours?" she asked.

"No. Aya are far too expensive to keep and feed so we rent them," Rai responded.

"What do they eat?" Grenin asked.

Rai pointed to some extra boxes the workers were placing on the platform on the aya's back. "A lot of meat, but we will try to find places with some wildlife to stop and let it hunt,"

Rai said.

After they set the last of the cargo upon the aya's back, the workers all lined up, bowed, and then sped off back to Twin Dari.

"Looks like we're ready to head off," Rai said, walking to the ladders hanging from the platform. He gestured for Grenin to climb up. The man grimaced but reached for the ladder.

Dock Town sank in the heat wave of the horizon and the ever-expanding sands. Rai sat at the front of the platform on the aya, feet kicked up, and looking out over the dunes. Grenin and Larina sat beside their stock playing some card game Rai didn't recognise.

"Ha! You couldn't bluff your way out of a river sweep!" Larina shouted, slamming down her cards. Grenin sighed and slumped back.

"Care for a game Rai?" he asked, waving the cards. "You can't do any worse than me."

Rai didn't look up. Grenin waited for a breath before mumbling something and then shuffled the cards again.

You can be an aya's stool sometimes, you know that? Fax said.

"I'm here to keep them alive and heading in the right direction. Not to keep them entertained," Rai whispered, using a dagger to dig out some dirt from under his nails. The Great Sun Eye was still high in the sky, so Rai had set up the tarp to shield them from the heat.

"Hey Rai. How do you know we are going the right way?"

Larina called.

"The aya knows the way. I just need to direct it when we get to a crossroads," Rai replied.

"Ooo! What a clever boy," Larina said, patting the platform beside her.

Do not correct her, Rai. It doesn't matter. Just leave it, Fax said.

"It's female," Rai said.

"Oh! What a clever girl," Larina said, patting the platform again.

Fax sighed.

The sands darkened with the sky, a phenomenon that only happened in Tarris. By the time the World Turner was watching over them with its crystalline Moon Eye, the sand would be black and will have hardened to an almost rock like solidity. Rai could already feel it hardening by the aya's gait. It would be the dark hour soon. The hour when the Sun Eye would pass out of sight and throw the world into an hour of only residual light before the Moon Eye would crest and light the world anew.

They will attack soon. You should warn them, Fax said.

"No, I don't want to scare them. I'll deal with their whimpering when I have to," Rai whispered, staring over the blackening landscape. Ahead, cliffs appeared on either side, a curving path snaking between them. *That's where they will do it,* Rai thought, his hands tightening around the aya's reins.

Wind caught between the cliffs rustled through them as they rode. Grenin and Larina fell silent, wrapped in the eerie twilight that had an other-worldly effect when out in the desert.

Creatures scuttled and darted into crevices in the rock. The pathway wound between the cliffs had enough space for three aya to walk side by side, but there was an unsettling closeness that contrasted the open sweeping sand dunes they had travelled on so far. Rai could see the tension in his clients.

They approached a crossroads. Another pathway converged onto theirs from the right and ahead, he could see the end of the rock formation.

Sand trickled down the cliff face. Glancing up, Rai saw nothing but the open sky between the cracked cliffs above. "Stay close to the boxes in the middle," Rai said.

Grenin jerked his head towards Rai. "What? Why?"

Rai lifted a finger to his lips. Grenin shared a glance with Larina before they cuddled up against the crates in the middle of the platform.

A feral scream shattered the quiet and Rai whipped the reins, launching the aya into a sprint, sending crates tumbling, and Grenin and Larina careening across the platform. Aya weren't particularly fast over long distances but could manage short sprints.

Thud. Someone landed on their platform.

Rai dropped the reins to duck under a dagger. He came up and punched the bandit in the face, knocking him over the edge of the aya. Another bandit clambered over the lip of the platform, having climbed up using the poor beast's fur. Rai unsheathed his daggers and bent in a relaxed fighting pose.

Grenin screamed nearby.

The bandit stood, pulling out her dagger and surveyed the platform. She was a tall woman, her hair tucked into a head wrap. The bandit snorted and nodded to herself clearly pleased they had only one guard aboard, a sinister grin lining her face.

"If we slit their throats and toss them out, no one will find them. We will even let you keep one crate. Whatever it is will be worth more than they are paying you, I'm sure," she said. Grenin squealed louder now, watching Rai.

He's a noisy one, eh? Fax said.

Rai surged forward, daggers first, unleashing a flurry of blows. She must have assumed he would take her bargain as her eyes flared in surprise, but her reflexes were fast and she deflected most of the attack, only taking a nick on her arm. She growled before kicking Rai in the chest. He fell back with a splutter but stayed on his feet.

The air cascaded around them as the aya continued its headlong sprint for the opening in the cliffs. Rai feinted, launching another attack with a now-unsheathed second dagger. The bandit took the bait, knocking the first swing wide only to be sliced across the leg. She roared in pain and threw that anger into a driving stab, which embedded her blade in Rai's shoulder. He hissed, pulling back, but she drove forward throwing a punch that cracked his jaw. Falling to the deck, Rai dodged several more strikes.

With another kick back, Rai's back hit the edge of the platform. The bandit smirked.

Rai... Let me help, Fax said.

"No, I got this," Rai said.

She brought her other dagger up, ready to plunge down, as Rai flicked his own into a defensive position, his shoulder screaming.

Ping. The female bandit stopped to watch as something fluttered in the wind after hitting the side of her face. They both turned to see Larina standing with a deck of cards in her hands and a snarl on her face.

I like her, Fax said.

Rai rolled back and launched himself, using the edge of the platform as leverage, right into the female bandit. She brought her arms up as Rai kicked her back. She tripped, slipping on the platform and fell screaming to the black sand below.

"We did it!" Grenin said, punching the air.

"Not yet we haven't," Rai said, gesturing back to where another aya was gaining on them.

Rai flicked the rein and their aya sped up. They burst from the pathway between the cliffs and back onto open sands. The heavy tromped footfalls shook the platform, sending the crates scattering across the platform. "Tie them down!" Rai shouted and Grenin and Larina jumped into action, collecting the boxes back together, and tying them down with some spare rope.

The other aya was gaining. *It must be fresh*, Rai thought. Their aya had been walking all day, whereas the bandits must have been camped in this area waiting for a signal from those who were watching in Dock Town.

Rai eased out the dagger in his shoulder with a hiss. Larina ran over. "Do you need help with that?"

"No, I'm okay," Rai strained to say.

Grenin appeared with bandages and a bottle of whiskey. "Here," he said, passing them to his wife. "Let her help. She helps patch people up where we are from."

Rai grimaced but nodded. "Be quick. They will reach us soon."

Larina wasted no time. She tore off the top of the whiskey and flicked a generous amount onto the wound. Rai let out a little grunt. "Oh quiet. It isn't that bad," Larina said, then handed him the bottle to drink from. She wrapped the bandage under his arm and around his shoulder until the top layer didn't have blood leaking through it. "There, as good as new," she said, standing back to appreciate her handy work.

"They're here!" Grenin shouted from further down the platform.

Rai rolled his shoulder, then pushed himself to his feet. His cloak flared behind him in the gusting winds of the aya's sprint. The bandit's aya came up from behind and the first of the mauraders jumped for their aya, grabbing its fur and climbing up as the landscape flew by around them in a blur.

"Stay by the crates," Rai said, as he cracked his neck and broke into a run.

3

A Gods Wrath

Uri's cronies lurched forward and the Sand Rats scattered. Nya launched from the rock she had perched on as one grabbed for her. She ran to the stolen stock, bundling it back into the sacks. The others were running circles around the cronies, who, despite their threateningly large frames and brutish faces, couldn't keep up with her younger, more agile crew.

A guttural growl from behind. Uri stood at the edge of the pit. He barrelled towards her. Scooping up the bag, Nya jumped onto the statue. She shimmied around the edge and clambered up the statue's wings. Uri leapt, fingers scraping against rock as Nya hauled herself upward. If she could just climb up the side of the statue, there was a hole near the roof that they wouldn't be able to follow her through.

"Stop or the rat gets it!" Uri shouted.

Nya pulled her eyes away from her escape. One of Uri's nameless friends had a hold of Jut. Nya hesitated. It was the biggest haul they ever pulled. Would they hurt him if she tossed it up through the hole?

"Give us the bag and you rats will still be able to pull a breath between your crooked teeth come dark hour," Uri snarled.

The rest of the Sand Rats were spread out around the temple, cowering behind piles of fallen rock. They weren't fighters, Nya knew. If this came to a fistfight, they would lose more than their score. Handing it over was the right choice. The only choice.

But this wasn't just Nya's food, it was her crew's and her mother's. And Uri wanted to tear that away from them.

Nya met Uri's gaze with a cold glare. Ragged breaths reverberated around the temple. Jut pushed back against the man holding him, but the Ghroban's arms were thick and unmoving.

With an exhale, Nya leaned against the wall and pushed, forcing her weight into the statue of the Nuian deity. It groaned, and for a second, she was worried it wouldn't give, but then she heard a *crack*.

It happened so fast after that. The statue toppled where Uri was standing. He dove out of the way, but not fast enough. Granite fell, crushing his right foot mid-dive. Fragments of the statue and dust flew in all directions, as Uri let out a scream.

They all watched in horror before breaking into action.

The brute holding Jut forced him face-first against the wall of the temple and Jut crumpled to the ground like a ragdoll.

One of the Ghrobans ran to Uri's side and the other stalked towards her, but Nya couldn't take her eyes off Jut until finally, he stirred. Nya let out a breath of relief as Der and Fro ran to his aid.

"Hey! Who's in there?" a voice called from outside. Guards. They must have heard the commotion and came to investigate.

The brute approaching Nya spun and, after deliberating, ran to help Uri instead.

"Nya! Guards! Come on, we need to go," Luk said, dragging her off.

The Sand Rats scuttled through the many holes in the building. Nya caught a glimpse of Der and Fro ushering Jut along before she followed Luk and slid through a hole, sprinting down the nearest alley. The shouting dimmed as they wove through the sand covered streets.

It was only early afternoon when they arrived outside the spice shop where Nya lived, but suddenly she was exhausted. The street was quiet. Most still taking their midday qed, a nap to sleep off the worst of the sun. Few worked under the fiery gaze of the Sun Eye at its strongest.

The spice shop was a three-story block building with a wooden structure holding up a tarp before the entrance where the owner would set up his stall. He had long taken his goods indoors, so Nya and Luk ducked into the shade.

"Those Duat damned Ghrobans!" Luk kicked up sand

and dust. Nya flinched at the curse. Duat was the name for the torment realms in the afterlife and people didn't throw around the phrase lightly.

"Jut…" Nya said.

"He's okay, I think. He had his eyes open when Der and Fro helped him away," Luk said, running a hand through his hair. "What do we do now?"

Nya looked at Luk. He was expecting her to come up with the answer. She couldn't lock up now. They needed her.

Nya let out a shaky sigh. "We lay low. Uri will be looking for revenge and we don't know if the guards had come because they saw us get away with the food or if they heard the statue falling," Nya said. Luk nodded, pacing.

"We meet up in a four days at the Bell Tower," Nya continued. "Not before. And only steal what you need to survive."

A set of guards passed around the corner. Nya and Luk leaned further back into the shadows, but the guards passed without a glance in their direction. They were chatting and on patrol, not searching for anyone.

"Four days. Bell Tower," Nya whispered after they turned a corner.

Luk nodded again and said, "I'll let the others know," before running off into the oppressive heat. Nya let her shoulders slouch as he passed out of sight and took a moment to collect herself.

The spice shop was closed, and the door locked. So Nya trudged to the side of the building and clambered up onto the window ledge, then to the second-floor window, heaving herself up and inside. She always left the window open so she could come and go whenever she wanted. The merchant still didn't trust her with a key, so it was this or be locked in for midday qed.

Planks creaked as she landed in the hallway. Nya crept down the corridor, past several doors, to the ladder at the back. Half in a daze, she climbed the ladder into their attic, shutting the hatch behind her. Two thin windows on either side lit the dust motes floating around the small, unfurnished room. Mother lay curled in a bundle of blankets under the far window, unmoving.

She won't have eaten today, Nya realised, then looked at her empty hands. An icy shiver worked its way up her spine. She must have dropped the bag when they ran from the temple. She gritted her teeth as silent tears ran down her cheeks. Nya cried as quietly as she could to not wake Mother. It came out in strangled grunts and gasps as the swell of emotion she had held in check for the Sand Rats hit her. The walls she built crumbling to dust in an instant.

In the end, it was for nothing. Nothing at all.

Wait.

When Nya had given her speech in the temple, she had waved a piece of bread about. She was sure she… yes. Nya ran her hands over her tunic until she felt a bump, then dug into her pocket. Tucked away was a piece of bread just larger than her palm.

Nya crawled over and laid it in front of Mother.

"Mother? Mother, you need to eat," Nya said, prodding her.

Her mother stirred, and her eyes fluttered open. She looked around as if unable to focus until she landed on the bread.

"Werin, is that you?" Mother croaked. She often mistook Nya for her father, who had left them before she was born. "You came back."

"It's me, Mother. Nya." Nya pat down a tangle of her mother's hair.

Mother's faced soured and she let out a groan, before reaching with a shaking hand for the bread.

Mother wasn't lucid much anymore. More often, she was in a state of semi-awareness.

Nya dragged herself to the other side of her mother and collapsed onto the blanket beside her. Her stomach ached, her eyes stung from the crying, and the weight of losing the food that would have fed her friends and Mother was the only thing that sat in her empty gut. But, as she drifted to sleep, Nya took some respite from the crackling her mother made as she ate the hard bread.

When Nya awoke it was dark out; the silvery gaze of the Moon Eye doing little to light the attic. Nya was lying on her side with something furry curled against her chest.

Dust.

Dust was a sand fox that her pack had abandoned. She had been left, too weak to move or search for food. So, upon finding her, Nya brought her to the attic and fed her until

41

she was strong enough to look after herself again. However, despite that, Dust always returned to the attic to spend time with Nya.

Nya ran her hands through Dust's fur. She was about the size of Nya's forearm with a long yellow and white brush-like tail. Dust's yellowy golden fur was soft, and her body heat had warmed Nya in the cool nights since helping the sand fox.

A sudden wave of nausea passed through Nya. She thought she might throw up if she had anything *to* throw up. Sweat beading her brow despite the cool.

Dust's beady red eyes glinted in the moonlight.

"It's okay," Nya whispered, although she wasn't sure if it was directed at Dust or herself. "It's all going to be okay."

Dust buried herself against Nya's neck and together they fell back into a restless sleep.

The next few days passed like the sand winds, abrasive but brisk. Nya did her morning tasks and then, in an effort to lay low, stole the bare minimum to survive, spending the rest of her time in the attic with Mother and Dust. The sand fox had picked up on the change in routine, and stopped by more regularly, as if to comfort her, staying with Mother when Nya went out to steal food in the morning.

The clamour of the morning market rung endlessly and the stink of meat roasting in the Sun filled the air. Nya slid another roll into her pocket as she passed the same stand again. That was two rolls now. With that, she veered into another street and hastened away from the vendor. In the distance, the bell tower rose above the buildings around her like a pillar holding aloft the sky.

The bell would ring out in warning if war was ever to come to Yontar. And while war was unlikely, the unrest in the city and threat of rioting was ever present. The rise in prices and taxes had already brought about protest. Nya didn't know much about the politics but saw the effects on the streets. Guards were quicker to beat anyone who stepped out of line. Gangs were at each other's throats making the dark hours too dangerous to be out in. And things were only getting worse.

Nya stared longingly at the tower. They were to meet at there in two days. How she missed her friends, but gathering would only make it more likely for Uri to find them.

She pressed on through the street and back to the spice merchant's shop. The less time spent outside would mean less chance of being spotted. Climbing up the rungs to their attic, she heard Mother muttering to herself.

She was sitting and adjusting the blanket across her legs, despite the heat. Her hair was a jumble of intertwined curls and knots. She had light brown hair, whereas Nya's was dark brown, almost black. And no matter how often Nya untangled her mother's hair, mothers tossing and turning would always entwine it again.

"Mother, is everything okay?" Nya asked.

Her eyes darted to Nya. *Seeing* her. "You little rat, running off in the morning when you should be here helping your Mother with the sewing." She wove her hands through the motions, catching the blanket, then letting it drop again. She had once been a seamstress. But that was long before the illness took a firm hold.

"Of course. I'm sorry Mother," Nya said. Nya bent down beside her and pulled out the roll. "I brought you something to eat."

"You think yourself some noble handing out to the poor when I'm the one working to keep us fed and sheltered!" Her mother snapped, but as soon as Mother saw the bread, her expression softened. She snatched it and crammed it in her mouth.

"You know, if it weren't for you, we would be eating like kings right now," Mother said between bites.

Nya sat beside her and ate her own roll. "I know, Mother. I'm sorry."

With her daughter put in her place, and food in her stomach, Mother seemed quelled for now. She stared off as her eyes glazed, seeing times past and promises unmet. "We could have lived in the palace," Mother said reverently. "You stole our happy life. Our life of luxury and security." With each word her voice became softer, lucidity fading as quickly as it came.

Nya leant back against the wall as Mother fell silent. She was right. Nya could never give Mother what she had stolen: a life without the constant pain in her gut, without the fear of whether they would be thrown out onto the street. A life without the regular beatings from guards who caught her trying to find food.

A life where Mother could get better.

This was Nya's punishment. Her own Duat. How she longed to lie down and go to sleep, and never wake up again. But what would happen to Mother? To the Sand Rats?

Some days a voice said, *To Duat with the lot of them*. That was insidious. A voice brought by the dark nights that she knew, if she could just hold out, would eventually pass. But the voice was a sandstorm eroding more and more every time it passed. But it did always pass.

Even if it was slowly hollowing her out.

Nya came to. She had been daydreaming again. Mother had fallen asleep beside her and the sky was darkening. At some point Dust had curled up on her lap. Nya smiled petting sand fox, who let out a gurgling purr.

I should get to sleep, Nya thought, yawning. How can doing so little make one so tired?

She lifted Dust, placing her carefully onto the blanket between her and Mother, then pulled back the blanket and slid under, already closing her eyes. Sleep came swiftly.

4

The Waypoint

With a roar, Rai tackled the closest bandit to climb onto their platform. They skidded back as Rai landed blow after blow across the bandit's face with the butt of his blade. His head rocked, and eyes rolled. *Another coming from behind*, Fax said as Rai threw the man off the aya.

Rai turned as hot pain seared across his back in an arc. He let out a yelp, swinging his dagger around wildly. This forced the second bandit back, as Rai got into a fighting stance. Dark hour had sucked most of the light away, throwing darkness over the platform, allowing Rai to only see some details of the bandit in the dwindling light.

Rai lunged, weaving his blades like snakes. The bandit frantically deflected what he could but he was on the back foot. They battled back and forth, trading blows, evenly matched in speed. But this meant Rai was going to lose. If he spent too much time fighting one of the bandits, the rest could steal the cargo and kill his clients.

A squeal sounded from the crates. A bridge cracked against their platform connecting the other aya to theirs. And two bandits were stalking towards his cowering clients. Well, Grenin was cowering. Larina looked like she might launch herself at them if they got any closer, but that wouldn't end well either.

The bandit thrust at Rai in his moment of distraction, but Fax warned him in time to step to the side. Overextending, the bandit left herself open. Rai buried his left dagger into the bandit's guts, while the right knocked the bandit's arm away, then in the same motion Rai flicked the blade across the platform and into the marauder reaching for Larina. A gargled intake of breath came from the bandit as Rai kicked her off the side of the aya.

Rai spun to see the dagger he threw sticking out of the toppled bandit's neck. *Nice shot,* Fax said.

The remaining bandit shouted to his crew and the two more crossed the bridge, leaving only one more on their aya.

Four left. You sure you don't want help? Fax asked.

"The last thing we need is these two talking about how their escort had a shadow that fought with him," Rai said.

Suit yourself.

The three bandits charged.

If they were of similar skill to the one he just killed, he had no chance fighting all three at once. *I'll need to break them up*, Rai thought and let out a sigh. He was not getting paid enough for this.

Rai ran and dove off the side of the aya, grabbing the wooden bridge the bandits set up between the two aya. Wind buffeted him as he pulled himself up onto the bridge that jittered with the momentum of the charging aya.

The bandits shouted something, but the wind smothered their words. A war cry erupted from the dark, announcing the charge of the bandit they left to guard their aya. Rai ducked under the swing and parried the second attack with his bracer. *This would be a lot easier with my second dagger*, Rai thought, thinking about how he left it in that bandit's neck. He pushed back with his bracer causing the man to stumble.

We are far enough away. Let me help! Fax offered.

Okay, fine, Rai thought, glancing over his shoulder. He couldn't make out their aya, but the sound of clacking wood from the bridge behind him indicated the other bandits were coming back across.

Fax shot out of Rai's shadow as a massive greatsword sized blade and tore through the bandit's chest. The bandit looked down in shock before his eyes rolled back and he collapsed onto the deck.

See, it's easy. What's all this tiring back-and-forth nonsense you do for? Fax said.

Two of the three bandits ran at him from the bridge. Rai parried a swish of silver, then kicked the first bandit into the second. As they tripped back, Rai ran to the bridge and cut the ropes tying it down, letting it fall away into the dark. Rai then sawed through the thicker ropes holding the bandits platform atop their aya. With a satisfying *thwack*, the taut ropes snapped and the entire platform lurched from beneath Rai. The bandits shouted as the platform shook uncontrollably.

A captain should always go down with their ship, Fax said.

Rai threw himself across the widening gap between the aya as more ropes broke and tossed the platform, and the two bandits into the haze of movement around them.

Rai's eyes watered as he flew through the air, hoping he was falling in the right direction. He hit the side of their aya, relief flooding him as he gripped its thick fur. Rai hated clinging and pulling at the aya's hair, no matter how many times people reassured him it didn't hurt them. It had to be uncomfortable for the beast.

Dry, rough fingers felt the edge of the platform. He began to yank himself up when the last bandit appeared over him. Even in the darkness Rai could feel the grin on the bandit's face. The bandit pressed his boot on Rai's hand. Rai screamed, more in frustration than pain. The bandit bore down with more pressure.

Fax snapped out of his shadow in the shape of a crow, its favourite shape when taking form, and dug black ethereal claws into the bandit's face. The last bandit squealed in pain, grabbing at his face and staggered over the edge in front of Rai.

The falling bandit knocked Rai's grip, and they both fell toward the black sands.

Rai's breath caught as claws wrapped around his bracer

and Fax lifted him upward above their platform.

Fax released its grip, and Rai dropped with a thunk onto the deck.

Grenin and Larina sat, mouths agape, but alive.

"You... you are like a hero from legend," Grenin said.

Fax shot back into his shadow and started babbling excitedly, *Wait, wait! This is your chance! Say something cool like they do in the stories,* Fax put on its best gruff hero voice, *Something like, I turned from the hero path long ago. I just do what I can.*

"Shut up Fax," Rai said, falling onto his back and letting out a pained breath.

Ova's Great Moon Eye finally broke the horizon, bathing the black sands in a silvery light. They had brought the aya back to a trot as Larina patched up the fresh cuts Rai had acquired, a lot of which he hadn't noticed. They passed a Waypoint, but there were no complaints when Rai suggested they keep going to create some distance between them and where they had been attacked.

Inhaling, Rai felt the tug of skin around his wounds. "Damn, that hurts," Rai said.

"Stop breathing so hard then," Larina said, lathering a green salve that left a burning sensation on his cuts.

Grenin came and slumped beside them after checking over their cargo. "Everything seems to be in one piece." He sat and tapped on the platform like an impatient child.

"Just ask." Rai sighed.

Grenin slithered over and crossed his legs. Even Larina sat back, awaiting answers.

"So… How did you do it?" Grenin asked.

"I'm a trained mercenary," Rai said.

"But the shadow that lifted you up?" Grenin pressed.

Rai looked over the sand dunes. It was so quiet out here. "It's a rare Tarrisian creature. A type of blackbird, but it moves so fast, people sometimes claim to be able to see right through it," Rai said, as if telling a great secret.

There's no way they're going to believe that, Fax said. Grenin and Larina both gazed around at the sky, searching out this impossible bird.

Come on. Seriously?

"Can we see it?" Larina asked.

"No, it's really shy and doesn't show itself to strangers often. You are very lucky to have seen it at all," Rai said.

He knew these foreigners would believe his cover story with the reputation Tarris had across the seas. A mysterious place of untold magics and creatures, and unexplainable happenings. Stories of thousand floor palaces that held secrets within secrets, lost libraries, and artefacts that did the impossible. Blades that could spit out fire or fly through the air and home in on their target.

Some of which were true.

"That's incredible. Truly a tale to take home." Grenin grinned at his wife and she smiled back with a nod.

"Yes, well, wait until you get home before spreading my secrets," Rai said, climbing to his feet and walking to the front of the platform.

The black sand desert was different from the golden sands of day. With its hardening, no specs brushed over the dunes in the breeze as it did during the day. No creatures scuttled through its soft sands. The black sand desert of night was a dead place. A place of myth and stories. If he had been traveling with natives, they would have begged Rai to speed the aya up so they could reach the Waypoint sooner. But the aya had been through enough. And Rai feared no place since visiting that spectral plane all those years ago. Even the flickering memories set off a tremble that could not be stilled.

A protrusion on the horizon caught the attention of Grenin and Larina. "What is that?" Grenin asked.

"That's the next Waypoint, and where we will rest tonight," Rai said, not taking his eyes off the cresting black dunes around them. He didn't fear them anymore, but he knew there was more than stories roaming the black sand dunes at night.

The Waypoint was a mud-brick hut with one door and no windows. It stood stark on the sands during the day with its dark brown colour, but at night it blended well into the black sands around it. Rai hopped down first and walked into the Waypoint.

The inside was barren apart from four cots that lined the back wall. Although given its small size, little else would fit into the hut. Dropping to his stomach, Rai checked under the beds. No one. The place was empty. He liked this Waypoint in particular, as it had nowhere for crafty bandits to hide. Rai had heard stories of larger Waypoints having bandits in wardrobes and lofts that snuck down during the night to rob and kill unsuspecting travellers.

Another reason he liked this Waypoint was that it was almost always empty. If they had stopped at one of the two they had passed already, he was sure they would be sharing with at least one other party crossing the desert. This one, however, was located long after most travellers stopped for the night.

A startled gasp came from outside. Rai tore back through the door to see Grenin standing at the bottom of the ladder.

"The sand is hard as rock," he said.

"So it *is* true," Larina said, landing beside him, then stomping around.

"We have sand on beaches back home, but they don't turn black at night or harden like this," Grenin said, tapping his foot and scoffing.

"Go get some rest. I will watch the cargo and the aya. We can eat in the morning." Rai waved to the Waypoint.

"What about you?" Larina asked.

"I'll doze out here," Rai said.

"You're a sleep with one eye open kind of guy, eh?" Grenin said.

"Two eyes," Rai replied.

I'm pretty sure sleeping with two eyes open is called being dead, Fax said helpfully.

Despite their excitement about the sand, Grenin and

Larina were worn out after the attack. They had eaten not too long ago and were exhausted, so they put up little fight before turning into the Waypoint.

Rai rounded the aya and checked it for any wounds, but luckily the beast was unscathed. He scratched under her chin. "Thank you," Rai said and the aya groaned in acknowledgment. "I'm sorry there is no wildlife here. I'll try to stop somewhere tomorrow."

Rai unpacked and set up a trough of food and one of water. The aya buried her face in the food while Rai dug out a small ditch in the sand and stacked some kindling, lighting it ablaze.

Only then, when the aya ate contentedly and his clients slept in safety, did he feel respite from the day. The desert cooled and a chilly wind played with the dancing flames. Rai sat crosslegged gazing into that orange haze, feeling the heat warm his weary bones.

The salve that Larina applied on his wounds worked wonders. It must have had numbing properties, as Rai only felt an ache of the previous stinging.

It's been sometime since we had to fight like that, Fax said.

"We knew it could be a dangerous job bringing foreign merchants inland," Rai said.

It is unusual. Maybe we should take a peek and see what they are selling, Fax said, and Rai's shadow stretched towards the unattended crates.

"No. It doesn't matter what they are selling. We're here to get them to Celabar. That's it," Rai said, and his shadow shrank back to the wavering echo of the flames.

You're no fun anymore, Fax said.

"I'm tired, Fax," Rai said.

They sat watching the smoke rise into the moonlit sky. That familiar quiet, haunting, and yet comforting. Even the aya relished the still, dead landscape, as it lay down having finished its food.

Rai wasn't sure how long he had been sitting in silence when Grenin pushed the door to the Waypoint open with a too loud creak. Rai grimaced, ears perked listening, but nothing stirred in the night. Grenin forced a smile and sat near the fire.

"You should get some rest. It was a long day," Rai said.

"Can't sleep," Grenin said. The fire crackled between them. "Thank you for today," Grenin said.

"Just doing my job," Rai said.

"Where I come from, that was above and beyond, so thank you," Grenin said as he searched the surrounding desert. The man always had a nervous air to him, as if he was waiting to be struck down. "I wish I could do what you do," he said. "I wish I could protect my wife the way you protected us."

Rai knew it wasn't his place to speak, especially with his past creeping as a shadow behind him, but he let out a breath and said, "I don't think she married you in the hope you would become something else." Grenin met his gaze. "She chose you the way you are. Don't become something you are not."

Grenin nodded but looked disheartened.

Ah yes Grenin, there is no way you can become strong like me and protect your wife, Fax said in its mock Rai voice. *You aren't great at this reassuring stuff, are you?*

"No, that's not what I meant," Rai said to Fax, but of course Grenin couldn't hear Fax, so assumed Rai was talking to him. Rai sighed and shook his head. Often Rai's words and meanings were only well-acquainted neighbours.

"It's okay, you're right. I'm not you. I'm not a fighter. My wife does a better job protecting me than I do her," Grenin said.

"What I meant was, you don't want to become like me." The word *killer* rippled through his mind, stirring memories. "You love each other and that's what is important. Life tends to tear away those you love when you aren't looking. Don't make it easier by stepping back. Grab hold of your loved ones and make sure you keep a firm grip. That is how you show strength. Not with these." Rai patted on his daggers hanging by his belt.

Grenin searched through the words, nodding.

I take it back. That wasn't bad, Fax said.

"Thank you," Grenin said again.

An awkward silence settled around them.

"Why did you come to Tarris to trade? I'm sure you know that most trade at Dock Town and return home," Rai asked.

"The sailor asked us the same thing," Grenin said. "Is it really that uncommon to do trade here?"

"Well, no. But most that do are well established merchants that have their own ships and mercenaries," Rai said.

Grenin nodded in understanding. "We are from a small town in Denpess. Most never leave the country. But we swore since we were kids to get out and see the world. Everyone in our village was happy living through stories, but we wanted more. We wanted to *see* the stories. Make stories of our own," Grenin said, beaming, lost in long ago and far away. "We have seen the Ever Growing Tree, we have waded through the snow in the Trosan Empire, and now we have battled bandits on the black sands of Tarris. Sometimes the best memories are the ones that terrify you in the moment." Grenin shook himself out of his reprieve.

Rai couldn't relate. He had been thrown into a life that should have stayed in stories.

"What about you? Any plans to leave Tarris?" Grenin asked.

"No, I don't think so. I'm tied to it," Rai said.

Grenin didn't press for details. Instead, they sat, unspeaking, as Ova the World Turner's Moon Eye continued its watch over the black desert.

5

For a Price

Night in Tarris was like being in another world. The colourful city of tan and alabaster sandstone had its colour sapped by the dark, and the light from the Moon Eye painted the city with a glossy silver. Merchants and meanderers traded for shifty cloaked figures that more closely resembled black sand phantoms than the people of Tarris.

Many walked the small hours doing business in an effort to avoid the heat of day.

But the night brought dangers too.

With the black sand and dimming corners came a crowd that lived for the dark. The gangs of Yontar ruled the night, and everyone knew it. Even the guards knew it, posting fewer patrols rather than more when crime was at its highest. People wore cloaks to fend off the cooler temperatures, which also happened to obscure their faces and play into the very specific businesses of Yontar at night.

Water sloshed in the bucket swaying at Nya's side as she stalked up the street. Normally Nya avoided the night crowds but it was the only time she could fetch water while wearing a cloak to hide her face without drawing suspicion. And Uri was sure to be keeping an eye out during the mornings when most queued at the wells.

Head dipped and cloak drooping over her face, Nya scuttled away the well. She glanced over her shoulder before stepping into a winding side street. During the day these narrow pathways between towering buildings felt reassuring. Nya could duck out of the busy crowds and into these alleys where she was more likely to come across a sand fox than another person. But at night, what was once reassuring was now menacing. These streets were a place gangs used to avoid what few patrols did walk the night.

Still, it was the fastest way home.

Nya followed the bend, sandstone walls on either side cloaking her in darkness.

A crash sounded to her right and she spun.

She let out a shaky breath of fake laughter. Just sand foxes, she told herself. The muted rumble of the city at night was a dampened sound compared to the raucous noise of day, making the quiet sounds of the city sharp and threatening.

Stepping up to the end of the side street, Nya peered down the main thoroughfare. Fiery hints of life lined shuttered windows and door frames. A couple city guards meandered their way along the street, yawning, and a hooded figure strode in opposite direction. Nya hesitated, watching the street a moment longer and letting the hooded figure pass out of sight before readying to leave her alley.

Nya was about to make her way down the street when Luk appeared from the mouth of another street torchlight illuminating his face.

Nya opened her mouth to call out but the appearance of another cloaked figure silenced her. The last thing she wanted to do was to garner the attention of others out at night.

Luk scrunched his brow and scanned the street, before passing into another alley. What was Luk doing here? There was a well closer to where he stayed. Was he out looking for her?

Holding her hood up with one hand, Nya jogged after him.

Darting around a corner, Nya was going to shout after Luk when he turned onto a perpendicular street. Cursing, Nya sped up.

Nya came to the corner. The sound of Luk's slapping footsteps halted and he spoke. "I never thought she'd do that with the statue."

Nya froze.

Who was he talking to? The statue that she knocked over?

"I thought she'd hand the stuff over when you grabbed Jut," Luk continued after the silence wasn't filled by whoever he was speaking to.

Nya peered around the corner. The alley was dark, the

60

surrounding buildings sheltering them from the Moon Eye's light. Three black shapes stood further down, barely visible among the shadows.

Silence held.

"Look, it's not my fault you didn't get the stuff. I told you where we would be and when," Luk said, irritation lining his tone.

Where they would be and when? A coldness crept up her spine. *No*, Nya thought. *Luk wouldn't have betrayed the Sand Rats.* He wouldn't have betrayed *her*.

They all leave in the end.

It was her mother's mantra. She chided Nya whenever she mentioned her friends. "You'll see," her mother had said, "It'll be a lesson hard learned." Nya hadn't believed her. Nya *couldn't* believe her.

Nya set her bucket down and crossed to the far wall, she inched over to the other side of the alley. Further up a set of steps led to a door on the second floor of a building. Nya pressed against the wall and crept along to the staircase.

"The deal was, I'd give you a cut when we got the haul. All I got from this deal was a broken foot," a familiar voice said.

Uri.

Nya crawled up the steps to the platform outside the door and peeked over the edge to the alley below. Leaning on a stick was Uri, and at his side was two of his usual cronies.

Nya's stomach twisted. She couldn't comprehend what she was hearing.

Luk had betrayed them. Ratted them out to *Uri* of all

people. Hot anger rose to meet the cold shock and grief of being betrayed.

Uri had found the Sand Rats temple awfully quickly after their heist. Luk must have told the Ghrobans about the job at the market and where they would find the Sand Rats after.

Nya's hands balled into fists.

"It's not my fault you couldn't steal it from a bunch of kids," Luk said, his voice wavering at the end like he was remembering who he was speaking to.

With a snap of movement, one of Uri's friends swept in and knocked Luk down.

"Easy now little rat," Uri said. "A rat among rats."

Even in the dark Nya could make out Luk shrinking away as Uri hobbled towards him.

"Now, if I remember correctly, our deal was that you tell me when and where I could find your 'big haul', as you called it, and I would let you keep a loaf," Uri said. "But we didn't get the haul now, did we?"

That's what she was worth? A loaf of bread? She had been friends with Luk for years and he sold her out for a *loaf of bread*. Anger flared inside Nya. After everything that was all it took to betray her?

"I'm sorry, Uri," Luk whispered. "I can fix this. We're meeting in a couple days. I'll tell you where if you let me go."

Uri tutted. His clicking tongue echoing down the alley. "You're right, we can fix this. I want to keep this partnership fair. I came out of this with a broken foot so you should come out of this with some broken teeth, at least."

The Ghroban holding Luk slammed his face on the ground with a sickening crack. Luk let out something between a strangled scream and a gargle. The Ghroban yanked Luk's head up by his hair as the other stepped in and pummelled Luk in the chest. Uri watched, indifference lining his neutral face.

Part of Nya revelled in Luk getting what he deserved. He had betrayed not only her but all of the Sand Rats. He had this coming.

He deserved this.

But Nya couldn't separate the small fragile boy crumpling under the beating with the boy she had at her side for the last few years. The boy she found crying and bleeding after some guards picked him as their target to stave the boredom. The foolish boy who had dreamed of becoming a travelling merchant.

Luk had betrayed her and she wasn't sure she could ever trust him again. But he didn't deserve this.

Luk's screaming had subsided to gasps. Nya doubted the people living nearby would even look out their windows. No one got involved in the goings on of Yontar's streets at night.

Nya sat back, cringing at the sounds of impact.

Would Luk have helped if the roles were reversed?

Probably not, Nya thought and lunged from the top step.

She crashed into the man hitting Luk, whose body folded and cracked against the dirt. Spinning, Nya swiped the knife she kept tucked into her belt at the man who was holding Luk slicing him up the forearm. The man squealed hopping back.

63

Uri growled and shouted something Nya missed in the fervour of the fight. He ran at her, but one firm kick to his stick and Uri toppled.

Nya ducked under Luk's arm and wrenched him upward. The boy groaned but stood. "Can you run?"

Luk hissed holding his ribs but nodded. This wasn't their first scrap, and Luk knew it was run or die. Those born on the streets learnt to build up a resilient hardiness against pain and suffering, not shunning away from it but accepting it as part of life.

Nya supported Luk as they ran back the way they came. Luk wailed, clutching at his chest with every step. He had probably broken a couple ribs.

Tearing through the alley and back into the thoroughfare, Nya heard shouting and footsteps ringing behind them.

"You heard?" Luk wheezed.

Nya nodded. "Save your breath. I don't think we'll shake them easily."

Being chased by gang and guard was an almost daily occurrence, but most of the time, Nya could wear her pursuers out. Her survival was a game to them. That wasn't the case now, though. Nya saw the hatred in Uri's eyes. He wasn't going to tire. He wasn't going to stop until he had Nya's corpse at his feet.

Lanterns swung throwing flickering shadows across the buildings as they bustled past. The speckled flames hung outside tightly shut doors. No one was going to open up for a couple street kids and Luk was already trailing behind, his injuries slowing him down.

Nya glanced over her shoulder. The Ghrobans hadn't made it onto the main thoroughfare yet, so Nya yanked Luk onto an adjacent street where they ducked behind a stack of crates.

Luk dropped back against the wall, eyes forced shut against the pain. Nya peeked around the corner, pulling back sharply when one of the Ghrobans tore out onto the main street.

"You should have let them beat me. They would've stopped eventually. Now if they catch us, we're dead," Luk whispered.

Nya faced the boy. She had just saved him and that was all he could say? Maybe she should have left this ungrateful, self-serving, sun-addled—

"No point hiding!" Uri shouted. "We'll find you eventually. Luk, if you hand her over, we won't kill you!"

Luk met Nya's gaze.

"Don't."

"I'm sorry, Nya."

"I know how we can get out of this."

Luk exhaled. "How?"

The quiet buzzed as Nya scrambled for a way out of this. They couldn't run from the Ghrobans nor could they hide for long. Nya had got the better of them with the element of surprise but if it came to a fight they would lose.

And no one was going to help them. No one would open their door to some street kids during the night hours.

The silence rose to a crescendo.

That wasn't quite true, Nya thought. There was one establishment that ran under the Moon Eye's gaze. One that had its doors open to the dark: the Night Theatres.

Opening after dark hour, Night Theatres spawned across the city. Ranging from high end to dingy back room gatherings, they sold seats in booths where one could sit and smoke and enjoy the evening's entertainment. This could be anything from dancers to story retellings to musical performers.

Mother had been a server in a Night Theatre for a while, but Nya had never been inside.

"You have to trust me," Nya whispered holding out her hand. "Please. Just a little further."

Luk bit his bottom lip as he stared at her hand. After a moment of deliberation, he blew out a breath and grabbed it.

Nya and Luk sprinted down the alley, their footsteps ringing out to Uri and his friends who shouted and chased after them. The darkened city flew past in a blur of motion. Luk staggered at Nya's side groaning, but he had committed now.

They darted under an archway engulfed in darkness, when Nya grabbed Luk and pulled him into a staircase leading down.

Nya and Luk burst through the door at the bottom. Immediately, they were hit by the earthy stench of smoke mixing with coffee and spices, all lingering in a thick, warm smog. Flames sat behind stained glass throwing vibrant colours across the room as dancers curved and coiled on a stage to the smooth flowing music.

Nya didn't have time to stop and stare as the man standing at the door shouted and dove for them. Yanking Luk into motion, they ran into the Night Theatre.

It was like something out of a dream. Colour seemed to fill the air, the stained glass lamps lighting the smoke. The intoxicating smell was making Nya feel heady as they pushed past a group of laughing people.

Uri wouldn't even consider that they fled into a Night Theatre. They were strict with who entered and would never allow some street kids in. He was probably already searching the empty streets beyond. A smile wormed its way onto Nya's face. From the fact they escaped Uri or from the fumes that were making the room spin, she was unsure.

Luk was at Nya's side staring wide-eyed and no longer holding his chest. The room was starting to swirl and Nya knew she had to get them out of there, but her legs felt slow like she was wading through knee deep sand. The fumes from the hookahs were taking effect. There were certain grades to the stuff they smoked. Nya didn't know much about it, but this must have been a high grade Night Theatre to already be feeling the effects.

There has to be a back door, Nya thought

A hand gripped Nya's shoulder and spun her around. The world continued to spin even after she stopped. A city guard was speaking to her. Saying words she couldn't understand. Then he towed her back towards the entrance.

What if Uri was still there? What if the guard was working

with Uri? Nya pulled back out of his grip and tripped on someone's feet.

The hazy room blinked to darkness.

6

A Flicker of the Truth

A scardrae sent almost imperceptible specs of sand trickling down the dune towards the Waypoint. People often thought scardrae were poisonous beetles because of their yellow blotched back, but Rai knew them to be harmless. Travellers avoided most of the wild creatures out in the open sands for fear of the few species that could do them harm. Some parties were outright hostile to the wildlife. Rai had broken a couple of noses because of such experiences in the past. The scardrae paused after realising it was being watched, before burying itself deep into the sands.

The door to the Waypoint ground open against the sand that the morning breeze had blown against it. Out stepped Larina, yawning wide, already wearing fresh clothes.

They broke their fast in the shade of the Waypoint. It took

no time for the desert to be smothered in heat now that the Sun Eye was on its watch. They sat in a circle around a stone pallet, covered with bowls filled a variety of colourful foods.

"I didn't realise warmth had a smell to it until coming to Tarris, but it does," Grenin said between bites of thick bread dipped into an aromatic local dip called krenchin.

Finishing his portion, Rai went to set up the tarp atop the platform for the day's journey while the merchants finished their meal, but the aya snorted to get his attention.

The aya was back to its normal self after its tiring sprint the night before. It bobbed around and made low rumbling noises to tell him it was hungry. They were incredible creatures that recovered quickly after strenuous activity. Rai envied them, still feeling the aches and tightness from the fight.

While the aya ate, Rai clambered onto the platform and slotted the tarp poles into place. As he fixed the last in place, Larina approached the bottom of the ladder.

"Before we go, is there enough spare water to wash with?" Larina shouted.

"I second that." Grenin ran a hand through his sweat-slicked hair.

"In Tarris we don't waste water for washing while traveling the dunes," Rai said. The two slumped forward. "However, we do have an aya."

They looked at him questioningly.

"Aya are great beasts for traveling long distances with little rest, but they have other perks as well," Rai said, jumping off the bottom rung of the ladder, then waving them to follow.

They walked to the front of the beast. It watched their every step with its beady, black eyes.

Rai brushed around its nose, and the aya opened its maw and ran its tongue over Rai, lathering him in saliva, letting out a mooing noise as it did so. The tongue was a dark red and covered in sucker-like bumps that moved independently from the fleshy base. With a slurp, the aya smacked its mouth shut, leaving Rai dripping.

Grenin and Larina lurched back, their disgust obvious.

"Their saliva has cleaning properties, and lessens your chance of infections," Rai said, moving to the aya's heavily furred legs, then rolling about on them until he was close to dry. His companions stared at him, unspeaking.

"I'll wash my face with some water, and that will be fine," Larina said.

The next two days passed as unchanging as the sands surrounding them. The dunes were occasionally broken by a copse of bone trees, white branched trees that grew no leaves. Bone trees were hollow and fragile and branches could be snapped between two fingers. A lone bone tree was seen as a bad omen among the people of Tarris, most growing in groups. The superstition stemmed back to a myth about a lost wanderer in the desert who sat at the base of a lone bone tree. Just when the wanderer thought his luck couldn't get any worse the bone tree was struck by lightning killing the traveller instantly, and birthing the phrase 'counting your bone trees is when back luck strikes'.

They passed through several small villages restocking their supplies. These desert villages were built near naturally occurring orchards, and therefore not on the direct trail from Dock Town to Celabar, but most took the more meandering route to pass through them and restock.

The orchards bristled with life. Water trees swayed in the breeze, their curved trunks creaking. Their massive palm leaves shielded water seeds, akin to coconuts in other countries, from the Sun's gaze. Water trees were deep-rooted and drank from the seas and streams deep below the sands. The water purified in their stems then filled bulbous shells that grew from the top of the tree. The seeds would eventually crack and leak the water upon the hardy foliage that often grew around these trees.

It was common for water to be sold in the seeds that grew from the trees, but the orchards had to be carefully managed to ensure the plant life got enough water to survive. More common was the use of wells. Orchards marked where water hid, and so the people of Tarris would build some of the deepest wells in the world to reach the caverns below. These small towns were the beating heart of Tarris and rarely got the praise they deserved. These were the people who carved a life around the water trees and cultivated them into sprawling orchards.

After arriving at the village closest to Celabar on darkening sands and sky, they stayed the night at an inn and set off to complete their journey at dawn.

By the time the Sun Eye was halfway through its cycle of

the following day, Rai's home broke the swell and fall of the horizon. It started as no more than a blotch but grew into a grand city wall.

"Is that...," Larina started.

"Celabar," Rai said.

Pillars protruded from the sandstone city wall, carved to match the natural curves of a tree. White paint snaked up each pillar like vines; as much a work of art as a shield. The wall was unrelenting. Only arrow slits gave any indication of the other side.

A tall, narrow gate squatted before a mass of people, a statue on either side. One was of Ma-atan, the Harbinger of Justice; the other Otil, the Raging Sand Serpent. Ma-atan was depicted as a skeletal creature, vaguely humanoid. Its arms ended in points like enormous blades. Otil, on the other hand, resembled a mix of a dragon and serpent. It had no wings and four feet stuck from its coiling serpentine body.

Tarrisians had once worshipped the gods. The corpse of those ancient times still clung to the foundations of their cities with the statues and carvings of their many deities. Few still worshipped the gods that once had been so prevalent in Tarrisian culture. But there were those who believed one day the deities would return.

"It's beautiful," Larina said, as the aya joined the back of the line.

Rai grunted.

They arrived early enough that the line wasn't the hours of crawling inch by inch Rai had experienced in the past. Even so, it wound over the dunes like a tail. Rai set down the aya's reins, reached over to his half-empty waterskin, and settled in to wait.

Ayas were the most common form of transport across the desert, but some people also rode yarens: potbellied creatures that had fin-like webbing between linking their limbs. Reins attached them to massive shells with two bladed runners beneath which helped carry the shell through the sand like the sleighs they used in the north. The yarens swam through the sand, pulling these shells.

There were also hyian. Hyian were much like horses, but with their longer legs and toed feet, they traversed the sands with a lot more ease than horses. They were light grey, short-haired with a face like a horse but without the mane.

The line dragged them towards the city gate. Rai peered through the throng and noticed a man he recognised at the gates. Harl.

Harl was a pain. He would often look for any reason to not permit traveller's entry to Celabar. Rai had run into him in the past, but it was unlikely Harl would remember him.

"Have you got all your permits ready?" Rai asked, walking over to the still-gawking merchants. Tearing their eyes off the chaos around them, Grenin nodded.

"Of course. They're here in this crate," Grenin said, pulling off the top of the nearest crate, which was firmly packed with Artonian ale.

Six bottles of the fine ale, clearly labelled. A wave of nausea passed over Rai. One reason The Sun Boat Inn was the only place to stock the ale was because of how difficult it was to get alcohol into Tarris. The monarchy had made getting the correct permits and tariffs to bring alcohol into Tarris difficult to dissuade merchants. Few drank it, and even less admitted to drinking it. They saw falling under its influence as a sign of having a weak mind.

"How... how did you get this past the dock workers?" Rai asked as Grenin slid out a piece of parchment. Rai read it over. It was a standard merchant agreement, with nothing about bringing ale into the country.

"The dock workers? The nice guy said he would waive fees if we gave him a bottle," Grenin said.

"The dock worker didn't have a right to waive these fees," Rai said. "You aren't allowed to have this in Tarris." Rai slammed the top onto the crate.

Grenin jumped back. "What? Why not?"

They were next in line now. Harl would give them the maximum sentence, Rai was sure of it. And bringing alcohol into Celabar was no light offence. Especially when Harl would assume they snuck it past the dock checks. The best they could hope for was getting tossed into a cell and forgotten.

"Next!" Harl's gravelly voice called.

Rai looked at Grenin and Larina. Grenin's face was slowly dissolving into fear as he realised the gravity of the situation.

"I said next!" Harl shouted.

"Stay sitting and don't let the guards see you," Rai said.

Rai guided the aya to the gate entrance. Exhaling, he clambered down the ladder. Harl was a well-built man with messy short brown hair. He wore an equally dishevelled uniform including a bronze jerkin with the Celabar guard crest upon his breast: a sword pointing down within a tree.

Two guards approached the ladder leading onto the platform.

"Wait!" Rai shouted. "Let me have a word with your commander first."

The guards glanced at Harl, who was watching Rai closely. He gestured and his guards went back to their posts, then he jerked his head towards the guard tower. Harl lead the way and held the door open, pulling it almost shut after Rai entered. The stone room was built into the city wall. A corridor branched off into darkness where it would connect with other garrisons and gates.

"What is this about, mercenary?" Harl asked.

"My merchant friends wish to pass without their goods being... disturbed," Rai said. "Perhaps we could come to an agreement."

Harl scratched his stubbled chin and asked, "What kind of agreement?"

"Eight derans as a token of my thanks for not damaging the goods," Rai said. Harl scoffed. "Ten derans," Rai corrected. Harl gave him a hard look.

"I will do a check personally, and if ten derans are on top of the crates, then I will only see them," Harl said.

Rai's hands tightened around the coins in his pocket. Ten derans was a lot of money, but as soon as Harl saw it was Artonian ale they were hauling, he would demand more, and

Rai didn't have more to give. He knew Harl didn't drink, no guard of his stature would risk their career on it, so offering him a bottle wouldn't work either.

He should let the guards arrest Grenin and Larina. This was their fault. It wasn't Rai's problem. He had tried and failed, so there was nothing he could do.

Rai sighed.

Harl wouldn't recognise the scraggy man in a tan cloak in front of him as the commander who disciplined him all those years ago. But Rai remembered. He remembered Harl being cruel to the poor of the city, wearing his uniform like a crown. He remembered Harl having other guards take the fall for his mistakes. He remembered the young boy Harl beat half to death for not bowing as he past. He remembered.

The foreign merchants who just wanted to see the world would be locked up while this man was free. Free to hurt others.

But that was the way of the world. The way it would always be if left unchecked.

Rai leaned in as if to whisper something to Harl, who in turn bent forward as Fax shot out as a razor-thin blade piercing Harl's neck.

Harl sputtered and gasped, but Rai put a hand over his mouth and watched as the shock drained from Harl's eyes and he fell into a wide-eyed, unseeing sleep.

Rai laid Harl on the ground. Sometimes the right path wasn't the one set by the ruling powers. Sometimes it was the dark path that ran red.

Rai threw the door to the garrison open and strode towards their aya.

"Right Gren, you are free to go!" Rai shouted, using a shorter name as to not reveal that they were foreigners. As long as they hadn't peered over the edge it was unlikely the guards spotted the merchants. Which meant when they found the body, all they would have to go on was a man in a tan cloak. Not much in a city of sand.

Grenin brought the aya back to a trot. The guards shifted uneasily but let them through. Rai saluted the guards as he hauled himself on board the aya.

The gate they had entered through brought them into the lower districts of Celabar. It was dark among the tall buildings, and cold. After being out in the open with only a thin tarp protecting them from the Sun Eye's heat, it felt like a cool night in the shaded district.

"Rai, what was that all about?" Grenin asked, laying a hand on Rai's shoulder. Rai spun. For a moment, his instinct almost took over as he grabbed Grenin's arm. Killing had put him on edge. With bandits it was for survival. But Harl? A man of the city? This was going to haunt him.

Grenin fell back beside his wife.

"I had to kill the captain," Rai said. "He would have arrested you both and thrown away the key."

Their faces shifted from fear to horror.

"You... killed that captain?" Grenin asked.

Rai nodded, slowing the aya. It was foolish to keep it at a trot. Not only was it dangerous, but it would attract attention.

They came round to The Last Grain, a lesser-known but respectable enough inn, and Rai knew the owner. He would look after the merchants and their stock. Rai brought the aya into a courtyard and climbed down. He waved to the stable crew and they moved in to unload the crates.

Grenin and Larina climbed down warily. "Stay at this inn. The owner will buy your ale if you tell him I brought you. The rest you will have to sell to merchants in the city," Rai said, and leaned in. Both Grenin and Larina took an involuntary step back. Rai saw the fear in their eyes. They no longer saw him as "a hero from legends". Rai knew he wasn't what they thought he was, but it was nice to pretend for a while.

"Do not show it to anyone else or try to sell it to anyone else or you will be imprisoned. Am I clear?" Rai asked.

They nodded.

"I'll be back for the aya later," Rai said, grabbing a crate as he walked towards the main street. Rai pivoted and lifted the crate. "An extra fee for the extra service." Both Grenin and Larina nodded again, not saying a word.

Rai sighed and walked onto the streets of Celabar.

The cold street was nothing compared to the cold that filled him after the heat of a kill. He swung the crate in one arm; it clinking with every step. Most of the shops were closed for the qed.

If Rai hadn't been on a job, he would have been sleeping right now, too. With that thought, exhaustion hit him like a punch to the gut. He had felt tired more often of late. A tiring of the soul that no amount of sleep could quell.

That's a shame. I really did like them, Fax said.

Rai said nothing.

They feared us, even though we saved their lives, Fax said. Fax was good at understanding humans, but occasionally it couldn't comprehend some things.

"People fear what they don't know. After we killed the captain, we showed them who we are," Rai said. "The truth of who we are. They caught a glimpse and realised they didn't know me at all. They never did."

7

Death's Breath

*D*rip. Drip. Drip.

Nya was going to lose her mind if she had to listen to that dripping any longer. She sat huddled in the corner of her cell, light pouring through the slit at the top of the wall. How they kept the cell so cold during the day was a mystery, but she had to rub her arms to fight off the chill.

And the Duat-damned dripping.

It must cost a fortune to have water drip all day like that. Unless it wasn't water. She didn't want to think about what else it could be dripping.

She woke in the cell and had no idea where she was being held. Its walls were green and moulding with putrid-smelling slime.

Nya had spent some time beating against the iron door set

into the far wall and shouting her voice hoarse, but eventually she grew tired. With the Sun still up, Nya guessed she had only gotten a couple hours of sleep.

Drip.

That isn't helping, Nya thought. She couldn't focus on anything with that damn dipping.

Ka-chunk.

Someone was at her cell door.

It swung open to reveal a guard in a bronze jerkin. "On your feet," she said.

Nya shuffled back against the wall. The guard sighed and swung the shackles at her side before saying, "You don't want me to come in there."

Inching forward Nya swallowed, hands shaking as she held them out. The guard snapped the shackles around her wrists and yanked Nya to her feet.

"Good choice."

Nya followed the guard through corridors lit by braziers; the flames chasing away the cold that clung to her. It felt good to stretch her aching legs, and with the diminishing dripping she could feel herself relaxing. Now, if only she had some water she could start to feel human again.

"Keep up," the guard growled, yanking the chain connected to her shackles. Nya jerked forward almost colliding with the guard.

They walked past arrow slits in the walls before heading up a flight of stairs. Nya guessed she was in the local guard tower. One of many tall, narrow turreted towers attached to the outer city wall that housed the patrolling guards for each district, as well as the petty criminals captured.

She was a petty thief and not worth putting in the palace dungeons. That eased Nya a little. Hopefully they would sentence her a few weeks of labour and then she would be let go.

They came to a door, the crest of the local district carved into the stone wall above it, with two guards posted outside. *This must be the captain for this district.*

The guards nodded to the woman leading Nya and pushed the door open.

The woman dragged her into a small room with a table in the centre. Shelves lined the left wall, filled with wrapped scrolls and ledgers. The room held the musky smell of old parchment, but there was no dust or clutter. The table was carefully arranged; parchment held open with carved rock paper weights, and reed brushes laid in height order beside an ink palette.

A man sat behind the desk. He sniffed and wiggled his nose as he ran a finger over the parchment laid out before him. His greying hair was parted down the centre and hung to his ears. He was shorter than Nya, barely able to see the glyphs at the top of the parchment without leaning forward.

He sniffed again. "Sit," he said with a thin voice.

Nya didn't have time to reach for the chair before the guard pushed her into it.

"What is your name, girl?" he asked. Nya thought about lying, but what difference did it make? Her heart thundered.

He didn't appear to be the type work with a gang, but...

"Nya," she said.

He met her eyes. "My name is Captain Winzl. So they caught you—" he leaned over his parchment again, running his finger over some glyphs Nya couldn't read. "Sneaking into a Night Theatre." The man tutted and shook his head.

"Well, lucky for you, I have some labour needing done around the tower. Instead of an extended sentence in the cells, we could put you up for a shorter one if you are willing to do some cleaning and errands around here. That is what the boy who was with you signed up for. What do you say?"

Nya clenched her teeth. She had been so distracted, she had forgotten about Luk. "Yes Captain, I can do that."

"Excellent!" he said, clapping. "We will put you up in one of the resident cells, but you will have to keep the shackles on, I'm afraid."

"Wait. I'll have to stay here?" Nya asked.

Winzl blinked. "Well, of course."

"I can't," Nya said, more by reaction than thought.

"You don't have a choice, girl. Its four weeks in the cells or two doing work," Winzl said.

"Two weeks?" Nya said, sweat lining her nape. "Captain, I look after my mother. She isn't able to go out and get food. Without me, she won't survive."

Captain Winzl barked out a laugh. "Do I look like I give an ayas stool about your mother, girl?"

Nya jerked away from him. He seemed pleasant enough to begin with, but now his personality shifted. His smile tightened and rose a little too high.

"Listen girl and listen well. You should be grateful for the opportunity to sweep up our leftovers. If you behave, we might even turn a blind eye to the disposal of said leftovers."

Was he suggesting she would want to *eat* their leftover meals?

The guard behind Nya cleared her throat. "Captain, we could send her to the... special project."

Captain Winzl sat back and picked at his teeth, then let out a hum. "The project... Yes... Tell you what, girl. I'm a kind man. I'll give you the choice. We have a way for you to leave sooner if you sign up for a project in the palace. It should only take a day or two."

Mother could survive a day or two without food. They had done so in the past.

"What... what is the project?" Nya asked.

Captain Winzl wriggled his nose and said, "It's a secret. You'll have to join it to learn more."

Nya saw the man hiding a smug expression. This was clearly not a standard project, if there was one at all. It could be that she was signing up to her death. But when was the last time she was without death's breath upon her neck? It was the stench she woke up to every morning.

"I'll do it," Nya said.

"Very well," Captain Winzl said, shrugging. "It was your choice. Remember that. Send her through the Blind Walk." He waved a hand and they towed her out of the captain's chamber, his sniffle fading behind the closed door.

The guard hauled Nya deeper into the tower. Down flight of stairs after flight of stairs, until there were no more windows, and the only light came from the roaring flames spaced along the walls.

"Are we *below* the city?" Nya asked. In all her life she had never been this far under the sands. Some places had cellars, but this just kept leading downward.

"Shut up," the guard said, tugging on her chain.

They continued down, passing openings; some leading into rooms, others to more corridors. The eerie quiet of a crypt rung through the dark. Nya pressed closer to the guard letting the chain hang loose as she searched the black.

Finally, they came to a chamber shaped like a gear, a large main chamber surrounded by little nooks. The guard led her to one of these nooks and unlatched her chain.

"Stay there," the guard said, walking back to the entrance.

Nya saw the lever too late.

The guard wrenched it down and the ground beneath Nya fell away. Her breath caught. She didn't drop far, landing hard on her back. Nya spluttered, choking on a cloud of dust.

"Keep walking and you will arrive at the palace," the guard's voice called from above and the hatch slammed shut, throwing Nya into inky darkness.

Nya sat up feeling for the side of the tunnel. She felt the rough stone walls on either side. It was a very narrow tunnel.

Breathing hard, Nya felt fingers of panic wrap around her throat. Her heart beat so loud she was sure her body was wrenching with each thump. What had the guard said? That this led to the palace? What if she couldn't find her way? What if they left her to crawl about in the dark for the rest of her life?

Breathe, Nya thought.

She needed to calm herself. Nya took some deep breaths, her heart slowing. Coming back to herself, she recalled the captain using the term *"blind walk."* She had assumed it meant she was going to be blindfolded, not tossed into a dark tunnel.

I can get through this. For Mother, Nya thought as she steadied her breath and pressed forward. Timidly, she led with one foot, feeling the ground. Her head throbbed and the disorienting dark left her dizzy. But she had to keep moving forward.

Nya inched forward, occasionally stopping to settle herself. The dark swirled and took shape, her mind playing tricks. Nya shrieked more than once at forms that weren't there.

She continued edging through the dark. She had no way to judge her progress, always squinting in the dark in hope she would see an end to this pitch black void.

At one point, Nya was sure Mother was standing ahead, smiling at her. "Mother?" she asked. Her mother's face curled into a snarl.

I should have left you to die, her mother said, her voice echoing off the walls around her. *I had the option, you know, but I was stupid and young. I brought you back to my home even after he left.* She turned and walked into the dark.

"Mother, wait!" Nya shouted, giving up on caution and

running after her. "I know, I'm sorry!"

Nya ran pushing off the walls of the tunnel.

Until finally, the black dissipated.

The old dead-end alleyway they had slept in when Nya was younger formed around her in swirls of memory. Exhaling, she glanced around the familiar surroundings.

Mother crouched, tongue poking out in concentration as she wove fabric together. Nya didn't know what she was sewing, but it always turned into something incredible when she finished. It amazed her that she could take nothing and weave it into something beautiful.

Then the alley lurched and Nya watched as time sped past. Mother's condition was worsening. She watched herself stroll into the alley, head hanging after not being able to steal food that day. Her bruises burned from the guards who caught her trying.

Mother was laying on her back, sewing discarded. Nya ran over and shook her. This wasn't the first time her mother had fallen into one of her states, but they were lasting longer and longer.

"No!" Nya shouted, the sound echoing down the tunnel.

Time rolled past again like specs of sand on the breeze as Nya spent the next week and a half making riskier moves to steal and sell whatever she could find until she finally had enough for the street doctor to make a visit.

Ravenous hunger churned in her gut, but she had to do something for her mother.

The doctor examined Mother and shook his head. An

illness of the mind, he had said. How was she supposed to treat that?

It was Nya's fault. She had always been a burden.

Nya spun around as the scene shifted once more. The doctor was gone and Mother scuttled around a corner out of their dead-end alley.

She ran after her mother, catching glimpses of her disappearing around the next bend. The outline of mother's back was becoming further and further away. Nya reached out. If she could just touch her... Nya snagged her foot on the rough terrain and flew forward, landing with a *crunch*.

Tears ran down her cheeks and she heaved as the cries bubbled out of her.

"Please don't leave me," Nya whispered to the unmoving dark.

She cried until her eyes stung and chest ached. Eventually the sobbing waned to a whimper, then to an exhausted exhale. When had she last slept? Was it night?

Nya pulled herself to her feet and stumbled through the dark, heedless of the pain in her ankle or the cuts screaming for her attention. Blood trickled over her lip and she wiped it away, tasting the metallic tang on her tongue.

I must have hurt my nose when I fell. The thought passing as quickly as it arose.

A pinprick of white cracked the black surrounding her.

Nya's breath caught. Was the black playing tricks on her again or had she finally reached the end? She pushed onward staring into the blinding white.

The light grew with every step until it was all-consuming, and Nya collapsed forward into it.

8

The Ear

*B**ut we killed those bandits for them?* Fax asked.

Rai approached the towering building he had called home for the last year. It shot up ten stories between two shorter buildings, a rickety stairwell zigzagging up the side. It creaked as Rai made his way past the other apartment doors.

"Heroes kill bandits and defend the weak, Fax. Monsters kill the innocent," Rai said, swapping the crate of ale to his other hand.

I'm not sure I would consider the captain who turns a blind eye to his guards beating thieves until their eyes are swollen shut innocent, Fax said.

"That's the problem, isn't it? There are no heroes, only monsters who won," Rai said.

Rai reached the top floor, where a long walkway led to his door. Bending down, Rai checked his tripwire, a thin cable leading to his apartment. It would snap triggering a chime in his apartment when someone was coming or had passed when he wasn't home. He flicked the taut cable. No one had passed since he left.

Pulling his key out, Rai slid it through the bolt and, with a series of satisfying snaps, the door opened and Rai stepped inside. He had paid a hefty fine to have this locking mechanism built into his door. It was a vast improvement over the single bar that had been installed previously.

The apartment was one chamber with a fire pit sitting in the middle of the room. In the left corner was a bed with a chest at its foot; in the right was a desk strewn with parchment and half rolled scrolls. Where some would hang tapestries, the stone walls were bare. The wooden floorboards unadorned by rugs or animal skins.

Rai placed the crate of ale down by the door as Fax shot from his shadow as a crow, landing atop the roof beams above.

Ah, that's much better. One needs to stretch one's wings now and then, you know? Fax said.

"You don't have wings," Rai said, unlatching the top of the crate and taking out a bottle of ale.

That's not what you told the merchants. You told them I was a rare black bird that was so fast some say they could see through it! Fax flew back and forth.

Rai sighed and cracked the top of the bottle open with the

rim of his table as he collapsed into his chair. The Sun Eye was still high, but with only one window, the room wasn't particularly bright. Rai lit the lantern on his desk, then pulled a piece of parchment from his belt.

The reason he took the job with Grenin and Larina wasn't solely for the money, but also to pick up this letter. He had waited so long for it. As soon as he heard a ship was coming in from the far northeast, he dropped everything to meet it at Dock Town. The fewer hands the letter passed through, the better.

Unravelling the parchment, Rai laid it flat upon the table, letting the flickering flames illuminate the scrawl. To most, it would look like nonsense, but Rai recognised the shapes of the coded glyphs. He got out another blank sheet and the key he had created and started on translating it.

A,

It has been a while since we were last in contact. I will try stopping by Tansen next time I'm in Tarris. As for the matter you asked me to look into for you: shadows that move and creatures hiding in shadows are rampant in folklore across the world.

In some, they are dark versions of those casting the shadows. In others, they are the sins that one has to carry. Different cultures all have their own names for them "The Nightwalkers", "The Tainted", and "The KaShut" in Tarris. But these are all legends and stories and I assume you didn't contact me to find some light reading so I delved into academic texts, historical records, bestiaries, and found nothing on creatures living in shadows.

I found several ancient traditions involving people lighting their homes with torches to minimise the shadows present, as they believed they were being watched from the shadows, but this is an ancient tradition and little is known about it.

As for the second thing you asked me to look into, this dark realm on the other side of a tear in reality. From what you described, it sounds like one of the Seven Torment Realms you could be banished to after being Judged upon dying. In particular, Reshim, the third layer of the Torment Realms.

I've attached some names of scrolls that discuss the Torment Realms in more detail, and where I found the ancient traditions, if you want to do some further reading. I'm sorry I couldn't be of more help.

Hope you and E are doing well.

H.

Rai took another swig of ale and let out a sigh. He had hoped for more. Something solid after waiting almost a year for this letter.

Rai glanced over the scrolls and parchment laid out on his desks, most of it containing legends and folklore. It was all he had found in the five years since that night. The night he passed into a dark realm and came out with a something lurking in his shadow.

"Any of that sound right to you?" Rai asked.

I don't know. To me, the dark realm was just home. We don't name things like you humans do, so I don't know if your people call it Reshim.

Rai had guessed as much. In the five years since they met, he had asked every question imaginable and had only grazed general details about the dark realm Fax had called home.

Something must have happened to create the tear between his realm and Fax's. Rai downed the rest of the ale. But what?

Bottles were drained and notes taken, as the Sun Eye dipped lower. Rai scribbled down connections between the scholar's notes and his own that he had pulled together researching the tear, along with the tomes and scrolls Harbeg recommended for further reading.

Setting down his writing reed, Rai reached into the crate of Artonian ale. He pulled the last bottle from the crate. Rai blinked. The last one? Already?

I'm not human, but I'm fairly certain that ale doesn't fill the requirements of proper nutrition, Fax said.

"Shut up, bird," Rai said, more slurred than he had hoped.

You said I wasn't a bird, Fax replied.

Fax was right. He needed food. He would save the last of the ale for later. Rai placed the bottle on his desk and rolled up the parchment, leaving the decoy parchments of historical events, and carrying his true studies over to his bed. He bent down, felt for the notch in the floorboard, then ripped up it. Dust flew and he waved it away before dropping the notes beside the rest he had written over the years, and then replaced the floorboard.

Standing on cramped legs, Rai hissed and stretched them out. "Come on, then. I need to catch up with The Ear and I'll grab food on the way."

It was dark hour when Rai approached the derelict building that housed The Ear. He ran his hand through his stubble, wiping away the leftovers of the wrap he had eaten on the way over.

I don't like this guy, Fax said, hiding in Rai's shadow.

Rai didn't respond. Whenever he came to speak to the Ear he tried not to talk to Fax.

He ducked under the collapsed door frame and gazed up. The building was two-stories, but the second floor had worn away over the years and caved in. However, there was a staircase at the back that led up to a small platform that still hung onto the supports of the second floor, an orange glow emanating from it.

"Ear, it's Rai," Rai called as he made his way over, under the rubble, and up the steps.

"I know. My brothers and sisters told me you were coming," the Ear responded, his voice echoing through the space.

Rai reached the platform and took in his surroundings. A stone firepit sat beside a grand window that looked over the neighbouring one-story buildings. No one sat around it.

"Come on down, Ear." Rai settled beside the fire.

Scuttling sounded from the roof beams and a boy no older than fourteen clambered down with animal-like prowess. He had light brown hair that fell in a tangled mess to his shoulders. His brown eyes seemed too wide, like he was in a state of perpetual shock.

"How are you doing, Ear?" Rai asked, picking up a pot and filling it with the coffee beans and water Rai had brought, then placing it onto the flames.

"Well, yes well. Busy. Lots of whisperings. Lots happening. My brothers and sisters bring back much," the Ear said.

The Ear heard everything that was happening in Tarris through his brothers and sisters, who happened to be params, furred creatures' only inches tall and resembling mice. But most importantly, they could listen then recreate any voice they heard with incredible accuracy.

As the Ear was a boy, Rai wasn't sure if he had trained the params, or if they truly were like family and just came back to him repeating anything they heard as he claimed.

The pot spat and whistled, so Rai took it off the flames and poured two cups of coffee, handing one to the Ear.

"I heard whisperings of a captain that was killed by a man wearing a tan cloak who was entering the city," the Ear said. Rai ignored the comment.

"Have you heard anything that will interest me?" Rai asked, sipping his coffee. It was smooth, an expensive blend from the river villages of Ossin. He always brought good coffee when meeting the Ear. Coffee was his favourite.

The Ear picked up his cup and sipped, then started bouncing about, laughing. "Yes, yes, nice coffee and interesting whisperings that Rai will like," the Ear said.

What he thought Rai would find interesting was not always so. Rai remembered the time the Ear went on about a rumour of a man who wandered the desert in bright colours laughing and claiming to be a god. The boy found it fascinating, Rai not so much.

"What is it?" Rai asked.

"Birds Rai," the Ear said. "Birds are flying northward to the fallen city. Scardrae are seen burrowing in its sands, and eyes from all around fall on Asuriya, the lost capital of Tarris!"

Asuriya was the capital of Tarris millennia ago, but after a catastrophic event that ripped the city apart, the people abandoned it. After, Tansen became the capital where the emperor or empress led the country. No records existed that said what caused the calamity that destroyed the old capital, but anyone who stayed became ill and died within days. Some said the city was cursed. Others thought it nonsense, claiming an infection lingered in the city. And yet, some still attempted to scavenge from the old capital. Most did not return, and those that did never lived long.

"There has been talk of taking back Asuriya since I was no older than your brothers and sisters," Rai said waving a hand.

"No, no, no, these are important people whisperings," the Ear said. "Nobles and overseers."

Rai raised an eyebrow. Retaking the old capital was common talk on the streets as a hope of a new life. It was unusual for nobles and overseers to discuss a return to Asuriya.

"What do they say of it?" Rai asked.

The Ear grinned, pleased he caught Rai's interest. "They say a man has taken residence there claiming to be the rightful Emperor of Tarris. He is housed in the Mad Palace and calling himself the Mad Emperor."

"He is mad if he doesn't think the Empress won't send a squad to execute him for even suggesting such." Rai scoffed.

After the unknown cataclysm that destroyed their old capital, four families rebuilt Tarris from the ashes, and the ruling powers of Tarris was split between them. Three monarchs and the emperor or empress to guide them.

But it was human nature to hunger for more. More than one civil war had broken out in the last thousand years for the title of ruler.

But what would it mean if the old capital was liveable again?

"What else? Anything about shadows like I asked?" Rai asked trying to focus.

The Ear threw back the rest of his coffee, making Rai cringe. *That must have burnt his throat.* Then the Ear scratched his chin, breathing hard and hopping in a circle.

"No, no moving shadows," the Ear said, biting his bottom lip.

Still nothing, Rai thought. It was about time he moved on anyway. He had followed all the threads he dug up in Celabar. It was time to root around for answers elsewhere.

"Thank you, Ear," Rai said, standing. "For your trouble and reliable secret keeping." Rai tossed the Ear some coins. The Ear sold his information to many clients in Celabar, but he was still loyal and never shared Rai's secrets.

The Ear picked up the coins and mimicked locking his mouth and throwing away the key. "Is Rai away then?"

"Yes. I'm not sure when I'll be back for our talks, I'm afraid," Rai said, and the Ear looked disappointed.

Rai dug into his pockets and pulled out the rest of the bag of coffee he had purchased and dropped it in front of the Ear.

"If I'm back in Celabar, I'll be sure to come and see you," Rai said, and the Ear grinned at the coffee, then at Rai.

"Yes do, much thanks Rai, yes, thanks," the Ear said, bobbing up and down and bowing at the same time.

Rai bowed back, then passed back out into the night.

Dark hour had broken with the Moon Eye beginning its watch over the world. The streets had filled with those avoiding the heat of day. But Rai paid them no heed, wrapped up in his own thoughts and separate from the world around him. He had hung around Celabar for long enough. Perhaps he should head south to Rizu or venture out to the smaller desert villages.

Rai sighed. Would he ever find the answers? It had been five years. But he had no choice. The other option was to return to Tansen and he couldn't do that.

Not yet.

"We need to pack," Rai whispered. "We leave tonight."

Shouldn't you, you know, sleep?

Rai suppressed a yawn. He usually slept the day after returning from a job, as out on the open sands he only let himself doze.

"Okay, we leave at sunrise," Rai said. He was exhausted. His legs were shaky and eyes heavy. Fax was right, a goodnight's rest was in order.

Climbing the steps to his apartment, Rai stretched.

Rai reached the landing and jerked to a stop.

What is it? Fax asked.

He bent down. Someone had set off his tripwire.

9

The Doomed Others

Nya's left cheek pressed against the cold stone ground. Her eyes fluttered open, battling against the light, to reveal a lattice cage. Mind racing, trying to orient herself, she remembered stumbling through the Blind Walk and falling into the light.

She barked out a cough and lifted herself to her knees. Her body throbbed. Between falling in the tunnel and hurting her nose, to sleeping on the stone cold floor, there wasn't an inch of her that wasn't smarting.

"You're finally awake," said a boy.

Nya turned her head, then hissed at the crick in her neck. *You would think I would be used to sleeping rough by now*, Nya thought.

"You know, most sleep on the cots rather than on the

floor," the boy said.

"Where am I?" Nya asked.

"The palace dungeons, I'm afraid."

Nya studied her surroundings. She was in a long, narrow chamber with five occupied cages, the brown-haired boy was in the one next to her. On the wall behind her was a narrow door set into a stone wall. Nya had come through that, she was sure. She bit her lip, staring at the door. The ever-dark tunnel was behind that frame. Nya suppressed a shiver.

"First time through the Blind Walk?" the boy asked.

"They put people through it more than once?" Nya squealed.

The boy's face scrunched up. "Of course. They use it to transport all the prisoners from their districts so they don't have to risk bringing us through the streets."

That made sense. Nya had rarely seen prisoners taken through the city but never thought anything of it. But the idea of having to go through that tunnel again was making it hard to breathe.

"I guess it's also part of the punishment," the boy said, shrugging. "The name's Kit. What's yours?"

The boy seemed awfully relaxed. Nya wasn't sure if she wanted to share her name with him. He was a prisoner and could be in here for any reason.

Then again, she was a prisoner too.

"Quit it, kid. This isn't a feast hall," said a gruff voice from the cage on the other side of Kit.

"I'm just trying to be welcoming," Kit said.

"Well, you're welcome to shut up," the voice retorted.

"That's Drak," Kit said, pointing to the man lying on his cot. Drak grunted. "He's annoyed because he didn't want to tell me his name, but I overheard the guard saying it," Kit said with a grin.

"Nya." Nya brushed the hair from her face and climbed onto her cot. She hissed as her cuts and bruises made themselves known.

"Nya! Welcome to The Doomed Others," Kit said, spinning with his arms outstretched.

"Here he goes again," said a woman. She must have been in the cage next to Drak.

"What are the Doomed Others?" Nya asked.

"That's us. I came up with the name myself," Kit said. "The Doomed Others being us, being doomed for being sent into this secret project that will, almost definitely, end with our deaths." He slumped, head held by his hands but still smiling, watching Nya.

She sat unsure what to say. Her mind was still waking and this was a lot.

"You have scared the poor girl," the woman's voice said from the far-off cage.

"I'm just making sure she understands the situation and doesn't get her hopes up, mystery lady," Kit said. "She refuses to tell me her name so I call her mystery lady."

"Will you lot shut up!" Drak shouted.

Nya cringed.

"He gets cranky near feeding time," Kit said in a whisper

that everyone could hear. A smile crept across Nya's face. She couldn't help it.

He grinned back, clearly pleased he got her to smile.

"Do you know what this secret project is?" Nya asked.

"They haven't said yet. But I'm sure we'll find out come dawn. It's not all doom and gloom though," Kit said, laying back on his cot. "The food here is incredible."

"Really?" Nya asked. Her stomach rumbled.

"No, not really," he said.

Just like Kit said, it wasn't long before a guard pushed into the room carrying food trays and water skins. He slid a tray through the slot in each of the five cages and left without a word. The other occupants descended on their trays with the ferocity of a starved animal. Nya heard movement from the fifth and furthest cage and realized there was another person here with them who hadn't spoken yet.

She pulled her tray over. On it was a slice of bread and a lumpy grey gruel. Her stomach screamed at her to eat but the thought of her eating while Mother, and perhaps the rest of the Sand Rats, went hungry churned her stomach.

She picked up the slice of bread and nibbled at the crust.

"Don't be shy. You need to eat and keep your strength up. Death is not to be undertaken with an empty stomach, my mother always said," Kit said between slurps of his gruel.

She did need to keep her strength up to survive this and get back to Mother. Nya took a bigger bite of the bread and before she knew it, she was halfway through the gruel too.

The gruel wasn't as bad as it looked but after eating half

of it, she started to feel sick. It had been a while since she had eaten this much and her stomach rebelled. She sat back, feeling better and sick at the same time.

The others had finished long before her and now sat in satisfied silence.

"Told you. Drak will be okay with a little talk now," Kit said with a wink to Drak, who scowled back at him.

Nya wiped the back of her hand across her mouth. She wanted to ask why they were in here but thought that might be rude. And she was afraid of what some answers might be. On the streets you didn't ask about ones past and she bet prisoner culture would be the same.

"When you said we need to keep our strength up, do you think we will have to fight?" Nya asked.

"No idea but it'll dangerous. As sure as the sands," Kit said.

"How do you know?" Nya asked.

Kit sat up and gave her a funny look. Then, putting on a grumpy voice not unlike Drak's, he said, "You have two options, dear Nya. Either we send you north to the mines where you will spend the rest of your life in the dark and worked to exhaustion, or you can do this secret project where, if you survive, we will let you go." Kit shook his head and his normal voice returned. "If it sounds too good to be true, it probably is."

"You were going to be sent to the mines?" Nya gasped. There were stories of course, of criminals being sent to mines to be worked to death, but she never thought they were true.

"Of course. What was your other option?" Kit asked.

"A couple weeks of service in the guards' quarters," Nya said.

Drak burst out laughing and Kit's face fell into contorted amazement.

"And you picked the almost certain death option?" Kit asked.

Nya felt her cheeks flush. Had she made a mistake? These people were serious criminals if they were going to be sent to the mines, and Kit's talk of certain death was starting to sink in.

Drak was still laughing.

No. This was the only choice. If she had the slightest chance of getting back to Mother, this was the path she had to take. She wouldn't let her mother starve alone. Nya owed her everything. Mother never abandoned her when Nya ruined her life. So risking her own was only fair.

"Shut up," Nya snapped. "If you lot want to die instead of going to the mines, that's fine. But I'm going to be walking out of this palace tomorrow. Alive."

The others fell silent.

Nya stood and stormed over to her cot, lying towards the wall so the others wouldn't see her eyes welling.

Nya drifted in and out of sleep. Dreams were strung out between gasps of being awake, only to be pulled back into the nightmares. It felt like drowning in an ocean.

She was running, always running through the streets of

Yontar with Luk. Then it all went dark and she was back in the Blind Walk, pushing through the black as Mother chastised her for being too slow.

Nya gulped down a breath, springing upright.

It was dark, and panic froze her. She thought she might be back in the tunnel until she heard a low whistle of sleep come from Drak. Nya exhaled, letting her heart slow.

"Hey, you okay?" Kit whispered.

Nya nodded and ran her hands through her hair.

"I didn't mean to spook you with calling us the Doomed Others," Kit said.

"It's fine," Nya said. She settling back into the cot, her forearm resting across her forehead.

"What's out there for you?" Kit asked. "I mean, what are you so determined to get back to?"

Nya could tell from his tone he wasn't being cruel but was genuinely curious. "My mother," she said without hesitation.

"Ah," Kit said with a sigh. "I can't say I'm that close to my parents. Does she make it worth it?"

Nya tilted her head towards where Kit lay on his cot. He was little more than a dark shape in the late hour. "What do you mean?"

"I just mean, it's a hard life for us. Does she make the fighting and dark nights worth pushing through? You need to have someone or something like that."

A coldness wrapped around Nya. No, her mind told her. She didn't.

"Yes," Nya said without emotion.

There was a pause.

"I hope you get back to her then. I really do."

10

One Last Job

Rai crept towards his apartment. Pausing at the door, he ran his fingers over the bolt lock. There were faint markings on the surrounding metal where someone had forced it open.

Rai let out a sigh, the chances of his good night's sleep was disappearing like sand in the wind.

I'll go have a look, Fax said. Its shadowed shape slid under the door, returning a moment later. *Four city guards. Two at the door, one at the window, and the other looking through your stuff. Want me to kill them?*

"No, I need to find out why they're here," Rai said.

Rai moved to the end of the walkway and climbed onto the railing. Jumping, he grabbed the lip of the roof and shimmied his way around the side of the building until he came to the back window.

With a swing, Rai crashed through in an explosion of glass, showering the apartment with shards. Rai slipped his dagger from its sheathe and dragged it across the first guard's throat, then launched it at another guard standing in wait.

Finally the guards reacted, the one rummaging around his desk shrieked and ran towards him, blade first. Rai parried with ease, letting the man run past him, then kicked him out the window. His scream ended with a *crack* and a sickening splutter.

Rai turned slowly and faced the last guard who stared back at him, blade trembling in the moonlight.

"Let me make this very clear: if you run, you die. If you charge me, you die. If you so much as crap yourself, you guessed it, you die," Rai said. "In fact, the only way you don't die is if you tell me who hired you to come here and why?"

The guard pondered that.

"I... You..." he stammered and took a step back, knocking over the crate and sending the last bottle of ale spinning across the room. It hit the wall and shattered.

The guard's breath caught. He dropped his sword and held his palms up. Rai exhaled and threw his second dagger, which embedded itself in the man's left eye. He dropped to the floor.

"My last damned bottle of ale," Rai said, rubbing his neck.

Well, that wasn't very smart, Fax said. *Now we have no idea who is after you.*

Rai walked over and kicked the closest corpse to turn him

face-up. "If they knew who I really was, they would have sent more than four guards who can barely hold their swords," Rai said.

This must be about the captain I killed, Rai thought. But it was too quick. The guards at the gate barely saw him. To track him down this fast meant one thing.

"The merchants," Rai said.

They must have caught Grenin and Larina, Fax said, sitting atop his bed as a crow. *We have to go save them.*

If they had waited one more day before they were caught, he would have been out of here. He could leave them, sleep on the road and get out of Celabar tonight. They had likely given up his name. True, someone could have tortured them to get it...

It was a risk to help them. He was supposed to be keeping his head down and breaking prisoners out would certainly bring eyes on him.

Rai thought of the days he had spent with the merchants. How Grenin hurt his nose learning that their doors were on hinges, Larina throwing that card to distract the bandit, and Grenin wanting to be a hero.

Rai slammed his fist on his desk. "Fine! I always hated Celabar."

Yes! Fax shouted and flew about the apartment.

Rai reached for a sack under his bed and pulled it out, then ripped up the floorboard and filled it with his notes. He made his way to the wall and punched it with all his might. A puff of dust spat back at him. Carefully, Rai pulled the loose stone out to reveal the thin space he had carved when he'd moved in.

In it sat a bow, quiver, two daggers, and a belt lined with labelled vials of blood.

Rai brought them out one by one, attaching the belt around his waist, sliding the two daggers into sheathes, and swinging the bow and quiver across his back.

Fax had stopped cawing and watched him intently.

"Let's go," Rai said.

The breeze settled, and Rai drew in a deep breath, then let it out, loosing the arrow. It tore through the sky, whistling across the street, landing in a guard's face who, with a spatter of blood, dropped to the ground.

It felt good to use a bow again.

Rai perched on a domed roof bearing down on the local guard headquarters across the street. It was a fortress of stone with two tall segments connected by a shorter middle section. Balconies lined the towers where guards watched on patrol, coming in and out. Well, they *had* come in and out.

Nocking the next arrow, Rai waited until the guard on the adjacent balcony appeared. He couldn't have him spotting the body and alerting the others.

Once, in days past, Rai would whisper a prayer for those he killed. That was a time when he thought the gods to be watching over him. Now he knew better.

A guard stepped out onto the balcony, illuminated by the flicker of braziers behind him. Rai waited until he was a couple of paces from the entrance and loosed an arrow.

As it ripped across the distance, the guard noticed his fallen comrade in the split second before the arrow embedded itself between his shoulder and neck sending him falling back.

Rai didn't take pleasure in killing, but he didn't feel pity anymore either. "Fax, you ready?"

Ready when you are, Fax replied.

Rai strapped his bow onto his back and pushed off the roof. A sudden rush of air threw his cloak back as he fell a storey, before Fax grabbed his outstretched hand. His shade couldn't carry Rai's weight for long, but it could help him glide downward.

They glided over the quiet street to the balcony of the fallen guard. Rai let go of Fax, landing in a crouch, wobbling a bit.

All those ales have not done you any favours, Fax said.

Rai slipped into the guard headquarters. Inside, a corridor broke off in three ways: left, right, and forward. "Any ideas which direction?" Rai whispered.

Yeah, you just take a right, then a left, and down a flight of stairs, Fax said. Then, *No, of course I don't know.*

Guards will patrol the outer corridors. Best to go in deeper, Rai thought, looking to his right where the second balcony protruded. Rai backed out onto the balcony and kicked over the dead guard. He was a little narrower around the shoulders than Rai, but not by much. Rai stripped him, taking his jerkin and uniform, sliding it on and stuffing his cloak into the sack on his back.

Rai rolled his shoulders. The uniform was tighter than he would have liked but it would have to do. Back straightening, Rai headed straight down the middle corridor, delving deeper into the heart of the building.

He knew they held prisoners on the top floors. The furthest point from the exit on the ground floor. In his studies, Rai learned of other countries that held prisoners on the ground floor or below, which seemed counterproductive. Placing them high in the tower kept them away from those entering the building, as well as keeping them at the furthest possible point from the exit.

So, Rai took the first staircase he saw and worked his way upward. A set of guards passed him, bowing.

I'll be honest, I didn't think the disguise would work. I have seen no guards with bows on their backs, Fax said.

"Most archers are on the city walls, the rest carry swords when working here," Rai whispered. "But there's no reason to question it. I could be in training."

Exiting on the next floor, Rai finally spotted doors with barred ports. Noting the empty corridor, Rai peered into the first dark cell. Empty.

He moved to the next, where a brute of a man sat against the back wall staring at him with hard eyes. Rai continued down the corridor, checking each cell, but none held either of the merchants.

"Hey! Where are you headed? These prisoners are meant to remain undisturbed," a voice called from further down. He was plump, his gut hanging out the bottom of his jerkin.

The man had the look of someone who wore his rank on his sleeve.

"I was sent to check on one of the prisoners," Rai replied, bowing. This pleased the man, who sniffed and nodded.

"I wasn't informed, but very well. What one, soldier?"

"Two merchants," Rai responded.

"Ah yes, the merchants," the man said, then scrunched his brow. "They are in the other tower. We only hold the violent ones here."

Damn it, a guard should know that, Rai thought.

The man pulled back, laying a hand on his sword. He looked over Rai as if only now noticing his inconsistencies: the bow, sack, and too tight uniform.

"What was it you said your name was?" he asked.

"I didn't," Rai said.

Fax surged forward. The man managed to pull his blade out and swipe away Fax's first attack, but then Rai's dagger ripped through his neck. The man dropped his sword, letting out a strangled cry before falling to his knees, then collapsing onto his side, blood swelling around him.

Hey! I had that, Fax said.

"Too slow," Rai said yanking the dagger out of the man's neck and wiping it on his soiled breeches. "We need to work our way back down, then through the connecting building to the other tower," Rai said, sighing. It had been a coin toss to which side he would check first. He should have known luck would work against him.

A startled cry came from behind him. Rai spun to see the

same two guards he passed earlier standing at the top of the stairwell.

So much for stealth, he thought. Fax shot off towards them in bird form, gliding its wing through the first guard's neck, cutting off his shriek. The other bolted for the stairs.

See, I can do that too, Fax said. *Should I go after the other?*

"No point. Any guards on this side will already be alerted by the shouting," Rai said. "Come on. We need to find another way across."

Rai broke into a jog, moving away from the stairs where the guard fled. Arcing around a corner, another guard ran towards him.

"Did you hear that? I think there is—" he called, but Rai drove his dagger into his gut. A look of shock and horror danced across his face before softening as the light in his eyes extinguished.

Rai kept jogging, slowing as he approached an open arch that looked out onto the second tower, connected by a middling section five stories below.

There's no way I can carry you all the way over there, Fax said. *We would glide down onto the roof of the middle building before we reached it.*

Rai weighed his options. Guards patrolled the roof below. If he was to drop down, he would have to fight six guards in the open, where others might see them and rush to their aid.

Shouting echoed down the corridor. *Not enough time to use my bow,* Rai thought, listening to the shouting getting louder.

"We don't really have much of a choice, Fax," Rai said,

reaching into his belt and pulling out a vial of blood. He then unsheathed his daggers and poured half of the vial into each of the dagger hilts, where it ran up the length of the blade through a cut in the centre.

A clamour of calls burst from behind Rai. Rai didn't turn, instead he slid the empty vial and daggers back into his belt and leapt.

Fax wrapped around his hand and brought him gliding down onto the roof of the middling section. The night air felt cool as they descended. The guards shouted from the arch above, causing those patrolling on the roof to spin around.

Landing with a crack, Rai lifted his head to see the six guards standing in stunned silence. He slid both his daggers out from his belt and rolled his wrists. He had been hoping it wouldn't come to this, but he had the attention of the entire guard headquarters now. If he wanted to get Grenin and Larina out alive, this was the only way.

With a war cry, the six guards sprinted at him. Fax darted to the left towards the two who had been covering the rear of the building. Rai broke towards the other four.

As the two closest neared, Rai flicked his daggers, sending arcs of flames tearing towards them. The first screamed as the flames sent them falling back, holding their burnt face. The other, with more warning, dove under the flames.

"Diera blades!" the man shouted to his comrades.

A well-read man, Rai thought. He didn't think anyone would recognise the rare weapons in Celabar.

Rai brought the daggers down as the man rolled back, the

blades catching a bit of his jerkin and setting it alight. The guard yelped, rolling until the flames had extinguished. By that point, Rai drove both daggers into his chest.

The fear of a man that saw death marred his face.

A cry drew Rai from the dying man as the one with the burnt face swung his blade. Rai ducked, parrying the second swing, and stepping back to create some space. The burnt man had a manic look in his eyes as he ran at Rai with the ferocity of a bull.

Rai deflected the hatred-fuelled flurry of attacks. The man had clearly heard his friend shout that Rai held diera blades, and he kept Rai on the back foot, not letting him throw more fire.

The two other guards were closing in. Rai glanced over to see Fax finishing off the two on the other side, but that cost him. The burnt man sliced wildly, catching Rai's arm. He hissed and pulled back. He had to kill this man. Now.

The burnt man struck again, hoping to get another hit, but Rai parried and kicked the man's knee. He squealed as it cracked and folded at a wrong angle.

Rai swiped both blades along the man's neck and let him slump to the side.

The approaching guards slowed as they came to the last ten paces, cautious now Rai was free to focus on them.

Rai was acutely aware that this was taking too long. If he didn't get across this roof and into the other side of the building, this roof would be swarming with guards.

Fax flew to him as Rai lurched forward. The first guard

came in swinging, feinting, and then going for the kill. Rai stepped in, battering away the attack with his bracer, and sliced his dagger over the guard's gut. The man froze, tilting his head down to see the red seeping out of the gash across his stomach.

He brought in a sharp strained inhale and drove his blade into Rai's side with a snarl, then keeled over. Rai stumbled back in shock, clasping the dagger in his side, the blood running between his fingers. Most were too busy dying to attack.

The last guard fell upon him with a thrust from his spear. Rai ducked out the way, the blade narrowly missing his face. The spearman growled thrusting the haft and cracking Rai across the nose. Blood splatted over his vision as he tripped back.

Rai landed on his back, the wind knocked from his lungs. He groaned, tentatively touching his face. Hissing at the pain, he wiped the blood from his eyes to see the guard preparing to drive his spear into Rai's chest.

Rai could only lie there wheezing.

Suddenly, a black shadow blurred Rai's vision and a blood poured from the man's neck. Rai blinked and the man collapsed.

Come on, this isn't time for a nap, Fax said.

The gash at his side wasn't deep, but he was losing a lot of blood, light headedness giving an almost dreamlike wavering to the world around him. Rai reached for his belt and pulled out another vial, this time putting it to his lips and draining the contents. Warmth burned through him. Rai pushed up onto his knees, then stumbled to his feet, gasping. His side throbbed where the man had stabbed him and his nose was a bloodied mess, but the pain was numbing with the effects of the vial, and he could focus again, lucidity snapping back into place. Shouting came from the stairs on the far side of the roof leading down into the building.

More are coming. Come on!

Rai half-ran, half-staggered his way across the roof. He pushed open a door and stepped into the other building.

These merchants better be damn grateful, Rai thought, clutching his side and moving up a sandstone staircase lit by crackling flames.

11

The Tear

Nya slept no more that night, but watched as the Sun Eye's glare came back around and lit Tarris anew. The rest started to shuffle and rustle about, but no one spoke. A sense of foreboding tightening around them with every passing breath.

The iron door swung open, and in came the same plated guard carrying the same five trays. He passed them out and made his way back to the door. But before leaving he added, "Last meal. Make it a good one." Then he slammed the iron door shut.

"A cheery guy, that one," Kit said around a mouthful of bread.

"You were the one who named us the Doomed Others," the mystery woman said.

Nya knelt beside her tray and started eating. It was the same bread and gruel from the day before.

"If you can't laugh at yourself, you have no right to laugh at others," Kit said.

"That is the dumbest thing I've ever heard," Drak said, tossing his finished tray back out through the slot.

"You do yourself a disservice, Drak. Dumb things being said are most definitely your area of expertise," Kit replied.

The conversation petered out after that, not having the same energy it did the day before, all of them wrapped in their own thoughts.

And if there would be a tomorrow.

Nya had barely set her tray down when, with the sound of metal grating on metal, the iron door opened and in piled seven plated palace guards. In the centre, stood a woman. She was as tall and broad as the guards, even without the plate, a scar running through her left eyebrow. Her gait and stance placed her as the ranking officer.

"Pitiful," she said under her breath. "Wrangle them up and follow me." She twirled her fingers, and the guards broke into motion.

"Hands," the guard at Nya's cage demanded. She slid her hands under the slot where her meal tray was passed through, and the guard clicked on a set of metal shackles, already the metal abraded her skin.

The rest were undergoing the same treatment, although Drak had two guards ready at his cage. And given his hulking figure, Nya couldn't blame them.

Their cage doors creaked open and one by one the Doomed Others were led in a line to the palace dungeons. A guard walked behind Nya, knocking her with a spear tip anytime he didn't think she was moving fast enough. But it was hard to not slow and gawk. She was in the *Thousand Floor Palace*.

Towering in the centre of Yontar was the Thousand Floor Palace, the second largest palace in the world. The first being the Mad Palace in the abandoned capital. The Mad Palace was rumoured to be made from the bones of Gods and said to always be expanding and growing more levels. But that was a firepit story. No one had set foot in the lost capital in hundreds of years. This, though, Nya thought, looking around, was a real palace. *The* palace.

The palace Mother always thought she would be living in.

The chambers walls were covered in ancient tapestries still vivid and distinct, despite the ages that had passed since their creation. Nya couldn't read, but she could guess some meanings from the glyphs and icons.

The tapestry depicted gods and monsters, but also merchants and farmers. It showed Ova, the great creature that turned the world and watched over them with its two eyes: the Sun Eye blazing, and Moon Eye glinting.

The chamber walls told a story spanning back to the First Days. Nya wished she could linger longer but any slacking and *thwack*—a spear butt against her backside.

Ahead, at the end of the corridor was an arched door and a guard standing on either side of it. Etched into the surrounding walls were symbols of justice, common among the prisons and guard towers around Yontar. Scales and human hearts appeared more than once, referencing the Judging after death. Atop the door was a painting of Ma-atan, the Harbinger of Justice, its bladed arms reaching around the door frame as if daring prisoners to try and escape. The Harbinger would be the one to rip your heart out and lay it upon the scales for the Judging.

The Judging terrified Nya. Her mother always said that her heart wouldn't balance on the scales and Ma-atan would banish her to spend the rest of eternity in Duat, the torment realms.

And Nya believed her.

The woman at the front of their group spoke to the guards, then the door was opened and they walked beneath Ma-atan. Nya cringed as if it would reach out and snatch her, but of course, it didn't. Still, her muscles eased after passing under it unscathed.

They worked their way through the palace. Up flights of stairs and down corridors. Some had ancient drawings on the walls, others were blank with braziers being the only thing breaking the constant sandstone around them. Sometimes they went back down a set of stairs just to rise again later.

Finally, they came to a stop before another door. Nya had no idea where they were or how far they had travelled from the dungeons. But after more whispered words, they passed through, the guards keeping their eyes forward.

The chamber inside was a hive of activity. Guards stood along the edges as scholars sped about, carrying parchment and scrolls between the mass of tables scattered on either side. At the back of the room was an enormous staircase that fell away, out of sight.

"Wait with them there," the woman said to the guards.

The guards pushed the Doomed Others into a corner and told them to get on their knees.

"Didn't even leave us time to digest our gruel," Kit said, dropping beside her.

Now that they were together, it was easier to see the other members of the Doomed Others. Drak was even burlier up close. The mystery woman was pale skinned with long dark hair falling as far as her waist. She held her chin high and somehow looked distinguished, despite being on her knees and in shackles like the rest of them. Past her was the fifth member, the one Nya had only heard the scrapings of while in the cells.

He was a man in his early twenties. His head was shaven, but stubble was starting to come in. His eyes were closed and head bowed, his breath was the only indication he was not a statue. He lifted his head and looked at Nya, his blue eyes meeting hers as if he had felt them on him. Cheeks reddening, Nya whipped her head around.

The woman who led them returned with a skinny man wearing the loose-fitting robe of a scholar.

"My name is Commander Ewyna, and this is Mirt," she said. A five-letter name? Ewyna had to be a highly ranked in the palace to have a name like that. "He runs this... research project."

Mirt scratched his elbows and nodded. "Yes, well, I am the one who is running it now," he said with a laugh. Ewyna scowled at him.

"Anyway," Mirt said with a clap. "Let's get to why you all are here. This is a rather unusual and unique research project and sadly, we have lost contact with our field team. So we need a small group for... retrieval; including two of my researchers, a couple guards, and the five of you to recover who"—Mirt cleared his throat—"or what you can."

Mirt clearly didn't think the research team was still alive. What happened to them? What had they been studying? And why were they, of all people, being sent to recover the research?

"We are not soldiers. Why not send more guards?" Drak asked, receiving a spear butt to the side for speaking out of turn.

"We don't waste trained guards on these sorts of things. If it comes to it, you will serve as a distraction so the scholars can grab the remaining research and run," Ewyna said.

"Run? From what?" Drak groaned as he sat up, receiving another batter from the guard's spear as he did.

"You could run into husks, or worse," Mirt said.

"Husks?" Kit asked, also receiving a spear butt to the back. He spun to face the guard. "Really? I'm just asking about the mission!" Kit shouted.

"Husks are creatures that, from what we have gathered, are similar to humans. Like a human-bat mix. Human sized, but with rough black skin and short wings," Mirt said.

The image sent shivers down Nya's back. There was something unsettling about creatures that were human-like. Those were always the stories that scared her the most, the monsters that could walk the streets and be mistaken for one of them.

"And that's not even the *'or worse'* encounter?" Kit asked. This time the spear cracked him across the head, sending him toppling over with a squeal.

Mirt let out a titter, running a hand down the back of his neck.

Four others wearing plate armour approached. They must be who the Doomed Others were escorting. Nya could tell the two at the back were the scholars by the way they walked in their armour, side to side as if trying to shake off the weight of the metal, whereas the two guards walked with an ease that only those used to wearing plate could manage. Nya had learnt to distinguish new guards from the older, more experienced ones using the same tells.

"We're ready," one of the guards said.

Even the scholars are wearing plate armour? Where are we going?

"These are the two you will be escorting. Just stick with them and listen to the guards, and if you make it back alive, we will set you all free," Ewyna said.

No one said anything. Mostly because they didn't want to get hit by a spear rather than not having anything to say. They still knew next to nothing about this *recovery mission*.

"Come then, let's get you into position," Ewyna said.

Commander Mirt, two scholars, and two guards made their way to the back of the room and down the stairs. The Doomed Others were poked and prodded to follow. Guards stood at the top of the staircase to keep people from going down or from coming up, Nya wasn't sure.

They descended the wide steps. The stairwell was wide enough that five could walk abreast. Kit came alongside Nya as the voices from the rushing room above faded and they delved deeper into the palace.

"What do you think?" Kit whispered.

"I think we need to stick together," Nya whispered back. If she had learnt anything on the streets, it was that there was strength in numbers. A pang of sadness overcame her with the thought of the Sand Rats waiting atop that tower for her and Luk. She shook it off. If she was going to survive this and get back to them and Mother, she would have to focus.

They levelled off in a chamber much like the one at the top of the stairs. Torches threw flickering light over the sandstone chamber that darkened towards the back where...

Nya's breath caught.

At the back of the chamber was a black tear.

It was a tear in the fabric of reality itself. A pure black crack rending the air, emitting soft warmth. It drank in the light around it, the torches closer to the tear dimming. Even the torches at Nya's side were trembling, as if fighting to stay alight.

The air felt thicker down here, and sound didn't carry the same. It was as though Nya had ducked her head underwater.

Two more guards waited at the bottom step, the furthest point from the tear.

Her mind screamed for her to turn and run back up and away from this pulsating break in the world.

"What in the Duat damned realms is that?" Kit asked, his voice sounding tinny and far away despite him standing near Nya.

"That is where you will be going to find our lost research team," Commander Ewyna said.

"You want us to *enter* that thing?" Kit asked.

The Commander ignored him and shouted, "Line up!"

The two guards and two scholars didn't move. They expected the Doomed Others to go first. It was dawning on Nya that they were here as fodder. Nothing more than meat shields. A tremor worked its way through her arm.

"Come on, forward!" the guards said, jabbing the Doomed Others forward. They crept towards the rent. With each step, the warmth in the air increased.

"Gods damn it," Drak said, looking down the line. They crept at a sands' trickle of a pace. "Fine." Drak approached it first.

He reached out, brushing in front of the tear. His fingertips warped, bending, and stretching. Drak yanked his hand back and tapped the top of his fingertips as if to check it was still there. Then with a roar, he charged into the black. His body rippled and pulsed and was *pulled* into the tear. Then he was gone.

"Drak?" Kit called but got no answer.

"He's on the other side. Move," a guard said, nudging them on.

The bald man who hadn't spoken went next. His face impassive as he casually walked up and into the tear. The mystery woman followed. Kit gave Nya a nervous glance.

"Ladies first?" Kit said, gesturing forward.

Nya sighed but edged up to the tear. There was a burning sensation on her skin now that she was close. She feared it might be too hot to touch or that it would burn her as she passed through.

Shaking fingers reached out, numbness seeping through her hand, then up to her shoulder. Instinctively, Nya held her breath as she moved into the darkness.

Then she passed into the dark place.

12

Out of Celabar

The fight on the rooftop must have drawn the guards out, as Rai made it to the top floor without passing another guard. He was grateful, given his injuries. It gave him time to wrap his side and staunch the bleeding.

"Fax, go ahead," Rai said, as he exited onto the third floor to check.

Fax darted down the corridor as a crow, hovering before each cell. The doors were made of iron, with barred ports at eye level letting in light. Fax hovered near the middle of the corridor.

They're here, Rai!

Rai pushed off the wall and jogged down the corridor. The blood he had ingested from the vial was taking effect and his side and nose were more dull aches than screaming pain.

But he had to be careful not to overtax himself. His wounds hadn't healed, the blood had merely smothered the pain, allowing Rai to ignore it.

Rai peered into the cell Fax hovered before. Inside, huddled together at the back of the cell, were Grenin and Larina. Grenin had been beaten, his right eye swollen and bruising.

"Fax," Rai said.

Fax slid down to where the locking bolt would be, slicing it in half and the door swung open. Light from the corridor poured in giving Rai a better look at the two. Larina had been crying. Her face was red with strain and cheeks damp with tears, but she was unharmed. Grenin, however, was injured worse than Rai had originally thought. Bruising covered his arms and legs and one of his shoulders sagged. Probably dislocated, Rai guessed.

"Rai?" Larina croaked.

"I know you two want to take stories back to your homeland but this is a little over the top don't you think?" Rai said.

"I'm so sorry. It was me. I told them your name," Larina said, more tears running down her cheeks. "They were hurting him."

Rai walked over and bent down beside them. They both leaned back, wild-eyed. "It's okay. I'm not going to hurt you. I'm here to break you out." Rai laid a hand on Larina's shoulder.

She let out a breath. Grenin's eyes focused on him. He

smiled, blood lining his teeth.

"I di-didn't break," Grenin stammered. "I didn't tell them. Kept firm grip of those I love."

Stupid, stupid man, Rai thought. Grenin hadn't broken under the beatings, so they hit him until Larina broke. *So much for not being strong enough*, Rai thought. Grenin was stronger than he gave himself credit for.

"Come on, let's get out of here," Rai said, putting himself under Grenin's good arm and heaving him up. Grenin yelped as Rai and Larina got him to his feet but he stood. Rai led him into the corridor where Larina gasped.

"You're hurt," Larina said.

"Just some scratches. Maybe you can help patch me up once we are out of here," Rai said, shifting Grenin so he could help him walk.

They made their way down the corridor to the staircase. It was a steady pace given Grenin's condition, but they wouldn't outrun any guards. Creeping down two flights of stairs, the thunder of boots on stone rung from further below. Rai gestured to Larina and they crept out onto a floor and started down the corridor.

They have blocked all the stairwells, Fax said, flying back to them.

"It's the bird!" Larina said as Fax flew beside them.

"We will need to push through then. I can put Grenin down and—"

They have a korhin too, Fax said.

An image of the huge blue, pot-bellied, circular-eared

creature stole Rai's attention. Fighting one of those fresh and with backup would have been a task but hurt and with Grenin and Larina… he had no chance.

They would need to find another way down. They pressed on towards the arch at the far end of the corridor, allowing Rai see how high they were. Still ten stories, at least.

"Could you carry Grenin down?" Rai asked.

Yes, but I can't carry more than one at a time, Fax said.

Rai leant over the edge and saw the nearby alleys were empty. An inn sat across the street, windows lit.

"Okay, drop Grenin behind those crates," Rai said, pointing into the alley beside them.

Rai held Grenin until Fax lifted him from the ground. Grenin groaned with the strain. "Gentle, Fax," Rai said, as Fax carried him over the edge and down into the side street.

A screech from behind indicated the guards had found them. Rai spun. Three guards piled down towards them.

At least it isn't the korhin, Rai thought as the korhin turned the corner.

You've got to be shoving sand up my-

Rai shoved Larina to the right and dove forward. The korhin's fist crashed down, cracking the floor.

Rai dragged his daggers across the korhin's forearm, it roared slamming down his other fist forcing Rai back again. Rai cursed. The lack of flames wracking the creature's slimy blue skin meant the blood in his daggers had run out. The korhin growled and the guards at its side backed up letting it take care of the intruders.

I was away for ten heartbeats, Fax said. *You can't stay out of trouble for that long?*

The korhin threw itself up and came crashing down fists first.

"Take Larina!" Rai shouted and rolled back.

He kept evading the korhin's attacks, which were getting more and more aggressive as he slammed his hands around like hammers. Finally, Fax and Larina crossed the threshold and dipped out of sight.

Rai knew he couldn't keep avoiding all these attacks. One would land eventually, and that's all the korhin would need to turn him into mush. He needed to slow the beast until Fax returned. Glancing around, Rai spotted on the cracks in the stone floor.

Rai waited until the korhin sent a fist sailing towards him, then jumped off the wall to gain more height and landed on its fist. Before the creature could register what he had done, Rai was sprinting up its arm towards its face.

The look of a shocked korhin was a sight Rai was sure he would remember forever. Rai drove his foot down on the korhin's face with a satisfying *crack*. The korhin roared and swatted at him, so Rai kicked off his chest and landed in the middle of the snaking fractures lining the floor.

He smiled as the korhin glared with fire and death in its eyes. It slammed both fists right onto where Rai stood. The blow ripped through the stone, sending an explosion of rock and dust spiralling into the air.

Then the ground fell away.

They plunged downward among a vortex of sandstone and dust. Rai knew the ruptured floor wouldn't last and was prepared for it to collapse. He fell with control avoiding large chunks of sandstone. Screaming sounded from all around, as everyone fell through.

The clouds of dust parted, Rai met the eyes of the korhin, whose face was a frenzied mess of pulsing veins and bloodshot eyes.

It was going to tear him apart.

There is little more frightening than an angered predator, and this thing was a heartbeat away from ripping off Rai's face to use as a dartboard.

Time to go, Rai thought turning.

Rai took off for the open arch on this level, as a deafening screech shook the walls. Fax still hadn't returned but there was no time to wait, so Rai dove over the archway and into the night.

The ground came at him with the speed of an arrow.

A claw wrapped around his wrist and he jerked, a sickening jolt went through him.

Aww you really trust me that much? Fax said as they floated down to the alley.

Rai blew out a breath, too relieved to answer.

Fax dropped Rai, and he knelt beside Grenin and Larina. Wasting no time, Rai heaved Grenin back to his feet and shuffled across the street to the inn.

"Quickly, follow me. Stay quiet, and don't meet anyone's eyes," Rai said, as he pushed the door open.

Light bathed them as they stepped into the busy inn. A flute whistled over the hearty laughs and buzz of conversation. Rai focused on the back door.

Heads turned and questions were passed around the tables as people noticed his group. They must have been a sight. A battered man in guard uniform, holding up an even more bloodied foreign man with an eye swollen shut, being tailed by a terrified woman who looked like she would rather be anywhere but this seedy inn.

They made it to the back door and passed through without interruption. It led out into a courtyard, just as Rai had hoped. The open space was surrounded by stables with a locked gate on the right side.

Rai led them into the stables, where an aya chewed contentedly on some meat. Luckily it still had its platform attached. Rai clambered up first and helped pull Grenin onto the platform, Larina following. Then with a whip of the reins, the aya trampled out into the courtyard.

"What about the gate?" Larina asked, as Rai flicked the reins again, and the aya barged through the gate wrenching it off its hinges.

They turned into the streets of Celabar as they heard the door swing open from the courtyard. City guards or disgruntled inn goers, Rai wasn't sure.

"Here." Rai unlatched a pouch from his belt and passed it to Larina. "It has bandages and a small bottle of alcohol so you can patch Grenin up."

Larina took it with shaking hands. "Rai..." she started

and stopped several times before deciding on, "thank you." Then she moved over to Grenin who sat against the side of the platform, head lolling back and forth.

No one gave them a second glance as Rai brought them to the city gate. It wasn't uncommon for people to travel at night to avoid the heat of day. Rai nodded to the guards who waved him on. Word hadn't travelled this far yet.

Thank the gods.

Rai kept them moving, following the city wall so they could leave from the opposite direction of the gate that they exited, hoping to throw off anyone trying to track them.

Soon, they were on the black dunes, heading west. Grenin and Larina talked in hushed tones but it was quiet once again. It always felt strange to Rai to go from the screams of battle to the silence after.

They passed two Waypoints before Rai thought it safe to stop. He hopped down and did his check of the Waypoint.

"It's empty," Rai called. "We should spend the night here. It's unlikely they will work out what direction we went for some time."

Rai helped Larina get Grenin inside and lying on one of the beds. He was coming in and out of consciousness, when Larina lay beside him, and Rai stepped back out to the aya.

He breathed in the fresh air.

You certainly know how to make an exit, Fax said.

"Can you watch for a bit? I need to rest," Rai managed as he climbed back onto the aya and fell asleep, unsure if Fax had agreed or not.

Something nudged his chest. Rai groaned, his body already sitting before he was awake. Everything ached and his throat felt as if he had been drinking sand. He strained against the glare of the Sun, trying to focus on what had awoken him.

"Here, drink this," Larina said, handing him a waterskin.

Rai took a deep draught before looking at the sky. It wasn't long after sunrise. He had slept too long. Fax should have woken him.

"How is Grenin?" Rai asked, bowing his head in thanks as he passed back the waterskin.

"He will live," Larina said. "We both will thanks to you."

"I was part of the reason they put you in there. I was only fixing a wrongdoing," Rai said, rolling his shoulder. Larina's face screwed up at the mess Rai had made of his bandages on the move last night.

"Can I?" Larina pointed to his blood-soaked bandages.

"Please," Rai said.

Larina peeled off the bandages around his side. Then she pulled out fresh bandages that Rai gave her the night before, ripping off a small cloth and dosing it in water. She dabbed and cleaned the wound, then re-bandaged it, sitting back with a satisfied nod.

"That's much better," Larina said.

"Thank you," Rai said, wishing she still had some of the salve that numbed the pain from the last time she patched him up. But at least they weren't afraid of him anymore.

"What now?" Larina said, worry worming its way onto

140

her face.

"We keep heading west. I have some connections in a small village where we can stock up on water and food, then we can decide the best way to proceed," Rai said.

Larina nodded. "I'll go see if Grenin has woken yet." She climbed down from the aya and disappeared back into the Waypoint.

Rai stood, stretching his stiff muscles.

"No movement last night?" Rai asked.

Nope. The black sands hardened before we were on the dunes, so there were no footprints for the city guard to follow, Fax said. *I doubt they will be able to track us.*

"They will probably guess we ran south, trying to get back to Dock Town and then on a boat out of Tarris," Rai said, as he tracked over the cresting dunes surrounding them. "That will make it difficult to get those two back home if they send men to watch the docks."

It's still an improvement on the prison cell, Fax said.

Sand trickled down the dunes as they travelled west, early morning travellers bowing as they passed. Grenin looked a damn sight better now that Larina had bandaged him up and he had some sleep. Even the swelling around his eye was coming down.

Gamo village stood stark against the desert with its patches of greenery. The village nestled beside an outcropping of rock reaching out of the sand. Water trees swayed in the breeze casting shadows across the lush vegetation, sheltering it from the harsh Sun Eye.

There were about fifteen buildings, all the same three-story height spaced out around the village. Out here life was much more relaxed. They didn't care about proving their worth by building taller and taller buildings. The people in the village of Gamo built what they needed and nothing more. Even the village elder, who looked after the vegetation, had the same size and shaped home as the rest.

Rai brought the aya to a trot. A handful of villagers were already out tending the patch of greenery under the water trees. Armed men paced the periphery to fend off thieves and bandits. They watched as the aya idled past; hands lifted to shade their vision.

The village had no inn so Rai reined in the aya, leading it into the shade of the first building.

"Wait here," Rai said, as he clambered down.

His feet crackled on the gravel as he trudged over to the farm patch, where an old man with an arched back and wisping white streaks of hair watched him approach.

"Here to rob a quiet village?" the old man asked. "Don't think we won't put up a fight."

"If I was, I'd have an army with me to bring this stubborn lot down," Rai said, and the pair smiled at each other. Elder Kalt pulled Rai into an embrace, laughing as he did.

"It's good to see you again, my dear friend," Elder Kalt said.

"And you," Rai said. Then, stepping back, he added, "You haven't aged a day."

Elder Kalt gave him a toothy grin. "Come, come! You have

arrived in time for the morning breaking of the fast."

"I have brought some friends with me."

It felt strange calling them friends, but the merchants didn't have any money to pay him, so Rai couldn't call them clients anymore.

Elder Kalt grinned at that. Probably as much from Rai's discomfort using the word as the fact itself. "Well, I'll be damned. Did you hear that, Syla? Rai has managed to rope someone else into believing he's not terrible."

"Stop teasing him, Kalt," Syla said, as she walked past them carrying a basket of fruit. The short, broad lady was Kalt's wife. She was given the title of maut, which meant mother of the village. Syla had the warm eyes of someone half her age and the spritely step to make one believe it.

"Can I?" Rai said, reaching for the basket.

"No," Syla said, burling the basket away from him. "But you can help Kalt with the rest."

13

The Dark Place

Nya knew she was somewhere else. Somewhere different. The air was thicker, like it felt around the tear. An oppressive humid heat filled her lungs, her mind reeling at the foreign bulk of it.

The dark took shape. Sharp edges of black rock formations reinforced itself onto the world around her. She was in a cave, with only the faintest light outlining the structures. Three silhouettes shifted in front of her.

Behind, the same tear that was in the palace chamber hung in the air. A rent where all light was torn from the world. Kit came through, his scream sounding before his body appeared.

"Shut up!" Drak said.

Kit stopped, standing still. "Am I dead?"

"We aren't that lucky," the mystery woman said.

One of the guards came through next, followed by the two scholars, then the last guard taking up the rear. They moved more surefooted than the rest, pressing forward towards where the light bled in.

"Everyone pass through okay?" the female scholar asked.

"There was a chance we wouldn't?" Kit asked.

The scholar ignored him. "Now, we must stay quiet," the scholar whispered. "The longer we can pass through undetected, the better."

A guard and the two scholars led with the other guard falling behind the Doomed Others to ensure they didn't escape. Not that there was anywhere to run off to.

The uneven rocky terrain brought their pace to a crawl, but the light was expanding the further they moved, bringing more detail to the surrounding cave. Nya gazed up at the black rock. Some of it looked to have been carved, almost manmade with its straight angles and segmented shaping. She had never seen anything like it. Where were they? They couldn't be in Tarris any longer.

Cresting a ridge, the mouth of the cave gaped like a maw in the black stone, giving them their first glimpse of the dark place.

Nya inhaled sharply.

The sky was a turbulent sea of grey clouds. They ran over and crashed into one another like raging waves. The ground before the party gave way in a downward slope of scree, rock, and sand that was black as night, with tinges of purple in the stone. They were fairly high up, giving them a good view of the craggy landscape. Further down, formations stuck up from the ground.

They stood speechless. Even the guards were slack-jawed. Clearly it was their first time here too, despite their confidence in the cave.

The roiling clouds rumbled and roared, not even a crack of blue in the swirling grey. Nya had seen plenty of sandstorms in her life, but nothing like this. It was all so foreign. She was brought up on the golden sands and blue skies of Tarris. This was not Tarris. It was grey and black, the sky a raging storm. And if the sky held the Sun Eye, Nya could not see it.

Drak snarled and dove for one of the guards. The guard was too busy looking over the landscape to notice, until Drak had cracked him across the nose, sending spittle and blood spraying. The guard's spear went skidding from him. Drak kicked the back of his leg, forcing the guard to his knees with a howl of pain. Then, sliding the man's sword from his waist, Drak held it to his neck. It all happened so fast. The other guard had barely turned by the time a blade glinted beside his partner's neck.

"What is going on? Where are we? Start talking or I'll slit his neck," Drak said.

"Shh! You mustn't! They will hear us!" the male scholar hissed.

"Who will? Where are we?" Drak said, tightening the blade against the guard's neck, causing a bead of blood to trickle down his neck.

"Okay! Okay!" the scholar said, eyes darting all around

them. "We don't know. That's what we're trying to figure out. We have sent several research expeditions here. We never hear from most of them again, but this most recent team sent a courier saying they found something and were coming back. That was three days ago."

"We really don't know much, but there are... things living here," the other scholar said with a shiver. "I've seen the state some corpses have returned in. Please, you must be quiet." Now everyone's attention was brought to the landscape, gazes passing between the land and sky. The thought of these humanoid bat creatures set a chill over the group.

"Let the guard go, Drak. If these husks are as dangerous as they make them out to be, we will need as many swords as we can get," the mystery woman said. "And it's not like we can escape. The only way home is through that tear, and through a palace surrounded by guards."

Drak stared at her. The fury in his eyes that would turn most away, but the mystery woman stared right back.

Finally, with an exhale, Drak tossed the guard forward and dropped the sword. The guard idling at the ready surged forward, smacking Drak in the face with his spear. The scholars helped the fallen guard back to his feet and returned his spear to him.

Nya cringed back from the beating. Facing away, she watched as the mysterious woman surveyed the landscape. Sure, Drak had the toned muscles of someone who knew battle, but the cool and collected sense of certainty leaking from the mystery woman was something else entirely. Nya wanted to stand next to her if anything was to happen.

The guards were more cautious after Drak's skirmish at the cave's mouth. Spears were gripped tighter, and the two guards at either end of the party kept a couple paces further from them.

Drak was badly beaten but none of the rest of the Doomed Others stepped in to stop the guards. Even after they started moving and Drak swayed, head down, spitting globs of blood every couple of paces, none of them approached him. But he didn't groan or fall behind, and Nya had no doubt the man would jump into action again if needed.

As they made their way down from the cave, the rock formations grew around them. Peaks and stacks jutted around them as solitary towers. Some rose as tall as buildings in Yontar, severely limiting their long-distance vision. Nya was on edge, watching the gaps between the cracked black rocks. Several times she thought she saw something moving in the corner of her eye, only to spin and see nothing but the dead landscape beyond.

They clambered through fields of rock that covered the dark land. Although, once they were on the rocks and could see into the distance again, Nya no longer felt free but vulnerable. Open to attack, and she was delighted to be back down and enclosed by rocks after passing through the stone run.

Now that they were out and away from their cave, a sense of restlessness permeated the party. No one dared speak in anything other than a hushed whisper.

Fingers curled around Nya's shoulder. She jerked away, spinning around. Kit lifted his hands, palms out. "It's just me," he said.

Nya blew out a breath, muscles relaxing.

"This place has me on edge too," he said, coming to walk beside her. "I have an awful feeling that something out there is—"

"Watching us?" Nya asked.

Kit nodded.

"Me too," Nya said, glancing over her shoulder. Everything around them was so still. The guard holding the rear glowered at her, so she faced forward again.

"Where do you think we are?" Kit asked. Nya shrugged. "I feel like we have fallen into one of the torments realms. Maybe we died in the Blind Walk after all, and this is the afterlife."

Back in the cell, Nya would have scoffed at that. But walking through this dead place beneath the storming sky, she could understand where he was coming from.

They hiked on in silence for a while, focused on their thoughts, when Kit spoke up again. "What happened to your father?"

"What?" Nya asked, baffled at the sudden change.

"You said you want to get back to your mother. I was just wondering what happened to your father," Kit said.

This boy had the manners of a sand fox at breakfast. But there was an innocence to him. Nya could see he was just used to talking about these things openly. Or at least, he didn't see his questions as prying like she did. It made her want to know what his life was like before this.

"I scared him off," Nya said.

"Scared him off?"

"Yeah," Nya said, her mind drifting through memories. "My mother worked in the kitchens in the palace. That's where she met my father. He was a palace guard, and they fell in love. He even invited her to move into the quarters with him. They spent every minute together. He got himself assigned to the branch that was nearest the kitchens so he could see her more." Nya's face darkened.

"That was, until Mother got pregnant. He didn't want me. Said kids were too expensive and would just tie them down. So he kicked her out when she started showing. Mother begged him to take her back, said she would get rid of me. Eventually, he got sick of her turning up when he was working and had her fired from her job and banned from the palace."

"It broke her. Ripped apart, only half of a whole," Nya said, remembering the exact words her mother told her. "She couldn't keep a job, so she ended up on the street. She wanted rid of me, but most of her money came from begging and people had looser purses around a pregnant woman. So she kept me. Begging went even better after she had me, too. A mother with a child brought more coin than a woman sitting alone."

"Then, as soon as I could walk, I got to paying back my debt to her. I did what I could with small jobs around our district, and stole what I could to feed her," Nya said, then shook her head, coming back to herself. "That's why I need to get back to her. I ruined her chance at a happy life, so I need to do what I can to make things better."

"That's awful," Kit said. "Duat take your father."

Nya snapped her head around. "My father is a great man!"

Kit looked puzzled. "But he left you and your Mother on the streets."

"Because of me!" Nya said, feeling a tear roll down her cheek. "It's my fault! They would have been together in the palace, living the life they deserved it if weren't for me."

Kit tried to say something and stopped, concern lining his face. "No, Nya that isn't your fault. Your father shouldn't have thrown out your mother. And your mother shouldn't have treated you like a sickness."

Nya was horrified. What did he know? He thought just because Nya summed up her situation in a couple minutes, he could judge her family?

Before she knew what she was doing, Nya hauled back and punched Kit in the face, sending him tumbling over a rock.

Glancing up, Nya realized everyone was staring at her. She looked down at Kit, who was groaning as he pushed himself up. Nya ducked her head, tears still streaming, and pressed toward the front.

They marched on, no one mentioning the outburst. The swell of emotion settled and Nya regretted hitting Kit, but she didn't turn to face him. She couldn't. He shouldn't have said those things about her family.

Finally, she came to walk alongside the bald man. She kept forgetting he was here. He was so quiet and stoic, as though unperturbed by their situation. She didn't talk to him and he didn't speak, but it was comforting just having someone beside her.

It was hard to gauge time without seeing the Sun Eye, but Nya guessed they had been walking for several hours before the scholar called the party to a stop. They ducked into an alcove in an escarpment of the same black rock that littered the land.

"We're close," the scholar said, after they came within earshot. "I think round that rock is where they set up camp."

There were sighs of relief all around. It had been a trek, but they hadn't run into anything that wanted to kill them, apart from each other yet.

"We don't know if they're there or not, but something has kept them from sending messengers, so we need to be careful," the scholar reminded them.

The other scholar was fidgeting with short sharp breaths. Nya saw concern in her eyes. *She knows someone on the missing team*, Nya realised.

"You five will go in first," the guard said, hand on the hilt of his sword and staring at Drak as if daring him to try anything.

"Let's make this quick," Drak said.

The scholar nodded, holding out a piece of parchment. "We sent a cartographer with them to make this map and come back with a copy as soon as they set up camp."

It was an incredibly detailed map with even the stray rocks blocked out. Nya ran her eyes over the route they'd travelled, remembering each section vividly.

This was a surprising sign of how far this mysterious project had reached. To hire a master cartographer to create a map like this showed the power and money that backed this.

The scholar pointed to a tiny indent on a block. "This is where we are right now, and this," the scholar said, pointing to crescent-shaped rock, "is where they made camp. In this curved rock to hide them from sight. You will break off into a group of two and a group of three travelling separate ways around the rock, then meet at the camp. If it's clear, whistle and we will come round."

Nya didn't like being sent in as bait. They were weaponless and armourless. If those husks were still there, they wouldn't stand a chance.

"Can we at least take a weapon?" Drak asked, hands outstretched to one of the guards. The guard cracked his spear over Drak's fingers, making him yelp and yank them back.

"This is it. We check the camp and walk back. If you can manage that, we will set you free," the scholar said.

This brought a thoughtful silence to the Doomed Others.

"Okay, I want to team up with him." Kit pointed to Drak.

"Good. It can be a boy team and a girl team then," the mystery woman said, winking at Nya.

Drak grumbled at that, but the mystery woman grabbed Nya and pulled her away before anyone could argue.

They crept down the embankment towards the back of the crescent-shaped rock. It towered over them, stomping out any plan of scaling it.

Sliding down the rocky terrain sent stones tumbling down in front of them, but the tumultuous rumbling of the sky masked the sound.

The mystery woman hopped the last of the way down and pressed her back up against the stone wall. Nya copied her, stumbling in beside the woman. With a nod, they both slithered around the bend.

"What's your name?" Nya asked.

The mystery woman looked at her. "What does it matter?"

"I don't want to keep calling you Mystery Woman like Kit does," Nya whispered.

The mystery woman smiled at that. "Styra," she replied. It wasn't a Tarrisian name, despite her looking like she was local.

"Nice to meet you, Styra," Nya said.

Styra nodded. "And you, Nya."

They passed the bend, eyes searching for movement. Nya followed Styra's lead, keeping her back to the wall and walking sideways. The rock was smooth but ridged under her fingertips. At least this way, nothing would creep up on them. Finally, they came to a sharp corner that fed into the centre of the crescent rock, where the camp should be.

Styra paused and took a few deep breaths before leaning around and peering into the open space. Nya waited, her heart pounding as she tried to keep her own breathing under control. Their party had made it this far without being attacked, but this was where the research team went missing. And being so deep into this strange land meant there would be no easy retreat.

"It looks clear, but it's understandable that the research team never made it back," Styra said, then inched around the corner. Nya closed her eyes and copied Styra's few deep breaths, then followed.

Torn patches of black fabric lay scattered about; the remains of four black tents. Two still had poles in places, but something had ripped big chunks out of the sides. They blended into the black stone encircling them, no doubt a purposeful decision.

And bodies lay strewn across the plain.

No body was whole. Pieces littered the ground in an indistinguishable mass of crimson and pink. Bile rose in Nya's throat and she spun, throwing up against the rock wall. Nya laid her hands on the wall to steady herself, breathing deeply.

"You okay?" Styra asked, resting a hand on her back.

"Yep." Nya swallowed back another influx.

"Don't signal anyone yet. I want to get a better look," Styra said.

Nya was about to argue; tell her it was dangerous to go alone, and the faster the others arrived, the faster they could all leave, but instead, she threw up again.

After her stomach settled, Nya straightened and swivelled around, pointedly looking at the sky. Styra ducked into one of the standing tents.

I need to go with her, Nya thought, but her body refused to move.

Nya coaxed herself forward, keeping her vision high so she couldn't see the mess on the ground. Her footsteps squelched and she almost threw up again, but with a moment of eyes forced shut and thoughts of elsewhere, she continued.

She made it to the tent, held up the canvas, and went inside. It was dark, allowing in none of the pale light from outside. Styra stood beside a table, flicking through pieces of parchment.

"Are those the research notes?" Nya asked, coming to her side.

What was left of a man lay on the desk, face half torn off. Nya yelped and lurched back.

"Yeah. They were pretty thorough," Styra said. "Testing how time passes here, trying to identify the rock types."

"The boys will be here any second. We should signal the rest," Nya said. Styra spun and gave a firm nod.

A whistle sounded. "The signal," Styra said, peering out the thin gap of light.

Together, they exited the tent to find the boys cresting the corner. Kit was pale and trying his hardest not to look at the bodies. Drak took in every detail, his nose upturned and disgust crumpling his face. The bald boy, however, was stoic as ever. How he managed that, Nya did not know.

"I don't like this," Drak said as they approached. "What creature would do something like this?"

"Not anything I know of. Only humans slaughter like

this," Styra said shaking her head.

"Let's get these damn notes and get out of here before we find out," Kit said.

"I have the research notes," Styra said, holding up a pile of parchment, "but I'm guessing they will want to look around before we head back."

Drak nodded. "We found the team. They better make it quick. I want to be back at the palace before it gets dark."

"*If* it gets dark here," Styra said, gazing at the sky.

The two guards crept into the camp, the scholars following close behind. Faces fell, skin lost colour, and something shattered in their eyes. The fidgeting scholar looked like she was going to faint.

Then she screamed.

She ran through the camp wailing and calling, "Riol!" Her heavy footfalls kicking up gore as she went. Nya watched as she yanked back the tent flap and collapsed to her knees. The half torn man.

The other scholar sprinted after her and wrapped himself around the howling female scholar, hushing her and holding her tight.

"Hey, do you hear that?" Styra asked.

Everyone stood still and tilted their heads, listening. It was hard to hear over the weeping and roaring of the clouds, but Nya thought she heard a... whipping sound?

Eyes widened with realisation.

Wings beating.

All eyes fell on the tent and screaming scholar inside.

"Someone needs to shut her up. Now," Drak said.

One guard ran for the tent, but it was too late.

A shriek blasted over the din.

14

Old Friends and Older Lessons

They huddled around the elders' table, bowls of fresh fruit and bread scattered across its surface. Elder Kalt had the village doctor see to Grenin and Rai, both receiving pain killer roots and fresh bandages.

The dining chamber was austere. A thick brown rug ran under the table, and a single tapestry depicting the village hung on the back wall. Their utensils were similarly plain and unadorned. Rai had come to envy the simple way of life in Gamo.

Rai scooped out a slice of melon. It had been a long night. Dal, the bloodhound, lay across his feet, looking up expectantly. He was an old dog now, his face drooping and eyes glazing. Rai sliced off a bit of melon and slid it under the table, scratching the dog's head as he chomped loudly, attracting a glare from Syla who had already fed the hound.

"So what brings you all the way out here?" Kalt asked.

Rai took a draught of water before saying, "I'm looking for a favour, I'm afraid."

"I'm sure we can arrange something for the saviour of Gamo," Kalt chuckled.

"I need you to smuggle these two out of Tarris," Rai said. Grenin choked on his water, eyes shooting up to Rai.

There was a beat of quiet.

"Done," Kalt said, then went back to eating as if Rai had asked to borrow a jug. "We have a shipment planned to go in a couple of days. I'm sure no one would notice a couple extra barrels."

Grenin and Larina shared a glance. "You can trust Elder Kalt and Maut Syla," Rai said to them. "I trust them with my life."

"I take Rai at his word and I promise not to pry into your business," Kalt said, hands outstretched.

"And if he does, you can remind him of that," Syla said. "He's become a right nosy goat in his old age."

Kalt scrunched his face up. "I have not!"

Syla twisted to face him, one eyebrow raised.

"Maybe a little," Kalt said.

"You're welcome to stay with us until then, too," Syla said to the merchants. "I can prepare the spare room."

"Ah, thank you!" Grenin stammered.

"That's very kind of you," Larina added as they bowed deeply from their chairs.

160

"Of course. Now eat and I can show you to your rooms," Syla said.

They finished the last of the food, and Syla led Grenin and Larina upstairs to their spare room. Dal lifted his head and watched them go but made no attempt to get off Rai's feet and follow. Silence descended around the table.

Kalt stared at Rai for a moment.

"This doesn't sound like keeping your head down," Kalt said. Rai said nothing. "I'm impressed you kept it down this long, to be honest."

"I'm heading south," Rai said.

"Still hunting for more shades?" Kalt asked, and Rai nodded.

Fax slid from Rai's shadow and perched on his shoulder as a crow. *I'm still your favourite shade though, right?* Fax asked, letting Kalt hear him.

"Of course." Kalt smiled. "When do you plan to leave?"

"As soon as it's dark," Rai replied.

"They will ask about you." Kalt jutted his head towards where Grenin and Larina had gone. Despite his best intentions, Rai had grown to like them, and he hated partings.

"You'll take good care of them?" Rai asked.

"Of course, of course," Kalt said, waving a hand dismissively. "It's not the first time I've smuggled people out of the country." Rai smiled at that.

"I'm more worried about you," Kalt said. "You look beaten and tired, my friend. Why don't you stay a while? Rest up and leave in a couple days."

Rai met his eyes, and Kalt sighed again. "Okay, I get it. But you don't work for her anymore. You don't need to be on the move, always chasing."

"Spending life waiting for tomorrow is a life waiting for its end," Rai repeating what Elder Kalt told him the first time he came to Gamo.

"Exactly," Kalt said. "At least stay the night. You will be better rested and be able to travel faster with a full belly and loose legs."

Kalt was right. He was always right.

The old man has a point. Plus, I like the noises he makes when he drinks too much ale, Fax said regarding Kalt's singing.

"I'll stay until I'm rested," Rai said.

Elder Kalt grinned. "Let me grab the ale."

"Has this guy ever told you about the time he defended this village against a pack of kirens?" Elder Kalt slurred, pointing to Rai.

They sat on the rooftop, where seating surrounded a fire pit all built into the stone roof of the elder's home. Flames reached into the black night, battering back the cool. Others in the village sat atop their roofs, lighting the village with embers flickering all around them like stars. It was common in the desert towns to eat and drink on rooftops around a fire after the Sun Eye had completed its watch, but it almost never happened in the major cities. Rai couldn't understand why, as sitting out in the open up here, with the breeze and fire battling for dominance, was the place Rai treasured most.

Dal lay belly facing the flames and snoring, the sides of his face rippling with each exhale.

Elder Kalt was well into his cups now and ever the storyteller. "They had been attacking our village every night for three days! On the fourth day, this fellow staggered into town." He flicked his head towards Rai. "That night there were thousands of glowing eyes in the dark surrounding the village."

"Packs only move with about forty," Rai said, but Kalt ignored him.

"It was the most they had attacked with. We thought ourselves doomed to an untimely death."

"What are kirens?" Larina asked.

Kalt's expression turned serious as he leant over the flames. "Kirens are like wolves but larger, enormous boulders for shoulders, and a long snout. Teeth the size of daggers. Vicious things. Took a liking to our farm patch over there, and a couple chunks out of some in the village too while they were at it."

"Anyway, this man single handedly—"

"With the help of the entire village," Rai added.

And me, Fax said. *You would've been dead without me.*

"—fought them off! Killed a good lot of them and sent the rest running back into the wilderness with their tails between their legs." Kalt laughed.

Grenin and Larina grinned, while Syla sat back, shaking her head, a smile pulling at her lips.

"How has it been in Gamo?" Rai asked, changing the topic.

Elder Kalt scratched his chin. "It has been a while, eh."

"Jok is all grown up now. I know you were fond of him," Syla said, sitting forwards legs crossed. "Double the size as when you last saw him. He started tending goats like his father, bought some off a merchant in Celabar and is selling the milk. Goats are rare around these parts," she said to Grenin and Larina.

Rai sat back and glanced over the village. Memories of the attack and the nights he spent here were bittersweet.

"Goats are incredible creatures," Kalt said looking into the flames. "Have I ever told you the tale of Tremedes the Kind Hearted?"

Grenin and Larina made the mistake of shaking their heads. *Great, here he goes*, Rai thought.

I love story time with Kalt! Fax said.

Elder Kalt grinned and cracked his fingers.

"Well then, this was back in the First Days when the ancient shapers, creatures as big as cities, roamed the land. Goats were around then too, you see. Now Tremedes was the eldest of the goat tribe. He was smart. Kept the tribe roaming and away from possible predators, not tempting fate. He broke the goat tribe up into smaller packs that moved separately whenever they came across one of the shapers. And because the giant creatures needed to eat an entire tribe to fill themselves up they often left the smaller packs that roamed the land, deeming them not worth the trouble.

"But one day, Tremedes and his tribe were travelling across the sandy plains when they heard a strange cry. The cry shook the sands at their feet and the trees quivered like flags in the wind. As they always did when coming across something unusual, the goat tribe split into packs and spread out before Tremedes and his group went to find the source of the cry.

"To their surprise it was Setto, one of the ancient shapers. It's said that shapers looked similar to tortoises but with mountains upon their backs. Anyway, Setto lay flat on his belly, face pulled tight in a grimace. *Tremedes, the kind hearted goat, said to put others before himself,* Setto called. *Something sharp has caught in my mouth and I cannot get it out. It causes me much pain. Would you be so kind as to pull it out for me?*

"Now Tremedes was indeed kind of heart, and couldn't leave Setto who was clearly in a lot of pain. So he clambered into his mouth and right enough, embedded into Setto's gum was a sharp bone fragment. *I've found it!* Tremedes called. He pulled on the bone trying to wrench it free but it wouldn't come loose.

"*Solus come help me,* Tremedes shouted. The second goat entered Setto's mouth but even with the two of them they couldn't pull the bone free. So they called in a third goat. Then a fourth, and one by one the goats lined up until the whole tribe was heaving on the bone.

"With a mighty pull they finally prised the bone free. Setto hissed but then let out a breath of relief. Tremedes pleased with how his tribe had come together to help another smiled and glanced down at the offending bone.

"Tremedes saw the end of the bone they had pulled free

curled into the shape of a goat's horn. And all went black."

Kalt leaned back. The others sat in silence.

"I don't understand," Grenin said.

Rai shook his head and met Syla's gaze, who had the same resigned look in her eyes she always did when Kalt told one of his stories.

"A kind heart has to be led by a smart mind," Larina said. Kalt clicked his fingers and pointed to Larina.

Rai knew the story was directed at him. Kalt had always warned him about doing the right thing for others and disregarding himself. But Kalt didn't understand. He thought Rai was searching for answers about Fax and the rend out of loyalty to the empress. She was the one who sent the Seven to find a mysterious 'weapon' the monarch of Yontar was said to be hiding. The empress had feared he was going to use it to take the throne and incite a civil war.

And that was one reason he had spent the last five years searching for answers. But not the only one.

Rai felt drawn to the rend. He couldn't shake it from his thoughts. The monarch was playing with powers he didn't understand. Rai had been to the dark realm and returned with Fax and still didn't understand it. But one thing was certain. Shades were a danger to Tarris. Even if the monarch had one soldier with a shade, the country's seats of power would be thrown into upheaval.

And there was something else. A presence in that dark realm. Rai could feel it even now. Something grander than Fax. Something that wanted freed.

A shiver ran up Rai's spine.

No, he wasn't doing this for the empress. He was doing this for Tarris.

"—and we had thought Rai was this shadow man from Yontar." Grenin laughed.

Rai's ears perked as he was pulled back into the conversation. "Shadow man?"

"Ridiculous right? But we had just heard of this strange man with strange abilities right before we met you," Grenin said.

"Yeah, they say his shadow stretches and pulsates like it's alive," Larina said.

Rai froze, his mind whirling. His breath stolen from his lungs.

"Where did you hear this?" Rai snapped.

Grenin frowned at the sudden outburst. "The sailor who brought us to Dock Town warned us about him. Said his brother left because things were getting too dangerous in Yontar and that we should avoid it."

A man with a moving shadow. This was the most notable thing he had found in his search over the last five years. Yontar was to the north and Rai tried to avoid the larger cities in fear of being recognised… But it was a big place. Plenty of places to blend in.

Kalt said something but Rai paid no mind to those around him. There was another. Someone else with a moving shadow.

Memories of that night five years ago flooded back. Of the seven that entered the tear, he was sure at least one other got out. Had they gained a creature like Fax in their shadow too? Or was this something else?

Rai's mind reeled with the possibilities.

The most promising lead in sometime, Fax said.

He had to leave. Rai glanced up to Grenin and Larina. They would ask too many questions he couldn't answer. He hated saying goodbyes anyway.

Rai cleared his throat and stood. "I'm going to take a leak." He made his way to the steps attached to the side of each building, patting Dal on the stomach as he passed. Kalt nodded knowingly as Rai jogged down the steps and out of sight, a soft sympathetic smile playing at the elder's lips. He knew what this meant to Rai.

Rai stood at the entrance to the elder's house. He couldn't linger any longer. The merchants were safe but the people of Yontar may not be. The rumoured shadow man could be another shade and Rai wasn't going to wait until the sands ran red for that fact to be proven right. He sighed peering into the Elder's home before spinning on his heels and walking out into the village.

Torches stuck out from the ground in front of each home and near the farmland on shoulder-high poles. Three guards on night patrol passed by, the closest bowing to Rai. Rai nodded and kept walking.

Rai found his aya head-deep in a trough of fresh fruit. It was a feast for an aya, who would normally be fed leftovers. The platform was still on its back, but the supplies that Elder Kalt had collected for Rai during the day were stacked around the aya's feet. Rai loaded the beast, tying down the supplies for the journey ahead. He was fixing on the last strap when a voice came from below.

"Rai? You up there?" Grenin shouted.

Rai paused and took a deep breath. He was hoping to avoid this. He slid down the ladder, almost landing atop Grenin, who stood squinting into the dark.

"Were you going to just head off and not say goodbye?" Grenin asked.

"It's just easier." Rai shrugged.

"Easier for you, Rai," Grenin said. "We can't very well pay you if you leave during the night without saying a word."

"Pay me? I—" Grenin cut Rai off, handing him a bottle of Artonian ale.

"I'm sorry we can't pay you more, but we lost our stock and earnings when they arrested us," Grenin said.

Rai looked at the bottle. "Where… how?"

"I asked Syla if they had any and well… Kalt has a hidden collection he thinks Syla doesn't know about," Grenin said with a grin. "Just don't let him see you with it."

Gods be damned, you aren't going to cry over a bottle of ale, are you? Fax asked after a moment's silence.

"Thank you Grenin," Rai said. "I'm sorry for wrapping you both up in all this."

"Sorry? This is the most exciting adventure yet. I told you out at the Waypoint that we are doing this to see and experience the world, not make a fortune," Grenin said. "And anyway, we should have been arrested at the Dock Town for not having the right papers. We would have lost everything either way." He paused. "I do have one question though."

"Yes?"

"What is that black bird thing?" he asked.

They had seen Fax lift them off the ground, and disappear and reappear in the blink of an eye. His tale of a rare bird wasn't going to hold up anymore.

"That's what I'm going to find out," Rai said.

Grenin thought over this answer before nodding. "And I wish you the best."

Rai reached out a hand. "Goodbye, Grenin."

"Goodbye, Rai," Grenin said.

Rai undid the knot that attached the aya to the fence, then clambered up the ladder. "Besides, you don't seem to need me anymore," Rai called down. "It was you who protected your wife in those cells."

Grenin beamed at the compliment. "Next time we meet, I'll be able to fight you off," Grenin replied, dancing around in what Rai assumed, was a fight.

Rai snorted and whipped the reins. "Your wife could still knock you into the sand."

Grenin shrugged. "Yeah, probably."

Grenin watched as they trotted through the village, backed by the incandescent glow of fires and revelry on the rooftops. Rai faced forward, away from the simple life he once thought he could have, but now knew better. The aya broke off at a canter, past the village and out onto the black sand.

15

Dark Wings Beat

"Run," Drak said. Styra grabbed his arm before he could break off.

"We won't be able to find our way back without that map," Styra said, gesturing to the tent. They stared at each other. Drak broke first, dipping his head with a sigh and nodding. Together they ran towards the torn tents and wails of the grieving scholar.

The shrieking was getting louder and the beating wings sounded like approaching war drums. Nya's heart thundered as she watched Styra and Drak run through the dead and into the tent.

They kept watch on the sky to the west but couldn't see far within the maze of cragged rocks. The guard beside Nya twitched, his face a mess of pulsing veins, scrunched flesh, and dripping sweat. Nya always thought of guards as immovable forces of nature, so seeing one about to wet his breeches brought a new level of panic.

Come on, Nya thought. *Hurry.*

It felt like an eternity before Styra, Drak, the guard, and the two scholars appeared from the black maw of the tent.

"Come on!" the guard beside Nya called to them.

They were halfway across the open space when a black blur barrelled from the sky and tore the guard from the ground. Nya's breath caught as it shot back into the air, the guard screaming in silvered claws.

A thud sounded a second later as the guard's decapitated head hit the ground.

They gazed into the roiling sky as more black forms descended. Some screeched, a high-pitched squeal that forced Nya to cover her ears.

"Run!" someone screamed. Nya's feet were already padding over the rocky ground away from the death, away from the monsters.

They tore down the scree, hurtling over rock and fissure. Ahead was a plateau, caves and indents cut into the rock. If they could find somewhere to hide, they *might* be able to lose their attackers.

"There!" Nya shouted, pointing at the plateau. She made the mistake of looking over her shoulder to check if the others were close.

The sky was now full of husks. They had black leathery skin, bat-like ragged wings, and long narrow faces, mouth and nose protruding in not-quite a snout.

Nya screamed, it was a raw, feral sound that she didn't know she could make, born of pure terror.

One swooped, racking a gash along Drak's arm, but he battered it on the nose, sending it squealing and flying off again. Drak gripped his shoulder, which was now a mess of blood and torn flesh.

Nya's foot caught in a gap between rocks, sending her tumbling forward, ankle flaring. She scraped along the scree, cutting her legs and forearms as she went. Adrenaline held the pain at bay, her mind reeling.

Flashes of the bodies in the camp assaulted her. That could be her next. She couldn't breathe. Turning onto her back, Nya watched as the guard ran past her, not even glancing in her direction. Next passed Drak and one of the scholars. Styra was some paces out, giving her a concerned glance. Nya saw the moment she chose to leave her behind.

Lastly, Kit and the bald boy ran at the back of the group, struggling to keep up with the older members of the party. Nya caught Kit's eye. He looked away.

They all leave in the end.

Yes, she was going to die here.

One of the husks dove.

Nya threw up her arms to cover her face and chest. Razor sharp claws tore into her forearms like they were parchment. She screamed.

"Back!" Kit shouted.

Tear blurred as shapes shifted in front of Nya. Kit was

shoving the husk away. He pushed it, barely moving it an inch. The creature spun. Kit stepped back, realising his mistake. He couldn't fight that thing. None of them could.

The bald boy shot through the air foot first, cracking into the husk's nose. It screeched, smacking into a rock face. The bald boy was as expressionless as ever, even after fighting off a demon from another world.

Kit sprinted over and held a hand out to Nya. She took it and was jerked to her feet. The three of them dashed across the rocky terrain.

The husks swarmed the sky, more cautious of swooping in now that they had seen their prey weren't as defenceless as they seemed.

"Over here!" Styra called from a shadowed crevice in the plateau.

The three threw themselves in that direction, with the careless forward motion of sprinting down an incline. Nya's legs felt like they were no longer attached to her body. Claws dug into her back and she squealed but didn't turn.

As the three of them approached the cave, they launched themselves into the dark. Nya crashed into the serrated rock of the cavern floor, slicing her legs and arms. Immediately she spun, gazing out of the mouth of the cave.

The sky was almost completely blacked out by dark wings. The surviving guard and Drak stood at the opening, spears snapping at any who came close to their crack in the stone wall. Husks plunged towards them just to end up with a spear through their shoulder or wing.

After a while, less made the dive. Instead, they shrieked louder.

"What are they doing?" Drak shouted over the clamour.

"It sounds like they are calling out," Styra said. That was a terrifying thought.

"We need to back up into the cave!" the scholar said.

Styra helped Nya to her feet. Nya hissed at the cuts and bruises that littered her body. Even breathing pulled at her skin and was painful enough to bring tears to her eyes.

They skulked further into the darkening cave. Drak and the guard backed up slowly, still stabbing out with their spears to any brave husks that tried to follow.

Soon, it was pitch black, the erratic breathing echoing around her was the only thing telling Nya she hadn't passed out. The crack of light shrunk as they moved, the shrieking of the husks dimming.

"They aren't following us," the guard said.

Nya let out a shaky breath.

"They… they're leaving," Drak said.

He was right. The chorus of calls was quieting. The husks were flying away.

Nya slumped against the wall and slid down until she was sitting. Now that the frenzy was fading, the ache and sting of her injuries came in full force.

"What in the Duat damned gods was that?" Drak roared, waving his spear around with his good arm. "We did not sign up for this."

"And you think we did?" the scholar said. "I found my

husband dead and my research partner was torn apart in front of me!" the scholar's voice was shaky.

Nya hadn't seen the other scholar pass her when she tripped. She hadn't even noticed he was missing. She should have been horrified at all the death, but Nya didn't have the energy. Instead, tired resignation sat on her like a stone.

Drak threw the spear, then leant up against the wall, clutching his clawed shoulder.

"Hey, you okay?" a distant voice asked, a hand touching Nya's shoulder. Nya jerked back, trying to kick away. "Hey, hey, we're okay now."

Nya breathed hard, making out the outline of Styra.

"Let me see your back," Styra said.

Nya faced the other way, loosening her shirt so Styra could inspect her back.

"The cut is shallow," she said. "But you will need to keep it clean to make sure it doesn't get infected."

A cold river of pain ran down Nya's back. She hissed, pulling forward. "Sorry. I'm just pouring some water over it," Styra said as the pain subsided.

Nya panned around to see Kit and the bald boy leaning against the far wall. Kit's head buried in his hands.

"Kit," Nya said, and he glanced up. "Thank you." Nya couldn't make out his expression in the dark, but after a pause he nodded. "Thank you too," she said, facing the bald boy, who bowed his head.

"There you go," Styra said, pulling Nya's shirt back down. "That's the best I can do for now." She stood and patted her hands together. "Drak, let me look at that shoulder."

Drak grumbled something unintelligible but didn't make a move when she walked over and begun cleaning his wound.

"What now?" the guard asked.

"We either wait then backtrack, or we go deeper into the cave in hope that it will take us to the other side of the plateau, where we can curve back around and find the path we used to get here," Styra said.

"There's no way I'm going back out there," Kit said.

"There's no promise this cave doesn't lead to a dead end," the scholar said.

"Or more of those *things*," Drak said.

"Husks," the scholar said.

"How far does the map go?" Styra asked.

The scholar slid the map out, unrolled it, and shook it flat. She studied it in the poor light before saying, "It goes as far as the end of this plateau. There is no way of telling if this tunnel goes all the way through or not. And if we do make it to the other side, we will be going blind trying to hook back around to the mapped area."

This elicited groans.

"Let's vote," Styra said. There were nods all around. "All in favour of waiting then backtracking, raise your hands."

The bald boy, the guard, and Drak lifted their hands.

"Safer the evil you know," Drak said. "They said there's worse out here than those husks, and I'd rather run into them in the open than a dark cave."

Nya saw Kit's arm twitch, but he didn't lift it.

"And those in favour of following the cave," Styra said, then lifted her hand. The scholar and Kit lifted theirs as well.

Nya couldn't face those things again. Her cuts burned at the thought of them. She put her hand up.

"That's that then," Styra said. "We continue through the cave until we find the other side."

Drak sighed, his shoulders crumpling forward in defeat, but he didn't argue.

After resting a while, the group made their way further into the black. The scholar took out some flint and using a rag torn from the guard's cloak, made a torch. The guard led, waving the torch to ward off the reaching shadows.

They wandered, unspeaking. No one willing to disrupt the still around them in fear of what it held. The flames threw flickering light around the same black rock that covered the land. Nya was beginning to hate that charcoal coloured rock.

The orange light brought details to their haunted faces. The scholar's face was drawn and blank. She ambled past Nya, clutching the provisions bag in a trance, only semi-aware of what was going on around her. Drak slowed to defend the back of the party, a manic look in his eyes as he stared into the dark. Even Styra's composure had slipped.

The rock walls and roof around them sank into the inky black as the cave expanded. Nya swallowed. The bald boy walked a couple paces in front. Nya still hadn't talked to him. She wasn't sure he did talk, but she sped up to his side.

"Thanks again for saving me," Nya said. The bald boy studied her a moment then bowed his head. "We haven't really talked. I'm Nya." She bowed back.

The boy said nothing.

"He is of the Urdahl to the north," Styra said, craning her neck around. "They believe in only speaking what is absolutely necessary."

Nya hadn't heard of the Urdahl, but her education was lacking and amassed little of the world outside Yontar. "Oh," she said. "Can you say your name?"

"He hasn't spoken to any of—" Styra started.

"Bas," he said.

Styra stared at the boy. Bas had kept his eyes forward but now turned to face Nya.

"You are fated. An aura of darkness surrounds you. Ova wanted me to save you," Bas said. "You are fated too." He added, nodding to Styra. "Lost and looking for something you know is gone and as unreachable as the past."

"Fated?" Nya asked.

Styra gazed at the boy, uncertainty lining her face. "They believe in a destiny and fate for all things. Some claim they can even see others' fate just by looking at them."

The guard hushed them from further ahead, pausing and waving his torch about. Styra stared at the bald boy, who gazed back at her for a moment longer before she moved to see what the guard had found. Nya and Bas followed.

The darkness had drank in the details of the rock and left nothing but a void around them.

"What is it?" Styra whispered.

"I saw something," the guard said.

The party stopped, straining to see into the unbreaking black. Then Nya saw a flicker of movement.

"There," Nya whispered.

"I saw it," Styra said. "Keep going, silently and quickly."

"Do you hear that?" Kit asked. Nya strained to hear a faint chirping sound.

They started off again at a jog. Nya's body flaring with exhaustion. There were more shifting shadows now, Nya's head pivoting back and forth trying to watch them all. Incandescent light reflected off a wriggling limb. The clacking chirp growing louder, filling the cavern like a thousand little insects calling.

They broke into a run, paying no heed to the uneven ground.

"Look!" the guard shouted. A fissure of white was on the horizon. The way out.

"Shh!" Styra said to the guard.

The clacking chirp silenced. The shuffle of movement stilling.

"Oh sh—" Drak said as a limb slapped down from the dark, flicking him across the cavern and into the wall. He screamed as five hands wrapped around him and pulled him inward. Blood poured out from where the fingers dug into him, his screams turning into a gurgled plea.

Hands consumed him, crushing him against the wall and tearing him to pieces, and the screaming ceased.

"Run!" Styra called.

Nya sprinted for the exit. All around, in the newfound

light, the walls squirmed and writhed in a mass of limbs. But they were all connected. Could this be one creature?

Another limb swung from above —Nya couldn't tell if it was an arm or leg. She ducked, and it arced past the front of Kit, missing him by a hairs breadth.

They were almost out.

In front, a hand burst from the slithering mass covering the wall, snatching the scholar. She squealed, terror-stricken. Styra ran for her, clawing at the hand, but with a vicious yank, it dragged the scholar away, enveloping her in the wall. Styra leapt back when it was clear the scholar was going to die, and Nya glanced away as the cracking gave way to a squelch.

The light was blinding compared to the dark of the cave, Nya squinting against it. The guard vanished into it, then so did Bas, followed by Styra only moments later.

Kit ran beside Nya. *Not far now.*

Cold crept up her spine. Nya screamed. It felt like something had a hold of her. She turned but nothing was there. Then the feeling was gone, replaced by a *presence*.

One of the flailing limbs reached for Kit. Nya called out and Kit met her gaze. His eyes didn't hold the terror the scholar's had. She saw sorrow and acceptance in his gaze. Somehow, that was worse.

It grabbed Kit, wrapping around him and dragging him away. Nya came to a sliding halt. The cave exit was right there. "Go!" Kit shouted, but she couldn't. Her legs wouldn't move.

Nya closed her eyes and screamed.

Then she felt it.

The presence jut out towards Kit. She opened her eyes and saw a long black ethereal spike sticking into the hand that held Kit. The monster let out a howl that shook the cave. Then it loosened its grip, and Kit slipped free.

Nya was stunned and confused, but Kit grabbed Nya's arm and together they bolted for the light. The creature sent more whipping limbs snaking out towards them. The attacks hissed passed them as they ducked and jumped through the cave.

Kit held Nya's hand, pulling her on. Past him, the white was expanding, and then it drowned out everything else.

They burst from the cave, throwing themselves onto the ground. Nya rolled onto her back and kicked further away from the cave mouth, but nothing came out after them.

Nya thumped her head against the ground. Her lungs ached from all the running and screaming.

Above, the sky stormed. She had never been so relieved to see a tempest.

A Black Blade

A deeper silence held the remnants of the Doomed Others. They walked and they listened, always for the beating of wings or scuttling of any other creature that roamed this Duat-damned land. The cragged landscape opened, letting them curve back round to the other side of the plateau, where they reached the mapped area. Luckily, Styra tore the map off the scholar before she was consumed in the cave. Nya couldn't help but wonder, had Styra tried to save the scholar or did she just go to retrieve the map?

They went back the way they came. What started as a group of nine had whittled down to a party of five. Styra led the procession with the guard at her side, followed by Nya, Kit, and Bas trailing behind.

Nya felt *heavier* now. She was sure it was the weight of the horrors she had seen, but a presence still loomed in the back of her mind. She needed to go home. Go back to Mother, and Dust, and the Sand Rats, and everything would be okay. It had to be okay.

They trudged over rocky plains and through fields of monolithic black rocks, retracing their steps with the slogged pace of a fallen army. The sky never dimmed as they climbed the incline. It was impossible to tell how long they had been in this dark place with the clouds obscuring Ova's Great Eyes, but it felt much longer than a day, and yet it never darkened.

Nya's stomach grumbled, but the thought of food made her want to vomit. She knew there wasn't any anyway. The scholar had been carrying their provisions.

Eventually, they stood at the base of the rise that housed their cave and only way back home. There weren't any cheers, no one sped up. It didn't feel like a victory after what they went through.

They plodded up the hill with the last of their energy pausing in front of the cave, panting and regaining their breath. "Give me the map," the guard said. Styra hesitated but handed it over. "When we go through, I'll do the talking," he said.

The remaining guard relit their torch, passing into the hollow. Walking into the cave, Nya felt a swell of panic. What if the tear was gone? What if they were stuck here forever? Her breathing increased as they made their way through the cave. It must have been louder than she thought as Kit came up beside her and asked, "You okay?"

Nya nodded, not trusting the tremor not to work its way into her words.

"I never got the chance to say, but I'm really sorry I said those things about your family. I know nothing about them and I made assumptions and—"

"It's fine," Nya said. Kit met her eyes and nodded.

The flames of the torch pushed back against some invisible force, as if fighting a wind they couldn't feel. Then the flames began to dim. Nya remembered back to the chamber, and how the braziers acted similarly. She let out a long exhale. They were going home.

The air grew thicker, and warmth emanated from the dark. Nya couldn't see the tear but she knew it was there. One by one they passed through, feeling the same strange numbness before the palace chamber flickered into view.

Guards shouted something, and a messenger sprinted up the stairs, but it was all background noise to Nya as she dropped to her knees, relief flooding her. They had made it.

Spear tips were levelled at their party. The guard who held the map shouted something, but the guards on duty ignored him and kept their spears level. Nya shook her head. She blinked, held her nose and blew until noise became sharp again.

"It's just orders," one of the guards on duty said.

"Orders? Sure, for the prisoners, but I went in willingly," the guard snapped. "I want to talk to the commander immediately."

"We have sent for her. There are precautions that need to

be taken after a trip," the guard said. "We need all of you to remain here until they have done so."

The guard who had come with them to the dark place launched into another tirade. Kit sat crossed legged, watching the guards argue, his eyes pitted and dark with exhaustion. Nya crawled over to him.

"What's going on?" Nya asked.

"We are waiting on some checks apparently," Kit said with a shrug. Nya waited for a jibe or joke. She could think of several using a probe but Kit didn't say another word. The dark place had changed them, and not for the better.

Styra stood off to the side, back against the wall, flicking through the research notes they grabbed in the camp.

"What do they say?" Nya asked.

Styra flicked past another page and sighed. "Not much. They didn't have time to finish their studies."

It was all for nothing, said a voice in Nya's head. Nya spun, but no one was behind her. It felt like the voice came from within. A presence in her own mind. *Doesn't that make you want to rage, to tear, and rend?*

"Nya?" Kit's voice asked, sounding far off. Nya turned to face him.

"Did you hear that?" she asked. Styra looked confused, and Kit shook his head.

"Hear what?" he asked.

"Never mind," Nya said.

The guards parted, and Commander Ewyna swept into the room with a handful of guards and scholars. She was as dismissive as ever, with only a cursory glance over them.

"Commander Ewyna, the rest of the—" their guard started, but Ewyna lifted her hand for silence.

"Hold them," she said.

A rush of guards flooded past her, two for each of the five survivors. They grabbed Nya and yanked her up, holding her against the wall alongside the others, a guard on each arm. She didn't have the energy to fight and made no attempt, yet they were still rough in pressing her against the wall.

"Commander Ewyna, I was on duty. I went there by choice. I feel this is unnecessary," their guard said.

"Silence," Ewyna said. "It's just protocol. Mirt?"

Mirt stepped from behind Ewyna, smiling. He held a dagger about the size of Nya's forearm. The blade was black, and the pommel was a dark purple, intricately carved with a design Nya couldn't make out. Mirt held it reverently between two hands. It wasn't a threatening grip, but still Nya pushed back. Something screamed that she needed to stay as far from that dagger as she could.

Mirt approached the guard first, holding the dagger out. The guard pulled back, but Ewyna's guards held him tight. He looked at the dagger, then at Mirt. Ewyna nodded and Mirt continued onto Styra.

Nya's stomach churned as Mirt made his way up the line. He waved the dagger in front of each of them until Ewyna gestured him on. What good did this do?

They hadn't hurt the others, so there was no need for concern. And yet, Nya's heart was increasing with every step

Mirt took in her direction. Kit leaned back, but Mirt stepped closer, hovering the blade in front of him. Ewyna nodded once again and Mirt faced Nya.

Nya's heart dropped when Mirt met her eyes. She felt like she had been dangling over the edge and she was now in free fall. Panic swelled inside riding a wave of nausea that threatened to drown her.

I have to get away. I can't let that thing near me, she thought.

Nya thrashed.

"Just be calm," Kit said. "They won't hurt you, Nya."

Nya ignored him, shaking and trying to pry herself from the guard's grip. Mirt was closing in, his face a nervous twist.

She felt like she was on fire, burning up from just being near that blade. It was like it was trying to scour her from the world. A realisation dawned that she wasn't going to be able to get free of these guards. She survived going to that Duat-damned plain and back just to die from a blade that never touched her. She wanted to laugh and cry and scream, but nothing came out.

Mirt held the dagger out.

"Her brother was murdered," Styra blurted out. "She found him with a dagger in his chest. It makes her nervous around them."

Nya could barely hear her over the deafening roar of blood filling her ears. Mirt glanced at Ewyna.

"Just a moment longer," Ewyna said, her scrutinizing gaze baring into Nya. "Press it on her."

Mirt pushed the dagger towards her.

188

The presence inside Nya howled and writhed. It wanted to rip through the guards and Mirt, but Nya kept it contained. Nya squealed as it came within inches of touching her and Mirt jumped back, startled by a messenger's voice.

"Commander Ewyna," someone said, "the Monarch needs a word. He said it's urgent."

Nya's head lolled, grateful the blade had backed up.

"I think we would have gotten a reaction by now, Commander," Mirt said.

There was a pause that lasted several heartbeats.

"Search them for anything from over there, then set them free," Commander Ewyna said, then marched up the stairs.

The guards loosened their grip and Nya fell to the floor. Kit swept in and grabbed her before she smacked her face off the stone floor.

"Nya?" Kit asked. "Nya, you okay?"

"Uh huh," she said, although she thought she might just close her eyes and sleep forever.

The guards did a quick pat down of them before escorting them up the steps. Kit helped her up, as Nya was sapped of energy. Styra watched her with concern. They passed through a blur of corridors, doors, guards waving them on, and the next thing Nya knew, she was out.

Out of the palace and back on the streets of Yontar.

Above Nya was a slate roof. Nya blinked. What happened? She sat, getting a better look at her surroundings. She was wedged between two buildings, lying on a rooftop with the lip of the neighbouring building arching over her, protecting her from the Sun Eye. Crates sat on either side, making the space feel almost cosy.

Nya rubbed her eyes, trying to recall what happened. She was burning, then they were freed of the palace. That was all she remembered, fragments and flickering faces.

She must have passed out, but how did she get here? Where were Styra, Kit, and Bas?

"Look who's finally awake," Kit said, waddling across the roof, bread and fruit in one hand.

Nya's stomach grumbled. He ducked under the lip of the roof, sitting cross legged in front of her.

"What happened?" Nya asked.

"We are free!" Kit said, gesturing broadly around him. "I'll be honest, I didn't think they would actually let us go even if we did come back." He ripped the bread in two and passed half to Nya. She bowed her head in thanks, then bit into it.

"The excitement was too much and you passed out," Kit said. "So I brought you here."

"Where is here?" Nya asked, mouth full of bread.

"Not far from the western gates," Kit said, eating his bread. "I crash here sometimes."

Nya glanced around. It was a convenient spot for someone living on the street. The eaves of the neighbouring roof kept the Sun Eye off, and it was nice and high so no one was likely to come across them.

Kit handed her one of the jacku fruit, a dumpy green shell that contained a soft juicy centre when cracked open.

"What about the others?" Nya said.

"Gone," Kit said with a shrug. "Styra was worried about you, but I said I would look after you until you woke."

Nya's thoughts started to sort themselves out. They had done it. They had survived and made it back. She looked at the fruit that she had already taken a bite out of, then up to Kit.

"Thank you, Kit," Nya said.

Kit stopped chewing and met her gaze. "Of course," he said, facing away, his cheeks reddening. He cleared his throat. "So what happens now that you're out?"

Nya dropped the last piece of her fruit, sudden realisation hitting her like a sandstorm. "Mother!" She jumped to her feet, smacking her head on the eaves. She grunted and rubbed the back of her head before scuttling along the rooftop.

Hopping down onto another nearby rooftop, then into a narrow street, Nya was already running when she hit the ground. Kit said they were near the western gate, so she turned south, skidding around a corner. Nya didn't know what time it was but the Sun Eye was high, and streets quiet so she guessed it was after midday.

How long had they been in that other place? Nya wracked her brain, but with no discernible night there, it was impossible to tell.

"Wait!" Kit called, trailing behind her, but Nya didn't stop.

Nya tore through the streets, kicking a cloud of dust up as she went. Startled people stared as she sped past. It was beginning to look familiar. She knew where she was; not far from the tower, where she was meant to have met the Sand Rats. That felt like a lifetime ago.

Her legs burned, and lungs stung, but the merchant shop came into view. It was closed. Nya ran and leapt, grabbing the window frame. She pulled herself up, throwing the window open, then battered down the corridor, uncaring if she was waking the merchant from his qed or not.

Nya threw herself up the steps at the back of the corridor, the hatch swinging open, and she clambered into their attic.

Mother was there.

She was lying, unmoving among a pile of soiled blankets. The smell made Nya flinch.

She was too late.

Mother had died here, alone.

There was a scratching sound. Nya looked up as Dust dropped in from the window. Dust stilled. She had cheese hanging from her mouth. The sand fox sprinted across the room and jumped into Nya's arms.

Nya held her close, tears streaming down her cheeks. Dust buried into her, rubbing her head against Nya.

"I missed you Dust," Nya said.

Nya picked up the cheese Dust had dropped. "Where did you get this?"

Dust pulled back. She grabbed the cheese and walked over to Mother, where she dropped it near her hand. Mother stirred.

"Werin?" Mother asked.

Nya sucked in air, her eyes watering. A warmness bloomed

in her chest and she collapsed beside Mother and wept. Dust buried her way between them, letting out a purr. The fox must have been looking after Mother, bringing her food while Nya wasn't there.

"Clever girl," Nya said, running a hand down the arch of Dust's neck, who leaned into it.

Mother was alive.

"Nya? You up there?" Kit called.

She had almost forgotten he was following her.

"Nya? I'm coming up," Kit said.

Nya glanced around. The attic was a mess and stunk of aya's stool left to boil in the midday Sun.

"No, wait. I'm coming down. I need to get water and food for Mother anyway," Nya said with a smile.

17

The Patched Cloak

The sand softened, its golden hue returning in the first light of the Sun Eye. And the city of Yontar rose from the desert. The place where it all began. And the place where it all ended. It had been a long journey from the small village of Gamo but finally, Rai had arrived. The aya let out a *moo* of relief now that the end was in sight.

Rai look. Rai! I'm like a real bird now, Fax said.

Fax darted about in the shape of a crow.

"You look more like a man falling from a roof," Rai said.

Fax flew past battering the back of Rai's head. He rubbed it, not taking his gaze from the city. Rai had made a rule for himself that he would avoid the larger cities like Yontar. Even Celabar straddled that line, despite being half the size of Yontar. But this was the best lead he had gotten in years.

If this man was like him, perhaps he knew more about these shades and that dark place with the storming skies. He would certainly be more helpful than Fax, Rai thought as Fax flew like an upside-down bird in a strange arcing spiral.

Fax had called that place both a home and a prison. It couldn't explain why, other than it felt like a prison and it knew it had to get out.

Sharp fragments of memories flashed into his head. Claws. Teeth. Black wings. Screaming. Death.

And something else. Shifting in the shadows. A presence greater than Faxs or even a thousand Faxs.

Rai?

Rai snapped out of his thoughts. "What?"

Don't you think we should have stayed with Kalt and Syla? I like them. I can tell you are at ease with them too, Fax said.

"We can't," Rai said. "We have a mission."

It's been five years of searching, Fax said, *can't we give up? If something was going to happen, it would have by now. Maybe the tear isn't dangerous.*

"We both know that isn't true," Rai said.

He didn't need to elaborate. It was dangerous. He didn't know where it came from, how it opened, or, more importantly, how to close it. But he couldn't have more people stumbling through it. And Rai was sure they would send scholars through to research the dark place. The curiosity of men was an insatiable itch that often bore unwanted scars. Humans would send people jumping from cliffs to see where the bottom was.

And although Fax assured Rai more shades like it wouldn't pass through because shades needed a host that was strong of mind to hold them, the idea of others with his abilities was terrifying.

That's why he had to see this rumoured man with the moving shadow. Yes, to see what he knew of the shades and of the dark place but also, if it came to it, to put him down.

They worked their way down the line leading into the city. Yontar was one of the seats of power in Tarris, which meant many were coming and going through its gates. The city walls were much like Celabar's in design but taller, grander, as if Celabar had been practice and this was the real thing.

Sandstone pillars protruded, white paint snaking them like veins. They were painted as such to blend into the desert and make it look like the wall was a line of giant bone trees to appease Ova the World Turner. The one who always watched them with its Sun and Moon Eyes, turning the world and giving them night and day.

Why an all-powerful deity would care that they built a wall was up for speculation. They lost the reasoning behind the design through the ages. Some believed it was to trick Ova, so it didn't know how far they had progressed as a race. Others said it was to show that no matter how they changed as a people, they would respect the planet as it was when they first drew breath, and not sully it for personal gain.

They trickled ever closer to the gates. Which were also colossal compared to Celabar's, with the line of people breaking off into five side-by-side lanes that were checked before each person was let into the city, like water branching at an intersection.

They waved to Rai. He brought his aya to a stop and climbed down the ladder to talk with the guard.

We aren't going to kill this one, are we? Fax asked.

"Morning traveller," a short stout, balding man said, noting something on a piece of parchment.

"Morning," Rai replied with a slight incline of his head.

"Any stock aboard?" the guard said, looking up.

"No, just a traveller here to see family," Rai said.

The guard sniffed and nodded. "Don't mind if we...?" he pointed to the aya.

"Go ahead," Rai said.

The guard waved two others on to search the aya. One clambered up to the platform and the other walked around checking underneath and among the aya's fur for other places where one could hide import.

"Any news from Yontar?" Rai asked.

The guard lifted his head from his ledger again, covering his face with his arm to shield from the Sun's glare. He inspected Rai before nodding to himself. "Movement with the gangs. They're all riled up of late. Best to not go out during the dark hours," the guard said.

"My thanks," Rai replied with a slight bow of the head. Yontar had always been an unsettled city. The monarch had a way of riling up the people with his poor decisions. But that had been going on for years. So were the gangs more active because of the shadow man?

The guard hopped down behind Rai and whispered to his commander. He eyed Rai one more time, running his tongue over the back of his teeth. It was hard to be inconspicuous when your shadow was darker than everyone else's.

"You are clear to go," he said, noting more down on his parchment.

Rai bowed, clambered back onto the aya, and whipped its reins. As Rai passed under the gate, he glanced at the huge iron teeth sticking out from above. The gates were like sleeping creatures, open and relaxed, letting people pass through for millennia, but if war was ever to stir and startle them, they would snap shut, the beast wakening. Rai hoped he would never see those iron teeth fall.

The aya trotted through the main thoroughfare. Following this street to the centre of Yontar would take one to the Thousand Floor Palace. It was a hulking building, the base wide enough to house another city. The palace became narrower near the top but never to a point, eventually flattening out and squaring off.

There was another wall around the palace to stop anyone from getting in. It was of similar height to the city wall and had a promenade built onto it called the Strip, wrapping almost all the way around, where upmarket merchants set up shops for nobles and those with plenty of spare coin to spend.

It was unlikely that the palace had a thousand floors. No one had counted the floors. It seemed trivial once it got to a certain height. And technically, it was only the second largest palace in Tarris. The first being the abandoned Mad Palace in the lost capital.

Still, the Thousand Floor Palace was a sight beyond sights, and people near the gate stopped to gawk at its grandness.

Much like Celabar, the immediate area around the lower gate housed the merchant shops and market streets. They were just as busy as the main thoroughfare, with crowds filling every available space like sand in a storm. The Sun Eye was still low, the heat not yet oppressive. Rai hoped he would be in the shade of an inn before it got much hotter.

Rai led the aya down one of the quieter streets, still filled with people but not as tightly packed. He had passed several inns already, but well-travelled folk knew the closer to the gates, the higher prices you would be paying.

Ahead, a man stumbled out of an inn, drunk before midday.

Perfect, Rai thought.

The inn sat on a corner, an iron sign depicting the outline of a square patch with lines woven through it. Below written in scratchy characters, the name read, *The Patched Cloak*.

Rai brought the aya around back in search of the courtyard and found it gated off.

Why would they gate off their courtyard at the busiest time of day?

He hopped down and walked the aya up to the gate. It was unlocked, so Rai pulled it open and led the aya into the courtyard. The stables held no aya, horse, or yarens and no stablehands roamed in wait. So Rai saw to his aya, pumping water into a trough and shutting it in a pen. The mud-clay gate creaked shut, then with a *crack* part of the hinge snapped, and it fell askew.

Perhaps we should have kept looking, Rai thought.

Rai headed over to the back door of the inn and tested the handle. The door was open. *So they aren't closed*, Rai thought, and he stepped into *The Patched Cloak*.

A sparsely lit corridor led down into the main common room. Rai passed a staircase leading to rooms upstairs. He paused, listening.

"You hear anything, Fax?" Rai whispered.

From upstairs? No. Someone is at the bar though, Fax said. Rai had come to the same conclusion.

The bar was a seedy little den that was in desperate need of a clean. Booths lined the far wall, dangling firelights hanging above each. To Rai's left was a stone counter. Leaning over it, Rai peered past the dark doorframe where the kitchen sat shrouded, rot wafting from the darkened space.

This place looks like it hasn't been used in over a hundred years, Fax said. Sometimes Fax's perspective of time was a little off, but in this case, Rai couldn't argue. The wood booths were peeling, the kitchen moulding, and the hearths burned out long ago.

On the right side, another counter stood as the bar. Bottles piled in precarious pyramids had the hairs standing on the back of Rai's neck. They were one exhale away from crashing to the floor. And arranging all this was a red-haired, pale-skinned woman.

Rai had never seen a red-haired woman before. She sped back and forth, picking up bottles lying on the bar, then shaking them. The woman tossed empty bottles into a metal tub and the rest lined on top.

Rai stepped up and cleared his throat.

"Sweet spilled rum!" she yelped and dropped one of the bottles. It shattered, sending glass skittering across the floor. "You thun-brained bampot!"

Her accent had a twang to it. Probably from Nuia, the mountainous continent to the north of Tarris.

She scowled at Rai, hands on hips like it was his fault she dropped it. The red-haired woman wore an emerald, billowing robe that was lined with creases and flowed with her movement. She was young. Too young to be running an inn herself.

"Bam... pot?" Rai asked.

I think that was an insult, Fax said.

"Who are you and what are you doing at my inn?" she snapped.

"I was hoping to get a room," Rai said.

"We're closed," she said, hands still on her hips.

"I can pay two derans a night," Rai said, slapping down two coins on the bar.

The woman gazed longingly at the coins, then up at Rai. It was double the asking price for a room in this district. She cleared her throat, emotions fighting on her face, before she grabbed the coins.

"Well then. We have limited services with it being closed

and all," she said, tapping the coins against the bar as if to check if they were real.

"That won't be a problem," Rai said.

The woman looked up at him. Her eyes matched the green of her dress.

"You will have to see to your own food, but we have plenty of drink if you aren't one of these Tarrisians that claims not to drink but then does behind closed doors," she said.

Rai smiled at that.

"But no trouble at my inn," she said, pointing at him. "No one pays this for an empty inn if they aren't wrapped up in something nasty."

Rai said nothing and she raised her eyebrows. "No problems at the inn," Rai said.

"Good." She nodded. "The names Illy."

"Rai," he said.

"Nice to meet you, Rai." She laid her hand flat, palm up in front of her. Now it was Rai's turn to raise an eyebrow. She sighed, leaned over and grabbed his arm, lifted it above hers and then dropped it, letting it fall and hit hers.

"It's how we greet each other in my country," Illy said.

"I see," Rai said, examining his hand. He was fairly well versed in Nuian culture but had never heard of them greeting like this before.

"You can take your pick of the rooms upstairs," she said, then turned back to sorting the bottles.

"I do have one question," Rai said.

Illy sighed, rubbing her hands on a cloth and spun around

again.

"If the inn is closed, who was stumbling out of here?" Rai asked.

"My bottle-brained nephew," she said. "No matter what I say, all he does is drink and who knows what else." She shook her head. "But he's family, you know?"

Rai didn't know. But this nephew was of interest. Unstable as he was, he could have connections on the streets of Yontar and Rai needed leads to find this shadow man.

"He doesn't partake in blood dealing or anything? I need to know I'm safe here," Rai said.

"He won't do you any harm," she said with a laugh. "A sand fox could pin my puny little nephew down. You aren't in any danger from him."

"My thanks," he said, bowing and making for the stairs. Illy nodded and went back to sorting the bar.

Rai climbed the narrow staircase up to the rooms. Tapestries filled in the walls between the many doors on either side. A thick layer of dust dulled the images and sand lay unswept across the floor.

Nice place, Fax said.

"At least we won't be bothered here," Rai said. "And we don't need to worry about being recognised."

Apart from maybe the params hiding in the walls, Fax said.

Rai grimaced. He didn't mind the little furry creatures, but he didn't want them where he was sleeping. And they could be listening. He learned to watch for them after learning about The Ear and how he had tamed and trained them to repeat what they heard.

Rai slid open the door at the far side of the hallway. The furthest room from the staircase meant the most warning if someone was approaching. The door swung open and Rai's nose curled. Austere would have been a kind description. More sand piled in the corners, and the only thing in the room was a broken bed frame.

I thought bigger cities would have nicer rooms, but your place in Celabar looks like a palace compared to this, Fax said, flying over and sitting atop the bed post.

And I'm paying two derans a night for this, Rai thought.

With further exploring, Rai found another bed and brought it into the far room. He closed the shutters, which clacked loudly, threatening to crumble and fall out the window. Finally, he swept out the sand, brushed his hands on his cloak, and stood back inspecting the room.

Well, now it closer resembles a room, Fax said.

The window looked over the front of the inn, letting Rai see anyone coming in and out of The Patched Cloak. Noise from below caught his attention and Rai adjusted the shutters to allow him to peek out. The drunk man, Illy's nephew, stumbled back into the inn as some merchants he had pushed passed cursed at him. He must have been in his early twenties, but already his eyes were yellowing and hair thinning. He had all the signs of a blood addict. Which meant he knew where the heart of Yontar's streets was.

"Perfect," Rai said. "Now we wait." He pulled up a stool he found in one of the other rooms and sat at the shuttered window.

Crack.

The stool collapsed under his weight.

Fax let out a cawing bird-like laugh.

"You aren't a bird!" Rai shouted as he rubbed his aching back.

And you, dear Rai, aren't sitting on a stool anymore.

18

False

Something was wrong. It wasn't the wrong of the dark place Nya had survived, but something else.

They had been back in Yontar for a couple of days, but it felt like a different place. Was this really the same Yontar Nya had left? They couldn't have been in that dark place for more than a couple of days. Dust had been bringing Mother enough food to survive, but she didn't know how much Mother needed. She couldn't have been gone any longer. So why did the city feel so different?

Nya fell back into her routine. She started her days by helping the spice merchant with pickups and deliveries. Then she spent some time with Mother, who came in and out of awareness, thinking Nya was the man who abandoned her, or realising it was the daughter who took everything from her. She stole food that she needed to survive at the morning markets, then returned home to clean Mother up and sleep before dark hour. She had looked for the Sand Rats at their usual spots to no avail. But Kit came by occasionally and they would eat and talk in the shade of alleys, much like she had with Luk and the other Sand Rats.

It was almost the same as before, but it felt hollow. Like she was playing a part in a street performance of her life. None of it felt *real*.

Perhaps she'd changed.

Nya pushed through the morning market carrying a crate for the spice merchant. The mix of spices she picked up from a trader passing through Yontar smelled intoxicating. Every time Nya inhaled, it smelled slightly different. One whiff brought sharp fruity scents, the next could be a duller woody scent.

The clamour of vendors blared above muffled haggling. Nya's arms burned as she shoved through the jostling crowd. How could a crate of spices weigh so much?

She dodged around people who looked through her, uncaring. She had timed this badly. Half an hour ago, this street would have been a lot quieter. Nya twisted to squeeze through the crowd, but someone backed up, bumping her and sending her stumbling. The crate toppled from her arms and scraped across the sandy street.

"Watch it!" the pompous man said, then stalked off.

Nya sighed and went to pick up the box. Two hands with the bracers of a guard wrapped around it as she approached.

Her stomach sank, but the guard straightened and proffered it to her. Nya took the crate, eyes downcast.

"Here you go," the guard said. There was a pause, then he asked, "Nya?"

Nya brought her eyes up.

"Jut?" Nya said. "You're a guard?"

A grin spread across Jut's face. It was him. He seemed taller and broader since she last saw him, although it may have been the guard uniform that gave that impression. "Guard in training," he said, gesturing to another guard a couple of paces behind who was talking with one of the vendors.

"What happened to you and Luk?" Jut asked, his face slackening. "You never came to the tower."

"It's a long story," Nya said. "I wanted to come. I really did."

Jut nodded, but his expression stayed grim. "We waited for you. We kept going back, thinking we had the wrong day," he said. "The Ghrobans were everywhere, so stealing enough to even survive was hard."

"I'm so sorry," Nya said, feeling a flood of emotion.

"Once we went to the tower looking for you, we overheard the guards saying they were recruiting. So we signed up," he said.

She was glad they had found a way to stay safe from the Ghrobans and get food in their bellies, but the city guard? Did he remember all the beatings they received from the guards? All the cruelty that was the lifeblood of their ranks?

"I'm glad you are all okay," she said.

Suddenly, a deep voice cut through the buzz of the crowd and said, *The Sand Rats moved on without you*. Nya looked around, but the market goers were giving them a wide berth, staying a couple paces away from Jut in his uniform.

The tumult around her dimmed, and the voice sounded again.

In fact, they are doing better without you. You thought you were looking after them, but you were just holding them down.

Faces glanced at her from the crowd.

And the worst part is that, deep down, you knew that but you refused to let them go. You were afraid of being alone.

"Nya, you okay?" Jut asked, a look of worry creasing his face.

"Yeah, yeah, I thought I heard something," Nya said.

It was the same voice as before. The presence.

"I was saying, I could ask and see if they are looking for any more recruits?" Jut asked.

How sweet. He's pitying you, the voice said.

"No!" Nya snapped, a little sharper than she meant. Jut leaned back at the outburst. "I mean no, thank you."

"Are you sure? You can't keep up what we were doing," Jut said.

Was he threatening her? Would he hand her in if she was stealing just to survive? He was doing the same thing not so long ago.

"I'm fine," she said, adjusting the crate she was holding.

Jut didn't look convinced. His mouth drew closed. Anger boiled in Nya's empty stomach. She hated being pitied.

"Jut! Come on. It's not a patrol if we stand about," the other guard called.

Jut glanced over his shoulder, then back to Nya and said, "I better get going."

Nya nodded.

"We can help, Nya. Come have a meal with us sometime," he said.

Nya fought to keep the sneer off her face. He wanted to give her charity now? Did he remember it was her that had been feeding *them*? She didn't need their help.

"Take care of yourself, Nya," he said and backed off into the crowd.

Nya watched him go. The throng went back to jostling her as they passed, now that the guard was gone.

Suddenly, Nya felt herself fall to exhaustion, her legs and arms shaking under the weight of the crate.

She trudged forward, ducking out from the mass of people to set the crate down and give herself a break. Leaning against a wall, she felt a heaviness despite having put down the crate, and her head ached. How could she have lost so much so quickly? She couldn't have been gone that long, but everything had changed.

You're nothing more than a burden chaining yourself to those you love, the voice said.

Nya regarded the empty alleyway, breathing hard.

"Shut up!" Nya screamed.

The shadows in the side street *vibrated* in answer to her. The dark rippled outward like disrupted water. It expanded, reaching and covering the reflected light from the Sun Eye, pulsating around the edges.

It circled her until it shrouded the alley in shadow. Darkness hung like a mantle for a moment. Nya stared, breath held. Then eventually the dark receded.

She watched as the shadows settled, returning to its normal size.

Turning, Nya watched people walk past the end of the street.

Had she imagined it? She ran a hand over her face. She was so tired.

Nya snatched the crate and sped back to the merchant's shop, silencing her thoughts, eyes downcast and focused on the ground in front of her.

The next step. Then the next.

Kit was waiting out front, under the shade of the streets tarp. He swayed on his feet, watching the bustling market. Nya pushed through and slung the crate onto a stack of others piled up outside the spice shop.

"Nya! There you are," Kit said. "I was wondering if you wanted to show me this temple that you and your friends used as a hideout."

He smiled, hands held out.

"Not today," Nya said, and made for the entrance of the shop. She was tired and done with the day.

"Come on," Kit said, running up beside her. "Please? Are you afraid the god is angry with you for using his statue to crush that thug's foot? He's probably thankful. That's the most any god has done in centuries."

"I said no," Nya said, pulling away from him. Kit stilled.

"Are you okay?" he asked.

She hated that question. It brought with it a rise in the dark sea in her mind. Her eyes started to sting.

"Fine," Nya choked and stepped into the shop.

The owner, an older man called Phen, was behind the counter weighing out spices on a metal scale.

Jars of spices lined the shelved walls in a busy mess of colours. There didn't seem to be any structure to how Phen arranged the spices, all randomly placed covering every patch of the wall.

"Nya, is that you? Did you get the thyme and red spice?" Phen asked.

"Out front," Nya said with an exhale, then she took to the stairs.

Nya wiped a loose tear as she went along the corridor and up to her attic. Mother was sleeping when she entered, so Nya lay beside her, holding down her swell of emotion.

She lay there for a while, listening to the steady breaths of Mother sleeping. Numbness swept through her as she stared at the roof beams.

Why was everything so much harder now? She had made it through that dark place and returned home. She should be happy.

Thoughts of walking into the desert plagued her mind. Being free from all this seemed like a dream.

But she couldn't. She had to look after Mother. She *owed* it to Mother. She was indebted to Mother. It was the reason she rose every day, the reason she risked her life stealing and working whatever job she could find.

But since returning from the dark place, it felt *fake*, meaningless.

Shadows lengthened, a coolness carrying on the breeze. Mother tossed and turned beside her. She mumbled something, then yanked at the blankets. They unfurled from around Nya and dragged half across her body, letting cool air caress Nya's arm.

"You trying to get your Mother sick?" Mother asked, pulling at them again until Nya had none covering her.

"No, sorry Mother," Nya whispered.

"You know, one time when you were sick I gave you a bigger portion of food than me, despite me being a lot larger than you," she said, eyes closed as if she was sleep talking.

Nya remembered that. She had a fever that lasted over two weeks. Mother had tutted every morning when Nya wasn't able to get up and work but she had given Nya the larger share of their rations.

It was to make sure you could get up and work, a voice said. It was probably right. Nevertheless, she remembered it fondly.

Nya lay on the cold ground. She should get up. They hadn't eaten today and she should go steal some food for her and Mother. She should apologise to Kit. She should check on the Sand Rats.

But she wasn't going to do any of these things. Instead, she pressed her eyes closed and drifted into the void.

19

Yontar's Underbelly

L ight drained from the sky like sand in an hourglass. The sand blackened and torches were lit across Yontar, giving it a surging radiant glow. Rai watched as nightlife picked up, bringing out all sorts now that they could be obscured by the dark.

I see upon the sands, something the colour of... blue! Fax said. There was a moments quiet. *Come on, Rai, something that is blue.*

"I'm not playing this game with you," Rai said.

Why not? Who knows how long this nephew will be, Fax said.

Rai didn't answer.

The street below had picked up now that the Sun Eye had dipped out of sight, more and more people had started passing by. Fax flew over and perched on the window ledge.

Why do you think this inn is in such a state? Fax said.

"I don't know or care," Rai said, not taking his eyes from the street.

It doesn't pique your interest a little? How about your fascination with risk evaluation? Don't you think they could be dangerous? Fax asked.

Rai sighed. "No, they aren't dangerous. They are from Nuia, just recently came to Tarris. You can tell by the fact their white skin is still pale as the snow sitting on the mountains of their homeland and not red, as most foreigners get once they stay for any length of time," Rai said. "And if you were paying attention, their rooms aren't much better than ours. They still have most of their clothes bundled too. And since they're related, and from the sounds of it, not seeing eye to eye, I doubt they bought the place to open it together. I'm guessing a relative passed away and they inherited the inn and are trying to decide what to do with it."

Fax whistled. *Not a bad guess. I still prefer my theory that they are ghosts come back from Duat trying to right their wrongs of overcharging at their crappy inn.*

"By overcharging us?" Rai scoffed.

It's a working theory, Fax said. *And you offered to pay that.*

A man in a drooping blue robe stepped out of the shadows. A hood covered his face, but Rai could tell from his stagger who it was.

"The nephew," Rai said.

That's right! He was the blue thing. Now your turn, Fax said.

Rai leapt to his feet, swept up his cloak, and left his room.

He went out the back, through the courtyard and round to the corner, where he watched the nephew pass down a side street.

Lit windows and torches outside of taverns and other establishments speckled some orange in the azure twilight of night. Revelry cheered in dulled spikes as Rai passed windows, the scent of furthing leaves pouring out in an earthy musk. Veering around the corner, the nephew peered over his shoulder. Rai kept walking. Stopping now would be suspicious. The nephew turned back, joining the crowded main street.

"Fax, keep on him," Rai whispered, and a piece of shadow darted among the feet of the throng.

Rai barged into the flow of people, heading towards the nephew. A stern look silenced those who grunted at him. Falling into the swell of the crowd, Rai waited, eyes searching. Fax slid back into his shadow.

He left the main street up here, Fax said.

Rai pressed through and leaned against a wall, looking sideways down an alley. The nephew was at the far end, rubbing his arms erratically, as he walked up to an old derelict building. *A blood den*, Rai thought.

"Looks like I was right about him being a blood addict," Rai whispered.

Blood was a powerful thing. Taken from the right species and boiled, you could get euphoric effects by inhaling the steam. Some creature's blood could knock one out for a week. Others would do nothing at all.

Those inside were probably smoking param blood. It was cheap, easy to get a hold of and, after a sharp sensation, lulled the smoker into a mellow catatonic state for a few hours. It also rotted ones brain and teeth. And yet so many turned to it during hardship just to be consumed by its addictive nature.

Of course, some blood did more than that, Rai thought, touching the diera dagger at his hip. But few knew about its true power, and less still had the connections and materials needed to utilise that knowledge.

With a paranoid spin of his head, the nephew hopped over the knee-high wall.

Blood dealing was illegal, but in every city, blood dens could be found if one knew where to look. Rai stepped over the wall of the old decrepit building. It must have been a place of worship, few other buildings would have this large a space around it.

The temple was a wide, domed building, torchlight pouring out of a squint door that no longer sat in its frame. On the second floor was a glass mosaic depicting a boy with a blade facing a burling shadow.

Rai crept forward. Even before reaching the door, the odour of vomit hit him, turning his nose. A quick glance inside revealed exactly what he thought he would find. A hall stripped of furniture and decoration and filled with empty-eyed people lying around with the blank faces of disassociated corpses. Most lay on blankets, but a good number sprawled out on the hard floor.

Inside held the muted noise of those not really there.

Whimpers mixed with laughing, but it was quiet enough that Rai could hear the creak of floorboards as the nephew made his way to the back of the temple.

He skulked along to the far wall, itching at his side, and eyes darting around, as he handed a coin over to a man, who handed back a pipe. The nephew already had it in his mouth before he made it to one of the candles and hovered it over, letting the blood come to a boil. The man who sold him the pipe ducked out into a back room.

If I'm going to find out anything about this shadow man, it'll be from him, Rai thought.

Rai headed around the side of the building. These old worship buildings always had a back door where the priests would enter.

The walls around the back of the garden were undamaged and rose to well above Rai's height. Dirt lay in patches of churned-up mounds, where gardens used to flourish. It saddened Rai to see what was, no doubt, once a sprawling, beautiful garden now rotted and ruined.

He turned. Someone was beside him.

Rai jumped back, sliding his daggers into his hands.

A man with scraggly greying black hair threw his hands up. A beard drooped from his face in wiry curls that broke off in all directions. He wore a short-sleeved tired brown tunic, with black breeches that had a rip across his calf, and he only had one boot.

"Who are you?" Rai asked. How had this man snuck up on him? Rai had been trained to be aware, but this older man somehow got up close to Rai and he hadn't noticed.

"I didn't mean to scare yah," he said, a hint of laughter in his tone. "I was just coming out to see what you were looking at."

The man didn't look like he was a blood addict. His face wasn't sunken and his eyes were clear.

"Who are you?" Rai repeated.

"The names Lem, pleased to meet you," Lem said, putting a hand out in offering.

"Why are you here?" Rai asked, ignoring the gesture.

Lem shrugged. "For the conversation. Gets lonely on the streets, you know."

Rai thought of the people inside, catatonic. *The conversation?*

"What about you?" Lem said, stepping closer, one eye wider than the other. "You don't seem like the type to turn to the red perfume."

Rai sheathed his daggers but didn't bring his hands far from them. "I'm looking for someone," Rai said.

"Aren't we all," Lem said, then peered at Rai. "Yes, you are looking for someone."

"What's that supposed to mean?" Rai asked.

The man laughed. "You wouldn't understand if I told you. You must look to find someone. You can't be told where they are or you haven't found them, have you?"

I think he has breathed in too much second-hand blood vapour, Fax said.

"I best be on my way," Rai said, heading around the building.

"Wait! Perhaps I can help!" Lem called.

The Moon Eye lit the side garden in a pale glow. They were alone, the buzz of the city sounding distant. Most inside were out of it and would be no use talking to. This Lem, however, was sober and spent time around blood dens and Yontar's underbelly.

Might as well ask and see, Fax said. *Worst case, we can kill him. No one's around.*

"Okay," Rai said. "I'm looking for a man with a moving shadow."

Lem's eyes widened, and he shushed Rai. "Shh!" He laid a dirty hand on Rai's mouth, his head swivelling around the empty garden. Rai spat after Lem moved his hand. It tasted of off milk.

"Come with me," Lem whispered, then pulled Rai round the back of the building.

The back garden had high walls surrounded it, unbroken. Patches of soil ran up the sides of a long, narrow pit, almost like a trough built into the ground. A pond, Rai realised. Although empty of water now, Rai could see where the water would have sat in the greenery of the garden.

Lem walked to the edge of the empty pond and hopped down. It only came up to his waist. He waved Rai to follow. Rai jumped down beside him and Lem bent so that he was below the lip.

"Duck." Rai raised an eyebrow but did as he was asked. "Anyone could be listening," he said. The pond certainly didn't have sound proofing attributes. In fact, standing in an empty pond would bring more attention to them if someone was to come out back, but Rai didn't say any of this.

"You ask dangerous questions, muscle man," Lem said. Rai looked down at his sleeveless tunic.

I think he wants a kiss, Fax said.

"The man you ask about is a demon," Lem said. "I seen him. I seen him when he first took to preaching." Lem peeked over the edge at the still empty garden. "I was just going about my daily walk around the city. Got to keep fit and healthy, you know." He nodded at Rai.

"Anyway, I was that way," Lem said pointing northeast. "And walking down a street to see an old friend, sleeping Siv. You would like him. He does a magic trick where he can steal your boot from your feet without you even noticing. Still haven't figured out how he does it." Lem paused, scratching his beard and sucking his teeth.

"You know, I don't think he gave me my boot back," Lem said.

"The shadow man," Rai prompted.

"Ah, yes," Lem said. "So, I was coming down this street and I heard shouting. Of course, I followed the noise. Gets boring, so anything like that I always go to see what's happening. And this cloaked man stood on a crate and was shouting about how the royals didn't care for their people anymore, and that they lied to them, and all that sort of stuff. Then he was talking about a… reckoning! That was it. A reckoning that would bring justice down on those who sat on thrones and ate their weight in fruit we would never taste."

"It was all very rousing. I was ready to maul some guards and the such, but he said this reckoning was coming and that he needed followers to help bring it about," Lem said.

He's recruiting, Rai thought. But what for? What was this reckoning?

"Anyway, I was about to leave, sleeping Siv was probably waking for his hour, so I had to be quick if I wanted to catch him awake, but then the shadow man did something I haven't ever seen before, or since," Lem said leaning in conspiratorially. "He lifted his hands and everything got darker. It was still early morning, Ova's Sun Eye high, but the street darkened like it was coming upon the dark hour. Shadows covered everything. Some screamed, others fell to their knees. I was going to clap, but no one else was, and I didn't want to be the only one. If someone else started clapping, I would have joined, but I didn't want to start and then be the only one doing it, you know."

Sounds like we found our man, Fax said.

It has to be another shade like Fax, Rai thought. He didn't trust this Lem, but this wasn't something he could make up. It fit what Fax could do exactly.

"And this man was in the northeastern part of the city?" Rai asked.

"Uh. That way," he said, pointing northeast.

"Thank you for your help," Rai said, standing. "Here, something for your time." Rai passed him a deran.

Lem stared at it, then bit it, lip curling in disgust. "What am I supposed to do with this?"

"It's a deran, Lem. You can buy things with it," Rai said. Surely the man knew how money worked.

"I gathered that, but what do I need to buy?" he asked.

"Another pair of boots?" Rai shrugged.

Lem's eyes lit up. "Now that's a good idea."

What a strange man, Rai thought as he climbed back out of the pond.

"Thank you, fine-booted friend. Next time we meet, I will be equally fine-booted," Lem said, grinning from inside the pond.

Rai bowed to the depth you would a friend, then marched out of the garden. A breeze rolled over his skin, filling his lungs.

One step closer to finding the truth.

20

A Dark Voice Whispers

Nya slipped a piece of fruit from the stall and slid it into her pocket. Her sleight of hand had improved over the years, but she still found herself caught more than half the times she stole anything. She kept walking, not speeding up or slowing as to not attract attention. No one called. No one shouted for her to stop. Nya let out a long breath.

She swerved around the market crowd, head low. Nya felt the fruit bulging in her pocket. This would be fine for today. The markets were busy with an influx of travellers bringing in the harvest which made it easier to steal food from the stalls with the mass of people to blend into. But it also increased the risk. If they caught her when it was busy like this, the guards would be sure to make an example of her to put off others.

She had seen the viciousness of their examples and would

rather be hungry tonight than strung up as a message to others tomorrow.

It had been a couple days since she saw Jut, and luckily hadn't run into him or any of the other Sand Rats again. She still didn't know how to feel about that. There was a distance between them, and it was growing each cycle, like parting ships that were set on slightly different courses. It all felt so sudden. And yet, running that heist in the market felt like a lifetime ago and only a couple of days at the same time.

Kit had come around twice and tried to coax her out, but she didn't want to go anywhere or talk with him. She couldn't pretend to be okay. Not yet.

Nya ambled with the flow of the market goers, sifting through her thoughts. It was only when someone bumped into her that the world sharpened again and she felt eyes on her. The hairs prickled on the back of her neck. Somehow she *knew* she was being watched. Nya had a keen sense, honed by years of surviving on Yontar's streets, but it was like a voice in the back of her head had whispered the thought to her.

Nya didn't turn. She knew better than to show whoever was tailing her that she was aware of them. She had to get out of this stream of people and break for the cover of the winding side streets.

Two of them, the voice said. Nya didn't start when the voice spoke anymore. It was becoming a part of her. Still, it scared Nya. It said and saw things she couldn't. Which was impossible when it was a voice in her head. She tried not to think about it.

Nya ducked under a crate, then squeezed between two cloaked figures. She made sure to not move too quickly, but she needed to create distance between her and whoever was following her. The raucous calling and clomping footsteps of the crowd masked any hint of if those following Nya were speeding up to keep her in sight.

Maybe it's Jut and another Sand Rat? Nya thought. *Or Kit and one of his friends.*

Was she being paranoid? The voice said no. Not so much with words but impressions. She didn't want her followers to catch her. Nya shook her head. How could she know that? Maybe she should just glance back and —

It was Uri and one of his cronies. Not one of his cronies she had seen before, but he had a similar girthy build to Uri and his other friends. And they looked right at her.

Nya spun and dove through any gaps she could find in the bustling crowd. She had been back for days and seen a couple of Ghrobans who hadn't recognised her, so Nya had thought herself safe. But, of course, Uri wasn't going to forget after she crushed his foot. That, hopefully, meant he wasn't able to move quickly.

Pushing and shoving through the crowd, Nya no longer cared about staying shrouded in the mass. She heard irritated people shouting and guessed Uri and his friend weren't kindly asking people to move aside either.

Nya wove through the throng like a needle through fabric. The shouting was getting further away. Nya ducked out into a side street and bolted around a corner.

Standing still, breath held and back against a wall, Nya listened.

"She went down here, I'm sure," someone said.

Cursed sands of the capital, Nya swore.

Nya pushed off the wall and ran on light feet. Buildings leaned over the alleyway like monolithic watchers as she dashed past. Wind corralled down the narrow streets, rustling Nya's hair and clothes, ushering her onward. Turning right, a group of sand foxes picking through trash scattered. Nya cursed. They will have heard that. Veering around the next left, Nya looked down a long straight ending with a dead end.

No.

Nya whirled around. She needed to take the right instead.

Just as she made to turn back, Uri and his friend crested the corner. Uri's lips curled into a snarl. Nya backed up, and with each step back, Uri approached. His friend stayed at the alley's entrance leaning against the wall.

"Hello little Sand Rat," Uri said. "We have missed you while you were in that cell. The rest of your gang may be out of our grasp, but you're who I really wanted."

Nya glanced down, but there was no bandaging around his foot. The last time she saw him, he could barely put weight on it.

"Oh, this?" he said, following her gaze and shaking his foot. "Varsep knows some tricks. Healed me right up."

Varsep?

Nya searched for words she could fashion into a shield and sword, a phrase that could save her. But Uri was stubborn and single-minded. There was nothing she could say to change his mind. He was going to kill her.

Nya's heel hit the wall, and she tripped. Uri's grin spread wider. She had nowhere to run.

Inside, the voice pulsed. It was a pressure on her mind that said, *bare your teeth*. If she couldn't hide, then she must fight. It didn't use words but the impression was clear. The presence buzzed with energy coaxing her to do something. Nya pushed back against it. She was no match for Uri in a scrap.

Uri unslung a bat from his under his cloak. The poorly crafted wooden bat looked like he had broken it off an old cart. The thick end was splintered and cracked like it had smashed against something over and over. Red stains had seeped into the wood and dried.

"Please Uri, I'm sorry," Nya said. "I'll do anything. I'll pay you back."

"Yes, yes you will," Uri said. "Blood for blood."

Nya slid down the wall, hands raised.

FIGHT!

I can't.

Uri paused, running his tongue over teeth and twirling the bat, loosening his wrists. He lifted the bat and Nya squeezed her eyes shut as her mind screamed at her. Everything came to a crescendo of piercing noise in her head as she waited for the impact.

Then there was a scream, and another, and a wet noise.

The black fell silent.

Nya's hissing breath whistled in and out, sounding over the nothingness. Tentatively, she opened her eyes. The alley was darker than it had been seconds before. Shadows crawled up the walls and flooded the ground.

A shadowed spike protruded from the wall and through Uri's head. He still stood, held up by the spike, his empty eyes staring. His mouth hung open as blood poured from his wound.

Nya screamed.

The spike receded slowly back into the wall, letting the body slump to the ground. Nya propelled herself to the side to avoid Uri's body. She sat a moment, watching as he leaked crimson, it pooling around him; the blood edging closer and closer to her.

Nya's breathing was erratic. She stumbled away before Uri's blood reached her. The ethereal darkness blanketing the alley unfurled its grip. Nya staggered away as it grew lighter. Coming to the end of the street, she saw Uri's friend, who had a hole in his head too, blood spatter covering the wall he leaned against.

Nya held back the vomit crawling up her throat and ran.

She lurched through the winding streets. She had to get away. Tearing through the alleys, Nya had no thought of where she was going. The walls on either side blurred as she ran.

Hurtling around another corner, Nya's foot caught on an abandoned crate, sending her tumbling forward. She hit the ground hard.

With a grunt, she rolled onto her back. She stared at the sky, blue and untainted, as she caught her breath.

It's exactly what happened with Kit in that cave. Was she causing these shadows? She must be. The thought was terrifying. What was wrong with her?

Nothing is wrong with you, Nya, the dark voice whispered.

Nya lifted her head, but of course the alley was empty. It was the voice, the presence.

"What are you?" Nya asked, feeling it stir.

I'm going to help you, said the voice. It was deep and was as much felt as it was heard.

"How?" Nya asked.

I'm going to help by showing you that you don't need to bend to the world around you, it said.

Nya paused. "But what are you?"

Your people have called us aspects or shades, among other things.

Nya had never heard of either of those phrases. Maybe she should have felt worried or scared, but she didn't. She had grown used to the presence, and there was little the world could throw at her that would scare her after the horrors she had endured.

The presence had done nothing but help her.

"How can I not bend to the world?" Nya whispered.

By bringing it to its knees.

Nya returned home as light seeped from the sky and the sand blackened. It was soon going to be dark hour. The gap when neither of Ova's Great Eyes were watching.

Nya felt a little better. The presence was no longer an unknown force. It said it had no name, so she had taken to calling it Bom to help separate it from herself.

Bom changed everything. She could now protect herself from the guards, the other gangs, and anyone else who threatened her or Mother. Finally the sands had fallen favourably for her.

Grabbing onto the top rung of the ladder, Nya pulled herself up into their attic. A hand snapped from nowhere, smacking her across the face. Nya toppled, banging her head on the ground. She blinked away the orbs specking her vision and saw Mother. She was standing. Lucidity in her keen piercing gaze.

"Mo-Mother?" Nya asked.

"You're late," she spat, then turned away.

The lantern was lit, drawing hard lines around everything in the room, and colouring it in reds and blacks pushing against one another. Mother hadn't been *here* enough to stand or hit her in weeks. She had spent some time sitting and coming in and out of awareness, but mostly she clung to the past seeing only her memories.

The blanket, that had been firmly wrapped around her every moment for weeks, was neatly folded, and the old cabinet was dragged from its corner. Its red, chipped paint was bordered by a gold swirling pattern, and lying atop it was Nya's cloak. A ragged grey piece that she wore whenever leaving during the Moon Eyes watch, to hold back the cool winds and curious stares.

"Mother, what are you doing?" Nya asked, sitting up. Another back hand snaked out, only flickering her head back instead of tipping her over this time.

"Don't question your mother. I'm patching up this cloak to make it acceptable." Mother turned and grinned at her daughter. "I have a plan to get us enough food to last us a lifetime," she said, then went back to stitching the cloak. "And maybe Werin will come crawling back."

Nya stepped over, keeping her distance from Mother but curious to see what she was doing. She had cut a patch from the sea blue curtains that sat untouched on the old cabinet. Mother threaded through the sea-blue fabric on one side of the cloak, attaching it in a blocky pattern.

"Don't just stare, hand over the next patch," Mother said, gesturing to the curtain lying at her feet.

Mother had already cut the curtain up into similar patches like the one she was sewing. Nya picked up the next one and handed it to Mother.

Nya ducked a little lower, staring at Mother. She could always tell Mother's mental state by her eyes. They were sharp with a firm grasp of what was around her. Mother looked up at her and Nya flinched back.

"So, what is this plan?" Nya asked. These episodes of lucidity could fade at any moment and she wanted to make the most out of being able to talk with her mother.

Mother finished attaching the patch with a flourish, then patted the cloak. She smirked, pleased with her work. It was half done, blue patches woven along one side.

It was pretty, Nya thought. Mother had always been a talented seamstress and had made most of Nya's clothes over the years. Recently, though, Nya had to make her own, and she wasn't nearly as good as Mother.

Mother tapped on the cabinet, staring at Nya for a moment. "You will be a lost noble's daughter," Mother said, taking a step closer to her. "One that will ask for aid from the palace guards."

A fist cracked across Nya's nose. She stumbled back, holding it, her hand turning red with blood. Nya looked at Mother with astonishment when the next strike smacked her across the cheek. This one caused the orbs of light to flash across her vision and then she was on her back again, Mother standing over her.

"They will take you in," Mother said as a foot rammed into her stomach, causing Nya to curl and suck in air. "And you will tell them I saved you from some thugs."

Another foot swung, kicking her in the face. Nya saw blood spray as she lay coughing.

"Please," Nya croaked. Mother kicked her again, and the room wavered, unconsciousness threatening at the edges of her vision.

"I'm sure the palace will be grateful that I brought them a noble's daughter. They will reward me well. Especially after the beating those bandits gave you," Mother said.

She hit Nya over and over. Nya dipped in and out of consciousness, her vision snapping from black to blurs to black again.

Andrew Watson

"You will never be able to give me back the life you stole, Nya," Mother said among more strikes. "But you can try."

A foot cracked her face and Nya lolled onto her back. Above, the silhouette of Mother approached lined in red and orange.

Yelping erupted from behind her and an unfocused haze of yellow moved about her mother's feet. Dust. She was snapping at Mother's ankles. Nya wanted to reach out and make her stop, but everything hurt. Mother shouted something and kicked Dust, who landed a couple feet away with a whimper.

A spike of rage jolted Nya. She had done everything for Mother. Mother had barely been able to function the last few years, and Nya had gotten her food and water at her own expense, often going without. She had gone to Duat and back just to feed Mother, but deep down, she knew it would never be enough.

This was going to be her existence. Repaying an endless debt that would eventually kill her.

The pain was secondary to the pit in her stomach. It fell to depths that Nya didn't know possible. But at the bottom was a flicker of something. Something hot and angry. It growled, growing into a roar as the pit filled with rage. It was a tempest of fury that filled Nya, fuelled her. She was angry at the world, angry at Mother, and angry with herself.

The blur of firelight around her darkened. The beating stopped and Mother said something that Nya couldn't make out over the rumble in her mind. It must have been dark hour as only the faintest light fought back against the surrounding black.

Nya sat, wobbling back and forth. Blood dripped from her lips. Mother spoke again and took a step back towards the lantern on the far side of the room. Nya was acutely aware that the darkness was reaching from her, smothering that light. Her body ached and mind throbbed, making it hard to think.

A snarl crept across Nya's face and a spike darted from the wall and tore through Mother's leg. She screamed. It was a dull quiet sound to Nya. Another spike shot through Mother's other leg, then one through each of her arms until it held her outstretched.

Nya lifted herself on shaky legs. She rocked, finding her balance, then dragged herself over to Mother.

More spikes erupted, severing tendons and arteries. Nya could barely hear her Mother's screaming.

She stared into her mother's eyes. Terror filled them. And she was lucid still, fully aware of what was happening. Good.

A spear burst from Nya's shadow, edging closer to Mother. Mother thrashed and shook but couldn't move with the other spikes holding her. Nya watched as this wider blade of shadow broke the skin and slid between Mother's eyes. Pain frenzied through Mother's face, then that eased to a blankness.

Nya stayed like that, staring at Mother's strung-up corpse for a while longer before the darkness receded. The spikes slid free and vanished into the shadows. The lanternlight brightened and Mother dropped to the floor. Nya sunk to her knees beside her.

A noise came from behind her. The spice shop owner, probably to see what all the noise was. A gurgle and he fell silent too.

Light got its hold of the room once again. The attic was a tapestry of red. Some of it Nya's, most of it Mother's.

Nya wrapped her arms around Mother. She didn't cry or wail but embraced her in the quiet.

Nya held Mother in that blood-soaked room until the Sun Eye rose and lit the horrors done by the dark.

21

Comfort in Company

The warm wind of late morning carried Kit up the steps and onto the promenade that wrapped around the palace wall. The promenade was named after the architect that built it, but no one called it by that. Kit couldn't even remember the architect's name, but locals called it the Strip.

To his left, a railing lead along the edge guarding from the drop into the city below. Standing over ten stories above the city, the view from the Strip was stunning.

On Kit's right was a line squat two story buildings. They were made with a darker sandstone than the lower city and had doors that were wider at the bottom and grew narrower near the top. Colourful lines and patterns were painted around doorframes and windows as ornamentation that you wouldn't find in the city proper.

These were upper-class merchants, who sold the rarest and finest goods for more coin than most residents of Yontar would ever see. Which also meant they did strange things like paint their door frames.

Guards stood like warding statues on either side of the top of the staircase leading onto the Strip. Kit flashed them a piece of parchment and they waved him past, much to the shock of the nearby nobles. The highbrows looked down their noses as Kit walked among them.

Kit passed across the thoroughfare, confidently. He was a boy in rags, surrounded by the richest in all of Yontar. He was as out of place on the Strip as a fisherman was on the dunes.

Usually he would savour this part of his journey, but today he was preoccupied. Nya had been acting strange of late, lashing out and coming up with ways to get out of spending time with him. This wasn't uncommon. Most grew bored with Kit eventually, but Nya was different, and she wasn't as much brushing him off but shrinking away.

Kit knew that feeling. After going to that strange black rock place with the bat-things and the cave monsters, his sleep was restless. He'd often wake lathered in sweat. That's partly why he wanted to spend so much time with Nya. There was something reassuring about her having gone through it too. He didn't want to talk about it, but just having that shared experience was comforting in itself.

Kit sauntered up to his destination; a shop much like the rest on the promenade. In fact, most of the shops on the Strip were indistinguishable aside from the signs hanging out front. This one had an iron outline of an arching tree which was the sign of a fruit shop, and that meant the best of the best from the orchards and rare fruits like that weird barbed green one that Reavs wouldn't let him touch. Kit just wanted to see if it was spiky or soft.

He heard a gasp when he entered the shop. Kit grinned. They probably thought he was going to rob the place.

Oh ignorant nobles, he thought. He was stealing from them, but not in the way they thought. True stealing was an art. True stealing didn't leave them confused about where they placed their coin purse, or shaking their fist as Kit ran off.

No, true stealing had them handing you their coins with a smile.

The interior of the merchant's shop looked like an orchard had grown through it. Green vines covered the walls. Plants stood tall and healthy in pots; some in sand and others in soil. Baskets were filled with more fruits than Kit knew existed. And the freshest scent in all of Yontar radiated from the produce.

Kit inhaled deeply. He loved rich people smells.

At the far side, Reavs appeared through a door draped in darkness.

"How can I... Kit? Where have you been?" Reavs asked.

Kit pulled his finger back from the barbed green fruit. So close.

"I had a run in with some guards. I'm back now though," Kit said.

"Well, I've had time to think about it and I don't want

to go through with this anymore. I'd rather just beat the competition the same way I've in the past," Reavs said. He brushed his fine tunic that was made of very thin fabric. It had a white robe base, then a dark red layer on top that fell across his shoulder and came down to a point at his waist.

"I go away for a couple days and you get sand in your eyes?" Kit said. "I took the long way around the Strip and went past the new fruit shop. There were several customers lined up, Reavs. *Lined up*!"

Kit hadn't taken the long way. The other fruit shop was on the opposite side of the Strip and it was too hot to walk that far today. Although he had been greatly exaggerating the new fruit shops popularity since he met Reavs. It was part of his job as a broker. He broke deals between high-end business and street gangs so they didn't have to meet. Kit's latest job was telling this Reavs about the new fruit shop and how he knew people who could... disrupt their stock.

"I don't know. I don't want to be singled out by this shadow man," Reavs said.

"Shadow man?" Kit asked.

"You haven't heard?" Reavs said, eyebrows lifting.

Kit was meant to be his eyes and ears on the street. To have his client, know something he didn't was an oversight.

"I've been away," Kit said with a sigh. He couldn't pretend he knew anything about a shadow man.

"Well, there is a man running about that lower city claiming he will reign fire and death upon the injustices of Yontar," Reavs said. "And he has been rallying support from your kind."

Your kind. Kit bit back a retort. He had to with these high
and mighty clients. He sent the first couple screaming for the
guards because of what he'd said to them. And no matter how
satisfying that was, he needed to eat.

"Does this shadow man have a name?" Kit asked.

"He calls himself the Harbinger of Justice, or was it he will
bring the Harbinger of Justice? I can't remember," Reavs said,
biting the inside of his lip. How many nervous ticks did this
man have?

"Okay," Kit said, pacing. "Let me go find out about this
Harbinger of Justice but don't make any rash decisions, like
not wanting to follow through with the plan. We get lots of
screaming fanatics in Yontar. I'm sure this man is just another
sun-sick sand-sniffer."

Reavs had his, *that disgusting lower city speak,* face on. "Very
well, but I want to know this man won't go throwing open my
door in the middle of the night before I agree to anything,"
Reavs said.

"That's fair," Kit said, nodding. "I'll be back in a couple of
days."

Kit made for the door when Reavs added, "And Kit, please
stop stalking down the Strip. People will talk if they see you
keep coming and going. I gave you that pass so you could get
past the guards, but can you at least *try* to be subtle?"

Kit bowed. "Of course."

He wasn't going to do that.

Turned out, this shadow man had been doing the rounds. Kit had met with several of his connections in large gangs and they had all heard of him. This shadow man wasn't approaching gangs though. He just appeared from nowhere, preached about a sandstorm that would scrub the land of pesky injustices, made a spectacle, and vanished.

He was the leader of the Decreed. A 'gang' that Kit had always thought was more of a cult. They had been growing over the last couple years and Kit could understand why. The Decreed preached about a better life for those on the streets and those struggling to get by. And how the country had enough food and water to easily feed its people and yet beggars starved to death every year.

It sounded like a good cause until they spouted nonsense about using ancient powers to level Tarris' hierarchy and tear down the monarchy. A sprinkling of sense means very little under a heavy dollop of crazy.

Kit had always known they were being run by a lunatic, and now that this shadow man had shown face, he was proven right.

People had been joining his cause though, tattooing scales on their skin in reference the Judging that happened after death when Ma-atan would weigh your heart to see if you'd lived honourably.

Kit was away for a couple of days and half the city was now a cult. Terrific. His mind raced with the cons he could pull and the money he could bring in. This shadow man was, no doubt, a con artist as well, so he wasn't tainting his soul by taking advantage but teaching the people of Yontar a lesson about trusting strangers.

"Thanks small head, narrow head," Kit said, walking out the Crusaders' hideout and nodding at the thugs on the door. They growled as they always did. Kit had taken it as a growl of acknowledgment, but their eyes always said otherwise. He would have used their names if they had ever offered them.

Kit spent all morning learning about this shadow man. He had to give the guy credit. He had made quite the impression on the streets in such a short period of time. People said he was Ma-atan's disciple, others said he was a dark god come to tempt them, and everyone talked about how he could manipulate the surrounding shadows.

All this talk of dark gods, and shifting darkness made Kit think about the place with the ever-storming sky. A chill trickled down his spine.

Don't think about it. Don't think about it. Don't think about it.

He needed to speak with Nya. She always settled his nerves. Kit pivoted from going back to his gap between the rooftops and decided to head for the spice shop.

It was midday, most sound asleep for qed. Kit loved midday. The streets were quiet, less jostling so he could get around easier, and the heat didn't bother him much. It was like a game; moving from patch of shade to patch of shade, avoiding the Sun Eye.

He wound his way south, watching as sand rats and params peaked out from their corners. Kit loved seeing the wildlife that came out during qed.

The spice shop sat on the corner of a dead market street. Kit pressed his face to the glass, but inside was in darkness. The merchant was probably sleeping. He was going to have to be careful not to wake him. The merchant had not taken a liking to Kit. Kit couldn't think for the life of him why.

Kit started by calling Nya at the side of the shop where the window to the attic was, but no one answered. She was normally back by this time.

I can't shout any louder without waking that spice man, Kit thought.

Grabbing a handful of small rocks, he threw them against the shuttered window. They pinged off, and several times Kit had to hop to the side to avoid them falling back on him. After a while, Kit threw the rocks down. Where was she?

He didn't know any of her friends' old meeting spots, so he would be searching the city blind. *I should check the attic first just in case she is asleep*, Kit thought, trying to put off the mindless wandering that was about to fill his afternoon.

Kit scaled the side of the shop, using the window ledges as he had seen Nya do many times. The shutters of the second floor slid open and Kit dropped into the corridor. Immediately, the stench of death hit him like a physical blow. It wasn't the first time that the odour rang warning bells in his head.

At the far end of the corridor the spice merchant drooped from the attic hatch, blood dripping like a leaking faucet from a wound in his neck. Kit looked away and swallowed bile.

Nya.

Pushing onward, climbing the ladder past the corpse, Kit eased into the attic.

The attic was a room from his nightmares.

Kit had seen some awful things with the fighting among the gangs in Yontar, but nothing like this. *Everything* was a splattered in blood. And in the centre of it all was Nya, holding her mother, Dust bundled up beside them.

Nya stared, eyes wide but unseeing.

Kit approached, each step squelching beneath his feet. His stomach dropped as he caught a glimpse of Nya's mother. Her pale corpse was covered in gashes and punctures that leaked the last of her blood into the pool at their feet.

"Nya?" She hadn't noticed him entering. "Nya?" Kit reached out and laid a hand on her shoulder. She spun, startled.

"It's okay, it's just me," Kit said, and she relaxed a little. He could now see cuts and bruising covered Nya's arms and face, one of her eyes was swollen black and green. "What happened?"

Nya turned and stared at her mother again. For a moment, Kit thought he was going to have to prompt her again, but she eventually said, "I killed her." It was a whisper, and Kit wondered if he had heard her right.

"I didn't mean to," Nya said. "She just, she…"

"Hey, hey, it's okay," Kit said.

What in Duat's seven torment realms happened here? Nya's mother was awful to her and Kit felt no sympathy for the woman, but she looked like an armoury's worth of swords and spears had torn through her. And Nya said she had done this? This wasn't an accidental death; this was butchery. Nya couldn't have done this. Could she?

Kit took a step back, wavering. No. He couldn't leave her like this. Maybe she was blaming herself, as she so often did when her mother was involved.

Dust ran over and passed between his legs, rubbing against his ankles. Kit bent to pet her, handing coming back red.

"Come on. Let's get you two out of here," Kit said, heaving Nya up.

Kit took them back to his rooftop, cleaned off the worst of the blood and flesh, then Nya passed out on his bundle of blankets without so much as a word. She looked exhausted; like she hadn't slept in days.

Dust sat on Kit's lap as he slung his feet over the edge of the rooftop, gazing down at the market that was picking up now that the Sun Eye dipped low. Dust was letting out a shrill purr as Kit scratched the side of her neck.

"What was that, Dust?" Kit said.

Nya was more beaten than Kit had realised. A layer of blood concealing further gashes and bruising. Kit had tried to clean them. He knew first-hand infection could kill.

He had to make sure she got better. Nya had saved him in that cave. He still thought about it. Dreamt about it. Being wrapped in that writhing hand with too many fingers, sure he was going to die, then Nya screamed and somehow made it let go. She had saved his life, and he was going to do his best, which may not be much, but it's all he could give to make sure she was okay.

Kit had gone out and spent the last of his coin, which he had saved up for a hot meal, on salve and painkillers, which he lathered onto the worst of Nya's wounds. If he could keep them from getting infected, he was sure Nya was going to be okay.

Well, her wounds would heal.

But that hollow look she gave him…

A deran and two silvers sat in Kit's hand. He rolled them around. It was all the money he had left in the world. Dust stretched and rolled onto her back. Kit smiled.

"I guess it's time to go steal us some dinner, Dust," Kit said, rubbing her belly.

22

The Man with the Too Dark Shadow

Nya hung suspended in the place between sleep and reality. In the place where time warped, some moments stretching into eternity and others fleeting, barely noticed. She was semi-aware of Kit and Dust. They took her to where Kit stayed, between the two buildings, under the shelter of the neighbouring eave. Nya had slept a lot, waking only for brief moments, some during the day and others at night making it hard to tell how long she had been with Kit.

She had killed Mother. She hadn't meant to, but Mother hurt Dust, and was hurting Nya, and in the confusion she'd lashed out. She hadn't meant for it to kill her. Nya just wanted her to stop. To stop the kicking. To stop the shouting and berating. And to leave Dust out of it.

She got what she deserved, Bom said.

Shut up! Shut up! Shut up! Nya thought back.

Bom had said that a lot. And the worst part was, she was beginning to believe it. She thought the presence was going to help with her problems, but it just made everything worse.

It's Bom's fault, Nya kept telling herself. But she knew it for a lie.

It all started in that dark place. She caught Bom then, like an infection, a residual evil that clung to her and she couldn't be rid of. And worst of all, couldn't control. What if she got overwhelmed and hurt Dust or Kit? She couldn't live with herself.

Kit dropped down in front of her, bringing her back to reality. "You're up," he said. "Here, eat some bread." Kit passed her a slice and tore into his own.

The Sun Eye was early in its watch. The morning markets filling the air with scents of coffee and spices, and the din of the people bringing life to the city around them.

Dust stirred beside her. Nya hadn't realised she was sleeping there.

"Don't worry, I got enough for you too," Kit said, tossing Dust an edge. She jumped and snapped it out of the air.

"Kit, thank you. I… I don't know what I would do without you," Nya said.

He looked up from his bread, taken aback. "Of course," Kit said. "You saved my life in that place. I owed it to you."

Would Kit have helped if she hadn't saved him? It didn't matter. Of course it didn't matter, but still, the thought twisted her stomach and she no longer wanted to eat the bread.

Kit finished his bread, brushed his hands off and leaned back breathing in the arid air. He coughed, then reached over to grab a waterskin and took a long draught, before offering it to Nya.

Nya sipped. She hadn't realised how parched she was. Despite it being warm, it was the best water she had ever tasted.

"So, it's been a week," Kit said, fidgeting. "Do you want to tell me what happened?"

Nya froze, the waterskin at her lips. She had talked a little over the last couple of days, but not much. And nothing about what happened in the attic.

"You don't have to if you don't want to," Kit said.

"No, it's okay. I want to tell you about it," Nya said and was surprised to realise she meant it.

He won't understand, Bom said. *He will hate you for it. Think you are weak, or a threat.*

Bom might have been right, but Nya didn't care anymore. She hated herself, so what difference would others hating her be?

"I did it," Nya whispered.

Kit didn't react, just stared, arms laying on his crossed legs.

"I killed Mother," Nya said.

"Did she hurt you?" Kit asked.

Nya had forgotten about her wounds. They melted into the numbness along with everything else. Her hands were dirty but washed of blood and covered in pale minor cuts.

Where had she picked those up? She didn't remember.

"You didn't deserve that," Kit said, a hint of a growl in his voice.

She had deserved it. And much worse now, after what she had done.

"I think I'm sick," Nya said. "I think I caught something in the dark place."

Kit knitted his brows. "In what way?"

"There's a presence in my head," she said. "It talks to me, whispers things."

"What kind of things?" Kit said.

Nya waited for Bom to speak. It didn't but she felt it listening.

"I thought it wanted to help me," Nya said. "It said it wanted to help me. That day, Uri and his friend found me at the market but it killed them. It came from the shadows. *My* shadow. And it killed them, Kit. *I* killed them.

"Then when I got furious at Mother it—"

Silence hung between them before Kit spoke again, "Could it... Could it attack me now?"

He's scared of you, Nya thought. *He doesn't want to be near you.*

"I don't think so," Nya said. "It's only appeared when I was angry or scared."

"And it's from the dark place?"

Nya nodded. "I think so."

Kit gazed out over the city and rubbed his face, thoughtful. Did he think she was lying? Nya wouldn't blame him, even she didn't understand.

"I bet that's why they waved that black blade about when we came back," Kit said. "You really didn't like it. I thought it was the stress of surviving that place. The guards probably thought that too, but I wonder if they were looking for something like that."

Nya hadn't thought about it, but she would never forget the burning she felt when the black blade drew close. She knew even then something was wrong, but she'd only wanted to get away and return to Mother. Back to something stable and familiar. Back home.

"Nya, look at me," Kit said, shuffling forward and taking Nya's hands. "What happened to your mother was not your fault."

Nya shied away, not meeting his gaze.

"Nya, listen. You had every right to be angry. If that *thing* interpreted it as a violence that was from *it*, not you. I haven't known you for long, but I'm an excellent judge of character. I know you loved your mother, even if things were"—Kit exhaled trying to come up with the right word—"difficult between you."

Nya had felt nothing in days, and now the sudden rush of emotion floored her, making it hard to focus. An uncomfortable warmth bloomed in her chest and seeped outward, bringing tears. Sympathy shone in Kit's eyes and Nya didn't deserve it. She knew she didn't. Guilt and grief swirled in her gut like a poison.

Dust nuzzled her thigh, stepping onto her lap and lay

down.

Kit's face scrunched and he said, "Wait. Did you say this thing came from your shadow?" Nya nodded, rubbing at her sniffling nose.

"I think there is someone we can talk to about this," Kit said.

Nya hadn't been to the northwest of the city before. They descended a steep staircase, under an arch and came out into an open area that reminded Nya of an inn courtyard, but it wasn't walled in. Open spaces like this weren't common in Yontar, even busy market streets were long and narrow.

On the way over, Kit told her about a man rumoured to have a moving shadow. Nya nodded gratefully but Kit didn't understand. There couldn't be another like her. She was alone in this world and left to deal with the shade herself.

"And why are we here?" Nya asked. Dust ran about her feet, never straying far in the unfamiliar location.

"There are rumours that he is going to preach today," Kit said.

Stalls lay in a grid, forcing people to weave around them. Most of the merchants were packing up their stock, the early morning crowd having finished their shopping and returned home to get out of the worst of the heat.

Nya sighed. She didn't want to be out here. Heavy with grief and hazy from sleeping so long on Kit's rooftop, all Nya wanted to do was rest.

"Let's stop here," Kit said, noticing her trailing pace.

They sat on the corner, backs against a wall, watching the emptying market square. A light breeze sent sand bouncing across the ground and the scent of freshly baked spiced goods wafted on the air. Nya inhaled deeply.

"Is it saying anything?" Kit asked. It took a moment for Nya to realise he was talking about Bom.

"Not right now," she said.

"Can you make it attack? Like when you saved me in the cave?" he asked.

Nya felt Bom listening like a breath on her neck.

"I don't know," Nya said. "That just sort of happened."

"Maybe there is a way to control it," Kit said. "If this shadowed man is like the stories say, then he can control it."

I hope so, Nya thought.

Even in the building's shade, sweat covered Nya's nape and forehead. The market had emptied not long after they arrived, but as time passed, more people appeared. Most were street-dwellers like her and Kit. They huddled in patches of shade. Some standing in circles whispering amongst themselves, others came alone, eyes darting around the filling square. Several guards crept around the edges of the market, watching the growing crowd.

"Do people normally stand around here?" Nya asked.

"No," Kit said. "Others must have heard the rumours too. And look, there's a man in a cloak standing over there. He has the outline of a mace-axe under it. I think he is with the shadow man."

Nya scanned the market until she saw the man Kit

described. He leant against the wall, trying to act nonchalant, but the hard look in his eyes separated him from the anxious crowd.

"Their numbers are growing. Call themselves the Decreed and they follow the shadow man," Kit said in a whisper.

The man met Nya's eyes. She immediately tore her gaze away, a flush of heat ran through her. She glanced back, but the man was staring elsewhere. Nya let out a breath.

Time passed as they watched the crowd build, the guards growing ever-more nervous.

This could get violent, Nya realised. She only knew what Kit had told her, but this shadow man didn't sound like a friend of the monarch. Few on the street were. Those who benefited from his rule were the nobles and high-end merchants.

The market square darkened.

Nya looked to the sky, expecting to see a cloud blotting out the Sun Eye, but the sky was crystalline. Her heart beat faster. Shadows leaked from where they should be, like spreading water. She reached out to Bom, but there wasn't a pull or push from it. Dust buried herself between Nya and Kit, a hiss sitting at the back of her throat.

People gasped and screamed, backing away from the oncoming dark. Others grinned and laughed, jostling their friends as if they had been proven right. Kit stared, a mix of shock and awe etched into his face. Nya realised he hadn't truly believed her until now. Even Bom flared in awareness.

Nya's heart thundered as ethereal darkness smothered the

last of the light.

A figure rose from the rooftop across from Nya and Kit. He was topless with baggy grey breeches held in place by a band of brown fabric. He wasn't muscular but rather skinny, with a boyish physique.

However, it was the mask he wore that caught Nya's attention: a black jackal baring its teeth, topped with pointy ears. The jackal represented many things in Tarris culture, but here, it could be nothing else but a symbol of death.

"People of Yontar!" the man shouted, but much like his physique, his voice was boyish. "Are you content being herded like cattle? Content chewing on the scraps of those who think they are your betters?"

Nya walked into the thickening crowd. Her heart hammered with the intensity of a blacksmith's hammer to anvil. There *was* someone else like her. Nya couldn't believe it.

He could help her control Bom so she didn't need to worry about hurting Kit or Dust or anyone else ever again.

Suddenly, the square was a hive of people. The crowd that had been slowly building now swelled to bursting with those hiding out of sight all rushing in at once. They all came from nowhere, pouring in from the side streets and pressing forward. Dimly, Nya heard Kit calling to her but lost him in the jostling.

"They say they rule for you, yet have any of you seen an outstretched hand from the monarchs of Tarris? Or the Empress herself?" the jackal-headed man called.

"No," he said. "They sit atop their mounds of food while

you starve! They send soldiers to resolve disagreements amongst themselves! They hide behind walls of stone and spears! We will no longer accept this. These are old ways. Ways that have aged like the decayed skeletons that bore them."

The man paused. "But I am here as one of you and I am not hiding."

The jackal-man brought his hands to his mask and lifted it from his shoulders. He looked to be in his early twenties. Dark, matted golden hair fell over his eyes. A stern expression rested on his face as he panned over the square.

"We will purify the sands of Tarris," he said. "We will sweep through them like a sandstorm that will wash away those of dark heart and mind. Scour this country until only the worthy have breath in their lungs. The time for a purge has come. Everyone will bow and be Judged and only the worthy will rise again!"

The crowd whooped and screamed. Some drew swords and lifted them in salute. It was easy to assume all agreed with the roar around her, but Nya saw conflicted to disgusted faces hidden among the crowd too.

But he's right, Nya thought. Mother and she had struggled their entire lives, and yet Nya had seen the plentiful food carted in to the Strip and nobles homes. All those on the street wanted was enough food to survive.

The man waved for silence and the shouting subsided to low murmurs.

"The time is near, my friends," he said. "Tell all who will

listen that a reckoning is coming."

He rose his hands and the shadows darkened further, blotting out Ova's Sun Eye and throwing them into the dark of night. More roars and cheers came at this. This display of power. Nya shuddered.

Snaking tendrils darted from the black, coiling around the crowd and plunged into a guard's chest, then forged onward splitting the next guard into two. Nya's breath caught.

Then the black mantle lifted from the square. Its shadow tendrils pulling back from the light. The man was backing up, preparing to disappear.

Nya watched in horror as the guard coughed up blood, his eyes glazing over. Memories from the attic smothered her. Panic crawled up her throat, and Bom stirred. Her emotions feeding it like water to greenery. She felt Bom leaking through, which just made it harder to contain her emotions.

This man was sick, like her. He couldn't help her. For a moment hope sparked at his words, but she was searching for a way to stop the pointless killing not fuel it. And just like that the embers of hope were doused.

Suddenly, she became aware of the vast crowd around her. She had to get away now, before she lost control again. What if she killed all these people?

Nya pushed her way through, breathing hard. Her mind screamed at her to run, to get to anywhere but here, where there were so many people. A stray foot caught her and Nya stumbled to the ground. A few people turned, but no one reached to help. Bom laughed and she felt it expanding out from her.

NO!

Nya leapt to her feet and tried to run when a hand clasped her shoulder. She tried to tear away, not bothering to look and see who it was, but the grip was firm.

"Wait," a deep voice said. "I can help."

Nya spun. A man in a cloak held her firm. He was broad of frame, arms thick with muscle.

Nya tried to pull away.

"I'm like you," the man said and his shadow flickered.

23

Familiar Faces

After meeting with Lem, Rai had spoken to others about the shadow man. They all said similar things: a man appeared, did some magic with the shadows, spouted some nonsense about justice, and then disappeared. The reactions ranged from some thinking him an ancient god, to others claiming he was trying to swindle his way into their pockets using tricks to block out the Sun. Rai knew better.

Rai walked down a narrow, winding street in the north-eastern part of Yontar. A breeze carried dust down an empty backstreet. The one interesting thing he found from each person he talked with was *where* the man had appeared. He had appeared all across the city, save for the north-eastern part of the city. Others had caught onto this too, starting up speculation that was where he would preach next.

"Would you be able to tell from afar if he has a shade?" Rai whispered.

Only if he uses its power, Fax said. *I can't tell just by looking at someone, but if they reach through the shadows, I will be able to tell if it's a shade or not.*

Rai nodded. From what he had heard, the man would make his talents known when he spoke.

Rai had scouted this part of the city for the last two days, trying to work out where the man would appear. He was certain it would be today, given all his previous preaching was exactly seven days apart.

But where would he emerge? Rai came up with three options, but upon talking with people, it seemed someone had already whispered the location. It was brave letting everyone know when and where you would appear, especially now that this man had made a name for himself. A reputation of rebellion, dark magics, and promise. The monarch was sure to station guards around the square to try to capture him.

Not that they would make any difference if he had a shade.

Rai arrived at the boxy market square. Stalls were still up as the last of the market goers spent their coin. Rai skirted the edges, noting ten guards and already a handful of people in corners waiting. A man stood at the intersection of the square and another busy street draining a water-skin and seemingly just taking in the morning, but Rai noticed the outline of a mace-axe under his cloak. Not a weapon the city guards used. Another three with the same weapon were spaced around the square, acting casual. This was the right place then.

Rai made it all the way around, then ducked into the seamstress's shop. The low-ceilinged room was cosy with the warm candlelight. The elderly lady nodded as Rai approached. He slid over a couple coins.

"Remember, no more than an hour," she said.

"No more than an hour," Rai agreed.

Rai climbed to the third floor, pushed open the storage room door, and walked to the window. The room was full of fabric, mannequins, stacked sewing needles, and other sewing implements, all of which were engulfed in a thick layering of dust. She *had* said she didn't use the room much anymore, Rai mused.

Rai grabbed a chair and dragged it to the window and sat.

Try not to break this one, Fax said.

Rai yanked open the old shutters, letting light pour into the room. The market was closing, merchants preparing to pack up their goods.

Rai monitored the square as the Sun Eye rose higher. Marketgoers thinned to little more than a trickle, but a secondary crowd was growing.

As soon as this man appears, the market is going to be packed, Rai thought, watching a group of beggars peering from behind a barrel sitting in an alley.

Baking bread filled the air as nearby homes fixed their morning meals. Rai's stomach grumbled.

"Should have grabbed something on the way here," Rai said, holding his gut.

The square darkened.

Too late now, Fax said. *It's beginning.*

The shadows expanded as a shade reached out from its host. It covered the market in darkness. Some screamed and cowered, others watched in awe. Those screaming were the smart ones. Shades could appear from nearby shadows so as the shadow man smothered the square in darkness, he extended the shades' reach to where it could appear and attack. Those in the square all stood in its grasp now.

Definitely another shade, Fax said. *More people must have gone through the tear.*

Rai needed to figure out how to close that thing, and fast. The idea of more people like him was unsettling. Although, from what Fax said, it was unlikely there were many, even after years. Shades could only attach themselves to people under certain conditions. They had to be strong of will, have weakened defences when they attach, and shades only picked those they thought worthy.

Still. Even one blade could draw blood. One kiren could kill a pen of livestock. And one shade could tear an empire asunder.

"People of Yontar!" a voice called. "Are you content being herded cattle? Content chewing on the scraps of those who think they are your betters?"

Atop the building to Rai's left, stood a man in a jackal mask. Rai shuffled his chair around to get a better view. The man looked and sounded to be in his mid-twenties. He wasn't built with muscle, but he was fit and toned. *Possibly a guard?* Rai thought, but something told him no.

The throng of people all bunched forward, wanting to get a better view. Those hiding in alleys and side streets flooded in as a rush, all vying to get closer.

Bells rang in Rai's mind. There was something familiar about the man's voice and his phrasing. Like Rai had heard it before.

The man let that sink in. "But I am here as one of you," he said. "And I am not hiding."

Then it clicked. Rai knew who the jackal-man was before he took off the mask. He slid the mask from his face and Rai stood sharply, sending his chair toppling over.

What is it? Fax asked.

"Kyan," Rai said.

Kyan gazed over the crowd. He had always looked younger than he was. Rai remembered joking that it matched his youthful optimism.

Kyan? Who's Kyan? Fax asked.

"An old friend. He was one of the seven that went into the tear with me," Rai said.

Oh.

"We will purify the sands of Tarris," Kyan continued. It had only been five years, but he looked a lot different from when Rai had last seen him. His face had stretched, eyes hollowing like he hadn't slept a wink in years.

Rai's mouth went dry and his gut dropped as he relived Kyan's death.

He had watched Kyan die in that dark place. And in a way he had, because the man in front of him was not the boy he remembered.

Flickering memories came unbidden to Rai's mind. He had always been close to Kyan. Rai had mourned him, grief still flaring with a familiar scent or phrase. Kyan was like a younger brother to him.

"I have to speak to him," Rai said, turning.

Wait! Are you sure that's the Kyan you know? Fax said.

Rai scrunched his brow. What was that supposed to mean? Although he had only been half-listening, phrases that Kyan preached rang in his head.

"The time for a purge has come!"

Kyan had always been an idealist, wanting to do more for the people, but this didn't sound like him speaking.

Not all shades are like me Rai, Fax said. *Some want to see this world burn, and they will use their hosts, intertwining their wants with their own until they are one and the same.*

"The time is near, my friends," Kyan said, his face now seeming even more twisted and warped to Rai. "Tell all those who will listen. A reckoning is coming."

A reckoning? What are you planning, Kyan? Rai wondered.

The darkness pulled back. *What do I do? Should I find out what he is planning before confronting him?* Rai thought. The mass was cheering and shouting below.

Rai, there's another shade, Fax said.

Rai's jerked his head up, scanning the crowd. There. A teen girl who had fallen over. Those around her wouldn't be able to tell, but from Rai's perch, he could see her shadow leaking like blood.

Andrew Watson

Kyan pulled away, stepping back away from the ridge. Rai couldn't catch them both.

In a split decision, Rai spun and hurtled down the stairs, passing the startled seamstress, and out onto the street. He barged through the crowd, tossing people to either side.

The girl was about to squeeze between two burly men when Rai grabbed her shoulder. She tried to break away, but he tightened his grip.

"Wait," Rai said. "I can help."

She turned, tears streaming down her cheeks. She tried to yank her arm free of his grip again.

"I'm like you," Rai said.

She faced him again, mouth ajar. Fax stirred his shadow subtly, so most wouldn't notice. The girl did.

Rai led her back through the crowd. She didn't fight, instead just staring at his shadow. They walked to the seamstress's shop. Rai made for the stairs, passing the older woman. The seamstress stopped what she was doing, fabric laid out on the table before her and raised an inquisitive eyebrow. Rai paused, sighed, then dug out a deran and tossed it to her. She took it with a smile and got back to work.

Rai opened the door to the same dusty room he had watched Kyan from and gestured for the girl to enter. In the dimming light of the hallway, Rai squinted noticing the bruising and cuts that covered the girl. *What happened to her? It looks like she's been in the fighting pits.*

The girl looked nervously in, then back the stairs.

She's going to make a run for it, Fax said.

She turned to regard Rai again before stepping into the room. Rai followed her in and closed the door behind him.

A strip of light painted a line down the middle of the room. The girl kept her emotion from her face, but her hands were clenched.

"I'm not going to hurt you," Rai said. "I'm sorry for dragging you here." He gestured around the room. "I didn't want the jackal headed man to see us."

"Prove it," the girl said, voice shaking.

"Prove what?" Rai said.

"Prove you're like me," she said.

I'm not a party trick, Rai, Fax said.

"No, party tricks are fun," Rai said under his breath. He closed his eyes, feeling Fax spread across the shadows around them. Then, as his eyes sprung open, the dark crashed down from either side of the chamber, enveloping the light pouring in through the window.

The girl spun around, trying to watch everything at once.

"Believe me now?" Rai said, releasing his grip and letting the dark subside.

The girl faced him. "You've been there too. The dark place." It wasn't a question. Rai nodded.

"Why don't you sit," Rai said, pointing to the fallen chair. The girl didn't move.

I need to make myself not a threat, Rai thought. "How about this," Rai said, pulling another chair from the dark. "You can sit in this one right beside the door, and I'll sit in that one by the window." They both moved to their respective chairs.

The girl was still cautious, not taking her eyes from him as she inched over and perched on the edge of the chair by the door.

"Why don't we start with names," Rai said. "I'm Rai."

"Nya," she replied.

Rai eyed the girl. "Do you know the jackal masked man?" The girl shook her head. "You had hoped the jackal masked-man could help you with your shade, didn't you?"

Nya nodded.

"Fax?" Rai said. Fax unfurled from his shadow as a bird, hovering beside him.

Nya's eyes widened, but she didn't move away. *Good, I don't want to scare her with too much too fast*, Rai thought.

"I can help you with yours," Rai said.

"Does it kill people like the man down there did?" Nya flicked her head in the square's direction.

"Only if I let it," Rai said.

"Do you let it?" she asked.

"I don't go around killing guards, if that's what you are asking," Rai said. The girl bit her lip and stared at the ground. She was hiding something. "Did you accidentally hurt someone?" Rai asked.

"*It* hurt someone," she corrected.

Rai regarded the girl. She was nervous and confused, but there was strength in her. There had to be to host a shade. Rai thought back to when he first realised something was in his head. It hadn't gone well.

"How about this. We can meet again tomorrow once we've both had time to think on it," Rai said. A lot was on his mind too, and he needed some time.

"I can show you the basic control methods I've come up with, and you can decide if you want my help or not," Rai said.

"How can I trust you?" Nya asked.

Rai didn't do any of the theatrics this time, but the room darkened. "If I wanted to hurt you, there are a million easier ways to do so than letting you go and hoping you will meet me tomorrow," he said. "I'm like you. We need to stick together so we don't become like the jackal masked man."

Rai saw the fear grip Nya as she folded away from the expanding dark around her. Rai let it dissipate and her breathing eased. With only a moment's hesitation, she nodded.

"Come to the Patched Cloak inn. It's in the western district. The door from the courtyard will be open."

Nya stood and scurried towards to the door, stepping backwards as to never leave her back exposed. She cracked the door open and slid through, her footsteps clattering down the stairs. Rai sighed. This is not how he thought today was going to go.

Do you think she will come tomorrow? Fax asked.

"I hope so," Rai said.

But until then, Rai had to think on Kyan. His old friend was alive.

"You said not all shades are like you," Rai said.

Fax landed on the floor at Rai's feet. *I've told you before, we are like any other creature. All very different in how we think and what we want. We are all one, but have different minds, different aspects. Especially when we separate and find hosts.*

"Kyan didn't agree with a lot of what monarchy was doing in Tarris, but this reckoning isn't like him. Or wasn't like him," Rai said. "He was always about finding the right way to do things. Could his shade have changed how he thinks?"

Change? No. Persuade? Probably. I can feel your desires, what makes you get up in the morning. There is an advantage to that. I could try to persuade you that the only way to keep Tarris safe was to kill that girl, for example.

"You think that thing has convinced him the only way to help the people of Tarris is to rebel?" Rai asked.

It's possible.

The people of Yontar had been stirring and pushing back on the monarchy for years now, with the widening gap between the rich and poor. But it hadn't been building long enough for an all-out rebellion. Kyan wouldn't be able to conscript enough people to make any real change. So what was Kyan planning? What was this reckoning?

If Rai could talk to him, convince him this wasn't the way. But he didn't know what Kyan had planned. He needed to learn that first. Which was going to be difficult when Kyan would recognise him. Unless...

Rai got up and swept out of the room.

24

Thieves of a Different Kind

Kit was nowhere to be seen, so Nya headed back to their rooftop. *His rooftop*, she corrected herself. The city was humming with energy. Guards had flooded the market place where the shadow man had preached. They were questioning anyone they could get their hands on, so Nya made sure to slip away discreetly.

She didn't know what to think of Rai. Could she trust him? Was he going to turn out to be like the jackal-masked man? Flashes of the coiling black shadow stabbing through the guards sent a shiver down her spine. Even if his intentions were true, the means were not.

Nya couldn't continue like this. She could have hurt a lot of people today. She would have to speak to Rai again, even if he did scare her. But what did *he* want? He wasn't going to help her for nothing, and he could see she didn't have money.

He will use you, Bom said. *Use you as a weapon*.

Nya paled but didn't respond.

She wove through the city towards Kit's roof. Her body ached, bruises and cuts flaring with every step. It was quieter the further she moved away from the square. Sand foxes, like Dust, ran through the shadowed alleys hunting for scraps. Murmuring voices dwindling to silence, and sand hissed as it scattered up the streets in the warm midday wind.

Ahead, an elderly woman laid down a deitan in front of a temple. A deitan was an offering to the deities, usually consisting of a palm sized plate containing edible roots, cheap fruits, spices, and incense. The woman wore a sunburnt orange robe and she bowed her head before retreating down the street. She hadn't even passed out of sight when a street kid appeared from nowhere, snatched up the deitan, and scampered off in the other direction.

Deitans weren't uncommon. People placed them in front of homes and business in hope of good favour from the deities. However, it was a dying practice. Once it would have been a sin to steal a deitan, but times were hard and the deities were falling from the minds of the people.

Nya hesitated in front of the temple. It was a grand structure with pillars on either side of a great two story opening, faded carvings of Ma-ilus, a deer like deity, etched onto the pillars. Nya had never thought much on the deities. They were no more than fanciful stories to her and most living on the streets. She had never met a devout follower. Starving, beaten, and struggling for survival made deities that were meant to look after the Tarrisian people hard to believe.

If there were once deities, they had abandoned the people.

"You can't be thinking about going?" Kit said.

Nya had returned to the roof to find Kit and she caught him up on what happened after they lost each other in the crowd.

"Why not? You were the one who wanted me to speak to someone like myself," Nya said.

"Yeah, but I didn't think it was like that," Kit said, waving his arms around, mimicking the tendrils that the jackal masked man called upon.

"That's exactly why I have to go," Nya said. "I can't hurt you or Dust."

Kit stared at her, picking bread from his teeth. "I'm coming too."

"No," Nya said. "It's too dangerous. I don't know what Rai wants."

"And that is exactly why *I* have to come too," Kit said. "I've been in my fair share of scraps." Kit hopped around the roof, arms raised, thrusting the occasional punch.

Nya tilted her head slightly. "Kit, you saw what we can do."

"Your shadow magic is nothing compared to..." Kit stuck his arm out and Dust ran up it and onto his shoulders. Had he trained her to do that? "Dust! The Yellow Demon! The Light of Yontar!"

Dust glanced at the two of them, sniffed, and then lay on Kit's back.

"Yeah, she looks like the true saviour of Tarris."

Dust yawned, closing her eyes.

"That's because I just fed her. Give her an hour and she will become her true demon self," Kit said.

Nya shook her head.

"Come on, sleepyhead. I'll be walking like those swaying water trees if you stay on my back any longer," Kit said, and reluctantly Dust hopped down. Kit then slumped into the shade and took a long draught from the waterskin.

Kit and Dust were why she was going to go through with this. Nya hadn't cared about herself for some time. Maybe she didn't deserve them. But she was going to gods damned fight for them. And that meant learning to control this thing inside her.

You hear that, Bom? I won't let you hurt them.

Nya ducked under the eave of the roof and sat beside Kit.

"So are we going to wait until dark hour?" Kit asked.

"He asked me to meet him tomorrow," Nya said.

"Yeah, that's exactly why we need to go today and scout the place out! It could be a trap."

He had a point.

Kit had to ask some of his contacts on how to find the Patched Cloak. It was an inn that had been closed down for some time, about a year, Kit's contact guessed. Time had eaten at The Patched Cloak. The rusted sign hung askew, shutters were closed tight, apart from where some had completely broken off, and the place gave no indication of life within.

"Are you sure he said the Patched Cloak and not the Paradise's Knife? At least that inn isn't falling apart," Kit said.

They leaned against the wall along a side street across from the inn. "No, this is the place. Where better to hide than a closed inn?"

"I can think of several," Kit said. "Most of which wouldn't have a param infestation."

Nya spun to face him and said, "You live on a roof."

Kit shrugged. "It doesn't have any dust."

Dust growled at their feet. "You don't count," Kit said. "I meant the dirty kind."

"Come on, let's head around the back and see if we can see anything," Nya said, walking across the street.

This was a busier part of Yontar, near a main gate. Many merchants rode aya to and from, making the most of the cooler temperatures now that the Sun Eye had fallen to the horizon.

Nya was halfway across the road when the smell of spices hit her like a wall. A scent that slung her to a not too long ago past.

One of the merchants that passed her was a spice merchant. The familiar fumes worked their way through her, freezing her to the spot. Wafts of paprika faded to cinnamon. She had been learning to distinguish them so she could help the spice merchant better.

He's dead now, Nya thought.

Phantom aromas followed; the smell of blood, a rusty fragrance, and of decay as she held Mother.

Distant shouting got louder. Kit barrelled into Nya sending them tumbling into the dirt. Nya came back to herself, lying on her back and looking up at the purpling sky. She hissed, her injuries aching as she sat up.

"Are you okay?" Kit asked. "You were almost crushed by that merchant's aya!"

A merchant cursed at them as he rode past on his aya. Nya only knew the meaning of half the words he threw at them. She hadn't seen it coming, lost in her own thoughts, and would've been crushed if Kit hadn't shoved her out the way.

"I got distracted," Nya said.

Lines marred Kit's brow and forehead. "Maybe we should head back."

"No, no, I'm fine," Nya said, standing. "Let's keep going." She couldn't go back to huddling up on that rooftop, no matter how badly she wanted to. Nya knew if she did that would become her life. A life of wallowing in grief, and always the promise of more death whispered from her shadow.

They walked around the side of The Patched Cloak. Flames burned in most surrounding shop windows, but the inn remained a darkened corpse. It was one of the bigger inns on the street with its own courtyard and stable for aya, hyian, and whatever else their customers rode.

The courtyard was as stark as the rest of the inn and the stables were empty aside from one aya.

Kit did a quick side-to-side check, then launched over the

gate. Nya did the same and Dust ran between the bars. Nya watched the aya carefully. She had heard stories of aya being trained to call out when thieves came close. But the aya only looked at her, munching on some... was that a stew? Nya edged closer until she could see into the trough. Inside was a meaty stew with nuts and spices, steam pouring from it. Nya's stomach gargled. Who fed their aya stew? It looked to be a better meal than most families ate.

Dust hopped up onto her haunches, glanced up to regard the aya, then back to the stew, before shoving her face in. The sand fox pulled back, face covered in a reddish brown, her tongue whipped around her mouth as she purred contentedly.

"What is it?" Kit hissed as he walked over. He hesitated, staring into the trough too. "Is that stew?"

"I think so," Nya said, watching the aya dip its head for another mouthful.

Kit looked at Nya, then reached in and scooped up a handful, shovelling it into his mouth.

"Eww!" Nya said, stepping backwards.

Kit smacked his lips, nodding appreciatively. "Yep, definitely a stew. A good one too."

The aya let out a low moo. It wasn't aggressive; it sounded more like the aya was agreeing with Kit.

"Right, you two, let's go before we get caught face-down in an ayas trough," Nya said, pulling Dust and Kit away. She bowed to the well-fed aya, who returned the gesture.

They stuck to the sides of the courtyard where the Sun Eye's light was at its weakest.

"What now?" Kit asked, licking stew from his fingers. Nya flicked her head towards the back door of the inn.

"You sure? I would consider this a successful scout," Kit said. "It looks like Rai is hiding in this inn. That's probably his aya, so he might not even be from Yontar."

"We need to know if there is more than just him," Nya said, already creeping across to the door. Kit sighed but followed, Dust trotting at their heels.

Nya gave the door a tentative tug. It was unlocked. She grinned at Kit, who smiled back before they passed into the dark.

Inside was an inky black. Nya felt walls on either side and thoughts of the Blind Walk came crawling from the corners of her mind.

"Listen," Kit whispered.

Nya could only hear the tromping of her heart at first until…

A woman humming.

They moved down the corridor until it opened into the common room. Booths sat in rows to their right, a dust slicked counter on their left. Nya leaned forward to see a red-haired woman behind a bar, noting something on a piece of parchment. Behind her was a bowl of stew.

"It looks like Rai is staying with his wife here," Nya whispered.

"A Nuian from the looks of her," Kit said.

"A Nuian?" Nya asked.

"Yeah, you know, a person from Nuia, the mountains up

north." Nya had never heard of such a place, but then again, she knew little of the world outside of Yontar.

"We should head back before we get caught," Nya said.

Kit nodded, and they were making to turn back down the corridor when Nya realised she hadn't seen Dust with them. She spun around. Dust sauntered towards the bar, heading right for the stew.

"Kit!" Nya hissed. He crept back, eyes widening.

"Sands suffocate me," Kit cursed.

Dust was already behind the bar.

"We need to get her," Nya said. She didn't know what Nuians ate, but sand fox meat was a delicacy and common in Tarris and she didn't trust this woman to throw Dust out. Kit let out a strangled exhale but nodded.

A writing reed hung from the red-haired woman's mouth as she read over the parchment. Dust was small enough to pass beneath her gaze, but they certainly weren't.

"We need to crawl to the bar, then go around the far side of it," Kit said. "We can sneak behind her and grab Dust."

Nya nodded and without wasting anytime, fell to her stomach and dragged herself towards the bar. She made it all the way to the bar where she jumped up onto her haunches, Kit doing the same beside her. They pressed against the bar, and Nya took a moment to calm her nerves before she crept along to the far side. Nya stifled a gasp when her sweaty back touched the cool sandstone bar.

The dark had obscured the booths, but edging closer, Nya could see the ripped up fabrics and scratched tabletops.

They stopped at the end of the bar. Nya craned around and saw Dust launching herself onto the tabletop behind the bar. The woman leaned over the bar, humming a jaunty tune that did *not* match how Nya was feeling.

Nya dropped back onto all fours and shuffled behind the bar. Dust started lapping up the woman's stew. Nya crawled faster. The woman looked up from her parchment, staring straight forward. Nya fought to keep her breathing under control.

Then behind was a scream.

Heads spun towards the noise as a startled man jumped backward. He must have been laying down in one of the booths. Kit leapt to his feet with a squeal too.

Crash.

The bowl of stew hit the floor, shattering and sending the broth spilling across the floor. The woman spun and saw Dust staring back at her, then turned and noticed Nya on all fours by her feet.

A silence held as they all stared at one another.

"You don't happen to have a room do you?" Kit asked politely.

25

New Boots and New Paths

"Lem!" Rai called. An undisturbed stillness had settled on the once-garden behind the blood den. The corners of the old temple garden sat in darkness. It was coming on dark hour; the sky a stretching hue of midnight blue to impenetrable black.

Rai met with Lem a couple of times since their first encounter. Despite his peculiarity, he had a lot of connections, and had been fairly reliable so far. Rai walked by the pond searching the black, when a hand grabbed his ankle. Instinctively, Rai kicked it off and hopped back.

"Down here," Lem said, standing in the empty pond.

"Lem, we've been over this. We don't need to hide. No one's back here."

Lem mimicked someone walking with two fingers on his

palm, then cupping his ear, and flailed his arms, ending with a flick of the wrist telling Rai he wanted him to come down.

The Pond Whisperer only speaks to those in the pond, Fax said in a mocking tone.

Rai dropped beside Lem, who grinned at him.

"Well?" Lem said.

"Well, what?" Rai asked.

"What do you think?" Lem asked.

"Think of what?" Rai asked. Perhaps he did need to rethink his confidant.

"Of my new boots, muscle man!" Lem said, trotting around. "They don't even have holes in them! Apart from the two you put your feet in, of course."

The new boots were a dark brown and came up to just above his ankle. "Yes, very nice," Rai said. "Now, did you find anything out about the shadow man?"

Lem's face fell. "If you don't like them, you can just say."

"No, no, they are very nice boots," Rai said. "I'm just in a bit of a rush tonight, Lem."

Lem puffed out a breath and shrugged, then leant in conspiratorially. "People are saying he's recruiting for an expedition."

"An expedition? To where?" Rai asked.

"No one knows. Just that he is looking for some... how did they put it? People who walk on the right side of the scales, I think they said."

"And how does one join this expedition?" Rai asked.

"Whispers say they are meeting north of the city," Lem

said. "They just sound like another gang to me."

What are you up to, Kyan? Rai wondered.

Kyan had always been one of the smartest men he knew. Nothing would have leaked out onto the streets that he didn't want known. If Rai wanted to learn what he was really up to, he would have to find this meeting place.

"Thank you Lem," Rai said. "I owe you one."

"I can try to join this gang if you want?" Lem offered.

"No, it's okay. It's too dangerous," Rai said, waving the offer away. The last thing he needed was Lem giving him up by accident.

The girl? Rai thought. *He wouldn't recognize her. She could get close to him.* Since she was like them, it was possible Kyan would want her at his side. *I would have to train her to defend herself first.*

Tilting his head, Rai noticed Lem was only a hair's breadth from his face. Rai jerked back.

"What are you doing?" Rai asked.

"You look funny when you are thinking," Lem said. "I was trying to see how close I could get without you noticing."

Rai really missed The Ear in Celabar.

"I better go," Rai said, passing Lem a deran. "If you hear anything else…"

"Light the temple's stained-glass window and you'll meet me back here. I remember," Lem said, nodding towards the old temple.

"And don't do anything that will put you in danger." Rai lifted himself out the pond.

"Living is danger, muscle man." Lem stared into the night.

Beautiful, Fax said in Rai's head.

"Please stop calling me muscle man. My name is Rai," Rai said.

"As you wish, Rai man," Lem said.

"Goodbye, Lem," Rai said, shaking his head.

Rai was deep in thought when he arrived back at The Patched Cloak. Dark hour had come, and lanterns were hanging outside of homes. Shrouded people hastened through the streets, scuttling past one another like params. Dark hour was always a time for caution. Almost all the city's crime happened in the two dark hours each day.

Nya would be safe, Rai thought. *She has a shade.*

Sending Nya to join Kyan and the Decreed was a risk. But it was the best option he had. She could join their ranks and learn what she could about Kyan's plan.

Rai hopped the gate and walked across the courtyard. His aya looked at him. Rai bowed and the aya went back to eating like it hadn't even seen him. It was probably the least trained aya Rai ever had the misfortune of acquiring. That included the time he was scammed and given a young aya that just wanted to run until it collapsed. When he was ready to leave Yontar, he would have to find a more accommodating aya.

Rai pushed open the door and walked towards the stairs, but voices made him stop on the bottom step. *That's more than just Illy and her nephew.* Rai spun on his heels and stepped into the inn's common room.

Sitting at the bar was Nya, a boy the same age as her, a sand fox, the nephew that Rai hadn't bothered to learn the name of, and Illy. Rai had been trained to be prepared for anything, but his brain stuck like a cart in deep sand.

"You okay, Rai?" Illy asked. Nya and the others turned to face him. They each had a bowl of stew, including the sand fox.

"I thought you said you didn't make food here?" Rai said.

"I said *you* will have to see to yourself. I like these three," Illy said. "They can't very well train with you tomorrow, living on the street and eating scraps."

Rai looked at Nya. How much had she told her?

"I was just telling Illy how you saved me and Kit from those bullies and you promised to teach us self-defence," Nya said.

Thank the ever-shifting sands, Rai thought. The last thing he needed was to try to explain all this to Illy too. "Yes, well, it was tomorrow you were to come by."

"I told them they could each have a room," Illy said. "It's not like I can sell this place anytime soon and they offered to help clean it up."

This new situation conflicted Rai. On one hand, it would be helpful having Nya close to train and keep an eye on her, but this close? In missions like this, having a place to retreat and step back to was vital. He didn't have that anymore.

"I see," Rai said.

There was a moment's silence.

"And it's unsafe on the streets now with this *shadow man*," the boy named Kit said. Rai tried not to glower at Nya, who went back to eating her stew.

"It's Illy's inn. If she says you can stay, then that is how the sands lie," Rai said, turning. "I will see you first thing tomorrow."

With that, Rai strode out of the common room and headed up the stairs.

Dimly, Rai heard Illy say, "Told you he couldn't make you leave."

You're angry about the stew, aren't you? Fax said as Rai slid his door closed behind him.

"No Fax, I can't say that's my most pressing concern." Rai slumped onto his bed.

The Moon Eye had begun its watch, bringing silvery light to the room. Rai had swept it and made it liveable. It was still bare, a temporary place with no soul of its own. But that was becoming Rai's way. He had found a rickety desk that he had dragged into the corner of his room, and laden it with decoy papers of histories like his last apartment. His true notes were hidden below the floorboards, along with his bow and blood vials. Rai was glad to have spent the time arranging the room now that two more were running about the inn.

Rai lay back on his bed, sinking into its soft embrace and gazing up at the cracked stone roof. He had once stayed in palaces, but before that, he had stayed places similar to this. It felt like he had returned to where it all began. Before he had ascended to the highest ranks, was used, and manipulated, then thrown away like a dull spear. She had lied to him or herself, he didn't know, but it didn't matter anymore.

He couldn't go back. Five years ago he was tasked with learning about what Yontar's monarch was hiding. He hadn't accomplished that yet. Rai was fulfilling his mission in researching the tear and shades.

And now that Kyan was still alive, he had to start by helping him. Even if that meant stopping whatever he had planned. He was a good kid, but fresh-eyed to the world. His shade must have pulled him to more radical thinking. The Kyan he knew wouldn't have killed all those guards as a display of power. That was the shade's influence, it had to be. Part of him knew that was just what he wanted to be true. Five years was a long time. People changed.

The small sounds of the inn made their way to Rai's notice; the clacking of the shutters in the breeze, the patter of params running around the empty places of the inn, and the low rumbling of the city. Rai listened as the others traipsed upstairs, Illy helping pick out the better of the rooms for Nya and Kit.

Illy was staying in the chamber another floor above Rai, built for the inn's owner to live in. It had access to the kitchens and common room directly without having to go through these living quarters. Nya and Kit chose adjacent rooms a couple of doors down from Rai's.

Noise at the inn settled to small sounds again before Rai's eyes sprung open and he stepped into the corridor. Passing down the hallway, Rai stopped in front of Nya's door and tapped lightly. He could hear her moving about inside.

"Kit?" Nya said, opening the door. She didn't look pleased when she found Rai on the other side.

"I have some questions," Rai said.

"Can't it wait until tomorrow?" Nya asked as Rai pushed into the room. Her chamber was much like his, the same shape and size. The only different was there was no desk in the corner.

Rai leant on the window and gestured for Nya to sit on the bed. Worry creased her face. He was going to have to train her to better hide her emotions.

"I want you to tell me the story of how you got to the dark place," Rai said. He had his guesses, but this was going to be the first thing he would have asked her tomorrow before training.

Nya shifted. "It's a long story."

"Start where you see fit."

Nya swallowed and begun her tale. Rai could tell she was holding back some information but let her continue.

Nya shivered despite the warm night and hugged herself as she told him of the dark place and the husks that attacked, and how the scholars had all been torn apart.

"Then after we came back through, the captain held us and waved a dagger near us and—" Nya said.

"A dagger? Describe this dagger," Rai said.

"Uh, the blade was black, and the handle was purple. It had designs carved into it, but I couldn't make them out," Nya said.

"In the pommel, was there an opening on the hilt?" Rai

asked. Nya arched an eyebrow. "In the bottom was there a hole?"

Nya looked down, searching through her memories. "There could have been, I'm not sure."

Rai scratched his chin. "And what did they do with this dagger?"

"They waved it in front of each of us."

"And did it do anything?" Rai asked.

"It," Nya hovered on the cusp of something, deciding if she wanted to say or not, then finally said, "It felt hot. Like it was going to burn me if it got close. My shade, Bom, was screaming in my head to get away from it."

A dagger that affects shades? Rai hadn't come across anything of the sort in his five years of searching. Could it be used to separate a shade from someone? Fax remained quiet.

"Was there anything else you remember about this dagger?" Rai asked.

Nya thought hard before shaking her head. "No, they got distracted and took the dagger away soon after. But I think they were testing for shades."

Rai crossed the window, scratching his chin. He had guessed the monarch would be researching the tear. The concern was if they knew about shades and how to test for them. It wasn't a stretch to think of how the monarch would try to weaponise shades. Finding people or soldiers able to host one would be difficult with shades being so picky, and it was a risk sending soldiers into the dark realm, so Rai doubted they had many, if any. Still.

Five years ago, the Empress sent Rai and the Seven to learn of a weapon the Monarch of Yontar was rumoured to be hiding. None of them could have expected to find a rend in reality.

"Rai, what is that place?" Nya asked, pulling Rai from his thoughts.

"I don't know," he said. "Somewhere dangerous. Dangerous to those who enter, but also dangerous to everyone in Tarris."

The monarchs each wanted the throne, and if one was to get access to a shade, Tarris could be thrown into civil war.

"Meet me on the roof at sunrise to start your training."

"I haven't agreed yet," Nya said.

Rai turned. "Nya, would you like me to train you to control your shade?"

"Yes, but I promised to help Illy with the inn first thing."

"I will talk with Illy. Training will be when the Sun Eye starts its watch. You can help with the inn during the afternoons," Rai said.

With that, Rai walked back to his room, aware that Kit was listening in on their conversation; his door cracked open a slither.

After getting back to his room, Rai sat on his bed.

"Well, Fax?" Rai said. "You know anything about a black dagger that affects shades?"

Fax slid from his shadow and flew over to perch on his desk as a crow. *I haven't, but I don't like this Rai*, Fax said. *Once we have picked a host, we can't leave them. The idea of being hunted with this dagger is...*

It didn't need to finish.

"Five years of cold trails and dead ends and now we have two clear leads. We will have to go back to the Empress," Rai said. "I always knew we would have to eventually, but first, we follow Kyan."

26

As the Sun Eye Rises

Nya woke in a bed. *In a bed.* She had only slept in a bed one other time, and that was when she was sick with a fever and Mother had taken her to a doctor after days and days of not getting any better.

Light tinged the sky, but there was still time before the Sun Eye crested the horizon. Nya rolled onto her side, rubbing her face against the pillow.

I should get up and find something to eat before meeting Rai, Nya thought, but the bed felt even more comfortable than it had last night.

It was strange having no one nearby when she woke, though. Kit was in the room next door, but that felt a city's distance away when she had spent most of her life sleeping in the same room as Mother and then Kit.

She lifted her head and saw Dust curled up at the end of the bed and smiled at the sand fox. At least Dust was with her.

Since leaving the attic, Dust had barely left her side. And really, it was thanks to her that they had gotten to stay at this inn. If she hadn't tried to steal some of that stew, they would be waking atop Kit's roof this morning.

Illy had been kind to them by offering a similar deal to what she had at the spice merchant shop; some help with cleaning in exchange for a place to sleep until they sold the inn.

Finally, with a sigh, Nya fell out of bed. She shook out her hair and threw on her clothes, then made her way down to the common room. Kit was already sitting in a booth across from Wenson, the innkeeper's nephew. Nya knew naming was different in other countries and that his long name didn't relate to his social standing, but she couldn't help but be a bit in awe of his name.

"Nya! Watch this!" Kit called, then turned back to Wenson, who was sitting forward, head in his hands. "You're a black sand-footed fool and smell of aya's stool."

A black sand-foot was another way to call someone an idiot in Tarris, referencing leaving your foot buried in the sand as it got darker and solidified. There were many cases, often travellers, stuck out all night unable to pull their foot free.

"Kit!" Nya said.

"Look, it's okay," he said, laughing and pointing to Wenson, who just nodded, and took a sip from his water-skin.

"He doesn't speak Tarrisian."

"Still, that doesn't give you the right to make fun of him," Nya said. "I doubt you speak his tongue."

"Nuian?" Kit said, gazing off in thought. He smiled, then said, "*Aytar yafa.*"

Wenson looked up, eyebrows knitted together and said, "*Ventora selan ceran.*"

His language sounded so strange to Nya. She nudged Kit and sat beside him in the booth. "What did you say to him?"

"I'm not sure. I knew a Nuian on the street and heard him say it once," Kit said. Wenson was scowling, so Nya didn't think whatever he had said was a compliment.

"You asked him where the money is," Illy said, amongst a yawn as she stepped out from the door at the back of the bar. She said something in Nuian to Wenson, whose face eased and he sat back.

"That probably explained why the Nuian was so angry. I thought it was a greeting." Kit shrugged.

"Rai was looking for you both," Illy said, leaning on their table.

"We were about to grab some food," Nya said.

"He said you would say something like that and that you can eat after," Illy said. "However, the man is a fool." Illy slid over two plates of bread lathered in a hazel spread. "Eat up. I won't take the blame if either of you are late."

Illy said something to Wenson and passed him a plate too, before walking off. Kit picked up the bread, inspecting the hazel spread, then took a bite and smiled.

Nya stared at her plate. Kit had gotten her food when she was in a bad way, but this woman didn't even *know* her and was feeding her. *Mother never got me food*, Nya thought. No, that was unfair. Mother did everything for her. She was sick and still had done everything for her.

"Hey, you okay?" Kit asked.

Nya realised she was crying again. Tears dripped onto the bread in front of her. She swallowed and nodded at Kit, using her robe to wipe away the tears.

After getting hold of her emotions again, Nya bit into her bread. It had a nutty flavour, but it was sweet too. She hadn't tasted anything like it.

"What is this?" Kit asked, sucking on his fingertips. How he had already eaten it all was a testament to the taste.

"Oh, you like that? It's called phia spread as it's made from phia nuts. I brought them from Nuia," Illy said, smiling at biting into her own slice behind the bar.

"It's incredible," Nya said, taking another bite. She had to be careful, as she had been eating less lately, and suddenly eating lots made her sick. "Thank you."

Illy grinned. "Eat up or I'll have to make some for Rai if he comes down."

They finished their breakfast and headed back to the living quarters where a sharply inclining staircase hidden in the far corner led to an open door. Stepping out onto the roof, Nya spotted Rai sitting cross-legged, looking out over the waking city.

The edges of the Sun Eye were peeking over the rooftops,

the sky a fiery pink. Golden light warmed the sandstone cityscape, and the Thousand Floor Palace stood as a giant on their right. It had always been an overbearing observer to Nya, with it being her mother's dream to live there. A constant looming reminder of her failures. And now that she knew some of what it held, it was even more of a behemoth horror. Nya shook off the clawing memories of the dark place.

"I said before the Sun Eye rose," Rai said. He sat on the far side of the roof looking towards the Sun Eye. His shadow sprawling long behind him.

"It hasn't risen yet," Nya said.

Rai stood and regarded them. He wasn't as threatening as when Nya had first met him. Something about having seen where he was staying, and meeting Illy and Wenson, softened the man's harder edges. Still, he was like her, and she knew that was something to be wary of.

"I have a proposition," Rai said. Nya felt Kit glance at her from the corner of her eye. "I will teach you how to control your shade. I can even teach you both self-defence, since that's what you told Illy you were here for."

It had been Kit who had told Illy that after she caught them in the inn. It sounded better than saying Nya was a monster and had to be trained or she could lash out and kill people by accident.

"In exchange, I want you both to join the Decreed," Rai said. Kit started to protest, but Rai raised a hand and his shadow flickered. "Let me finish. You won't be in danger. I need someone to learn what they are planning."

"Why can't you join them?" Kit asked.

Rai stared at him with the quiet intensity of Ova's Great Eyes. "Because I can't risk being seen. I need you two. It will be for your benefit too."

"And how is that?" Kit said.

Rai's shadow stretched towards them. "You would know if you would stop cutting me off every time I try to speak." Kit fell silent, taking a step back from the shadow. Nya stood her ground.

"Whatever he is planning will affect everyone in Yontar. He has been building his Decreed for years. This isn't just a gang wanting to cause a scene in the streets. The jackal-masked man is smart. He has something bigger planned," Rai said. "You don't have to decide now."

"I'll do it," Nya said a heartbeat later. Kit spun to face her.

"Nya! We should at least think about this. You don't know what these Decreed do," Kit said. "I've seen what they are capable of."

Nya ignored him and held Rai's gaze. Learning to not hurt the ones she loved was the only thing that mattered. If that meant joining and spying on a cult, so be it.

"I'll go myself if Kit doesn't want to," Nya said.

"Nya!" Kit shouted.

"It won't be easy," Rai said.

"I know," Nya replied. Easy had never been an option in her life. She could never repent for the things she had done, but she could try to stop herself from hurting anyone else.

Rai watched her for a moment before nodding.

Kit slapped himself in the face.

"You don't have to come, Kit," Nya said.

"And leave you to go in with only the advice from this guy, who hasn't spent a night on the streets in his life? No, I'm coming," Kit said.

"The sands have settled then," Rai said. "Shall we?"

Kit sighed.

Rai proceeded to train them relentlessly in the morning Sun. Even after it grew past the time most would return indoors for qed, they continued. Rai claimed that they wouldn't get to pick the conditions when it came to life or death. He trained them in hand-to-hand combat; how they should stand, how and where they should watch their attacker so they were ready to deflect, and how to throw a punch. As it got hotter, it grew harder to concentrate, and more than once Nya's vision blurred.

Nya felt sick when they finished. Kit looked little better. But she had spent the day focused and doing *something* to improve her situation. And not once had her mind drifted to dark places or Mother.

Nya lay, cold but sweating under the blankets on her bed, signs of sun sickness. It had been a long time since she was out in the Sun Eyes gaze all day, and her body wasn't used to it. She shivered, pulling the blanket tighter. Dust had been out when she returned, but as soon as she got back, Dust sat dutifully at her feet.

A light knock sounded at the door and Kit slid in. He came

up to her bedside and handed her a full water-skin. "How are you feeling? I brought you some water. You need to drink," Kit said.

"Thank you," Nya said, blinking away a dizzy spell then taking slow sips of water.

Kit sat on her bed and ran a hand over Dust's stomach, who purred and rolled over, not opening her eyes to see who was petting her. "Nya," Kit said.

"Before you say it, I know today was tough," Nya said with a shaky inhale. "But it was the first day. I'll get used to it."

Kit gave her a pitying look. She hated that look. "These Decreed have been appearing more over the last couple years. To start with, they were just another new gang that no one paid any mind to but now… Nya, they have slaughtered some of the biggest gangs in Yontar. They have meticulously invaded other territories and expanded their own. And this was all before the shadow man even made an appearance. He is like a war overseer on a playground. And I don't trust Rai either. The way he spoke about the shadow man was like he knew him."

"Kit, if you don't want to come—"

"Listen," Kit cut in with a sharper tone than Nya had ever heard him use. "We have been to a Duat-damned Torment Realm and back. If you want to sign up for a bloodthirsty gang, I'll be at your side. I just want to make sure you are doing this for the right reasons."

Kit turned and gazed out the window. Nya had pulled

back the shutters to let the cool breeze in. She was regretting it now as she bundled under the blanket.

"I know you saved me in that place and I kept telling myself that was why I wanted to stick by you but I've been lying to myself. I've had... nightmares." Kit bit his bottom lip.

"Of the dark place?" Nya asked, and he nodded.

"Of *that thing* in the cave," Kit said, and Nya saw the blood draining from his face just talking about it. "Nightmares where you leave me or I can't get out of its grip. And I don't know. Having you near when I wake is reassuring. I don't need to wake you and talk about it, but knowing you're there and you understand is enough to settle my nerves."

Nya stared at him, but he wouldn't meet her eye. She hadn't realised he had been struggling. Nya had been having nightmares about Bom and Mother, and knowing Kit was there helped her, too.

Kit faced her. "I don't need you to look at me like a wounded sand fox," he said. "I'm not any different."

"Sorry," Nya said, turning away.

"I'm here for you," Kit said. "I can't understand what it's like with this shade, but Nya"—he grabbed her hand and made her look at him again before continuing—"if you are doing this to punish yourself for what happened..."

Nya yanked her hands away.

"It wasn't your fault what happened and you don't *need* to do this," Kit said.

Nya's face wrinkled with disgust. "You have no clue whether it was my fault or not," she said.

It had been her fault. She still felt the anger that had filled her, how she lashed out, how she killed the woman who had done everything for her and gave up her life to look after her.

Kit raised his hands. "Okay, you're right. I'm not going to begin to try to understand. I just don't want you throwing yourself into a sinking pit because of what that *thing* did. What that *place* did," Kit said. "I know I said some harsh things about your mother in that dark place, but I know you loved her. You wouldn't have hurt her on purpose."

Tears tickled as they fell from Nya's face. *But I did*, she thought. She felt the stirring of fury in her gut. *And I might hurt you too.*

"I want you to leave," Nya said.

"But—"

"Out!" she shouted.

Kit looked hurt, but he stood and made his way to the door. He pivoted and added, "You deserve better than this, Nya," before stepping out and closing the door behind him.

Nya dropped back onto her bed, letting the last of the tears fall. Kit didn't understand, *couldn't* understand. He hadn't been there. She had talked to Rai about the shades, and he had said she could control it. She could rein it in. But she hadn't. She had wanted it to hurt Mother.

Nya wasn't afraid of Bom. She was afraid of what she was able to do because of Bom.

27

Blood and Bruises

Nya focused on her breathing, feeling it rise and fall. She let the air fill her lungs, then pour out her nose, where she paused before the next intake of breath. They had been training for a few weeks now. Kit would take part in the combat training and then help Illy in the afternoons, while Nya did her shade training with Rai. So far, that had involved a lot of breath work and meditation, with only occasionally talking with Bom and commanding it. She had managed to get it to expand her shadow, but little else.

"Good," Rai said, sounding as if he was in another room, despite him standing beside her on the rooftop. "Now, expand your awareness. Listen to each noise you hear individually. You don't need to think about what they are, just focus on the sound."

Nya listened to the scraping of Rai's feet as he walked across the dusty rooftop. She heard indistinct voices from the surrounding city, and the crunch of Rai's aya eating in the courtyard below.

"Being able to tune in to your surroundings is vital. You need to be aware and master your environment," Rai said. "It's also important to be able to clear your mind of thought. Especially when you start to get overwhelmed. Your shade feeds off your emotions. And being under stress and pressure will lead to misinterpretation and lashing out."

We don't feed off emotions, Fax said. Fax had begun to let Nya hear it talk. *But we feel them like you, making us want to act on them.*

It was strange to hear his shade chat like they were friends, when she could barely get Bom talking.

"I wasn't being literal, Fax," Rai said.

Good, because you would have been wrong, Fax said. Nya snickered.

"Right, that's enough for today," Rai said.

Nya opened her eyes. The Sun Eye had been high when she had closed them, but now it was almost dark hour. Fax perched on Rai's shoulder in the form of a crow as Rai rolled his neck.

"How are you so different from my shade, Fax?" Nya asked, standing.

We are different aspects of a whole, meaning we are the same and yet completely different. Your shade might not be as intelligent, Fax said.

A rush of air took Nya's breath away, and her shadow shot towards Rai. Fax crashed into it, and it slunk back into Nya.

"I'm so sorry!" Nya said, standing back and covering her mouth.

"It's okay," Rai said, brushing off the dust that the velocity of her shadow had kicked up. "Although your shade is influenced by your thoughts, you are influenced by its as well. Which is why we are practicing on clearing your mind."

Nya nodded, looking at her feet, her cheeks flushing.

"Come on," Rai said, waving to the door leading back down into The Patched Cloak. "You still have work to do for Illy."

Nya walked into the common room of the inn. It was a lot less musky that it had been when they first arrived. Over the past week, Nya and Kit had scrubbed the place, and it was looking decidedly better. Booths glinted in the firelight, where before dust would have dulled their reflections. And Nya was no longer afraid to let her feet down under the booths after sweeping the sand from underneath.

They had ripped boards from shuttered windows letting the winds stream through, forcing out the stale air. And they had begun cleaning the kitchen, but there was a family of params that needed evicted before they could do much more.

Dust lay snoozing on the bottle shelf, slid into a narrow gap where a bottle should have been. She didn't bat an eye as Nya approached. Illy was behind the bar, counting bottles and making notes on a piece of parchment. Creases lined Illy's brow like the numbers weren't adding up and she had a restless energy to her.

Nya dropped onto a stool. "You okay, Illy?"

Illy startled. "Yes, all fine. Kit is out cleaning the stables. You can help him tonight. I still need to find wherever those params are getting in and block it up," she said.

"Are you sure you're okay?" Nya asked as Illy sped about.

She set the bottle down, rubbed her head, and glanced at Nya. "It's Wenson. He would normally be back by now. He doesn't stay out for dark hour," Illy said. "I know he is in with bad crowds, and he can't speak the language, and I just... I worry about him."

Nya placed her hand on Illy's. "I'm sure he's fine," she said with a smile.

Illy sighed and smiled. "You're right. I've been so busy with the inn I haven't had the time to spend with him, and I'm worried his habits are getting out of hand. But every time I confront him about it he shuts me out."

"I'm sure Wenson is just working through stuff," Nya said. "Losing family is tough."

Nya swallowed.

"I wish he would speak to me about it. We were never close, but I hate seeing him like this," Illy said, absently tapping on the piece of parchment. "But I'm not his mother. He isn't much younger than me, so if he wants to spend his life getting drunk and wandering around the city, so be it."

Nya could tell Illy didn't mean it. She cared for Wenson. And Nya knew first-hand the pain of watching a loved one decline and not being able to help. But sometimes reaching out to someone in sinking sand was just as likely to push them further in. You just had to be there, hoping they will pull themselves out or be ready if they hold out their hand.

Illy shook herself out of distant thoughts. "Sorry Nya, I didn't mean to drop family troubles on you," Illy said.

"No, it's okay. You have done so much for me and Kit already," Nya said, and squeezed Illy's hand.

"You better head out and help him in the stables, or he'll complain for the rest of the night," Illy said.

Nya scoffed as Illy turned back to the bottles, though her movements were less sharp and agitated than they had been.

Making her way through the back towards the courtyard, Nya ran her hands across the walls to help guide her. This corridor sat in shadow and could have done with a sconce to light it.

She pushed open the door to the courtyard and a surge of hot air swept down the corridor. Above, a dark blue sky ran towards pure black, with dark hour almost upon them. A free-standing brazier flickered in the stables like a candle in a darkened room. Nya smiled and crept over.

Hunched over and scraping back the sand built up in the pen was Kit. He ran his forearm across his head, wiping away the sweat. Nya hopped onto the pen fencing and launched herself at him, letting out a high-pitched feral squeal. Kit screamed, throwing his hands up as she tackled him. Then Nya burst out laughing, watching his terrified expression in the firelight.

He sat back against the wall and held his chest. "That's not funny. You could have stopped my heart," Kit said, which just made her laugh more.

After catching his breath, Kit did eventually smile. He had gotten her enough times with the same trick that he couldn't complain.

"So, how was your extra training?" Kit asked. That's what they had been calling the shade exercises for Illy's benefit. Rai had made a passing comment in front of Illy about Kit having some knowledge already, and that Nya would need extra time to catch up.

She wrinkled her nose. "I don't know. I don't feel like I've got any more control than I had."

"It's only been a couple weeks," Kit said. "I'm sure you will get it."

He was right. They weren't in any rush. She would have to join this Decreed eventually to see what they were up to, and she wanted to be able to at least defend herself against the jackal-masked man when they did, but there was still time.

Nya nodded with a half-hearted smile. Then Kit dragged himself back to his feet and Nya strode to the far side of the pen to pick up the other brush.

Shouts and thumps of impact rang out in the street beside the courtyard. Kit's face screwed up as he looked in that direction. Muffled voices cursed and more cracks of impact followed.

Kit brought a finger to his lips.

Together they crept across the courtyard to where the waist-high fence led onto the main street. Peering over, Nya saw shadows at the far end. Three shapes were bearing down on a person trying to crawl away.

"We need to do something," Nya whispered.

Kit's face was hard. "We can't fight off three people."

"We can't just leave whoever that is," Nya said.

They watched as the three figures continued to kick at their victim, who was struggling to stay upright. One of them cracked their foot across the crawling person's face, sending them slamming into the wall. Then the three descended again.

That was all Nya could watch. She hopped the wall and stalked down towards them. Nya could feel the phantom aches from beatings she had endured over the years strengthening her resolve. "Hey!" Nya shouted, and felt Kit fall in at her side.

The three shapes looked up but sadly didn't flee as they made their way towards them.

"Back off. This is nothing to do with you," a voice growled.

"I was trying to nap and you lot are making a racket," Kit said. "So it very much has to do with me."

The three straightened. Two had tall, broad frames and one was skinny and short. As they got closer, Nya realized two of them were woman and one was a man. And the person lying semi-conscious was... Wenson?

Kit took a sharp intake of breath, coming to the same realisation.

"We are teaching a customer what happens when you don't pay what you owe," one woman said.

Wenson had been back to the blood dens. Illy had warned

Nya and Kit about her nephew's habits but he had been getting better. Or so they thought.

"It looks like he learned his lesson. How about you leave it at that?" Kit said.

The three laughed. "This one is going to be a warning to others. He'll be strung up and put on show come the Moon Eye's watch."

They were going to kill him. "We can't let you," Nya said, her voice coming out hard.

The three laughed again and stepped forward. "I guess we better back off then," the man said. The three were larger than Nya and Kit. Deadly silhouetted black cut outs, highlighting their broad physiques.

Bom, I know we don't get on, but I need you now, Nya thought. She glanced over her shoulder to the inn. By the time she ran back and alerted Rai, Wenson would be dead and possibly Kit too. She needed Bom.

"Just leave him and we won't hurt you," Kit said.

"That's cute. Do you think we could take that one home? We could do with a new pet," one thug said to his friend.

A woman snickered. "He even has a little bite in him."

"Will you two shut up!" the third snapped, then cracked her neck to the side.

The three stepped forward.

"If you have a plan, now would be the time Nya," Kit whispered.

"I'm trying!" Nya said.

Come on, Bom. If I die, you die. She wasn't sure if that was true or not, but it was worth a shot. Bom stirred but didn't move.

The three were in front of them now.

Kit, with a quick glance at Nya, screamed and charged. He ducked under the first swing, but a second caught him on the side of his head, and they threw him to the side. Kit and Nya had been training, but it had only been a couple of weeks. They couldn't fight off three thugs.

Bom!

"What about you, girl?" the woman asked. "Your friend is going to have to die now too, but I'll still let you go."

Nya's heart thundered in her chest. She saw Kit crawl over to Wenson and check on him. "No, please. Just let us go," Nya said.

"Just kill her and get this over with," the other woman said. "It's getting late."

With that, one of the woman lunged forward. Nya dodged the woman's grab and threw a wild punch. A splatter of blood sprayed from the woman's nose. She howled, grasping at her face.

Nya looked at her hands. It had happened so naturally. Rai's drills were clearly making a difference.

The other two marched towards her.

Not that much of a difference.

Bom, please!

The other woman threw a punch, and Nya closed her eyes, but it never connected.

Something black wrapped itself around her fist. It twisted

and tossed the thug back with a flick. The woman glanced around, perplexed. Nya reached out in her mind but it wasn't Bom.

Then an onslaught of shadowed shapes darted from the black around them, battering into the three thugs. They were tossed around and knocked to the ground. One of them started swinging at nothing but the shade's tendrils snaked up his arm and struck him in the face with his own fist.

Nya backed up.

Rai dropped from nowhere, and Fax stopped attacking, letting the groaning thugs push themselves to their feet. Fax wrapped around Rai, making him a black blur, when details should have been clear. He was more creature than man, with swirling shadow permeating from him.

One thug ran off, another stared in horror, the third dropped to their knees.

"We didn't know they were Decreed," the one on his knees said to Rai with a terror-stricken voice.

They thought Rai was the jackal-masked man.

"Go," Rai whispered, but it had the power of a shout in the quiet.

The other two scrambled away, bowing and running between apologies. After they were out of sight, Fax turned into a crow and flew over to Wenson and Kit. Rai and Nya rushed over too.

Wenson had been badly beaten. In the dim light, Nya saw pooling blood and purpling bruises. Kit was holding his chest but seemed to be okay.

Rai slid under Wenson's arm and hauled him up. Wenson hissed.

"Run ahead and tell Illy to get water and bandages," Rai said, walking back to the inn.

Kit sped ahead, Nya trailing.

Illy and Rai stood around a battered and bloodied Wenson. He had passed out, his face fallen slack, blood dripping down his cut lip. They had laid him out on a booth, where Rai had taken command and was cleaning him up. Illy was inconsolable when they first entered, but Rai had given her simple tasks to distract her and keep her mind focused.

Nya and Kit sat in a booth on the other side of the common room, not wanting to get in the way, but unable to leave. Kit grimaced, holding his chest as he shifted in his chair.

"Are you okay?" Nya asked.

"Yeah, fine. Think I cracked a rib though," Kit said.

"Do you want me to get you something?" Nya asked.

"Nah, I'm good, thanks," he said, breathing slowly.

"I should have jumped in and fought," Nya said, shaking her head. "I thought I could control Bom, but I was useless even after training with Rai."

"Hey, it's not your fault," Kit said. "You would've just gotten hurt too."

Nya knew he was right, but she should have been able to do more. Despite all her training, she couldn't do anything. It wasn't enough.

"Do you think he'll be okay?" Nya said, looking back at

Wenson lying on the table as Rai discarded another blood-soaked rag behind the bar.

"Yeah," Kit said. "He has lost a lot of blood, but I've seen people come back from worse."

"Rai! He's waking!" Illy called.

They sped over. Wenson's eyes fluttered open and closed as he tried to drag himself back to the waking world. He looked a lot better now that they had washed the blood off him.

Wenson tried to speak but cut off in splutters. Illy whispered something in Nuian that sounded reassuring.

"Keet? Neeya?" Wenson said between coughing.

Kit stepped forward and clasped his hand. "We're here," Kit said.

Wenson's eyes focused for a second on Kit, and he half smiled. "Black sand fool," Wenson croaked.

Kit let out a laugh. Illy was smiling, tears streaming down her face.

Later that night, Nya lay in bed staring at the shutter rattling in the breeze. A chill carried into the room settling in for the night. A scuffle could be heard from the common room of The Patched Cloak as Illy fussed over Wenson in the late hours. Beyond that the city hummed.

Nya knew she hadn't been training long but the fact she couldn't do *anything* to help Wenson was disconcerting. She had seen what shades could do and yet she couldn't defend herself against a couple of thugs? Kit told her it would come with time but what if they didn't have time?

They all leave in the end.

Illy and Wenson had made it clear that they planned to sell The Patched Cloak and move back to Nuia. Rai was here to stop the Decreed who could make their move any day now. And Kit was only here out of some debt he thought he owed Nya for saving him in the dark place. They could all leave tomorrow and Nya would be alone.

She had always been able to banish dark thoughts with the light of purpose. That purpose was to care for her Mother but she was dead because of Nya. So what was she to do now? What was she to do when they all inevitably left?

Nya pulled the blanket tighter squeezing her eyes shut. *At least they will be safe from me.* The thought was supposed to bring her comfort. Instead, she felt nothing.

28

A Lit Window

It was beginning to feel like days long passed. Up before sunrise and training until dark hour. The routine was good. It reminded Rai of simpler times. He hadn't even had a drink in... what felt like a lifetime.

Four days, Fax said.

"I told you, I don't like it when you listen in on my thoughts," Rai grumbled.

He had left Nya and Kit running through sparring drills on The Patched Cloak's rooftop. They were coming on well. Rai had trained guards with less tenacity than those two. *A hard life has left them fierce and determined*, Rai thought. But was that enough?

Rai had to ramp up the training. Which was why he had them working under the Moon Eye's watch. He needed to get them as ready as he could before sending them into the Decreed.

Kyan was a meticulous planner, but it had been five years. If he was showing his face now, it meant something was about to change. He was about to make his move.

Rai was on his way back to the inn with herbs bundled under his arm for Wenson. The man was a blood-addled fool, but he was Illy's nephew, and Rai needed to keep them safe, so he had somewhere to stay and train Nya. However, Wenson was getting better and Rai guessed he would be on his feet within the week.

Moonlight bled into the street in strips between breaks in the buildings. The city was alive, people making the most of the cooler temperatures. Kids chased one another down alleyways, carts trundled past laden with goods, and guards watched.

Rai had read of other countries that feared the night. After the Sun fell from its watch, they went inside and locked their doors, only those with ill will appearing under the Moon Eye's gaze, but not in Tarris. Here it was commonplace for the streets to be busier during the early hours of night. Night markets sprung up and families sat out in the cool. Dark hour being the only exception.

Rai strode through the crowd, mind running through training exercises for the following morning, when Fax said, *Rai look.*

He turned to the right and sat perfectly aligned between buildings was the blood den where he met Lem.

And the stained-glass window was lit.

"Looks like our friend wants a word," Rai said.

Rai made his way to the blood den. Soft groans came from inside as he hopped the crumbling wall surrounding the building. Rai took a second to look at the stained-glass window, now lit from within. A boy stood in the centre, holding a black blade, facing down what looked to be a creature with seven limbs. Each limb was a different colour, and it had no distinguishable body. It may have been depicting one of Toks' stories, the immortal boy. But Rai didn't remember any descriptions matching the thing he faced. Either way, it was a beautiful piece; he thought as he made his way around to the dead garden.

Lem was waiting in the dried-up pond, his fingers tapping against the pond wall, head swilling around, eyes searching. His gaze landed on Rai and grew wide, and he waved emphatically for Rai to hurry over.

"Is everything okay, Lem?" Rai asked as he jumped down.

Lem stepped forward, uncomfortably close to Rai, and said, "He's moving! Tonight!"

Rai tore through the city and back towards The Patched Cloak. He had worried about Kyan doing something against the monarchy, but he hadn't thought he would be leaving Yontar anytime soon. *I should have gotten Nya into the Decreed earlier*, he thought, skirting a corner.

He threw open the door to the inn and marched through the common room, barrelling up the stairs, and bounded through the corridor to the second staircase leading to the roof. Illy peaked out of one of the rooms to see what all the commotion was about.

"Rai? Is everything okay? Did you get the herbs?" Illy asked.

"Yes, I'll be back in a second," Rai said as he jogged up the stairs to the roof. Nya and Kit were drinking from water-skins and looking out over the moonlit city.

"Pack your things," Rai said. "Kyan's moving tonight."

They both stared at him, startled.

"What?" Nya asked.

"I was just informed that the Decreed have been buying aya and stock for a long trip, and they plan to leave Yontar tonight," Rai said.

Nya clambered onto her feet, legs shaking from the hard day's training. "What do we do?" she asked.

"Pack for a long trip and meet me in the common room," Rai said. They continued to gawk at him.

"Now!" Rai shouted.

It wasn't long before Nya and Kit were trailing behind Rai through the city, as he marched to the northern gate. They struggled to keep pace lugging sacks with provisions that Illy helped throw together. Rai had said to Illy that he didn't have time to explain, and that seemed to be enough for now, but later he would have explaining to do.

"Why now?" Kit asked. "And why so suddenly?"

"And where is it they're going?" Nya added.

"I don't know," Rai said in almost a whisper. He didn't like this. He didn't like not knowing.

They made their way through the city, the Moon Eye watching from above.

The northern gate towered above the surrounding buildings. It was mammoth in size; around the same as the southern gate, despite the fact that it wasn't often used.

When Yontar was built, the northern gate would have been used as much, if not more, than the other gates, as it pointed towards the old capital, Asuriya. However, now most used the western gate as it led more directly to Tansen, the new capital of Tarris.

Rai heard the shouting and shuffling of those about to depart before he saw them. The space around the gate was full of aya, men, woman, and a handful of hyian.

Those in charge barked commands as people darted about, carrying packs of food and water. Chains of people tossed sacks onto the aya's back, while others attached saddlebags to the hyian. Palace guards watched from a distance, but they weren't breaking any laws.

The Decreed had their own guards watching the chaos, subtly placed along the perimeter around the gate too. Cloaks pulled tight, the faint outline of weapons bulging at their sides.

"I can't go any further," Rai said, turning to Nya and Kit. They tried to act calm, but Rai noted their restless twitching.

They're just kids, Rai reminded himself. What was he doing? He didn't have a choice now though. They could look after

320

themselves, as long as they weren't head-to-head with Kyan.

"It's going to be okay," Rai said. "I'll tail you. Wherever he takes you, I won't be far behind. As long as you keep your heads down and ears perked, there won't be any problems."

"Unless all these followers are here for a ritual sacrifice," Kit muttered, but Nya elbowed him in the chest.

"You might have to convince them to let you join. Just try to regurgitate phrases from Kyan's speech," Rai said.

"We'll be fine," Nya said.

"I know," Rai said. "Be safe."

Nya nodded, and together with Kit, they jogged down towards the gate. Rai watched until they passed out of sight and into the mass.

They grow up so fast, Fax said.

"Shut up, Fax," Rai said.

He knew they would be fine. He kept telling himself so, but part of Rai knew he was sending them into the unknown. And into the arms of a trained killer.

Kyan wouldn't hurt them, Rai thought. He knew the man, and he only used violence as a last resort. After all, of the seven of them, it had been Kyan who tried to negotiate with that cannibal cult six years ago. He almost lost an arm.

But in the market... Black tendrils ripping through those guards just doing their job. That wasn't the Kyan he knew.

As if naming him was enough to summon the man, Kyan stepped out from a shadowed street, two of his Decreed at his side. Rai ducked around a corner. It was unlikely he would look this way, but his shade could be watching. Some heads bowed as he passed them, however, most didn't even acknowledge his passing. Kyan had never been one for basking in the centre of attention.

Rai slid down a street and made his way towards where Kyan had come from, sticking to the narrow, unpopulated paths. He didn't look too out of place with other curious bystanders walking by and watching from side glances, wondering about the happenings around the gate.

Slipping from the shadows and onto a road, Rai felt a solitary breeze carry down a street undisturbed by people or carts. While others weren't brimming with traffic at this hour, this street was completely empty. No lights filtered from shuttered windows, not a soul wandered up its sand covered road, and a silence clung to the road and walls.

At the far end was the northern gate and the mass of people, but they were all too caught up in readying to depart to notice as Rai creep up the street, walking with his back to the buildings.

Why would this street be empty? Fax asked.

"They all got up and left," Rai said.

Oh, you think Kyan used this as a base and bought off the entire street?

"More likely recruited or killed off, but yes," Rai said. "I just need to figure out which building he was staying in."

Rai passed several inns with a variety of names and types, none of which struck him as somewhere Kyan would base himself. Being so far from the more frequented gates around the city, and therefore, rarely used by travellers, the inns were rundown, some having fallen into disrepair. One called *The Dripping Bucket* was little more than a skeleton of what it once was.

Rai slid back into shadow and watched as a man towing a hyian stepped out from a side street and addled up to the northern gate. Rai waited until he joined the shuffling mass before creeping on.

A metal compass sign hung from the next inn, with the name, *The Cartographers Rest*.

Kyan was always buried in a book or studying a map, Rai thought, and pushed on the door.

Locked.

"Fax," Rai said. Fax slithered past the door and sliced through the locking mechanism. Rai spared one last glance down toward the procession readying to depart before slipping into the inn.

The bar was on his right, and tables were scattered to his left. The bar didn't have bottles of alcohol on show like the inns Rai frequented, rather glass vials and tubes of varying shapes and sizes for brewing coffee and tea. A map of Tarris covered a large section of the far wall with mud brick shelves lined with books at either side of it.

Rai passed through with little more than a cursory look over and found the stairs at the back left. Jogging up, he felt as if he was being watched. He spun, looking around, but no one was there and no sound trickled in from the surrounding inn.

"Fax have a little look around, would you?" Rai whispered. Fax shot on ahead.

Turning into the corridor, one by one, Rai threw open the bedroom doors. They all looked to have been inhabited recently. Thin blankets lay crumpled on beds and belongings were still stacked in the corners.

So they plan on coming back, Rai thought, poking through a pile of clothes.

Fax returned, saying, *We have the place to ourselves*.

Rai nodded to himself and continued checking the rooms.

He was coming up to the last three, when a door thrown open revealed a man standing by the window. The chamber was dark with moonlight shining through the window, lighting the edges of a familiar frame.

Rai froze.

I swear he wasn't there a moment ago! Fax said.

"Akarai," Kyan said.

"I thought you were dead," Rai said.

"And I you," Kyan said. He turned, still shrouded in shadow. "You didn't go back, did you?"

Rai didn't respond.

"I thought not. Did you get sick of being used too?" Kyan said.

Rai scanned the room as Kyan spoke. The room was simple and unassuming, much like the places Rai had been living. Notes lay scattered across his bed. Rai needed to get a better look.

"Why didn't you come to me after the rally?" Kyan asked, hurt masked in his voice, but Rai knew him too well for Kyan to hide it.

"I'm sorry Kyan. I wasn't sure if you were being controlled," Rai said.

Kyan laughed, lifting his head to the sky, and Rai edged towards the bed. "Controlled? No Rai, I'm not being controlled. Not anymore."

"I see that now, but what are you doing? You don't seem yourself," Rai said. "Those guards at the market—"

"Those guards were puppets," Kyan snapped. He cleared his throat, tempering his rage before continuing, "They're no better than those sitting on the thrones, Rai. Can't you see that? They chose to be there.

"Did you know what their orders were? I have someone in the guard's ranks, so I could keep tabs on them. They were to kill me and those who followed me and to beat anyone else they had the time to wrap their stubby little hands around too, as a warning. Innocent people," Kyan said, with a wave of his hand and false humour lining his tone. "We have studied the laws, Rai. Was I, or any of my followers, breaking any of them?"

"Not yet, but your rally could be considered as inciting rebellion," Rai said.

Kyan scoffed. "If speaking the truth is inciting rebellion, then the problems are in the system," he said. "But we both know that first-hand."

Rai stared at the boy he once knew, twisted and jaded from wandering a worn path that Rai knew well. "Sometimes I wish I hadn't brought you into the Seven," Rai said. "You deserved better. An easier life. One with your books and words instead of blood and daggers. I'm sorry."

Kyan's face softened for a moment, and Rai saw the Kyan he'd once known take hold. The kid with grand ideas of making a better world. Then it hardened again, a snarl curling at the edges. He turned back to the window. "You know, if you didn't pull me from the streets to train me, I'd likely be dead. Or a blood peddler," he said softly.

Rai crept the last couple steps and peered hard in the light reaching from the window at Kyan's notes. There were pages of scrawl and a map of Tarris. Routes had been drawn onto the map with times and dates at certain locations. The route covered the whole of Tarris, wrapping around on itself, avoiding all the major cities. But it didn't have a start or end position, it just looped around and around.

"You saved me from that life and I will always be grateful," Kyan said. "And now I must pass on that goodwill and save those who can't save themselves."

"How do you plan to do that?" Rai asked.

"By ridding the world of those who let it decay and fall into this state in the first place. By bringing justice to those who care only for the coin in their pocket," Kyan said. "They have grown complacent and lazy. It's time to remind them what the world is truly like."

He spun back around. "Stand beside me. It would mean everything to have you with me when we cleanse this world anew."

Rai regarded his friend. His words rang true in many ways. And being told that it would mean everything to Kyan to have Rai by his side stabbed into parts of Rai he thought long dead.

But how Kyan went about serving justice was a different matter. Those guards Kyan killed were following orders. And he had killed them before the guards had even attempted to harm Kyan. How did he know they would follow through with the orders?

Even if they had, the guards believed what they were doing was just. The guards trusted their supervisors who said Kyan was dangerous, and that there was good reason to stop him. Did that trust make them deserving of death?

Where was the line?

Rai thought about lying, about going with Kyan, and trying to bring him back to his old self, but he knew Kyan would see right through it. He could never lie to the boy.

"I can't," Rai whispered.

They let the words settle between them.

"That's a shame," Kyan said, sounding genuinely saddened by how this conversation went. "I would have liked you to have been with me. It's lonely when people don't understand, and you always did."

Rai knew no words would sway Kyan's conviction and found none that could reach the old him either.

"When all this is done, we can sit in that cafe on the Strip again and talk of small things without worrying about who will next wet our blades," Kyan said.

"Don't do this," Rai said. "Not everyone is corrupt."

"I know that. That's why they will be Judged," Kyan said.

Rai stretched out to lay a hand on Kyan's shoulder, but he fell to the ground like a dropped blanket. Then his shadow shot out the window.

Rai stepped forward, watching as a patch of black sped across the abandoned street and towards the gate, where the true Kyan stood.

"He had his shade project a copy of himself and use his voice," Rai whispered.

I didn't know we could do that, Fax said.

The northern gate was still a mass of motion, impossible to follow. But standing in the middle, staring directly at Rai, unmoving, was Kyan. He bowed, slow and deliberate, before turning and disappearing into the crowd.

Rai snatched Kyan's notes and ran for the door, Kyan's words ringing in his head.

They will be Judged.

29

The Unrelenting Path

The road declined to the northern gate, adding to the sense of inevitability. The courtyard around the northern gate was a like a snake pit, everyone weaving in and out of the rest preparing to depart. Firelight moved like fireflies among the writhing mass.

As Nya and Kit approached, a man, hooded with a long nose sticking out from the shadow, lifted a hand. His cloak shifted revealing a mace attached to his belt.

"Where do you two think you are going?" he asked.

"We want to join," Kit said.

"This isn't one of your street gangs, kid," the man said.

"We know. We were roused by your leader's speech and want to be a part of what he has planned," Nya said, remembering what Rai had told them to say.

The man clearly hadn't expected that answer and took his time to think it over. "I'm glad you see the importance of the mission, but we can't take on more. We don't have the supplies," he said.

"We have our own," Nya said, shaking the bag on her back.

The man eyed the sacks and sighed. "Look, I can see you are serious about this, so let me be serious too. We can't take kids. This is going to be a dangerous journey. Watch for our return and perhaps we will have a place for you then."

He flicked his hand dismissively and was about to walk off when Nya grabbed his cloak. She didn't know what made her do it, and immediately regretted it when he turned back, stern-faced.

"We can help," Nya said in almost a whisper. She felt Kit's eyes boring into her. She had been hoping not to reveal this so early, but it would be meaningless if they couldn't even join the Decreed.

Nya's shadow flickered. Just subtly so most who saw would think it a trick of the light. But the man understood, his face paling. It was all she could do with her shade with any reliability, but he didn't know that. He stared at her a moment, then nodded.

"If you can find an aya with space, get on it. If not, come speak to me and I'll make space," the man said. "Just ask for Cer." And with that, he rushed off into the crowd.

"He's going straight to Kyan to tell him," Kit whispered.

"Yeah, I know," Nya said. "We will learn more about what

they are up to if they think we are important though."

They skirted the edge of the people until they found a quieter section. A short line of sorry looking souls clambered up onto an aya, which was patiently watching all the happenings in the courtyard. They joined the back of the line of solemn looking individuals. Well, all apart from one who was grinning from ear to ear, and talking to the person in front, who didn't look to be listening. And curiously, he only wore one boot.

Climbing atop the aya's platform, Nya got a better view of the ever-moving mass. There were even more people than she had originally thought.

"Come on, shift up," Kit said, prodding her leg.

Nya stopped gawking and clambered onto the platform. The others sat in a line. Two at the front, clearly the ones in charge, murmured to each other, overlooking the procession.

Unslinging her bag, Nya dropped, letting out a puffed exhale and rolled her neck and aching shoulders. She knew they didn't know how long they were going to be away for, but the bag felt like it had enough supplies to last her the rest of her life. Kit sat beside her, his eyes constantly flicking towards movement.

Slowly, the rushing settled and, with no ceremony or word from Kyan or anyone else, they started filtering through the northern gate and onto the open black sand dunes. Nya felt her muscles easing as they passed under the gate. All the running around and shouting had put her on edge, and the easy march alleviated some of that tension.

Nya peered across the rolling dunes. The ebb and flow was mesmerising. Some rose to sharp ridges, whereas others were flatter and wider, but they all connected seamlessly together like brush strokes on a painting. Nya had left Yontar a couple of times with Mother. They travelled all the way to Karbari once, to see the ocean. Not so much in later years when Nya had to look after Mother, though.

I miss her, Nya thought.

Sitting with her dark thoughts, Nya noticed her sack *moving*. She sat up, glancing down the line of others. Some were already napping, some were watching the passing dunes, but none were looking her way. Even Kit slumped over and was staring out at the arching line of the sand.

Nya unlatched the tag and pulled back the top of her sack.

Dust jumped out of the bag, landing beside Nya on the platform. She shook and stretched like she had just woke from a pleasant nap.

"Dust? What are you doing here?!" Nya said.

"Dust?" Kit said.

"She must have snuck into my bag," Nya said, peering into her bag. Her spare clothing that Illy had lent her were crushed into a ball and covered in hair. "We have to take her back."

"Good luck with that," Kit said. They both turned. Yontar was little more than a speck behind them.

"You sneaky little sand fox," Nya said, shaking her head and petting Dust.

Dust curled up beside her as if to say, *well, of course*.

Nya scratched her head. Part of her was pleased she was with her, but a bigger part knew the possible perils they could face, and Dust was someone else to worry about.

"Best to get some sleep," Kit said, placing his pack down and laying his head on it. "Who knows what tomorrow will bring. Maybe Rai will climb out of my pack and make us breakfast."

Nya clacked her dry tongue, blinking against the light of the Sun Eye as she woke. Her neck ached. Sleeping on her pack didn't do much for neck support. Sitting up, she unlatched her bag and got out her waterskin, drinking deep. The dry desert air sailed through her hair, carrying an earthy aroma unmarred by the stenches of the city. Dust sent her paws out and ducked her head into a stretch, before coming over and rubbing her head against Nya.

"Here you go," Nya said, giving her some water.

Yawning, Nya rubbed her eyes. Someone had set up the tarp, so it shaded them from the Sun. Most were still sleeping, but a couple others were awake and digging into their packs for food.

More aya walked in front and behind theirs in a long procession across the desert sands, easier to see now in the daylight.

Something smacked Nya across the cheek, landing in her lap. She looked down and saw a piece of bread.

"It's about time you woke up," Kit said. "We need to talk."

Nya scooted over to sit beside Kit at the back of the

platform so they could talk without being overheard. She ate her bread, still overcoming the fuzz of sleep.

"I know we agreed to do this," Kit said. Nya glanced over her shoulder to make sure no one was listening. "But I don't trust Rai. He isn't telling us everything. He knows this jackal-masked man. He called him Kyan, despite there being no word on the streets of the guy's name."

Nya rubbed her forehead. It was true Rai had named him Kyan a couple of times while training, but she had assumed it was common knowledge.

"That isn't known by the gangs?" Nya asked.

"Nope," Kit said. "I asked around. No one knows the guy."

"I know I agreed to do this with you, but this is getting dangerous. We don't even know where we're headed," Kit said. "We were suddenly rushed away at night. And the more I think about it, the more I worry. What if Rai is in on it?"

Nya shook her head. "What would he gain from lying to us and sending us away?"

"I don't know, that's the problem," Kit said too loudly and several heads burled to stare at them. Kit held up an apologetic hand. "We could just leave. Nothing is holding us to Yontar. We could go to Tansen, damn it, we could head south to Dock Town and leave Tarris if we wanted.

"Why are we doing this?" Kit asked.

Nya let her head fall forward. "I don't know," she whispered. "I'm scared. I'm scared I'll hurt more people. All I've ever done was look after Mother and now that she... I don't know what to do anymore."

"Nya—"

"No, I don't want you to tell me Mother was a bad person. I don't want to hear that it wasn't my fault. I don't want to hear that I can move on, because I can't," Nya said. "I have done nothing but try and try and everything ends in pain. I don't know if it's me or just the way of the world, but I'm done trying to pretend like it will end any other way. So what if Rai knows him? I just don't care anymore, Kit. I'm tired."

Kit stared at her for an extended moment. Nya felt like she had spent everything she had and was ready to lie back down. Kit opened his mouth, about to say something, when a voice cut in.

"You two," a gruff voice said. They turned and one of the Decreed who stayed up front had walked over. "The Leading One wants to talk to you."

Nya and Kit met each other's gaze.

Kyan.

30

A Truth of the World

Kyan stared across the open sand. Yontar had long sunk into the horizon but he knew it was there. He knew Akarai was there. Kyan shouldn't have been surprised that Akarai had survived the trip into the dark realm. He was too stubborn to die. Kyan was sure if you dropped the man into a desert he would drink the sand and will it into water.

But Kyan hadn't connected Rai the mercenary—the man who had been asking about him on the streets over the last week—with his old friend and mentor, Akarai.

Seeing his old friend again had warmed Kyan. He had spent years believing Akarai was dead and finding him here lifted a weight of grief that Kyan hadn't realised he was carrying. *He should be here with me*, Kyan thought. But no matter. They would be able to catch up soon enough.

After Kyan had wiped Tarris of injustices.

The Decreed fell behind Kyan in a line of aya that marched over the black sands. The chosen few who would be there when the new Tarris was ushered in.

He had come so far and it had all stemmed back to sitting in his bedroom window. Where Kyan realised he would have to make the changes he wanted to see in the world.

Those days held strong in his mind. Kyan would never forget them because they forged him into the man he was today.

I can make it, Kyan thought glancing down at the two-story drop. His hand tightened around the ledge. It wasn't the drop that stayed him from swinging his other leg over. It was that there would be no turning back once he had.

The city of Tansen spread out in front of him, glistening in the moonlight. Before him was freedom. Freedom to help those who needed it.

Kyan glanced over his shoulder at his bedroom: an opulent chamber with a large bed and dresser, and a bookshelf against the far wall. He had always thought his room and life to be normal. How could he not when it was all he knew?

It was only during recent years he had learned the truth of the world.

Just over a year before, Kyan's father took him out into the city, to a bookshop that was said to have ancient tomes from the old capital. It was Kyan's birthday and a visit to this bookshop was all he had asked for.

As they delved deeper into the city and away from their home, Kyan had asked his father why some of the boys and girls wore rags. More and more children peeked around corners or scattered at the sight of them. Where were their robes? Had they been naughty and this was their punishment?

His father had laughed. *Laughed*. And said, "In a way."

His curiosity piqued, Kyan wanted to meet one of the ragged children to learn what they had done to be forced to wear such humiliating garb. Later, while his father was distracted by the shopkeeper, bartering over the price of a rustic tome Kyan had picked out, Kyan snuck out the shop and found a young boy around his own age.

He didn't have to walk far to find one crouched in the shade, head slack around the side of the bookshop.

"So what did you do?" Kyan asked the boy.

The boy startled and looked around eyes wide, then cowered back from Kyan.

"It's okay," Kyan said. "Here." He slid off his outer jacket. It was a thin blue waistcoat, far too warm to wear today anyway, and held it out to the boy.

"I stole from my father's wardrobes once, too. He made me go to the Strip wearing his oversized robe as punishment," Kyan said.

The poor boy looked terrified and hadn't said a word. But with a wiggle of the waistcoat, he reached out with a shaking hand and snatched it from Kyan. The boy stared at it like Kyan had handed him a live snake.

"You can put it on if you like," Kyan said.

The boy swallowed, then slid one arm into the waistcoat.

Suddenly, Kyan was yanked backwards as two of his father's guards swept in tearing the waistcoat off the boy. The guards threw him to the ground and started beating him.

Kyan spun around and his father dropped down to meet his eyes. "Are you okay?" His father had asked.

Kyan glanced over to the boy and watched as he was beaten bloody. What were they doing? He had only given the boy his waistcoat, which he didn't truly need anyway. The shopkeeper was apologising profusely to his father, saying he normally kept the area clear.

That was Kyan's first lesson on what the world was truly like.

That memory stung still. Kyan was so ignorant. But he understood now. Since that day he had learnt the truth about how most people in Tarris didn't have a bookshelf in their room. They didn't have a manor with servants and its own well. Some didn't even have food to eat.

His parents had said it was the will of the gods. But that couldn't be right. Why would they be so cruel?

Then Kyan was taken to his family orchards and he realised that their wealth was born on the bent and broken backs of those same people in rags. That was when Kyan knew he had to run away.

He had to make a change, and he couldn't do that going into the family business of oppression.

Taking one more glance into his bedroom and the world he was leaving behind, Kyan leapt from the window and slipped out into the city he would save.

31

The Sword

12 years ago.

Kyan hadn't forgotten the face of the boy. It had been over a year since his trip to the bookshop where his father's guards beat the child, but Kyan had thought about it every night since.

He was going to find the boy and make this right.

Kyan stole off into the night. Dark hour had passed bringing the glow of the Moon Eye. Darting between the manors, Kyan ran south into the city not allowing himself the chance to look back and change his mind. Soon, the familiar stone manors with bevelled rooftops, towering pillars, and decorative rock gardens changed for simple side-by-side two story mudbrick homes.

Everything was so *close* here. Buildings leant against one another, narrow paths snaking around them. Kyan could hold his arms out and touch the buildings on either side of the street. It was a stark contrast to the vast spaces of the manors in his estate.

But then Kyan heard it: the din of the people. Jovial voices clashing with cheers and laughter. He hadn't been allowed out of the estate come dark hour, but out here was a thriving world.

Kyan stepped into a wide thoroughfare and gaped.

His parents had spoken of cloaked spectres, creatures skulking in shadow, and danger around every corner. But it couldn't be further from the truth. Children chased each other up the street, weaving through the crowd. Torches blanketed the area in warm firelight holding back the settling chill. And more light and laughter filtered out from coffeehouses.

It was so full of *life*.

Those who lived in Kyan's estate only left their homes to visit another. They would never wander the streets like this.

A smile crept onto Kyan's face as he stumbled out into the crowd. He was jostled and barged past, not understanding the flows and streams of people. The scent of cooking meat wafted from inside and shook Kyan out of his stupor. He hadn't eaten and had planned to share out what little provisions he had stolen from the kitchens before he ran off.

Ducking out of the throng and down a quieter side street, Kyan spotted a group of kids a little older than himself in the same dirty rags the boy wore all those years ago. Kyan nodded to himself and stalked towards them.

The group of four sat backs against the wall talking quietly and shooting furtive glances at any who past.

Kyan dropped to his haunches and said, "Hey, I want to help. You hungry?" He unslung his bag and cracked it open, pulling out dried meat strips and proffering them to the closest of the four.

The closest young man had stubble on his chin, ragged hair falling in a tumble over his face. He studied Kyan before turning to his friends. They nodded to him and he snatched the meat out of Kyan's hands.

"That's awfully kind of you, stranger," he said, then stuffed the meat into his mouth. His face fell slack and then pulled into a grin and he faced his friends.

"I have enough for everyone, just—"

The group rushed Kyan as he dug in to get more. One grabbed the bag and yanked it from him while another shoved Kyan to the ground. The last two swept in, one stealing the air from his lungs with a firm kick to the chest, the other cracking a foot against his face, dizzying his vision. Then they sprinted off down the street.

"Wait! I need that." Kyan's voice trailed to a whisper as he sat up clutching his head.

Those walking down the street veered around Kyan as he sat in the dirt. No one reached to help him up.

The food was better off with them anyway, he thought. That was why he brought it. Kyan just wished he had eaten some of it first.

Kyan couldn't blame those boys from stealing what little was offered. He had seen the state of the streets and those who stole or starved. *You got caught up in the bright lights and lively streets*, Kyan scolded himself. The fortunate few had a duty to help those who struggled. And their desperation showed that no one was even trying. People like his parents left the poor of Tarris to wallow and starve. It was no wonder that they had become defensive and paranoid.

The streets had emptied and now an eerie quiet settled. The scent of coffee pouring out of the coffeehouses had drifted away in the breeze, leaving behind the unwashed stink it had masked. The Moon Eye was nearing the apex of its watch but somehow the city seemed darker than it had been earlier.

Kyan pulled himself to his feet and trudged on.

Days past and Kyan realised he was a fool. On the first night the same group of boys came back and stole his robes, leaving him to wear the thin rags of those he wanted to help. He grew hungry and resorted to stealing by the second night. A line Kyan had promised himself he wouldn't cross. But he didn't know how debilitating hunger truly was. It stole the strength in one's limbs and the thoughts in one's head, leaving only *want*.

Kyan had learned quickly stealing was no easy task and was caught and beaten by guards. He had tried to explain who his father was but the guards laughed and redoubled their efforts.

Thoughts of home clouded his mind. What was he doing? Kyan was out of his depth.

Kyan trailed through the streets, stomach growling,

crowds thinning as the night grew late. He hadn't walked with a destination in mind but found himself back at the bookshop he'd visited for his birthday. Kyan stared up at the building. The shutters were snapped shut against the cool night.

He had rushed into the city hoping he could help. But what could he really do? Kyan couldn't even look after himself.

He thought he needed to see what the city was like to aid it. Like a doctor diagnosing a disease from the symptoms. Instead, all he had done was catch the disease.

A scuffle of movement caught Kyan's attention and he spun. A boy. *The* boy. His nose was crooked, face a little more gaunt but Kyan knew it was him. He had the same straggly blond hair and tired eyes.

The boy glanced at Kyan before continuing down another alleyway. Kyan chased after him.

"Wait!" Kyan called.

"My gang is around this corner!" the boy shouted.

His gang? Did he think Kyan was trying to rob him?

"No wait! I'm not trying to steal from you," Kyan shouted.

Buildings rose on either side as dark monoliths leaning into the street and blocking out the night sky. The boy spun to face him and Kyan skidded to a stop. The boy smiled. Maybe he did remember Kyan?

A foot came down on the back of Kyan's knees and he dropped. Rough hands pinned his arms behind him and someone yanked his hair back. Only then did the boy approach. Kyan was too startled to struggle. The boy's gang must have been hiding in the shadows.

"I did warn you," the boy said. He pulled a shiv out from his pocket. "Pat him down."

"No, wait, please," Kyan said. "Don't you remember me?"

Hands searched his rags but they wouldn't find anything. He had nothing left to give.

"Funny, you do look a little familiar," the boy said. He ran his thumb over the end of the blade and searched Kyan's face. "You beg round these parts?"

"No," Kyan said, shaking off the others. "Years ago I tried to give you my waistcoat outside that bookshop back there."

The boy tapped the flat of the blade on his palm. Then realisation dawned on him and he burst out laughing.

"Oh, how far the mighty fall," he said. "I'm going to enjoy this." The boy pointed the blade at Kyan.

"Wait no! I didn't know the guards would do that! I really did want to help! I *do* want to help. Please," Kyan said. "Let me join your gang. I know things."

The boy looked up at his friends who were all behind Kyan. "Like what?"

"I... I can read," Kyan said.

He burst out laughing. "What good are words to us?"

"Please, I'll do anything. Let me prove my worth."

The boy considered this. "I'll tell you what, if you can steal something for us we'll let you join."

Kyan wasn't very good at stealing, evident by the bruise on his side and lump on his head. But what choice did he have? At least being part of this gang would be a start. Kyan nodded.

The boy's name was Ter, and his gang was called the Lockless. And they wanted Kyan to steal a sword.

"No one would dare question us if we had a sword," Rek, one of the Lockless, said.

Ducked into an alcoved doorway, the Lockless and Kyan sat in a circle.

"It would be a show of true power," Ter said. The other three nodded emphatically.

If Ter's shiv was anything to go by, a sword would be threat enough to keep them safe from other gangs. "But where would I find a sword?" Kyan asked.

Ter pointed over his shoulder and Kyan leaned out the doorway. Across the street was the local garrison. Two tall buildings connected by a shorter one in-between. His father made sure Kyan knew where they were and what they looked like, so if he was ever to get lost in the city he could find help.

"I can't steal from the city guard!"

"It'll be easy. They have a ton of swords and won't even notice," Ter said.

"And what if I get caught?"

"You won't get caught. The armoury is empty at night."

"How do you know?"

Ter grinned. "Follow me."

They scuttled around the back of the garrison, keeping clear of the watch guards at the door. A wall boxed in a courtyard at the back of the garrison, topped with arrow head spikes. Ter flicked his head towards it. Kyan opened his mouth to say something but was hushed.

Two of the Lockless ran off before returning rolling a barrel the size of Kyan. Together they tipped the barrel upright against the wall. Ter hopped onto it first and peered over the wall before turning and whispering, "Clear." He then pulled himself atop the wall, careful to avoid the arrowheads and leapt over. There was a thud and Ter said, "You next, noble."

Eyeing the barrel, Kyan bit his lip. This wasn't right. They were breaking into the *city garrison* to steal a *sword*.

"The noble is as skittish as a sand fox," Rek said, and the others chuckled.

Kyan's face hardened. He couldn't make a difference if he was too afraid to even try. A failed attempt was as much a step forward as a successful one. And he refused to stand still.

Kyan ran and jumped onto the barrel. His small hands fit between the arrow heads as he pulled himself up and over the wall, dropping beside Ter.

Ter rose an eyebrow at him. He hadn't thought Kyan would follow, Kyan realised.

The garrison's training ground was marked by chalk circles for sparring, and targets for archery practice in the far corner, but it sat in dark disuse at this late hour. Garrisons preferred to train in the heat of day so they would be ready to fight in any condition.

Ter and Kyan crept towards the garrison building keeping close to the outer wall where the dark was thickest. As they approached, Kyan could hear conversation and laughter through the walls. Kyan's heart quickened. If they were caught, a beating would be the best outcome. Kyan swallowed and sped after Ter.

Ter stopped beside a narrow opening at the bottom of the wall. "What is it?" Kyan asked.

"Look and see."

It was common to have these narrow windows to bring daylight into basements and lower levels. Kyan ducked and peered inside. Within, the garrison's armoury lay in darkness. Racks of swords and spears leaned against walls adorned with shields, and open crates held piles of arrows. Arrowheads and dulled swords lay atop a work bench. Kyan had always thought rooms like these would be neat and awe inspiring, but this looked like a messy storeroom, weapons, crates and barrels scattered throughout.

"See," Ter whispered. "Empty. Just squeeze through and grab a sword, then you can join us."

It seemed easy enough. But why hadn't Ter or one of the others already stolen a sword if it was that easy? Were they just afraid of getting caught?

If Kyan was caught, he could explain who he was and hopefully they wouldn't throw him in a cell. His bruises pulsed with how well that had worked the last time.

A step forward, Kyan told himself and sent his legs out easing them into the armoury.

Thud. Landing on the hardpacked dirt sounded unbelievably loud in the quiet. Kyan stood ears perked but no movement came from above. He edged into the armoury, searching the dark. His breath came out rattled and shrill.

Kyan was sure the guards would rush in at any moment having heard the battering of his heart.

Reaching the work bench, Kyan glanced at the sword. It was duller than the racked ones on the far wall, but wasn't that a good thing? He didn't want the Lockless to kill anyone with it, just dissuade others from attacking them. So he carefully, one hand under the blade, the other under the pommel, lifted the sword. There was no clang of metal or swish of steel.

Kyan smiled. He did it.

Suddenly, something wrapped around Kyan's ankle and pulled his leg from under him. He squealed as he fell and the sword slid from his grip, clattering to the floor. Kyan tried to crawl towards the window but something pressed into his back.

A screech tore through the quiet with a rippling call. Of course a garrison would have a screecher or two. The long-limbed monkey-like creatures were often employed by the rich to protect goods from being stolen. They had dark brown fur and could be trained to pin intruders and call out with their signature cry that gave them their name.

"Ter! Quick! Get this thing off!" Kyan shouted. Screechers weren't fighters and if they made a run for it without the sword it wouldn't follow.

A sneer and look of pure repulsion stained Ter's face.

"You want to help, noble? Then die with the rest of your kind." Ter spat into the basement before turning and disappearing into the night.

All the fight drained from Kyan's body and he went limp.

350

Ter knew about the screecher. That's why they hadn't stolen a sword. Guards barged into the room and the screecher slid off Kyan, replaced by firm hands that hauled him to his feet.

Kyan only half paid attention to their threats and punches. He had only wanted to help. He wanted to make things right.

Light illuminated the garrison proper, momentarily blinding him. As his eyes adjusted, Kyan found himself in a small chamber where three guards sat around a table playing cards.

Kyan was tossed to the ground.

"A little thief in the armoury," the guard behind him said.

The commander, evident by the patch on his shoulder, slapped his cards down and stepped over, picking his teeth. "The armoury, eh?" He bent down to stare Kyan in the eye. "You want to see what a sword can really do? Hear the cries of pain you can pull from a man with one?"

"Commander, maybe we should hear what he was doing down there first," said one of the other men at the table.

The commander scoffed. "You're lucky he's here or I would show you what a blade can really do," the commander whispered, quiet enough that only Kyan could hear. "You're right of course, Akarai," the commander said. *A six letter name?* "Take him to a cell."

The guards behind Kyan dragged him to his feet again and pulled him from the room. But not before Kyan caught a glimpse of the man who had saved him. Dark eyes met his. Who was this Akarai?

32

A Gathering Storm

Warm winds rustled the tarp, extenuated by the tromping footsteps of the aya. Rai shook out the map he took from Kyan's room. He ran his finger over the coarse parchment and folds in the page, but all he could see was the look on Illy's face when he left the night before: a mix of anger, fear, and confusion. He hadn't had time to explain everything to her, just that they had to go, and tonight. Wenson was recovering well and should be up on his feet in no time. But still, that hurt look was burned into his mind. He should have been used to it by now.

Rai sighed, lifting his head from the map he had been staring at all morning. The aya trotted over the sands at a steady pace, but it had taken some prompting. He had never met an aya this lazy before.

Kyan and his Decreed were ahead, hidden somewhere amongst the heat haze and cresting dunes. He had been tracking them from afar, staying out of the horizon line but close enough to follow their tracks before the breeze smothered them.

I see upon the sands, something the colour of... tan, Fax said.

"Fax, we are in the desert," Rai said.

Just guess! Fax said.

Rai let out a breath and said, "Sand?"

Nope, Fax said.

Rai scrunched his brow, looking around. "What else is there?"

There was rock back there, Fax said.

"And how would I know that now that we've passed it?" Rai snapped.

You should have been paying better attention, Fax said.

Rai went back to reading the map. It didn't make any sense. It was a map of Tarris, with dotted lines marking a route that wrapped around the country in a wide arc, passing a lot of the major cities, and even going through the lower part of the lost capital, Asuriya. But what was the purpose? Why did Kyan note this route?

He trailed his finger up from Yontar to where it intersected with the sketched line. *Is there something along the route or is Kyan going to follow it around the country?* Rai wondered. And how did this all tie into bringing justice down on the nobles and royals of Tarris?

I guess we'll find out, Fax said.

353

"Five days until we reach the line marked on the map," Rai said, gazing up at the horizon again.

Does that include taking cover from the storm? Fax asked.

"Storm? What…" his voice trailed off as he focused on the winds whipping around them.

Rai had known that they had been picking up since the Sun rose, but he had been too preoccupied with Illy and the map.

Kyan must have had about a hundred and fifty following him, Rai thought. *How is he going to protect that many from a sandstorm?*

It was slow moving and it could be several days before the sandstorm reached them, but there was no way around it, and few places to shelter from it. His thoughts fell to Nya and Kit.

Had he sent them to their deaths?

33

A Blend of Truth and Embellishment

The late morning heat was oppressive but being out in the desert let the warm summer winds have free rein, and Nya was grateful for it. Others had risen on their aya and now sat around chatting quietly and eating breakfast. The man with one boot, however, was far from quiet. He laughed deep and loud, slapping people around the shoulder like they were best of friends, despite them looking at him like he was insane. Perhaps he was.

The thud and scrape of hooves galloping through sand caught Nya's attention. One of the Decreed rode a hyian back to their aya, towing another two for her and Kit. Nya had never ridden a hyian before, but it was the only way to get further up the line without stopping the entire procession.

She had always thought aya looked majestic with their

scale and power. Hyian, however, were strange looking creatures. Short grey hair and similar shape to horses, but they didn't have a mane. It made them look shaven, like they were missing something. And their beady black eyes always stared blankly, like they hadn't held a thought in their lives.

They didn't smell great either.

The Decreed lined the hyian up at the bottom of the ladder and called for them. Nya peered over the edge at the rider who kept pace with their aya.

"Go on then," one of the Decreed at the front called.

With a gulp, Nya swung her foot over the platform edge of the marching aya and climbed down. Reaching her foot out tentatively, Nya felt the soft touch of flesh and fur.

"It can take the weight of fully grown men with no issue. Don't fear jumping onto it," the rider holding the hyian in place said.

So with a deep breath, Nya let go of the ladder and landed on the hyian. She swayed, but its flat back was easy enough to keep balance on. However, before momentum stole this victory, she sat down in the saddle.

The rider pulled her hyian out of the way and the third one took its place. Kit hopped onto his hyian with only a little wavering, before dropping into the saddle. And soon they were being led up the side of the procession.

Sweat budded across Nya's forehead now that they were out of the shade of the platform. She lifted her head, feeling the wind brush over her, but in the Sun, it did little to fight off the heat. Kit looked up the line at what was to come, a serious expression of hard lines etched onto his face. Nya was trying not to think about meeting Kyan but seeing Kit prepare for the meeting made her stomach flutter.

This man is a killer, Nya reminded herself. She needed to be careful with what she said. And somehow, get on his good side.

After some time, their line of travellers came to an end. Ahead of which, two scouts rode yarens. They sat in shell-like casings that were pulled by reins connected to the yarens, which dove in and out of the sand like riverfish careening upstream. Both arcing out wide in either direction, surveying the oncoming landscape.

The rider who held the reins of their hyian led them up to an aya and gestured for Nya to climb off and onto the ladder. Doing so, she felt her heart batter in her chest again. What was Kyan going to do now that he knew she had a shade too? It was possible he led her here just to kill her. She had powers like him and could be seen as a threat.

No, no, it's more likely he wants me at his side, Nya thought, unsure if she believed it or if she just wanted to convince herself it was so.

Clambering atop the platform shielded her from the Sun Eye, and she let out a breath, thankful to be out of its burning gaze. The platform was the same as any other, but with fewer people. Three people sat cross-legged around a pot at the front of the aya. Crates stacked on either side of the platform acted like walls, so even in the early mornings or late afternoons, they would be sheltered from the Sun. Nya waited nervously for Kit to join her before stepping up to the group. They exchanged a look of determination but spoke no words.

The smell of coffee came calling as they walked up to the indistinct murmur of conversation. At the far side of the coffeepot sat Kyan. He wore a dark blue sleeveless robe. It wasn't fancy but had the look of expensive fabric to it. The jackal mask was nowhere to be seen. "Ah, you must be the new two," Kyan said. "Come, sit."

The two others; a woman looking to be in her late twenties with braided black hair and a dark red robe, and a man the same age with dusty blond hair wearing a tan tunic and white breeches, slid around towards Kyan making space for Nya and Kit. With the deliberate slowness of one who walked into a predator's den, Nya and Kit sat as far from them as was acceptable.

"I'm glad you've joined us," Kyan said. "My name is Kyan. This is Pyna," he said, gesturing to the woman, "and Jip."

Kyan waited expectantly. He had been honest about his name, which surprised Nya. But Kit and Nya were no threat to him, especially out here in the desert, so he didn't need to lie. He wore a pleasant expression and had kind, soft eyes. A stark contrast to the fire and darkness that burned in them during his speech at the market.

"My name is Nya, and this is Kit," Nya said, clearing her throat of dryness.

"Where are my manners? Would you like some spiced coffee? It's my own recipe," Kyan asked. The other two had yet to look at them, instead staring forward at the coffeepot.

"No tha—" Kit started.

"Yes please," Nya said.

Kyan bowed his head before leaning over and pouring out a mug. Kit tilted his head at Nya, who kept her eyes forward.

"I've heard you are like me, Nya," Kyan said, handing her a mug. Nya shifted uncomfortably.

"It's okay, you can tell me the truth. It may seem like a curse, but I can show you how it can be a tool," Kyan said.

"I hear a voice in my head sometimes, and I can manipulate shadows," Nya said. Best not to share too much. "Are they okay?" Nya asked, nodding towards Pyna and Jip who were distractingly unmoving like breathing statues.

"They're fine. They just took some furthing leaves," Kyan said. "Pyna, Jip, why don't you go see how the others are doing?"

Pyna nodded, smiling, and both got up and walked off. Nya had seen many blood addicts on the streets who often looked completely unaware, eyes rolling, but Pyna and Jip could function, and were aware of their surroundings. Nya even watched as they climbed down a ladder onto a hyian. She didn't know much about furthing leaves, other than they were smoked and could have a euphoric calming effect. Some doctors were said to use them too.

"Sorry about that. It can get dull traveling for so long, furthing leaves and some discussion around a coffee pot helps the sands pass," Kyan said.

Realising she hadn't tried the spiced coffee, Nya put it to

her lips and drew in a sip. She had to get Kyan to trust her and building trust was a two-way street. If Nya was open and acted like she trusted him, hopefully he would do the same. Nya hissed, jerking back.

"Be careful, it's hot," Kyan said with a chuckle.

Nya had only tried coffee a couple times and thought it was pleasant enough, but not something she would seek out. However, this coffee was delicious. It was spiced perfectly, leaving a smooth and not too bitter taste.

"It's good," Nya said, somewhat surprised herself.

"I'm glad you like it," Kyan said. "Are you sure I can't offer you a cup, Kit?"

"No, thanks. I don't drink coffee," he said. It was a lie, but he was probably right in his caution. She trusted him to keep an eye on her if there was anything else in the coffee.

"So, how did you get your shade?" Kyan asked.

Nya and Kit recounted their carefully curated tale of how they were arrested together and sent to that dark place. Then of their return, and how they were set free, whereupon Nya started hearing voices, and how shadows acted strangely around her.

"That's when we heard about you and hoped you could help. We saw your rally at the market and resonated with a lot of what you said," Nya said.

"We have lived on the streets all our life and have never had help from Yontar's monarchy or any of the Tarrisian royalty," Kit added.

The tale, much like the coffee, was a blend of truth and

embellishment. Kit had come up with the story claiming the best lies were rooted in truth, and with his experience in convincing high-end merchants and deadly gangs to work together, it was an effective one. Kyan listened intently, his face revealing nothing of what he thought.

Once they had finished, Kyan regarded them for a lengthy pause that held no comfort. "Then you can see how important my mission is," Kyan finally said. "The palace used you as distractions. You were nothing more than expendable shields."

"That's why we knew we had to do what we can to help you," Kit said. He believed them. Nya felt an unfurling of tension in her gut.

"And when did Rai come into this?" Kyan asked.

They fell silent. Nya's stomach dropped like the ground beneath her had fallen away.

"Who?" Kit asked.

An all-knowing grin spread across Kyan's face. "You didn't think I would realise? I knew as soon as I heard that two others were trying to join just as we were leaving," Kyan said.

Nya noticed Kit's white-knuckled hand reaching for the mug that was sitting between them. She sent out a poke into the dark corners of her mind and Bom stirred. She wasn't sure if it would listen but it was at least aware.

"Let me guess. He said my shade is poisoning my mind, and that I was putting good people in danger," Kyan continued. "But his shade is miraculously not affecting him?

There are no studies done on shades. Yet." He leant forward and lowered his voice, as if he were afraid they would be overheard, despite no one else being on the platform. "But I can tell you, they don't change who you are."

Nya shivered. *They don't change who you are.* That couldn't be true. She wouldn't have hurt Mother. That was the presence. That was Bom, who had done that. Not her.

"You know, he used to be my mentor. Rai, I mean," Kyan said. "Did he tell you to spy on me and learn what I have planned?"

Nya and Kit remained unmoving, calculating what to do next. Getaway plans filled Nya's mind, but none of them had much chance of success.

"I don't know why he went through with all this bother. It's exactly what I have preached for the last month," Kyan said. "I want to tear out those who stroll through life upon the backs of others. Does that make me a bad person?"

"What about the guards?" Nya asked. Kyan looked questioningly at her. "The guards at your rally. The ones you killed."

"Those guards were going to kill me and whoever followed me. I broke no law in preaching, but I have Decreed inside the palace and those guards had been told to *kill*," Kyan put extra emphasis on that last word. "They were told to send a message by beating people in the crowd, too. It could have been you two they beat senseless. Do they sound like good people?"

"Are you going to kill us for being bad people?" Kit asked.

Kyan regarded him with a sympathetic sigh. "You're not bad people though, are you? You have tried your best just to be beaten down over and over again. You have done what was required to survive. I do not think that makes you bad. I think that darkness reflects on those who left you in that situation, don't you?"

He was right. It was like he was saying back what Nya had been thinking for weeks now. All she had ever done was her best. It wasn't her fault. It was those who put her in that dark place to get infected that had killed her mother. Those who didn't even know her name but tossed them into a dark realm to die.

"I am not who Rai has told you I am," Kyan said. "If you wish, you can have two hyian, and you can return to Yontar. We will even give you spare supplies if you need them. But you're also welcome to stay and be a part of something greater. Something that will punish those who have wronged you and many others."

He took Nya's hands. "And I can teach you what shades can truly do," he said in a whisper. Suddenly Kyan *split*. Another darker version appearing beside him, pulsating, and then in the blink of an eye, it was gone again.

"You don't need to decide now," he said, sitting back again. "A storm is coming and we will pass the nearest Waypoint soon. Shelter with us and you can decide where the sands will take you when it settles."

The same rider took Nya and Kit back to their aya. They

stayed quiet, roaming their thoughts. It wasn't until the rider had taken away the hyians and Nya and Kit had slid backs against the aya's platform that they began to talk.

"I think we should take his offer," Kit said, staring onward at the others who sat in a circle playing some sort of game. The man with the one boot was winning. And... was Dust being spun around in his boot? She looked like she was having fun.

"I agree. We should see what he has planned," Nya said.

"No, not that. I meant we should take the hyian after the storm passes and ride back to Rai, tell him what we know, and say Kyan caught us, then we can get back to Yontar and out of this mess," Kit said.

"You didn't trust Rai and now you've change your mind?" asked Nya.

"I don't trust either of them!" Kit said.

"Kyan could have thrown us to the desert after finding out about Rai," Nya said.

"He could still," Kit said.

"Aren't you sick of being kicked into the dirt by that city and everyone in it? Do you really want to go back to that?" Nya asked.

Kit ran a hand through his hair. "Of course I am, Nya. But I don't see how a man who has an angry shadow is going to help that."

"Let's find out. We don't need to trust him. Let's just see where this takes us," Nya said.

Kit ran his tongue over the back of his teeth, holding Nya's gaze. "Okay, but if things go badly, we grab a hyian and make a run for Rai."

Nya nodded and reached for her bag, her appetite having returned. Kit kicked his feet out and lay back in the shelter of the tarp, the wind playing with his hair. Dust trailed over and nuzzled Nya's side.

This was the right choice. They had to at least see what Kyan had planned before disagreeing with it. Nya blew out a breath and ran a hand through Dust's fur.

All the while, the storm grew ever closer.

34

Unremembered Memories

The storm rode at Rai's back for the following four days. It took shape as a blustering wall on the horizon that kept growing. Dust plumes extended out towards him like reaching fingers. It rose into the sky blocking out the Sun Eye and consumed all it passed. To fall into that would mean a death Rai wouldn't wish upon his worst enemies. He had seen how it ripped skin from bone, and devoured flesh until there was little left to mourn.

It will be over Yontar by now, Rai thought, whipping the reins, although the aya seemed to have felt the sandstorm, and was racing onward.

There was a nearby Waypoint that they could make it to if they were quick. But the next Waypoint after that was about a day's march north, and Kyan was only half a day ahead. The sandstorm was sure to catch them in the open.

Maybe he has one of those shelters you can build into the sand? Fax offered.

"Those are huge mud brick planes, and I didn't see them packing anything like that at the northern gate," Rai said.

Yeah, but I don't trust your eyesight. You didn't think that rock a couple hours ago looked like a smiling face when it did, Fax said.

No, he was certain they didn't have the portable shelters. They were rare and expensive and, although Rai was sure Kyan had the funds and connections to get them, he knew Kyan wouldn't have picked them. They were bulky and heavy, and would impede their pace, not to mention risky even when set up correctly. Rai knew of entire squads of soldiers who died when their portable shelters had failed them. Kyan wouldn't take that risk.

At least we won't lose distance on them, Rai thought, holding the map tight in the winds. *They will have to take shelter somewhere. Perhaps he scouted a cave.* It would have to be a vast cave to fit them all in, but it wasn't impossible given the rocky escarpments in this part of the desert.

The air was fresh and almost sweet as he breathed in through his cowl.

Rai lifted his cowl to cover his mouth, and shield himself against the worst of the sand. Nevertheless, the sand stung as it cut into his hands and scraped up his forearms.

Although the aya's fur would give it some protection, Rai wished they had sped up earlier, and had been at the Waypoint by now for the aya's sake. But it was a balancing game of not being seen by Kyan and his Decreed. Kyan no doubt knew Rai would follow him but it was better to stay hidden and decide his next move.

They were at the edges of the storm when they came to the Waypoint. Sand whirled around them in a cutting cloud. It was as if the winds were made of sand themselves. Rai had covered himself as best he could, but still, a new set of cuts marked his arms and face, where the sand had snuck under his cowl. And they had almost wandered past the Waypoint with the lack of visibility, but Fax had spotted it and led them over.

Rai dropped from the aya, ignoring the ladder, and trudged over to the Waypoint, unlatching the barn doors and throwing them open. He didn't need to prompt the aya who tumbled through.

Of course, now you listen, Rai thought, shaking his head at the aya and shutting the doors behind it.

He had to shove the door closed and slam down the latch after entering. As it clicked shut, the noise quietened and Rai could hear his heavy breathing.

The dust coated Waypoint was one of the larger Rai had been in. It was high-roofed to connect to the stable section that could hold up to four aya. A fire pit sat in the far-right corner, cushions laid out around it and closed slits in the roof above that could open to let the smoke escape. Rai ran a hand over one cot lining the right wall, and it came back covered in dust and dirt.

I think the stables looked cleaner, Fax said, sitting as a crow in the rafters.

"There is little reason to come this way through the desert anymore," Rai said, opening a cupboard, params scattered to reveal no rations. "There is nothing out here apart from the lost capital to the north. No villages either."

Do you think that's where Kyan is headed? The lost capital? Fax asked.

"I don't know. The route he drew on the map fell just south of it," Rai said. Rai stepped into the stable where his aya stood yawning. He ran a hand through his fur as he passed and climbed up onto the platform to get his supplies. Rai dished out some meat into the trough for the aya and slipped some cheese and bread into his pocket before making his way back to the main room.

He sat around the unlit fire pit and ate, staring into the hollow. It wasn't cold enough to need a fire, and he certainly wasn't going to open the air slits with the storm raging outside. Rai listened as the sandstorm buffeted the Waypoint. It was a particularly bad one from the sound of it.

It will have caught up with Nya and Kit by now, Fax said. Rai didn't respond. Kyan didn't make oversights. He must have created a plan in case of a sandstorm. Rai was sure he would, but it didn't stop the little voice that said he sent Nya and Kit to their deaths.

What was he like? Before I mean, Fax said.

"Who?" Rai asked, shaking out of his stupor.

Kyan, Fax said.

Rai slipped another piece of cheese into his mouth,

thinking of times best left unremembered.

Akarai walked out into the Sun Eye's gaze. The heat bore down on the training grounds where Neyla and Tysar sparred. White lines marked the dusty square that sat surrounded by squat palace walls on three sides. The fourth, an arch, lead to the palace gardens, signalled by the fresh scent the wind carried from that direction.

Blows passed between them as they fought for footing. Sweat dripped from both of them as they grunted and clicked their wooden training spears together.

Neyla stepped forward, scraping the spear off the ground, and flicking it up in a spray of sand and dust. Closing his eyes and swiping in front of his face, Tysar tried to clear his sight but it was too late. With another firm sweep of the spear, Neyla knocked Tysar from his feet.

Akarai was grinning as he walked onto the training ground. Neyla held out a hand, which Tysar ignored and clambered to his feet, coughing and rubbing his back.

"You should have backed up. Best to create space when you lose visual," Akarai said.

"Or just don't give me the chance to do it in the first place," Neyla said, raising an eyebrow at Tysar.

"Easy to say when you're standing in the shade watching," Tysar mumbled.

Neyla was bronze skinned, lean muscled, with keen brown eyes that demanded attention. Tysar smirked at her and pulled her into a kiss. He had a similar lean build but was a head taller than Neyla, his long brown hair falling to his shoulders in wavy curls.

Shaking his head, Akarai looked across the courtyard.

"What?" Tysar said, laughing. "The true battle is of the heart, Akarai."

"If you practiced with a spear as much as you did your *'battle of the heart'* you wouldn't be knocked into the sands," Akarai said, and Neyla hit his arm. "Isn't Kyan meant to be training with you?"

"Yeah, he was," Neyla said.

"He'll be buried in his books and scrolls," Tysar said with a scoff.

"His spear work was coming along though," Neyla said. "He will knock Tysar down in no time. Not that it takes much to get to that point."

"Put a sword in my hand and I'll cut through both of you working together," Tysar said. "I will never understand why anyone would pick these tiny, bladed sticks over a good sword." Tysar's face screwed up as he hefted the practice spear.

"I'll go find him," Akarai said, and strode towards the door he exited from. He should have known Kyan would sneak off, but he couldn't keep babysitting the boy.

As he entered the Atef Palace, Akarai heard Neyla and Tysar arguing, until there was a scuffle and they were fighting again. *At least if they are fighting they're training*, Akarai thought with amusement.

The hallways of the palace were always a source of awe for

Akarai. They were made from dark sandstone, and through the stone golden veins branched and snaked like roots in the rock. The origin of the gold veins was lost to time, with scholars unable to figure out what they were. Had they had woven it into the rock as a design? Was it a type of rock with gold veins naturally occurring? If so, why hadn't they found more like it?

Akarai liked to run his hands over it when he was walking alone. He could swear the gold had a coolness to it that the rock didn't.

Servants swerved around him, bowing as they passed. They wore dark red robes with ornate golden web patterns in reference to the walls of the palace around them. It had become a synonymous symbol of the Tarrisian capital, Tansen.

Akarai made his way through the lengthy corridors and up two flights of stairs to the reading room that overlooked the palace gardens. Sunlight streaked into the room from the grand windows, and dust motes floated carelessly in the glare. Shelves covered the walls.

More shelving stuck out perpendicular from the walls, covered in scrolls and books as old as the palace they sat in. It wasn't as grand a selection as the Tansen Archives, however, it contained some rare pieces, many with untraceable origins. The palace often received scholars wishing to delve into the collection.

Kyan sat at one of the long narrow desks, shoulders slumped and engrossed in pages of old. Short golden hair glinted in the light, as his boyish frame didn't move. He was the only one in the reading room and hadn't made any move, but Akarai was certain he knew he was there.

"You know, if a man charges at you with a mace, parchment will not deflect it," Akarai said, standing behind him.

Kyan didn't turn, but his muffled voice came from behind the arm he leant on and said, "What good is knowing how to stab if you don't know who your enemy is?"

"Your enemy will be Overseer Ulial if you keep missing training," Akarai said.

"But I think I'm onto something here, look," Kyan spun, holding out a piece of parchment. It was weathered, frayed around the edges, and discoloured with age. Written across it was the Old Tongue, a script Akarai knew, but few others did.

Ma-Eiko has woken. I didn't think in my cycles I would see one of The First. No one in living memory has seen them. They have become a legend in the eyes of most. But I have seen…

It cut off with only half a character coming to a tear in the parchment. Akarai placed the parchment back on the desk among the books and scrolls stacked in front of Kyan. He had notes written in a scrawl that spoke of many hours of reading and thinking.

"Ma-Eiko the guardian of The Rock Pass. People still lay out offerings for it in smaller villages before undertaking long journeys," Akarai said.

"Yes, but this is a first-hand account of someone seeing the creature. People think of it as a deity, something ethereal.

An icon. But what if it existed? What if it really did protect people?" Kyan said, words pouring from his mouth faster and faster. He often got like that when discussing something that interested him.

"It's likely there was once something that sparked the stories," Akarai said.

"Read this part again," Kyan said, running his hand over a certain passage. *No one in living memory has seen them. They have become a legend in the eyes of most.*

"What if they still exist? We know of a few creatures that live for hundreds of years, and what do they all have in common? They have to sleep for a long time. Sometimes tens of years. But this, a creature said to be hundreds of thousands of years old... It wouldn't be a stretch to say they would need to sleep for hundreds or thousands of years," Kyan said.

"It's possible I guess but—"

"I've been tracking different deities and first-hand accounts of them, and with each one there are enormous gaps where there are no sightings," Kyan said, spreading his notes out to reveal sketched timelines and webs of notes.

"Kyan, this is interesting, but look, you have very few first-hand accounts and even then, the validity of these scraps should be questioned," Akarai said.

"Yeah, I know," Kyan said, a defensive tone leaking into his voice. "It's just a theory at the moment."

"It's an interesting study," Akarai said, trying not to put the boy down. "But you can't shirk your duties to study. You are part of the Seventh Sceptre now, and that means you need to be the best. One only becomes the best with *regular* training."

Kyan grumbled something under his breath.

"What was that?" Akarai asked.

"Yes, okay. I will train with Tysar and Neyla this afternoon," Kyan said.

"Good," Akarai said, rustling the boy's hair. He shook him off and shot him a scowl. "They could do with someone to keep them from killing each other."

Kyan grimaced as he piled the books in front of him.

Rai bit into a piece of cheese. "He was just a boy with big ideas and the means to make them true," he said, after finishing.

The sandstorm rumbled and shook the Waypoint.

35

A Sombre Song

The storm chased them across the dunes. It hounded their backs like a pack of rabid kirens. They rode harder and faster, but Kit was convinced they were doomed.

I'm usually such an optimist too, he thought, peering over the back of the aya's platform.

The party had broken from their line into a mass of charging aya, kicking up sand that fed the oncoming storm. Kyan had reassured them that they would make it to shelter long before the storm reached them. But that's exactly what Kit would tell a group stupid enough to follow him into a sandstorm.

"Don't look so glum, lad," said a voice from behind. "I heard dying in a sandstorm is a good way to go."

Kit pivoted around and stared at the man. He had the

unhinged look that Kit had become incredibly good at spotting. Although it wasn't difficult to tell he was a little mad with the unkempt curly beard and greying black hair, not to mention the fact he only had one boot.

"I'm not sure being slowly cut apart and having your skin ripped from your bones by sand is a *good way to go*," Kit said.

The man scrunched his brow. "You know, you're right. I never thought about it. See what happens when you just take someone's word for it." He shook his head. "The names Lem."

Kit was tempted to give him a false name, but he would just overhear Nya calling him Kit. The aya platform wasn't big enough to remain anonymous, and who knew how long they would be riding together.

"Kit," he said with a slight bow, Lem mimicking the gesture. "Why do you have only one boot?"

"I don't have—" Lem looked down then burst out laughing. "How does he do that?! Sleeping Siv," Lem said with a shrug, like that answered the question.

Shouting broke out from ahead. They spun to see others on the platform standing and pointing. Jogging over, Kit saw what they were looking at. Ahead was a rock formation, and at its base was a cave.

They trotted the last of the distance and wandered into the cavern not stopping at the entrance but continuing to wade through the dark. The aya slowed, unsure of the terrain but soon the Decreed were lighting torches; incandescent light revealing the far rock walls of the cavern. It was more spacious than the mouth of the cave implied and continued deeper still.

They were safe from the sandstorm in here. Deep enough that only a dull wind and trickling of sand could reach them. However, the cave was all too reminiscent of Kit's nightmares of the dark place. Kit's heart raced as his eyes searched the shadows for movement. He couldn't help but imagine that mass of limbs reaching out and grabbing for him.

"Hey, it's okay," Nya said, laying a hand on his arm.

"Yeah, I know," Kit said, trying to sound nonchalant, but he knew he wasn't fooling anyone.

Eventually, they were called to a stop. Kit relaxed when more torches were lit and set up around the area where they would set up camp. There was shouting and shuffling as men and woman darted around, setting up tents and fire pits.

Climbing down from the aya, Kit, Nya, and Dust dodged around Decreed carrying tent poles and supply crates. Everyone seemed to know what they were doing and was going about their tasks with swift efficiency.

Kyan appeared from the mass of people, smiling and holding his arms wide, Jip trailing behind him. "We will be spending some time here, so get comfortable," he said. "I took the liberty of having a tent set up for you both over there." He pointed to one near the rock wall, facing onto a fire pit being set up.

He's trying to gain our trust, Kit thought.

"Thank you," Nya said with a bow, and reluctantly Kit did the same, although maybe not as deep as would be customary.

"Of course. There will be a food and drink soon, and I would like to talk to you both after you've eaten," Kyan said, then with a bow he sped off talking with Jip.

Kit watched as he walked away, no longer hiding his scowl. Then, realising Nya was walking towards their tent, he jogged to catch up.

In a hushed tone, Kit whispered, "He's trying to use you. Trying to build trust. I do the same thing when I work with gangs in Yontar."

"Or he's just being nice. I know it's hard to believe, but I have heard there are people like him. And anyway, we're trapped in a cave by a storm and surrounded by his people. He doesn't need to be nice to us," Nya said.

Kit glared at her. How can she trust this guy so easily? "Unless he wants something from you," Kit said.

Nya stopped and regarded him. "Have you seen what he can do? I can make my shadow flicker. I don't think he needs me for anything," Nya said, then marched off.

Tossing open the tent flap, Nya disappeared inside. Kit breathed out, then noted the others around them. None *seemed* to be watching them. Lem smiled and waved. He had a tent with two others just across the fire pit from them. *Great.* With a tap of his feet, Kit ducked into his tent.

Fires rose around camp, carrying the aroma of spiced stews. Chatter buzzed and songs were sung around the curling flames. Around their fire sat Nya, Kit, Dust, Lem, and four others who had been on their aya. One of the Decreed had come over and was stirring a pot held above the fire.

After being in the burning Sun all day, the cave felt damp and cold, so the fires were welcome as they all huddled around waiting for the food.

The Decreed poured the stew into ceramic bowls and handed them out. Kit took it with a bow of the head and was slurping it down by the time Nya got hers. The stew was okay, maybe a little bland, but it was hot. It had been hours since they had eaten, so the contents of the bowl vanished before Kit would have liked it to.

Nya had barely touched hers, only taking small spoonsful. She was a slow eater, but Kit didn't mind. Remembering how he found her in that attic, and how long it took for him to get her to eat anything, he was just happy she was eating something.

Lem had finished his too and was now humming a jaunty tune and stamping his foot on the other side of the fire. It wasn't a song Kit recognised, but Lem had talent for melody and rhythm that was rare among the hardened people Kit found himself around. He had underestimated the strange old man. It was a haunting melody that rose and fell telling a dramatic tale with no lyrics.

Nya nudged him. "You ready?"

"Huh?" Kit said, turning. She had finished her stew and was flicking her head in gesture to go. He had been so wrapped up in Lem's song that he hadn't realised she had finished.

"Yeah, okay," Kit said, standing.

Together they passed through camp where men and woman sat around fires eating, drinking, talking, and singing. It was almost nice. It wasn't the cult activities Kit thought he was going to find. No sacrificing, preaching, or bloodletting of any kind. Not even a single creepy chant. Just the discordant singing that reminded Kit of some gangs in Yontar who sang to their victims as they tortured them. But the only ones being tortured here were the people sitting around the fire having to listen.

Kyan sat at the furthest point they had delved into the cave with a handful of others, including Pyna and Jip.

"Ah, Nya, Kit, come sit. You already know Pyna and Jip. These two…" Kyan said and introduced the other two, but Kit wasn't listening. Instead he watched the shadows at Kyan's feet for movement.

"And this is Bis," Kyan said, gesturing to a man whose face was a mess of scars. His jaw sat crooked and nose squashed. "He was in the fighting pits of Rizu until he heard of our mission and came to Yontar."

Bis grunted.

Delightful company, Kit thought.

"Anyway, sit, sit," Kyan said.

They sat on one of the long benches surrounding the fire pit, Kit keeping his awareness on the shadows around them. At any point Kyan could kill them. Kit hated how helpless he was.

"Have you thought on if you will stay?" Kyan asked. The others all turned to regard them.

"We are still undecided," Nya said.

"I see," Kyan said, lacing his fingers. Firelight flickered over his face, casting him in deep oranges and blacks. "Come morning, I will take a selected few onward. The rest of camp will stay here until we get back or perhaps come and meet us depending on what we find. We shouldn't be too long, but I'd like to invite you both to come with us." Kyan held his hands out, gesturing to those around the fire.

"To where?" Kit asked.

"To knowledge," Kyan said. Kit hated people who spoke like that and would have spat at him if he wasn't such a scary guy. "There is a... relic deeper in this cave that I need to visit. I can't tell you more about it unless you choose to come with us. I hope you understand."

"Why us?" Kit asked, crossing his arms.

"I see potential in you both. You both understand what it's like to starve while others feast. And with your abilities Nya, you could join me and our mission of bringing justice to those think themselves untouchable," Kyan said.

I knew it, Kit thought. "You just want to use Nya!" Kit shouted.

"No, I'm giving you a choice. Like I said, you can leave as soon as the storm passes and I won't stop you. Run back to Rai and tell him I figured you out. He won't harm you and will probably let you be on your way when he realises you aren't useful anymore," Kyan said with a shrug. "But I think you want to help. I think you know that corruption runs rampant, guards abuse their power, rich are made richer while the poor starve, and I'm offering you a way to help stamp it out."

This was the sort of cult talk Kit had expected. The kind that sounded too good to be true. He looked over at Nya but her face was inscrutable.

"I'll do it," Nya said.

"Nya!"

"Look, Kit. We aren't doing this again. You keep criticizing my decisions, but you don't need to come! Either come with me or don't, but stop telling me what to do. I can make my own choices," she said.

The others around the campfire whispered amongst themselves, some disappearing to refill mugs.

Kit was stunned. "Why can't we just go back to the inn? Back to training and eating and laughing with that idiot Wenson and Illy?" Kit whispered. Those had been days when he felt he belonged. That short couple of weeks or so. They were *right*. Not perfect, no days are. But right.

"I can't Kit," she said. She didn't look angry or frustrated with him, but instead, she looked sad. "Kyan is right. I can't sit aside and let more people go through what we did. Living on the streets, being tossed into that dark place, the consequences that came because of that." She clenched her fists. "It was their fault. It was that captain that sent me through the Blind Walk, and the one that sent us into the dark place. They were the ones that killed Mother, and it's time we taught them that they can't just get away with it."

Kit was aware that Kyan was watching them, so he lowered his voice and said, "I can't follow you, Nya. This isn't right.

Blood will be spilled and it'll stain you. Killing always stains. Come back with me."

Tears were welling in Nya's eyes. "I'm already stained, Kit. You don't have to be, too."

Kit shuffled closer. "You can't actually trust him, do you?"

Nya brought her voice to a whisper. "No. But I need to know if this is will fix it."

"Fix what?"

"I don't know. Whatever is wrong with me. Whatever keeps me from being happy. Since Mother died… No, even before that, I've felt hollow. Empty. I should have been happy staying in that inn with you and Illy and Wenson but I wasn't. I'm not. Maybe fighting against those that took Mother from me is what I need to do."

"This isn't the answer, Nya."

"It's the closest I've come to one."

"You're welcome to stay in camp," Kyan said from through the flames. "We shouldn't be too long. You can wait here until we finish what I set out to do."

Kit stared into Nya's eyes, where firelight danced and darkness hid. She was as unmoving as the black sands. Did she really think he was trying to tell her what to do? He just wanted to help. He had tried, every step of the way, to dissuade her from this madness, but she still didn't see it. Perhaps she never would.

Kit stood. He had been through enough negotiations to know when he was beaten. After a moment's pause, he stalked off back towards their tent. Nya reached for him as he passed.

"Wait for me," she said.

Kit pulled his hand away and trudged through the camp. He didn't glance back.

He trawled back slowly, the revelry around him feeling far off and blocked.

Dropping back at his spot in front of the fire pit, Kit rubbed his forehead. Dust lay sleeping where Nya should have been. The others around the fire pit sat huddled together deep in conversation.

"Sombre song for the broken heart, my boy?" Lem asked, breaking off from the group and sliding over to Kit.

"I don't love her," Kit said.

Kit glanced over his shoulder to where Nya and Kyan sat close together in deep conversation.

"I think I'll sing the song just in case. It's a good one. It's about a lover who kills another lover for taking another lover while setting out to sea. And it's raining. And there's a dancing squid," Lem said, then cleared his throat. "It's called *Sad Love Song Number Two*."

And then he broke into song.

36

The Nightraven

8 years ago.

Kyan stalked around the sparring circle. His opponent, Tysar, matched his slow dance around the edge and grinned at him. The high vaulted ceiling echoed their rasping breaths. Tall narrow windows bathed the Tansen training hall in golden light that glinted off the sheen of sweat lathering Kyan's face, and the fetid stink of worked bodies filled the hall.

Tysar was lean but muscular and a fair bit taller than Kyan. His bulk and size had proven advantageous as Kyan was tossed from the circle or pinned into submission in every round they had sparred so far. Even with all the sparring lessons his father paid for and the training at the garrison over the last couple years, he was no match for Tysar. Akarai stood at the side, his face unreadable.

"Start," Akarai said.

Kyan ground his teeth and dove for Tysar. Head tucked, Kyan tackled him trying to force him back and out of the circle, but it was like crashing into a wall. His body crumpled against the strength of his opponent. Tysar held strong, grappling Kyan before knocking a leg from beneath him and throwing him from the circle. "Akarai, I think this one would do better fighting someone closer to his skill level. One of the plants in the garden for instance?" Tysar laughed.

Panting, Kyan wiped the sweat from his brow. He glanced to Akarai who didn't react but Kyan's face still reddened in embarrassment. This man had seen something in him. It was favour from the gods that Akarai had been in the garrison when he'd been caught four years ago. He had sat down with Kyan in that cell to hear his story when most would have brushed him off as a petty thief and beaten him. Then Akarai took him under his wing, showed him he had to be strong to bring about the change he wanted to see. He found a place in the garrison for Kyan and regularly checked in on him.

Then Akarai had invited him to Atef Palace to spar. Was this some kind of test? If so, Kyan was failing it.

"Kyan." Akarai beckoned him over.

"I'm sorry, Akarai," Kyan said. "He's just stronger than me."

Akarai leant in and lowered his voice. "Fighting isn't about who is strongest but who better understands their enemy and themselves. Do you understand your strengths? Do you understand your weaknesses?"

Kyan furrowed his brow. Before he could fully comprehend what Akarai was saying, he shoved Kyan back into the ring and said, "Start."

Kyan's eyes flashed up to Tysar who was yawning. Tysar underestimated him, Kyan realised. That was a strength. Still, it wouldn't do much good when they were face to face.

Kyan was fast. He had charged in every round hoping he could use that speed to catch Tysar off balance or win by a stroke of luck. But speed was useless when it came to a battle of strength. Kyan needed to use that speed a different way.

Kyan tread lightly around the sparring circle. Tysar matched him walking on the far side. When Kyan didn't charge, Tysar smiled. "A new tact?"

Kyan ignored him, continuing his watchful prowl. "Very well," Tysar said.

Tysar lurched, fist swinging. Kyan side stepped, knocked the attack wide, and then countered with a jab to the face. Tysar stumbled, holding his cheek uncomprehendingly. He blinked at Kyan and confusion melted into a smirk.

"That's better, little noble boy!"

There goes the advantage of him underestimating me, Kyan thought as Tysar cracked his neck and fell into a fighting stance.

Tysar swept towards him, faster this time. Too fast to evade. Kyan lifted his arms to shield his face as an onslaught of jabs harried him to the edge of the circle. He couldn't keep giving ground like this. He didn't have the strength to knock Tysar out of the circle but he didn't need to.

Kyan ducked under the next swing, letting it carry past him and elbowed Tysar in the face, then he grabbed him by the scruff of the neck and forced his head down. Disorientated and off balance, he was in Kyan's grasp now and Kyan took a moment to enjoy it before he kicked Tysar's legs from beneath him and he tumbled out of the ring.

Astonishment flashed on Tysar's face and then he burst out laughing. Kyan glanced at Akarai who nodded. Kyan beamed.

"Strength is in one's technique and mind as much as their muscles," Akarai said, holding out a hand to Tysar. "Thanks for doing this, Tysar."

"I'm always up for some sparring." Tysar ruffled Kyan's hair. "I need to meet with Neyla. But I want a rematch," he said, pointing to Kyan. "And I won't go easy on you next time, noble boy."

He left the training hall and everything went quiet aside from the sound of Kyan's heavy breathing. He was exhausted and dehydrated, blood singing in his ears. His body ached now that the fury of the fight had drained out of him. Kyan wanted nothing more than to drop to the ground and rest but he had to find out what this was all about.

"Why did you invite me here to train today?" Kyan asked.

Akarai eyed him. "Walk with me."

Together they wound their way through the Sun-streaked hallways of the Atef Palace. Golden lines spread throughout the sandstone walls like fine twine made of pure morning light. Servants in red went about their duties bowing their heads in deference to Akarai. Kyan still couldn't believe he was in *Atef Palace*, where the empress ruled over Tarris.

Arches on their right led out to a courtyard with a rock garden. A pond centred the space with a statue of Otil, the Raging Sand Serpent breaking the surface of the water.

They passed through a stone door entering a new wing of the palace. Here, it was quieter with fewer servants wandering the corridors.

Akarai broke the silence. "What do you think I do here?"

Kyan thought about this. "An overseer of some kind?"

With a six-letter name, Akarai was one of the most powerful people in Tarris and must have connections to the empress herself. Given he spent time at the garrisons, an overseer seemed right. It was likely he managed all of the garrisons in Tansen.

Akarai smirked. "Not quite."

The corridor ended with a silver statue of a nightraven glinting in the firelight of the braziers. The nightraven stood proud, wings outstretched, majestic and threatening in the shifting torchlight. It was only then Kyan realised this corridor had no windows, the only light shining from the braziers.

The bird was twice Kyan's size, and if the records were to be believed, this could have been a scale model of the creatures that had once flown the skies hundreds of years ago. Emperor Osinious was said to have two at his side during his conquest of the tribes to the north. He would send out his nightravens into battle and they always returned bloody, earning him the name the Red-beak Emperor.

390

"I command the Seventh Sceptre."

Kyan flinched coming back to himself. He glanced over to Akarai who stepped up to the statue.

Had Kyan misheard?

Akarai ran a hand behind the nightraven's wing and there was an audible *click*. Then the snapping and groaning of a mechanism rumbled in the walls and the statue swung towards them on unseen hinges to reveal a passageway.

The Seventh Sceptre were a rumour, a ghost story. They were said to be an honour guard for the empress, a secret task force sent on missions across Tarris. They were supposedly highly trained, the best in their field. Kyan had heard they could fend off an army between the seven of them.

But they were nothing more than a story. Right?

Akarai led him down a short corridor that opened into a grand chamber. A skylight shone onto a marble floor inlaid with a crest Kyan hadn't seen before: a swirling sphere surrounded in seven swords. Steps at the far side of the chamber led up to a circular dais where a stone table was surrounded in curving bench. Seven empty weapon mounts hung on the walls around the dais.

Kyan stared in awe. The chamber held the majesty that only something ancient could produce.

"You made it your life's mission to help the people of Tarris." Akarai's voice echoed around the chamber. Pillars towered on either side of them reminding Kyan of some of the ancient temples he had visited. His mind whirled with incoherent thoughts as Akarai walked to a bookshelf on the right, pulling a book from it and handed it to Kyan. The leathery tome was inlaid with the same symbol on the marble floor. Kyan opened the book.

"Change comes as sure as the wind. It's inevitable. Sweeping over everything. But wind can be corralled. Wind can be guided by stone. We are the stone that steers that change," Akarai said.

Kyan dropped into a chair by the bookshelf as he started to read. Inside the book was the history of the Seventh Sceptre. Kyan couldn't believe what he was reading. He pretended to be part of the Seventh Sceptre with his friends as children. They were heroes from legend. They were the ones who slayed the monsters in the stories. They weren't *real*.

Rulers and their Seven were listed going back hundreds of years. Flipping through, Kyan stopped when the current empress' name appeared and below it read, *Akarai*.

"Kyan, will you join the Seventh Sceptre?"

37

The Echoing Silence

Nya stayed in a spare tent around Kyan's group's fire that night, not wanting to return and face Kit. He had looked devastated when she said she was going with Kyan and she couldn't understand why. He had helped her because she saved his life in the dark place, so they were even now. He was free to do what he wished. What difference did it make if she didn't want to go back with him?

And how was a chance to get back at those who had done them wrong over the years not the right choice? She needed this. She needed something. A purpose. A reason to go on now that Mother was dead.

Nya held up the flap of her tent. Jip, Pyna and a handful of others were around the fire eating breakfast.

The flames crackled in the quiet. The camp was dimmer

than the night before, the firelight not roaring flames but subdued grumbling. Nya sat beside Pyna. She wasn't particularly chatty but was nice enough. Jip walked over with a bowl and handed it to her with a bow. She bowed back, wishing him good morning.

The bowl contained some sort of oat-based dish. It wasn't bland, however. They added cinnamon, and something else Nya couldn't put her finger on, giving it some flavour. The anticipation of the day made it hard to eat, but she tried to eat at least half of the serving.

Kyan hadn't told her much of what they were setting out for today, other than it was something of greater value than anything else in the world, and that it had been lost to time. Instead, they had talked about how they came to be there. How the Decreed had formed and expanded over the last five years.

Then of shades.

Kyan had a very different approach to shades than Rai. He spoke of leaning into the surges of emotion, letting them flood through her and directing that strength, rather than noting them and letting it pass over her like Rai instructed.

The sandstorm must have passed during the night as the rumble of the winds whipping at the rocks no longer sounded under the din of camp. The camp was sluggish, most still in deep sleep after the late-night celebrations.

One man walked through camp. A dark silhouette shifting among the tents like a stalking predator. Kyan. He came trawling back to their fire pit, his face serious as he flicked through a stack of parchment.

"Did you sleep last night?" Pyna asked once he came into hearing distance. Kyan looked up, blinking at her with bleary eyes.

"I couldn't sleep, so I walked and went through my notes again. I don't think we have much further to go," he said. "But we should leave soon."

Pyna nodded and got up to prepare. Kyan scratched his chin as he read.

"Can you tell me where we are going now that I have agreed to come?" Nya asked.

Kyan blinked at her, then smiled. "Have you ever heard of the Lost Library of Nenelan?"

They packed their supplies and left camp while snoring still rung from most of the tents. The party comprised of Kyan, Pyna, Jip, and Nya. Pyna and Jip walked a couple paces ahead leading the way deeper into the cavern. They walked in a warm torchlight lighting the immediate cave walls around them, before fading to an unseeable and unknowable path ahead.

"The old capital, Asuriya, was said to have a grand library. There are scattered references to this library and notes on how it was the largest and widest collection of knowledge in the world," Kyan explained. Nya had never heard of it, but you learnt little about books and history when you lived on the streets. They had stories, of course, but they were of heroes, and probably far from the true retellings.

"After the calamity destroyed the old capital burying large parts of the city under the sand, it was believed that the library was lost because no one could find it. Even in recent years, there have been expeditions to try to locate the Lost Library of Nenelan." Nya was coming to realise Kyan made a lot of hand gestures when he was talking about something he was passionate about.

"But the problem was that the few mentions of it we do have traced it back to different locations," he said.

"And you figured out which one was right?" Nya asked.

"They were all right," Kyan said.

"What do you mean?" Nya asked.

Kyan grinned.

The echoing silence filled the space where the noise of camp should have been. Low murmurs came from Pyna and Jip in front, but Kyan had gone quiet, refusing to elaborate on what he meant. Not that she minded. Since last night, when she had agreed to go with Kyan, a sense of surety and purpose propped Nya up. It had been so long since she felt like she was on the right path, or any path. It didn't matter how long the journey to come was. The sense of progression of moving forward was enough for now.

They marched on through the cave. Time trickled by and their surroundings constantly changed but always somehow stayed the same. Caves were like that, Nya supposed.

Darkness pooled and walled off their surroundings, their small sphere of firelight shifting through the almost tangible black. As a child, Mother would tell her that there was nothing out there in the black. Nothing hiding in the dark places of the world. But now she knew better.

"Kyan, we might have a problem," Pyna said. They had only been walking for a couple hours, but as Kyan and Nya caught up, they saw the way was blocked. Lifting her torch, Pyna lit the sandfall that rained down, covering the entire back wall of the cave.

Nya had never seen a sandfall before. Sand continuously fell from a crack in the cave roof, somehow replenishing itself to create a constant flow. It was mesmerising to watch as the sand dropped in a hissing blur. A tan sheet of constant movement. Sandfalls, however, were dangerous and impassable. There was no way of telling how far the other side was, or if there was another side at all. She had heard horror stories of people convinced they could pass through, only to be buried alive.

The cave walls drew in and narrowed towards the back, where the sandfall whispered. An impenetrable dead end. Kyan stepped up and reached out, letting the edge of his finger brush over the sandfall. He yelped, pulling it back to reveal scrapes across the tip of his finger, and blood drawn.

"There were some branching tunnels further back, maybe if we—" Jip started.

"No. It's straight through here. I'm sure of it," Kyan said, sticking his bloodied finger in his mouth.

"We could run back to camp and get something to try block off the flow of sand? It would burst eventually but," Jip said, trailing off as Kyan shook his head.

"No. It's a test. A way to keep people away," Kyan said, biting the inside of his lip and studying the sandfall.

He isn't thinking of jumping into the sandfall, is he? Nya wondered. Pyna and Jip exchanged a worried glance. *He is*, Nya realised.

"It's too risky," Pyna said. "Let's—"

With a sharp inhale, Kyan broke into a run. Pyna squealed, but Nya just watched in utter shock and amazement as he threw himself into the sandfall. He vanished, immediately consumed by the sands. The three of them stood and stared at the sandfall. Pyna had her hands clasped over her mouth.

"I'm okay!" Kyan's voice came from behind the sandfall. "It's as I thought, just a thin barrier. And you need to see what is on the other side."

Nya puffed out a breath. The sun sick fool just threw himself into a sandfall on a *hunch*. Luck was often the difference between dedication and stupidity.

Neither Pyna nor Jip seemed eager to follow. Nya sighed. She was committed now, so if that meant jumping through sandfalls, so be it.

With a running start, Nya launched herself into the sands. Less than a second passed before she broke out the other side and skidded to a stop. Pain blossomed across her skin, the grating sands leaving their mark with a smattering of cuts.

A musty, stale scent of age hung in the air as Nya inhaled sharply, her arms and face stinging.

"There is an ancient tradition," Kyan said, "To weaken those who step into places of importance like temples, palaces, and libraries. I've read about it." He scratched his chin. "Although, I read they drew blood by cutting across your palm. This is certainly a creative way of doing it I hadn't heard of."

The grand cavern around her was beautiful. There was no other word for it. The walls were tiled with intricate patterns and splashes of pale reds and yellows throughout. Glass orbs lit the space with white light, evenly lighting the entire cave like daylight. Stone benches were lined in rows looking out to the back of the cave where the cavern continued, falling away into unknown darkness.

Kyan was coaxing the other two through as Nya walked to the edge of the void. Peering out, she could see nothing but endless darkness all around, even to her right and left. *It must be a cavern larger than the one we're in*, Nya mused. Had something once been in this huge dark space? Or was there something out there no longer lit by the orbs?

Nya heard a sound. A low rumble coming from the darkness. It echoed through the black.

"Don't get too close Nya," Kyan called. Nya stepped back.

"What is it?" she asked.

"It's a tunnel," Kyan said, walking up beside her. "It wraps around most of Tarris, I believe."

The rumble was getting louder. It sounded like something was scraping against the rock. "Do you hear that?" Nya asked.

"Yep. Come on, let's sit down and wait." Kyan made his way back to the benches where Pyna and Jip were nursing their cuts.

Nya sat beside Kyan, her head pivoting around, marvelling at this ancient wonder. Squinting, Nya noted that the glass orbs didn't flicker like fire would, and this cave hadn't been disturbed in hundreds of years, maybe even thousands, so how would a fire stay lit? What was fuelling these strange lights?

"What are the light orbs?" Nya asked.

"I don't know," Kyan said. "There is so much we don't know about before the calamity that destroyed the old capital. There is so little of the times before. Notes and references to things we still don't understand."

Kyan was the most learned individual Nya had ever met. Talking to him was like talking to a noble. So if he didn't know what they were, she doubted anyone would.

Nya had thought little about the history of Tarris. It wasn't something she knew much about or had the ability to learn about. Of course, she knew about the catastrophic event that destroyed their old capital, Asuriya, and how they weren't sure what had caused it. And that they had lost of lot of history from that time before because of the scattering of their people and destruction of recorded histories. But she knew little else that weren't stories of heroes.

As they waited on the cool stone benches, the reverberating and grinding noise grew louder, until they had to almost shout to talk to one another. Nya looked around, but the others weren't bothered by the growing noise. Kyan wandered around the cave, stopping by a unique tile on a pillar like protrusion coming from the right wall.

Nya's eyes widened as something crested the corner of the darkness.

It was stone and carved similar to the walls around her, and it was *moving* through the tunnel. Nya watched in awe as a building slid across the empty space, filling the dark unlit cavern just beyond their own. The structure was ancient, ornate carvings of some bird-like deity inscribed onto its surface.

Kyan was laughing, and the others cheered. How something that size could move itself, Nya did not know.

A door came into sight. A golden design snaked across it, resembling roots of a plant.

They could enter this building?

Once the structure had covered the entire back wall where the dark cavern had once been, Kyan pushed something at the tile he stood beside and the building eased to a stop. The rumbling subsided, and only the trickle of sand could be heard in the cave.

They moved to the door, unspeaking. Kyan reached it first and fervently ran a hand over its huge bar handles.

He turned, meeting everyone's eyes before inhaling and pushed hard on the door. It swung open with a gasp, sending dust and sand out in an acrid gust.

Nya coughed, turning her head away, and waving in front of her face. It smelt of age and disuse. When she opened her eyes, the doors were open, and a sandstone corridor lead further into the now still building. The walls were lit by the same white orbs as the cave they waited in.

Kyan stood taller as he spun back to face them. "This place hasn't been tread in for over two thousand years. It may contain dangers and traps we can't even begin to fathom," Kyan said. "Stay behind me, and if anything happens, get out as fast as you can."

"You should let me or Jip go first," Pyna said. "If you fall, so does everything."

"No," Kyan said, lifting a hand as she tried to step in front. "I brought us here. What leader sends his people into a danger that he brought on himself? That is what we are fighting against."

Nya saw a passionate ferocity in his eyes. He truly was trying to change things for the better. How she longed for that passion. That sense of meaning.

Pyna didn't stand down immediately, but eventually bowed, stepping back.

Kyan leading, and the rest close behind, they crept carefully inside. They passed through the well-lit sandstone corridor cautiously slow, eyes darting to the blank walls. The end opened up and a couple paces forward was a balcony, an ornate waist-high railing signalling the drop.

Nya paused, gazing over the balcony railing, awestruck. In front of her were *hundreds* of floors leading down so far that Nya couldn't make out the bottom. On each floor was shelving two stories high, stacked to brimming with books and scrolls. All perfectly lit by the mystical orbs placed around on the walls.

Above them was one great orb shining like the Sun Eye,

and as big as some buildings Nya had seen. Gold rings spun around it, making a low whirring sound.

Pyna and Jip laughed and clasped into an embrace. Kyan gestured dramatically and said, "Well, Nya, welcome to The Lost Library of Nenelan."

38

The Facade

8 years ago.

The Seventh Sceptre approached the village of Wile. Tucked into the base of a plateau, Wile looked more like a stronghold than a village. And in a way, it was. High mudbrick walls protected the vast farmlands within.

Wile lay in the shade of the plateau hidden in shadow. *They must grow subterranean foods*, Kyan mused. Sunlight wouldn't reach the village even at the apex of its watch, so it was likely they grew roots and fungi, as well as managed livestock.

Akarai and Kyan rode to the gates on hyian. The other members of the Seven finding more creative ways to enter the village unseen.

Trawling up to the iron gate, Kyan could see movement on the walls. The gate was raised and they entered the village.

"Why didn't anyone call out?" Kyan asked Akarai.

"We don't pose much threat since there is only two of us," Akarai answered. "But they'll be keeping an eye on us. Wile isn't on any trade routes and they'll want to know what we're doing here."

Passing the threshold of the village and into the shadow of the plateau, a cool met them washing away the clinging heat of the desert. Inside its walls, Wile was much like any other desert village. Ramshackle homes that didn't rise above two-stories and where the cities would have buildings leaning on one another, here it was open and breezy with plenty of space around each property. Where the cities air stank of the unwashed bodies all crammed in, here it was fresh and unscented. Faces peered from windows and a woman ushered her child away from them.

A guard stepped in front of them making it clear they weren't to come any further into the village. Akarai swung his leg over his mount and dropped to the ground motioning for Kyan to do the same.

"What brings you to Wile, travellers?" the guard asked. The man's eyes were sharp despite his age. His hands were rough and veins bulging along his arms, marking him as someone acquainted with swinging the sword at his belt.

"My son and I are setting up an inn in Tansen and are looking to make supply deals with local villages," Akarai said.

Son? Kyan bristled but kept it from showing. Akarai liked to tease him about looking younger than his years.

The guard eyed them. "You'll have to take that up with

the elder. Leave the hyians here and I'll take you to him." He jerked his head gesturing for them to follow.

The guard led them through the main thoroughfare. The village had the ease of those away from the bustle of the bigger cities. Men and woman pushed carts through the street or carried baskets of goods, and children played.

Why are we here? Kyan wondered. It was his first outing as one of the Seven and during the briefing Akarai explained that they believed there was rebellion brewing in the village of Wile, but Kyan couldn't see how these peaceful people would want anything to do with a revolution.

However, this could all be a show for their benefit. Thin human skin pulled over a monster beneath. The empress' spies thought something was happening in Wile and who was Kyan to question them. The other five where no doubt already within the village limits searching for any sign of rebellion.

"–been wanting to open one for a while. The simple life's hard to find in the capital, you know," Akarai was saying.

"I'm glad I escaped that constant bustle. Better way of living out here," the guard said. "Here we are."

Backed against the sheer rock face, the elder's home was a long simple building, unlit braziers on either side of the entrance. "The elder will–"

A scream rang out over the din of the village.

Kyan spun to the sound. Smoke curled from the farmland. Others in the village stopped and stared, fear tightening their faces.

The guard glanced at the smoke and reached for his sword but Akarai was faster. Kyan blinked and the guard had two daggers protruding from his gut. Akarai ripped his daggers free and the man crumpled to the ground. Nearby more shouting and screaming, and the scent of burning carried on the breeze.

"Let's go," Akarai said and kicked down the door into the elder's home.

Kyan chased after him. "I thought they were waiting until we found evidence!"

"They must have found something by the farmland." Akarai wouldn't meet his eyes.

Flames flickered in the dark, throwing light over an austere corridor. Living in the shadow of a plateau would require them to be on all day. Akarai motioned through signs that he was going to go right and Kyan was to go left. Kyan couldn't remember the affirmative sign so he just nodded and Akarai slunk off into the black.

Kyan took a deep breath and crept down the corridor. This all felt so sudden. He had thought they would take their time searching the village for proof of rebellion. Not rush in killing and burning farmland. Straining, he heard noises outside rise to a cacophony of shouting and screaming but in here it was silent.

If anyone was here, they probably ran out to see what's going on, Kyan thought. So it would be empty in the elder's home. Still Kyan kept the furtiveness in his steps.

Dipping his head into a room, Kyan glanced over the

study before stepping inside. A candle swayed beside an open book. Crossing to the desk, the hair of the back of Kyan's neck prickled as a feral scream shattered the quiet and a woman dove at him, knife in hand. Training kicked in and Kyan side stepped, snatching her arm and knocking the blade free before twisting her arm behind her back and forcing the woman against the desk. She groaned trying to shake herself free but she was no fighter.

Akarai tore into the study blades raised, letting them fall to his side when he glimpsed at Kyan. "The rest of the house is empty."

"Take what you want just don't hurt anyone, please," the woman pled.

"We aren't thieves," Kyan said. Akarai ran a hand over the book and scrolls laid out across the study desk.

"Then what do you want?" she asked.

Kyan didn't know how to answer.

"Let her go," Akarai said.

Kyan blew out a breath and released his grip. Perhaps the spies had made a mistake because Kyan found nothing to warrant this idea of rebellion in the village. The woman straightened and Akarai slammed his dagger into her gut, covering her mouth to mask her screams, then after her eyes glazed, he slowly laid her across the desk.

A cold panic plunged Kyan into a frenzy. "What are you doing?!" He stared at the woman's corpse as blood puddled on the table and dripped onto the floor. Terror flooded Kyan at the sight.

"They were the target, Kyan, and this is the evidence." Akarai held up a scroll.

Bile threatened at the back of Kyan's throat as he took the scroll. It was plans to expand Wile, creating more farmland and bringing in more livestock. Kyan blinked and reread the scroll. "I... I don't understand."

"Look at who signed it," Akarai said.

Rikun.

"Rikun?"

"He's an Ossin overseer. Why do you think an Ossin overseer would care about expanding food supplies on the outskirts of Tansen?"

"I don't know. To help with the supply chain?" Kyan's head was spinning.

"To feed soldiers. The monarchs are always angling for a foothold against the empress and having somewhere loyal to their cause this close to the capital would be invaluable."

Kyan scanned the scroll. "It says nothing here about feeding soldier."

"They wouldn't be stupid enough to write their intentions down. It's painted as an expansion on food production to hide their true intent. A façade. The people don't know how close we are to a civil war. The monarchs have been eyeing the throne for years, Kyan."

"There's no proof! This is ludicrous Akarai! These people are farmers!" Kyan shouted.

"For now. They are still a threat," Akarai said. "You knew we were assassins."

"This is all a political game," Kyan said. "The empress' paranoia is killing these people!" Kyan felt dizzy and grabbed the desk to steady himself.

"This is the way of the world," Akarai said.

"You once promised me that we could change things. You said we were the stone that could guide the change," Kyan whispered.

Akarai laid a hand on Kyan's shoulder before taking back the scroll.

"Guiding is not controlling."

He wandered into the village, where the screams of a massacre rang out and flames curled and consumed.

39

Light on the Black Dunes

Rai, someone is coming, Fax said. Rai started awake, blinking the daze away. These long days must be getting to him, if he was dozing off without realising. Eyes searching, he whispered, "Check it out, Fax."

Fax shot off as a darkened patch as Rai hopped atop the cabinet in the Waypoint, then jumped, grabbing hold of one of the rafters. Rai pulled himself up and sat surveying the Waypoint beneath him. Params had nibbled at the leftovers of what he had been eating the night before. Sand covered the floor and piled in the corners, as it often did after a sandstorm. No matter how you blocked shutters and door frames, sand always found a way to drift through during a storm. It was why he wore his cowl over his mouth even inside the Waypoint.

Three guys. The same ones that have been following us since Yontar, Fax said, returning. Rai had known Kyan would send some men to follow him after running into him at *The Cartographers Rest*, but to have them approach him? Was Kyan testing him?

He should know better, Rai thought.

The worst of the sandstorm had passed, but winds still rattled the Waypoint. The aya crunched as it ate leftovers and the door creaked as it eased open with the care of someone wanting to pass unnoticed. Two Irdu warriors entered from the front. They wore nothing on their top halves, revealing thick muscled torsos, and loose white breeches wrapped with golden bands around the waist. Their unsheathed curved blades were held loosely in a ready grip.

Yeah, I don't think they are here to talk, Fax said.

Rai suppressed a scoff. Irdu mercenaries were all show. He had fought them before, and although they were better than your average guard, they certainly weren't what their reputation painted them to be. They would protect you from bandits with little bother, but if anyone with genuine connections or skill wanted something from you, and you had Irdu warriors as your guards, you may as well hand the goods over and save the money.

After they passed, Rai dropped onto the mercenary at the back, knocking him to the ground, where he hit his head and went limp. The other spun, eyes wide. Sliding his dagger from his belt, Rai swiped the mercenary, parrying his attack. They traded blows as Rai got a feel for his technique and loosened stiff muscles.

He was preparing to finish off the warrior when hot pain shot along his shoulder. Rai yelped, jumping to the side. The third mercenary must have snuck in after the fighting started.

I did say there were three, Fax said.

"And you didn't think to warn me that he was behind me?" Rai grunted, holding the gash on his shoulder.

You were getting too cocky. Sometimes you need a reminder that even a blade in a child's hand can kill, Fax said.

The two warriors stalked towards him as Rai backed up to the wall.

"Was this really the time for a philosophical lesson, Fax?" Rai snapped.

Always. Need to keep you in fighting condition. Not to mention, you keep telling me what a great fighter you are and that you don't need my help.

Sunlight poured in as beams through cracks in the Waypoints walls. The smell of sweat and unwashed aya hung in the air, but despite it, Rai took a deep breath and lunged forward.

Ducking under the swipe from one mercenary, Rai kicked the other in the chest. He spun, dagger out, nicking the first as he stepped in to thrust at Rai. The warrior grunted but arced his blade around and Rai jerked back; the attack narrowly missing him. Then swiped his dagger over the mercenary's throat. He gurgled, grasping at the wound as he toppled over.

The other screamed, running at him. He had lost all his composure after seeing his friends die, so Rai easily stepped to the side and drove his dagger into the man's back.

The warrior inhaled sharply as his blade clattered to the floor. Rai held him up and pressed the dagger deeper. The man screamed. He was going to die, but Rai had stabbed low enough to avoid the man's heart and instant death.

"What did Kyan say?" Rai whispered into the man's ear.

The man spluttered blood and groaned. Rai forced the dagger deeper, and he screamed again.

"Slow," the man managed between gasps.

"Slow?"

"Slow you down," the man croaked.

Kyan sent them to slow me down? Rai thought, tossing the man forward. He must have been hoping to finish whatever he was up to before Rai caught up.

"We need to hurry," Rai said, walking to the stable. "This is no longer just a scouting mission. Kyan is planning on doing something, and soon."

Rai rushed together his belongings and threw open the stable doors. The high winds battered him as he ushered the aya out. The winds weren't bad enough to hurt them anymore. He might have waited a little longer if given the option. But after hearing that Kyan wanted to slow him down...

Rai clambered atop the aya and whipped the reins. They started ploughing across the dunes as the Sun Eye drifted closer to the horizon.

The sky dimmed, and the sands darkened and hardened under the aya's feet, as Rai rode hard over the black dunes.

They had been moving fast for a couple hours, and still found no sign of Kyan or his party. The sands were now completely black and dark hour was approaching. Rai knew he couldn't keep pressing on through dark hour. It was dangerous for the aya. With only residual light from the Sun Eye, the sand black and solidified, the aya could easily topple and hurt itself, and that would leave them stranded.

And Rai knew of the creatures that came out during dark hour.

Kyan can't be much further, Rai thought. They continued on, despite the dark. It was foolish, and Fax made sure he knew that. The next Waypoint was a while off yet according to the maps of the area, but if he could just push through dark hour they could reach it before first light.

What do you think Kyan is doing? Fax said.

"I don't know, but if he's sending mercenaries to slow me down, it's fair to say it won't be something I agree with," Rai said.

That's a fair assumption, Fax said.

"Keep an eye out for movement," Rai whispered.

Okay. What about light? Fax asked.

Rai knitted his eyebrows. "Light?"

Yeah, like the one coming from that cave, Fax said.

Fax had better sight that Rai, especially in the dark, but Rai could make out the faint glow coming from a rock formation further up. Jerking the reins, Rai directed the aya to duck into the rising rock formations long before the cave mouth.

Although he was certain no one could spot him during

dark hour, and he doubted they would post scouts during the hour where no one dared to travel on the sands anyway, Rai still wanted to make sure they didn't spot his aya later.

Rock stuck out like toes from a plateau, allowing Rai to tie up his aya in an enclosed space. He set out enough food and water to last the aya a good while and scratched it under the chin. "I won't be long," Rai said.

Hopefully. He made sure to set the reins high enough so if the aya was to try free itself, it could.

Rai crept along and peered into the lit cave. There was no one in the immediate space, but the light was coming from further within, tinting the corners of the rock with an orange glow.

They must have hidden in here from the sandstorm, Fax said.

"Kyan is meticulous. He would have checked to see if a storm was predicted with the sky readers before setting out. He planned to get to this point before the storm hit," Rai whispered.

That begs the question...

"What's in this cave?" Rai finished and crept towards the light.

Cheers and revelry echoed from around the bend. The damp smell of the cave intermixed with the scent of smoke and spices. The terrain was slippery and uneven as Rai edged onward. However, after turning the corner, the glow of fire bathed Rai in light.

Aya and hyian were lined up on his left, which gave way to a mass of tents and fires sprawling out on his right. Singing and laughing echoed around the high ceiling cavern as they shovelled food into their mouths. Rai's stomach rumbled.

It would be funny if you were caught because of your stomach, Fax said.

Two scouts sat on the edge of the corner, but neither were paying attention. Instead of being spaced out, they sat together and were eating from bowls and only glancing up occasionally. Arcing around to the aya, Rai moved past the scouts with ease. Plenty of people moved between fires and passed around camp, making it easy to blend in once he was in the camp proper.

Rai made sure to avoid getting too close to the fires. He was sure no one would recognise him, or realise he wasn't just one of the Decreed, but best to be safe. Those in charge stood by a command centre discussing a map with stern faces. But Kyan was nowhere to be seen.

Would they have left the cave and continued on, or gone deeper, Rai wondered as he looked into the darkening end of the cave, where the campfires fizzled out and the cave led on.

Just as he was about to duck between the aya to think about what he was going to do next, someone bumped into him.

"Hey! Keep your eyes on your black sand feet fool," a man said, as he righted himself. The man was drunk and had just pulled his breeches up after relieving himself. He looked at Rai and squinted. "I haven't seen your face around here."

Rai's thumb slid atop his dagger, and although he never took his eyes from the man, he searched the sides of his vision, deciding if he could kill and pull this man into the shadows before anyone noticed.

"Lem!" Lem shouted as he passed between them. "I was wondering where you ran off to." Lem faced the disgruntled man and leaned in. "He can get a bit confused. It was one of the reasons why our mother named us the same. It's less confusing for him."

The man looked between Rai and Lem. "Less confusing? Surely that would just make it more confusing," the man said.

"How's that?" Lem asked, genuine confusion in his voice.

"Because you wouldn't know who she is talking to?"

"She would look at whoever she was talking to?"

The drunk man stared at him a moment, uncomprehending on how Lem didn't understand that having brothers with the same name would be confusing. He blinked, started to form words, and stopped, deciding it wasn't worth the hassle. Then, with a snort, he backed off towards one of the fires.

Rai waited until he passed out of sight and grabbed Lem, dragging him further away from the fires. "What are you doing here, Lem?"

"Helping you, of course," Lem said. "Also, this cult gang thing isn't too bad when they stop talking about justice. This is the second night of fresh stew and songs."

Rai let someone pass before whispering, "These people are dangerous."

"I know. I've been careful," Lem said. "They aren't all bad, though. You should come and meet some of my new friends."

"No, I don't need a repeat of what just happened. Where is

the jackal-masked man, Kyan?" Rai asked.

"He left this morning. I've been keeping an eye on him for you. Saw him sneak off down there first thing," Lem said, pointing further into the cave. That made sense. If he was going to leave the cave, then he would've taken his procession with him.

"What about two teens? Have you seen two teens anywhere here?" Rai asked.

"Nya and Kit?" Lem said. "Nya left with Kyan. Haven't seen Kit in a while, not sure where he got off to. He asked me to look after their sand fox for a while. It was following me—" Lem looked around spinning erratically. "It's gone! Oh, no. Oh no. Kit is going to kill me."

"It's fine, Lem. Dust does that. I'm sure she's around here somewhere," Rai said, rubbing his forehead.

Kyan must know she has a shade. Probably took her as his prisoner to keep an eye on her. And wherever Nya is, Kit is never far behind, Rai thought.

With a sigh, Rai laid a hand on Lem's shoulder. Despite asking him to stay, this crazy old man came to help him. He hadn't known Lem long, but he had joined the Decreed and travelled for days to help in any way he could. It was a kindness and sense of loyalty that was rarely found outside of story and song. He owed this man a lot. Rai could have wasted hours scoping out the camp to ensure Kyan, Nya, and Kit weren't still here. "I'm grateful you are here Lem, thank you," Rai said.

Lem snapped a salute, and Rai slapped his hand away

before anyone saw.

"Sorry," he said.

"Stay in camp," Rai said, and with a pat, he turned and headed towards the back of the cavern.

He made it past the last fire without so much as a second glance, then picked up a torch used to light the back wall and wandered into the black.

Rai moved quickly. He was almost an entire day behind Kyan, and he didn't want anyone to spot his torch moving away from camp.

Rai had been hoping for a hint of what was special about this cave as he wade through it, but it was decidedly unremarkable. The flames on the torch threw definition over sharp edges, and creatures who fled from its glow. Cracks in the rock walls made for possible other passages branching from the main one, but Rai stuck in the main tunnel. His stomach gargled, and he wished he had picked up some of the stew Lem had talked about.

Rai found no sign of Kyan's passing, no hint that anyone had come through here, but he trusted Lem. The strange man had earned his trust.

That trust seems to be paying off, Rai thought, seeing light further ahead.

Lightening his footfalls, Rai inched forward. A silhouetted figure holding a torch stood in front of a grand sandfall pouring over the back wall of the cave.

40

What Hides in Ancient Places

"It's beautiful," Nya whispered as she gazed out over the library. Even as someone who couldn't read, Nya was in awe at the space. Leaning over the balcony, the floors seemed to fall away forever, and looking across the chamber, shelves led in all directions. It was endless.

The shelves were made of a pale stone. Luxurious high-backed chairs collected in bundles under the light of the white orbs. Deep red runners laid out winding paths among the shelves and seating, disappearing into the endless stacks. Nya couldn't imagine the time required to build something like this.

Kyan blew a layer of dust off a particularly chunky tome that sat on a pedestal by itself. He waved away the dust and coughed before peeling back the cover and flicking through the contents.

"What does it say?" Nya asked, coming to his side.

"It's an overview directory. Each floor will have their own directory in more detail, but from what this says, we want to go down seventeen floors and head to the right wing," Kyan said.

"What are you looking for?" Nya asked.

"The resting place of Ma-atan," Kyan said without hesitation.

Nya couldn't believe what she was hearing. The depiction of Ma-atan wrapped around the doorframe back in the palace dungeons flared in her mind. "The Judge and Weigher of Hearts?"

"One and the same," Kyan said. "Come, I don't know how far we will have to walk. Hey! Touch nothing!"

Jip jerked his hand away from one of the light orbs, bowing his head, chagrined.

"We need to be careful. The ancient times are still a mystery, which means we are walking through here blind to what we might find." Kyan shook his head.

They moved down the spiral staircase that wove its way through the floors. Each floor was several stories tall, so passing down seventeen flights took some time. As they passed the opening archways, Nya couldn't help but peer in at the majesty of the place. There was so much variation between each floor; some with back-to-back shelves, others were spaced apart, and lined with glass cases containing a myriad of items Nya didn't recognise. Some shelves even *floated.* They had the same banded rings rotating around them like the great orb by the entrance had. Nya wondered if they were connected somehow.

"So you think Ma-atan is in our world?" Nya asked, jogging to catch up with Kyan, who lead the group with haste. Ma-atan was said to live between worlds, on the border of life and death, so Nya was certain it didn't have a resting place.

"I believe it once roamed Tarris. I think most of our deities did," Kyan said.

"But the legends speak of it waiting for you at Duat's gates, to decide if you're to be sent into one of the seven torment realms or into the reed fields of Aru," Nya said.

Nya kept glancing down, as she often did on steps, but these were perfectly cut and even. Each step felt to be the exact same size as the one before it, making it easy to traverse. How did an ancient civilization create such wonders that they couldn't match today?

"Not before the calamity. I think Ma-atan used to make its judgments here in Tarris before needing to fall into a long slumber. I have a theory that creatures with long lives need periods of extended sleep. We see this already with some species and I thought what if deities are the same? The stories then rode the generations across time, adapting and losing fractions of meaning, all adding up to a completely different tale that resembled the truth, like a coast compared to the land it used to be," Kyan said, then regarded Nya. "Doesn't speaking of a creature that judges you after death sound like something a parent would say to scare their children?"

Mother had used the stories of Ma-atan to keep Nya in line when she was younger. Her spirits dampened thinking about her mother, and guilt bubbled up. If Ma-atan was standing waiting to pass judgment on those who died, Nya would definitely end up in one of the torment realms. And if Kyan was right and found Ma-atan here in Tarris, then that may happen sooner than Nya had thought.

"Don't look so doom and gloom," Kyan said, as if he could read her thoughts. "Ma-atan can tell what is in your heart. You needn't worry. I know you're true hearted, even if you don't believe it yourself."

Nya forced a smile and nodded. Part of her wanted to believe him. Could she be blamed when they had thrust this shade upon her? Yes, Nya could be blamed, and she was lying to herself if she thought otherwise.

"Here we are," Kyan said, coming to the next landing. "Seventeen down."

They walked under an arch large enough for half of Yontar to fit through. It opened into a space not unlike the previous floors, shelves arrayed around them with a main thoroughfare running through the centre, marked by the red runner trimmed in gold. Some areas had wide open spaces, where shelves floated around in circles on an axis, those same rings spinning around them.

Another directory book sat on a stone pedestal. Kyan lifted the cover and flicked through the first couple pages before saying, "Yeah, this is the right floor. We need to go that way."

His voice sounded strange and it took a moment for Nya

to realise what was wrong. In this grand space, his voice should have echoed and reverberated like it might in a cave, but instead it was dampened and didn't carry, as if they were all in a close room together. The others noticed too. Jip even called out, but it was the same and sent no echoes.

"Strange," Kyan whispered.

They walked deeper into the library. It held the eerie silence of a held breath. It was as if the library was frozen in time. *In a way, it was before we got here*, Nya thought.

The floating shelves let off a low rumble as they spun, and Nya was grateful to have something to fill the quiet.

Nya stared down each aisle at the endless shelves of books. No one was there, no one *could* be there. This place hadn't been stepped in for thousands of years, but she couldn't help but feel like they were being watched. The others walked with the same trepidation, glancing around uneasily. Only Kyan marched on like there was nothing to be concerned about.

All the shelves looked the same to Nya. The only way she could tell they were making progress was to look back at the arch to the stairwell as it shrunk in the distance.

Down the next line of shelves, the end stood in darkness. Nya started. The entire library was perfectly lit by the white orbs, until now.

"Look," Nya said. They stopped and stared into the darkness.

"Maybe some of those orb things broke?" Jip offered.

"If you touch them, they feel like glass. It's possible," Pyna added.

Kyan's face was unreadable, but after they started up again, the pace he set had quickened.

The next few aisles also led into darkness, and the more they continued inward, the closer the shadows reached.

They stopped at the end of a row, and Kyan studied the markings carved into the shelf, before inclining his head and starting down between the shelves. Nya hesitated, watching the dark sitting further down the aisle before following. Hopefully, they wouldn't be going that far.

Kyan was mumbling under his breath as he walked sideways, running his finger over the spines of the books. Eventually, he came to a stop and slid a book from the shelf. Nya let out a breath. They were still some distance away from the darkened area.

"I found references to this ancient book. A bestiary written by Tokil that was said to have some of the elder bloods recorded in it," Kyan said to Nya, who watched curiously as he scanned the book.

"Elder bloods?" Nya asked.

"It's an old phrase for some of the oldest known creatures. Others call them The First, said to be some of the first living things on the planet," Kyan said.

A grin spread across his face, and he slammed the book closed with a puff of dust. "This is it. Let's go," Kyan said.

Just then, something crashed.

It came from further down in the dark. Heads burled, and they all stared into the shadow. Nothing happened for a moment. Then, *crash*. One of the light orbs shattered, extending the darkness.

Another shattered, the dark edging closer.

"Run," Kyan said in a whisper.

The orbs exploded one by one as the darkness reached for them.

"Run!" Kyan shouted, this time shaking them out of their stupor.

They bolted back into the main thoroughfare and back towards the stairwell. The sound of orbs shattering was getting closer. Their footsteps slapped against the stone ground, but much like their voice, they didn't echo. Nya peered over her shoulder. The darkness was almost to the end of the aisle.

"We won't make it," Nya said between gasps.

Kyan had a quick look too, then shouted, "Split up!"

Nya could tell by Pyna and Jip's faces that they didn't like the idea, but they were panting too hard to argue. The four of them broke off, running into different sections of the library.

Nya shot off, tearing around turns in the shelving. She ran under floating shelves and through some areas where tables and heavily cushioned chairs were laid out. Narrow spiral staircases lead to balconies atop the shelves, where more seating stretched out, but Nya didn't risk going up in case it led to a dead end. Her legs and chest burned. Stepping around into a new row of shelves, Nya dropped down, breathing hard.

What was that? Nya wondered. Something had to be hiding in that shadow.

The Ahmune, said a voice. It took a moment for Nya to

realise it was Bom who'd spoken.

"Ahmune?" Nya whispered.

An ancient creature, older than this library, Bom said. An image flashed into Nya's mind and she had to stifle a scream. Sinewy flesh stretched out over a thin bone structure in slabs of meat, almost like plates of armour. Ridges of its spine stuck out from its back, leading up to a long snouted face and antlers that stuck out like bone trees atop its head. Its eyes were white, contrasting its grey hide and black surroundings.

Nya held her hands to her mouth to stop her from making any noise. Around her was the eerie quiet again. But in here sound didn't travel, and she had run quite far. The others could be torn apart just around the corner, and Nya doubted she would even know.

"What is that?" Nya whispered. "And why are you helping?" A rational part of her said not to add that second question, but her mind was in a frenzy, and it was out before she could think.

You're my host, Bom said. *Death for you would be death for me. Although not in the same way.*

Nya wanted to keep it talking and learn more, but this wasn't the time. "What should we do? Can you fight it?"

No, Bom said. *You need to get out of here. It swims in shadow and can appear anywhere where it's dark. You must stay in the light. Go now.*

Stay in the light, Nya thought, her breath beginning to slow. *Go quickly!*

Nya stood and leaned around the corner. Orbs lit the rows

of shelving. In her panic, Nya had sprinted away with little thought of direction, but Bom left the impression that going that direction was the way to the main staircase. So with a ragged exhale, Nya broke into a jog.

Eyes darted up and down the rows. Everything sat in light and stillness. At the end of the row, Nya cautiously panned around the open space under the floating shelves, but again, nothing was there. The erratic hiss of her breath and thrum of the floating shelves above her was all she could hear. She hated not being able to hear. She hadn't realised how much she had relied on that sense, thinking it was more what she could see that linked her to that which was around her. But she felt like she was wandering blind. The Ahmune could sneak up behind her and finish her off without her even knowing it was nearby.

Jogging under the floating shelves, Nya dove into another aisle. She crept on when she heard a smash. Her heart stopped, and she craned her neck towards the sound. It had to be close if she could hear it, but it was difficult to judge distances. Nya turned back the way she came and ran.

She didn't dare take the time to look over her shoulder until she had made it under the next group of floating shelves and ran down another two rows.

As she sat there catching her breath, tapping came from a nearby row. Footsteps.

Nya stayed at the edge of her aisle, bent down with only the tip of her head poking out. A couple of heartbeats later and Jip tore out of one of the rows, his face a terrified rictus of horror.

He spotted Nya. Their eyes meeting for a second, before a crashing sound, and he was thrown into darkness.

Nya pulled back as she heard his guttural screaming, the snapping of bone, and wrenching of flesh. She wished the sound damping would have smothered it, but it ripped through the quiet like stone on glass.

Then it stopped. What sounded like a satisfied sigh followed.

Nya held her breath.

I feel you, a voice said. It was *wider* than Bom's and came from all around, rather than within. It was a raspy, low voice that felt like it shook the air it passed through. *One of his champions? But he is no longer here. Locked away in times to come*, it said.

Nya froze to the spot. She wanted to run away. She wanted to scream and run, but fear fixed her to where she sat like nails pinning her down. The shattering of more light orbs made Nya start to shake.

But you're here somehow. Interesting. Has he found a way to return?

Ahmune's voice swirled around her like a snake, sending shivers down Nya's spine.

Not speaking? It chuckled. *Very well. He must not be back then. Not completely anyway. Which means he won't know when I tear you apart, piece by piece. It's been so long since I've had proper food. Being locked in here leaves little to eat, you see. But I can survive a very long time with very little.*

Nya dared a peek around the corner. Darkness covered where she had run from. Something slithered in the inky black.

Pop.

Another light orb shattered a couple of rows over. She covered her mouth, sweat lathering her nape and running down her face. Bom buzzed in her mind with the fearful ferocity of cornered prey. It wanted to charge, rend, and destroy what was threatening them, but they both knew the outcome if they tried fighting. She needed to move, but as soon as she did, it would find her.

Breathe, Nya thought. *Think.* She sought a void of calm, but it kept slipping from her like sand between her fingers. Then a thought arose.

"Bom, can you knock a book over on a row on the far side?" Nya asked.

She felt reluctance from Bom. It hadn't ever been commanded before.

Another light orb smashed, and the shifting shadow jumped closer. Bom didn't move. Nya blew out a breath, readying herself to make a run for it, when she felt Bom slide out from her shadow.

She listened with bated breath. Then there was a *thud*. A swish of movement came from the shadow as the Ahmune careened away from Nya and towards the sound.

Nya felt Bom return and she stood and ran. A hissing roar erupted from behind her, but it was already diminishing with the distance. Nya sprinted up aisles, ducking under ladders that leant against the shelves, and through small domed chambers under brass spheres connected together that hung from the ceiling.

Sliding around a corner, she almost ran into Pyna, who was crouched, back against the shelves. Pyna tripped back, trembling, but she settled when she realised it was Nya.

Nya held out a hand. Pyna hesitated before taking it, and Nya pulled her to her feet. She opened her mouth to tell her about Jip, but then closed it again. It would only slow Pyna down. She could tell her if they got out.

When we get out, Nya corrected herself.

"Have you seen Kyan?" Nya asked.

"Not since we split up," Pyna replied. Nya hoped he was okay.

"We should head for the staircase."

"Do you know where to go? I've been completely turned around," Pyna asked.

Nya nodded and started off down the row. They passed some darkened areas, making sure to give them a wide berth. But as they continued, it remained a still and soundless library, lying undisturbed, as if it didn't have a creature roaming its halls.

They scurried down, past the dusted books, through elevated seating areas that had railings around them, and eventually they found the main thoroughfare that led to the staircase.

They broke into a jog, always watching for oncoming darkness. Their footsteps were heavy and slapping, but with the strange acoustics, they didn't worry about being heard, instead focusing on getting to that staircase swiftly.

The great archway stood at the end, beckoning them to safety. Seeing it spurred them on and gave Nya a jolt of energy as they pressed harder.

Hopefully Kyan already made it to the entry floor, Nya thought.

Against the far wall, and deep into the shelving on their right, a light went out.

Nya's stomach dropped.

It was too far to hear anything, but another patch of light blew out, then another, and another. Soon, it was as if the dark was making for the arch too. Lights blinked out, running along the back wall towards the staircase.

The dark was going to make it to the arch before them. Nya was sure of it. She started to slow. "Pyna! Look!" Nya shouted. But Pyna kept running.

"Pyna!"

Pyna turned her head and saw it, eyes widening. "We can make it!" she shouted and ran harder. Nya came to a stop, watching her bolt off. She was fast. Faster than her, and Nya thought Pyna might just make it.

Pyna's legs turned like spokes of a wheel, kicking up dust in her wake, and the dark hurtled onward. It was close, Nya thought as she looked between the two.

Hastening and throwing everything she had, Pyna reached the arches only a second before the approaching black. She was under the arch, half turned around, a smile on her face, when the area flickered into darkness.

There was no scream, just a dulled crunch and a faint chuckle.

41

Shadows Clash

Light from the torch drew a dark cut out of the figure pacing along the far side of the cave. Rai could hear the faint noise of muttering under the hiss of the sandfall.

"Fax," Rai said, and it slid over to investigate.

It's Kit, Fax said a couple heartbeats later.

Rai sighed and walked over. Kit was too focused on the sandfall to notice Rai approaching. Laying a hand on his shoulder, Kit screamed and jumped back, waving his torch around.

"Rai?" he asked.

"Quiet boy," Rai said, hushing him.

"Well, don't sneak up on me," Kit said.

Rai stepped up to the sandfall. It covered the entire wall. There was no way around it or way to tell if there was another side.

Dust nuzzled the back of Rai's leg. *So this is where you got off to*, Rai thought, glancing down at the sand fox.

"What are you doing here?" Kit asked.

"Where are Kyan and Nya?" Rai asked, ignoring his question.

"They came this way, but they must have turned off one of the other pathways. I've been checking the edges of this sandfall and I can't see any way around it," Kit said.

"They went through," Rai said.

Even in the thin light, Rai saw Kit's face screw up. "Through?"

"Why weren't you with them?" Rai asked, walking up scanning the ground.

Kit followed behind him, staring at his feet. "Nya wanted to go with Kyan."

Rai spun to face him. "She went with him willingly?"

"Yeah," Kit said. "He talked about punishing those who did them wrong and all that nonsense. It was clear to me he just wanted to use Nya, so I tried to persuade her otherwise, but…"

Rai should have accounted for this. Kyan had a way with words. He spoke like some men sparred and could wrangle anyone into submission.

"We will get her back," Rai said, laying a hand on the boy's shoulder. Kit gave him a firm nod. Turning, Rai kept walking along beside the sandfall. "Here. We have to jump through."

"Excuse me?" Kit asked.

"Look at the ground," Rai said. Sand lay scattered around their feet. Of course, there was sand all around the edge of the sandfall, but at this part, it stretched out further. "They jumped through here."

"You can't be serious," Kit said.

"Come on kid, where is your sense of adventure?" Rai said, backing up. "Don't you want to save Nya?"

Then Rai sprinted and dove through the sands. He barrelled out the other side into a roll before coming back up to his feet, daggers in hand.

Rai's breath caught. He stood in an ancient chamber bright in colour, with orbs affixed to the walls that produced a pale glow. Stone benches rose in lines, like a stadium all looking onto the grand door on the far wall. Rai wracked his brain for the chambers purpose, but he had never seen anything like it.

"Rai? You dead?" Kit called.

"No, hurry and jump through," Rai called back. More light shone from inside the great door at the back of the chamber. *They must be in there*, Rai thought. *But what is this place?*

With a squeal and a series of thuds, Kit appeared at his side carrying Dust, and nursing lots of little bleeding cuts. "Couldn't Fax have just held up the sand for us to walk through?" Kit asked.

"Maybe if it was a thin stream and not a wall like that," Rai said.

Plus, it's good character building, Fax said.

Kit muttered something about a damn bird under his breath as Rai walked across the chamber. A door was surrounded in ancient scrawl: scrolls, eyes, and Ma-nivi, an owl like deity. *A place of learning*, Rai thought. They were all symbols of knowledge and scholarly pursuit.

Rai peered into the open doorway, a narrow corridor led in before opening up to a wider space lit by the same mysterious glass orbs. "Stay behind me and keep quiet," Rai whispered, and Kit nodded.

They crept down the passageway, ears perked, but all Rai could hear was the trickling sandfall they were leaving behind. As he passed the white orbs they gave off a low thrum, and radiated a little heat, but other than that a silence held.

The hallway opened up into the grandest library Rai had ever seen. And then he knew where he was: the Lost Library of Nenelan.

Kit let out something between a gasp and a groan. Rai laid his hands on the balcony railing, it was the smoothest cut stone he had ever felt, and gazed down at the floors that fell away, seemingly forever. This place was meant to be lost under the rubble of the abandoned capital, but here it was, and untouched by the calamity. Fax flew out over the balcony edge and to the other side, where more shelves and reading spaces sat in wait, as they had done for thousands of years.

Rai made his way to the directory that lay on a stone pedestal. *The dust around it has been disturbed,* Rai noted.

They had directories in the Tansen Archives, but they were barely used, most just asking a clerk to help them locate whatever they were searching for. But in here you would need a battalion of clerks for each floor, given the scale of the place.

"Wow, what's that?" Kit asked, pointing at the great orb that floated near the high ceiling. It resembled the other light orbs but it was much larger and had bands of gold spinning around it.

"I don't know," Rai said, opening the directory. It was in an ancient script, but Rai could read most of it and figure out the rest with context. Scanning over the text, it was apparent that the library lived up to its name of having books and scrolls on every imaginable topic, from maps to bestiaries, histories to inventions, and even journals. And according to the prescript, there were even more directories detailing other topics, and narrowing down those broader areas like history, on other floors.

How am I going to find Kyan in all this? Rai wondered. *Think Rai. What would he be here for?*

They could hide by the exit and wait for Kyan to return, but that was assuming he was coming back this way. Rai was sure there were other exits out of the library.

"How long would it take you to search a floor Fax?" Rai asked.

Hard to tell. They seem to be rather large. A couple hours for a preliminary search maybe, Fax said.

That was too long.

Kit leaned over the balcony edge. "There must be hundreds of floors," Kit said. "Is this what I think it is?"

"The Lost Library of Nenelan," Rai answered.

Kit laughed. "Incredible. Do you know how many books I've sold to sun-sick nobles that I said were from here?" He paused, grinning at Rai. "A lot. Being a street kid that can read has its perks."

"Did Kyan mention anything that might give us a clue to what he was searching for in here?" Rai asked.

Biting the inside of his lip, Kit hummed. "Not much more than what he said at that rally. He wants to bring justice to the royals and monarchy. Maybe a weapon or something?"

A coldness shocked Rai. *Bring justice. They will be Judged.* How had he not thought about it before?

"He thinks he can find Ma-atan," Rai whispered.

"What? The deity?"

Everything slid into place in Rai's mind. Deities had always fascinated Kyan. He'd always thought they were still here, just locked away and sleeping. If he loosed Ma-atan on Tarris, it would tear through the continent, killing those it saw as unjust.

Frantically, Rai flicked through the directory again.

"He wants to bring Ma-atan to Tarris?" Kit asked.

Rai slid his finger over the contents. Bestiaries, seventeen floors down. "No, it's already here. He wants to wake it up."

Whirling around, Rai located the stairwell and jogged down the steps, Fax flying on overhead. Kit followed, shouting and using language Rai was going to have to talk to him later about, as Dust bounded down at Rai's side.

Sixteen... seventeen.

Coming down to the seventeenth floor, the immediate area was cloaked in darkness. Rai could see through it to where the rest of the floor was lit.

Something is wrong, Fax said. Although it didn't have to say it. Rai could feel Fax's unease, and through it, sense a presence in the shadows. Dust growled at their feet, baring her teeth.

Panting, Kit caught up and bent over, holding his knees. It didn't feel like whatever was hiding in the shadows was nearby, so with a deep breath, Rai entered the seventeenth floor.

The darkness was cool and thick, like an obscuring fog around him. It was unnatural and felt like it was holding him, coalescing his skin. Rai shivered as he passed out the other side.

The library was silent. He had noticed coming down the steps that his footsteps didn't reverberate as they should. Some sort of noise suppression, Rai guessed. He knew the ancient civilizations referenced things they didn't understand today, but he had never imagined them to be so advanced.

Kit appeared at his side, looking over his shoulder back into the darkness. "That... This isn't right," Kit said.

"I know," Rai said. "Something is in here with us."

Kit stared at him. "No one has been in here in thousands of years. How could anything survive?"

"With the size of this place, there is probably an entire ecosystem living in here. Even on the seventeenth floor we are comparatively near the exit, but further in? Probably creatures and animals that haven't been seen in a thousand years roaming around," Rai said.

Kit raised his eyebrows and ran his tongue over his teeth.

Rai and Kit walked along the right-hand side of the wide

thoroughfare, so they could dive into a row of shelves if they spotted anyone, or anything.

Stale air held the taste of time's passing, confirmed by the blanket of dust covering the surfaces of the library. Patches of darkness blotted areas, but they never got close enough to see if anything hid among it.

"What's the plan when we find them?" Kit whispered, but probably didn't need to, given the sound dampening.

"Find Nya and get her out. I will take care of Kyan," Rai replied.

"Good, simple plan. Easy to remember. I like it," Kit nodded.

At the end of the rows of bookshelves was an elevated seating area that had padded armchairs around circular tables. They were metal framed chairs with plush red cushioning. The tables had light sandstone legs holding up a darker stone tabletop. Beside it, another directory book sat on the same ornately carved podium that held the other by the entrance. Rai flicked through it.

The closest exit out of the library is two floors down, Rai read. Kyan had definitely come to this floor. The disrupted dust on some of the other directories and markers confirmed that, but if they found no more traces of him, the exit two floors down was their best bet. Perhaps he had already found the book that held Ma-atan's resting place, if it even existed. The more he thought on it, the more Rai worried Kyan was right about Ma-atan being in Tarris, and what waking such a creature meant for the country and their history.

Justice is fluid. Everyone fights for what they think is just. And Rai didn't have faith in an ageless creature having a modern moral compass.

The directory indicated a way to the lower levels on their right, so they skirted around the edges of the seating area and continued inward. They passed wonders, but they didn't have time to gawk; shelves floated in circles, huge four-plated doorways with no handles or way to open them were inset into walls, globes floated with metal bands spinning around them, and so much more.

Walls corralled them into a narrow section, where shelves were only a story high and balconies hung above them on the walls. Rai watched their darkened areas warily. Ahead, the space opened to an atrium, revealing the scale of the library once more.

And on the other side of the open space was Kyan.

Their eyes met, Kyan's betraying his surprise, but only for a second before composure flattened it. He was alone and held a thick leatherbound book.

"Go find Nya," Rai said.

"Uh huh," Kit said, with a nod and ran off, Dust trailing behind him.

Rai stepped up to the railing. Fax whipped out across the space to where Kyan stood. Kyan's shade lashed out, deflecting Fax's attack. *At least this time it isn't a trick.*

"Just had to check it was really you this time," Rai called.

"I should have known that even with a storm and mercenaries you would catch up," Kyan said with a sigh.

"It sped me up, if anything. It was an insult sending Irdu mercenaries," Rai said.

Kyan chuckled, and for a moment, Rai saw the boy he knew all those years ago.

"Come with me," Rai said. "Let the leaders of this country tear each other apart. We can live a simple life." He realised he meant it too. He could give all this up. Give up trying to learn what shades were, give up trying to help Tarris. Rai was tired of chasing and worrying. A simple life flashed before him, with Kyan, Kalt, and Syla in Gamo village tending the orchard and drinking around the fire pit at night.

Kyan shook his head. "You know I can't do that. This is what I was spared for that night five years ago. I survived so I could help those that I couldn't help as part of the Seventh Sceptre. I'm not content hiding with my eyes closed to what is happening like you are, Rai."

"And releasing an ancient creature we have little knowledge about is the smart way of helping the people? The Kyan I knew thought through all the possibilities. You can't tell me you haven't thought about all the horrors this Ma-atan could unfold on Tarris," Rai said.

"We have lost our way in Tarris, Rai. We have for some time. Perhaps an ancient creature not bound to the way we think will grant us the type of justice we need," Kyan said.

"What if its first act is to slaughter you and those who follow you?" Rai said.

Kyan shrugged. "Then so be it. It's certainly possible after what we did in the Seven over those last couple years."

Rai felt cold. Memories of the last couple years in the Seventh Sceptre coming unbidden to his mind. Screams echoed in his ears. Yes, he was certain this Ma-atan wouldn't judge them kindly. That simple life flitted away. Rai knew he wasn't meant for that life, but sometimes the dream was more important than the reality to come.

"You know I'm going to have to stop you," Rai said, thoughts of Grenin and Larina swirling in his head. Would they be safe from Ma-atan?

Kyan depressed a little, shoulders slumping. "I know."

Then Kyan ran and jumped over the edge of the atrium. He fell over ten floors before his shade appeared as a glider, and they drifted across the enormous expanse, that dropped to oblivion.

Rai laid his hands on the railing and kicked his legs over, falling after him. Air rustled his cloak as he shot down.

Rai landed atop Kyan, knocking his shade from his grip, both of them falling further until their shades caught them. Fax lifted Rai onto the closest floor's railing, where he stood holding a support pillar that ran the length of the atrium.

Kyan stood on the railing one floor up, looking down at Rai, a mix of sadness, frustration, and anger in his eyes. "You don't have to do this. Just go back to whatever you have been doing these last five years!" Kyan shouted.

Fax lashed out as a dark tendril, but Kyan parried the blow with a wave of shadow. Rai jumped, arm outstretched so Fax could grab him and flew upwards, kicking Kyan in the chest.

Kyan flew back into the floor with a grunt, the leatherbound book sent skittering away.

"Do you have any idea the number of people this could hurt? Innocent people, Kyan," Rai said.

Kyan sat coughing and rubbing his chest. "If they are innocent, they have nothing to fear. And what of the innocents we killed?"

"We were following orders," Rai said.

Kyan grunted and an onslaught of razor-sharp attacks launched at Rai. Fax countered as much as it could, but some cut through, leaving a gash on Rai's arm and thigh. Rai pressed in, and for a while they traded shadowed blows.

It seemed their shades were evenly matched, making any hit a matter of chance. A cut sliced across Rai's face, and he growled. Rai ran and dove under the fighting shades, tackling Kyan to the ground.

Kyan's eyes widened in surprise as they fell back, Rai pinning him. "We could go back together. Make changes the right way," Rai whispered.

Kyan struggled. "You know you can't. Not with her still running everything."

Kyan took advantage of the distracting mention of empress, and head-butted Rai. With a *crack,* blood gushed from Rai's nose. He rolled off, clutching at it. Kyan swung his leg around to catch the side of Rai's head, but his training kicked in and Rai caught the leg, twisting it. Kyan squealed, trying to follow the unnatural arc as Rai tossed him back. They lay for a couple heart beats groaning.

"At least you listened when I talked about distracting an

enemy that's stronger than you," Rai said, dragging himself to his feet and wiping the blood from his face.

"I always listened to you," Kyan said, hissing when he put pressure on the leg that Rai twisted.

"Well, not always, or we wouldn't be here," Rai said, diving in for another attack.

As Rai stepped in, Kyan unsheathed a curved blade, swiping it in a wide arc. Rai dodged, stepping back, but felt the air ripple as the blade just missed his face. Rai had purposely not used his weapons, hoping to incapacitate Kyan instead of doing any actual harm. Kyan clearly didn't hold the same reservations.

"I'm sorry it had to end like this," Kyan said.

Kyan rushed him, slicing diagonally. Fax jolted over and smacked the slash away, as Rai followed it with a kick in the gut.

Kyan's shade ripped into Rai's back and he screamed, falling forward. Falling to his knees, Rai hissed, but part of him felt relieved. Kyan's shade could have killed him right there and then, which meant Kyan didn't let it.

Rai unfurled from his huddle, whistling through his teeth at the pain. Glancing up, he watched as Kyan stepped back onto the railing, book in hand.

Kyan grimaced at Rai, then jumped, his shade darting off and materializing as a glider again.

You okay? Fax asked as Rai forced himself to his feet.

Rai broke into a run, launching over the railing in pursuit.

42

A Flame Ignited

I know you're near, champion of the shadowed one, the voice from the dark whispered.

Pulling books off the shelf, Nya squeezed through the gap and crawled over to the far wall. The stone ground was cold on her hands as she padded across it, and Nya wriggled her nose against the dust. One sneeze and the dark would be upon her.

She glanced over her shoulder through the shelves to where a swirling darkness covered a space where glass boxes held strange objects. Every time she looked at that darkness, panic rose up her throat. Nya tore her gaze away and steeled herself.

Focus, Nya thought. *Just keep moving. Don't think.*

Edging along the far wall, Nya came to a brass door. She

448

cracked it open and slid through.

Bom flared warning and Nya came to an abrupt stop at the edge of a massive cylindrical chamber. It dropped endlessly with the occasional light orb lighting patches of the pit.

Nya eased the door shut and skirted the edge of the drop. As she peered into the hole, Nya noted that the walls of the drop were covered in light orbs but most were cracked and broken, only a few still producing any light.

"What is this place?" Nya asked, and unlike the library proper her voice echoed into the dark.

The Ahmune's prison, Bom said.

"That thing was imprisoned here?"

How had such a creature been trapped in this chamber? Who had trapped it in here and why?

"Wait, if it was locked in here could we lead it back in and trap it?"

The light orbs, Bom said.

Nya looked down into the pit again. *The light orbs had kept it in here*, Nya realised. A creature of shadow weakened and held by light. At some point over the thousands of years since the calamity the Ahmune must have figured out a way to destroy some of the orbs and free itself. Or perhaps they had broken or faded themselves with times passing. Either way, with no one maintaining the light, the chamber couldn't hold the Ahmune any longer.

Back against the wall, Nya slid down to seating and placed her head in her hands. "How did I get into this mess?" Nya whispered.

It felt like just yesterday she had been running around Yontar with the Sand Rats. Now she was in a library, said to be lost to time, being hunted by ancient creatures straight out of legend.

It all stemmed from going to that dark place. If she hadn't been arrested to escape those Ghrobans, would her life have been normal?

All Nya wanted was to survive, but in doing so, she had lost everyone. Mother. The Sand Rats. Kit. Dust. *They all leave in the end.*

She let her feet hang over the edge and peered down into the black.

What was the point in going on? What did she see for herself? Distant days held no promise.

Kyan would've gotten out and he would find a way to punish those who made her life a living torment realm. That would have to be enough.

Nya let her eyes and mind glaze over as she stared into the impenetrable dark.

The door behind her creaked open and something soft rubbed against her back.

"Nya?"

Nya lifted her head, coming back to herself. She wasn't sure how long she had been sitting there.

"Are you okay?" Kit asked.

Kit?

At first she thought it her imagination, but she spun to see

Dust pressing against her back.

Nya's heart dropped. They should have been safe back in the caves. Not here. "What are you doing here?"

"You can thank Dust. She ran off. Must have smelled you," Kit said bending down onto his haunches beside her and holding out his hand. "If we can find you in a library that no one has stepped in for thousands of years, I don't think you should worry about us not finding you wherever you go."

"You shouldn't be here," Nya snapped.

Kit's face dropped. "We came for you."

"It's not safe. We need to go. Now," Nya said. Energy flared through Nya as she stood. She couldn't be the reason these two died too.

"I don't understand," Kit said, as Nya leaned against the door, peeking through the gap.

"Come on," Nya whispered and slid back out into the library.

Kit was about to say something else when Nya shushed him. She had to get them out. The look on Pyna and Jip's faces and the cracking that came from the shadow echoed in her mind. She couldn't let the same happen to them.

Nya crept along the bookshelves, waving Kit and Dust to follow.

"Nya, stop. What is going on?"

"You shouldn't have come for me," Nya said.

"We couldn't just leave you," Kit said.

"You should have!" Nya said spinning to face him. "You don't understand, you damn fool! I'll just pull you into darkness."

Kit stared at her a moment. "Or we could pull you out of it."

The words hit like the heat of the Sun Eye. Emotion welled in Nya's throat.

Nearby a light orb smashed, blinking out of existence.

"It's here." It was too late. "Run!" she screamed, and the three of them broke into a sprint.

Behind the dark was closing in.

"What is that?!" Kit screamed as they tore down the library.

A roiling wave of black rushed at them as they barrelled forward, past shelves and more glass cases holding mysterious items. Light orbs shattered behind them, growing louder as it drew closer.

Dust padded ahead of them, galloping, and leading the way. Blood pumped in Nya's ears, her legs burning.

Smash… smash… SMASH!

Nya didn't need to glance over her shoulder to tell it was on their heels.

With another crash, darkness engulfed them.

It wasn't like extinguishing a lantern. This darkness felt like a smog, heavy and thick. The next light orb looked dimmer and further away, as if seen through a tinted lens. The Ahmune laughed, a deep rumble that bounced around in the dark. Its voice was clearer now she was in there with it.

Panic flooded Nya. She could have faced this alone, but the thought of Kit and Dust befalling the same fate sent icy terror through her veins.

A breath of hot wind blew over her neck. It was there.

Bom poured out, feeding on Nya's emotions, and lashed out behind her. She didn't turn or slow, but awareness of what Bom was doing was there. Like how she knew what her arm was doing without looking at it. It struck something. And the Ahmune grunted in pain. Surprise blossomed in both Bom and Nya's mind. They knew it had to have a physical form. Bom had shown her what it looked like in her mind, but neither had expected to be able to fight it or cause it injury.

Bom then threw everything it had at the beast.

Tendrils whipped out, arching blades in the dark, as they continued to run. The Ahmune hissed and growled in frustration. Ahead, Nya saw the area open to an atrium where two specs darted about over the drop. It was Kyan, and he was fighting… Rai?

"Hey!" Nya screamed. Kit spotted them too and joined the shouting.

Kyan and Rai noticed them just as the darkness reached the atrium and threw the entire space into the gusting black.

Nya huddled with Kit and Dust at the railing where Bom battered away anything that came close. Peering into the dark, Nya couldn't make out Kyan anymore. The blustering black covered everything.

Nya pulled Kit and Dust closer, eyes fluttering against the gales. Then in the dark a flame lit. It was small and a good distance away, born into a world trying to extinguish it. But it burned brighter, flared higher, until it burst outward into a flaming vortex, spiralling and shooting outward.

The flames reached out and Nya felt the heat. The Ahmune squealed and it grew a little brighter. Bright enough to see Rai standing on the railing across the atrium, slashing and swinging around his daggers that sent waves of flames into the dark. The incandescent glow lit his frenzied eyes, and firm, determined expression. Even Kyan, who stood a few paces away, watched in awe.

Kyan jumped and ran along the railing, positioning himself across from Rai, and shouted something to Rai, but Nya couldn't make out what. Rai nodded, sliding his hand down into his belt, then tossed a small vial of something red to Kyan, who unstoppered it, and poured it into the end of his dagger.

A breath later and flames erupted from Kyan's daggers too, tearing through the black. Nya saw an outline of a creature in the darkness. Pale plated skin that looked like armour.

The Ahmune.

A vicious roar cut through the din as the dark thickened, trying to consume the flames.

An idea sprung to her mind, and Bom reacted immediately, shooting off towards the Ahmune. With it distracted, Bom could make a move. The shade cut into its hide, sliding between the plating.

The Ahmune let out a scream of pain that shook the foundations of the lost library. Nya cupped her ears, squeezing tight against the violent sound that ripped through the air.

I will kill — the Ahmune started, but two plumes of flame

battered against its form. It squealed again as it threw itself over the balcony edge, falling with its too thick darkness into the abyss of the library.

They watched as it dropped out of sight, a cloud of swirling black shrinking as it fell.

It was gone. For now.

It was still dark, the nearby light orbs having been destroyed, but it wasn't the ethereal darkness of the Ahmune. Nya drank in the air like she had been locked up in the attic, with its musty thickness, and this was the first breath of fresh air she had in days.

Rhythmic panting sounded around them. Rai shot over the distance, knocking Kyan down. Rai pinned his arms while Fax wrestled Kyan's shade.

"We don't understand the horrors of the past Kyan! Can't you see that now," Rai said.

Nya studied the two as they fought. Her breath steadying as she got up and approached. Kyan's eyes were bloodshot and wild.

"The horrors of the past might be what we need to fight the horrors to come," Kyan said.

Rai glanced up at Nya. "Nya, quickly, I have a vial in my belt that will subdue him." Kyan thrashed against him. "Quickly Nya!"

Nya looked between them. If she helped Rai she could return to The Patched Cloak with Kit and Dust. She could go back to training on the rooftop with Rai and eating dinner with Illy and Wenson.

But that wasn't enough. Nya couldn't control the shade inside her and it could hurt those she loved. Kit and Dust almost died to the Ahmune and they were only here because of her.

Flashes of Mother being impaled by darkness sprung to Nya's mind.

The emptiness would remain if she returned. This hollowed out feeling that consumed her. Guilt for killing Mother. Guilt for not being able to be normal. Guilt for not finding joy in the simple things like Kit could. The darkness was eroding her from the inside and she wouldn't let it reach her friends.

And they would all leave soon enough anyway.

The Harbinger of Justice would end it. Nya would be killed for her crimes and they would be safe in a world better off without her and those who made her like this.

Bom whipped out and lashed Rai, who was sent flying and cracked against a support pillar.

He was staring at Nya, betrayal lining his face, when Kyan's shade cracked him across the face and he went limp.

Nya swallowed then ran over to help Kyan to his feet. "Is he going to be okay?"

"He's just knocked out." Kyan pulled himself to his feet. "He'll be fine."

"Nya?" Kit's voice was weak and scratchy. She spun to see him standing gingerly, Dust staring at her from between his legs again.

"I'm sorry," Nya said, and Dust growled at her. *Growled*

at her. "Dust?"

"I don't like Rai. You know this. But this is wrong, Nya. I know what he is planning," Kit said, flicking his head at Kyan.

Nya was staring at Dust, who bore her teeth at Nya. She had never in the entire time Nya knew her done anything remotely aggressive towards her before.

Darkness pooled around Kyan, his shade preparing to attack.

"No, don't," Nya said. "Leave them."

She met Kit's gaze. "Forgive me," she pleaded, reaching out again, but Dust snapped this time.

Nya's heart sank. Kyan was walking away and called to her. She looked over at him, then back to Kit and Dust. With tears filling her eyes, she turned before they could see and jogged to catch up with Kyan.

Kyan led her, unspeaking, through the library and to an arch not unlike the one that led into the staircase.

Dust had *snapped* at her. Nya couldn't get the image of her out of her head. Was it because she hurt Rai? Because she was leaving with Kyan?

Nya wiped the tears from her face.

Kit waited until they were out of sight before running over to Rai. He dropped down beside him. Rai's eyes were shut but darting back and forth, staring at nothing Kit could see.

That can't be a good sign, Kit thought. Kit shook him lightly, but he didn't stir.

"Come on, Rai," Kit said. "You can fend off a giant shadow demon, but a bash to the head floors you?"

He's not responding to me, Fax said, sitting as a crow beside Rai.

Rai's face was tight. Dust brushed against his leg.

"This isn't working," Kit said, then slapped Rai across the face. "Wake up, you damn leaking bucket. I swear if you don't, I'm going to come in there and show you how we fight on the streets. None of this forms and drills nonsense!"

Rai lay, unseeing, a haunted look creasing his paling bronze skin.

43

Light Winds Howl

L ight glinted between the leaves shifting in the breeze. The Green Leaf Orphanage was known for the tree in its courtyard. A wealthy patron that had once been an orphan had gifted it to the orphanage. And it was Rai's favourite spot. He had found a perfect nook in the roots for him to sit in and shield himself from the Sun Eye's gaze.

The orphanage was a three-story stone building, with regular shuttered windows for the many small rooms it contained. Some other kids ran about in the courtyard between Rai and the orphanage, but they would go inside soon before it got too hot.

This was Rai's resting time. He had worked out all morning, doing pull-ups on the tree branches, and some other movements he'd read in a book. He made a vow to himself to get strong so he could defend himself and those he loved.

This pushed away the other kids though, most didn't want to do gruelling workouts in the early morning. They wanted to play.

Rai didn't mind.

The long sliding doors were open, revealing most of the ground floor of the orphanage. Maut-Eln, the mother of the orphanage, was rushing around inside. Maut meant mother, but it was used for motherly figures rather than the one who gave birth to them. Often small villages in the desert had a Maut. Someone who cared for the others like they were her own.

But Maut-Eln was a stern and unrelenting middle-aged woman. Which was probably the reason she was beginning to grey at the edges of her dark hair. Rai avoided her when he could. She wasn't cruel, but if you caught her in a bad mood, it was difficult not to do something that wouldn't end in a lashing.

She busied herself passing back and forth, making sure all the children had done their chores and that the place was clean. This type of dashing around meant one thing: they were going to have a new member at The Green Leaf Orphanage.

The breeze brushed through the roots of the tree in a calming rustle of the branches and leaves. With his eyes closed, Rai would still imagine the green canopy above him flowing in the light winds. This was his favourite part of the day, so he savoured it a moment longer, before pushing himself up and making his way inside to start his chores.

Best not to be found idling about when Maut-Eln was on the prowl.

Rai was sweeping the sand from the hallways when the new one arrived. Some guards dropped him off, Maut-Eln ushering him inside. The new ones face was drawn, and his sagging eyes showed many sleepless nights. He was of an age with Rai, eight or nine years old. The boy looked up, catching Rai's eye before Maut-Eln led him away.

It wasn't until after qed that Rai saw the boy again. They were in the feast hall, as Maut-Eln liked to call it, but in actual fact, it was no larger than other rooms in the orphanage, and all of the children crammed in around the three narrow tables to eat.

They had all hunkered down for afternoon mealtime, when Maut-Eln clapped twice and the room fell silent.

"We have a new family member," Maut-Eln said, her voice prim and proper, curling around each word's inflections and sounds like it was a speech test. "This is Kon."

The boy had dusty, dirty blond hair, left long and unruly. It fell in strands over his face and he had to brush it back regularly. Nervously, Kon bowed, probably hoping it would speed the ordeal up. "You must all make him feel welcome and introduce yourselves before dark hour. Okay, you can go sit now," Maut-Eln said, nudging the boy forward.

Rai saw Zin and his cronies whispering and staring at Kon, who sat further down at the table Rai was at. They were probably going to recruit him into their club. They had tried the same with Rai when he first got here. Rai declined, and they made his life a living torment realm because of it. Rai should warn him. Tell the new kid to join their damn club.

No, best to not get involved, Rai decided, sniffing and turning back to his food. He had survived so far by keeping his head down, and he planned to keep on surviving.

As the Sun Eye was nearing the end of its watch, they were allowed to go outside and play. Rai had finished the last of his chores and stepped out to spend some time relaxing at the base of the tree, when he noticed someone had already taken his spot. Kon. While the other kids played games and ran around, Kon had a book propped on his legs. He didn't glance up, enveloped in whatever he was reading.

Rai sighed, making his way around to the side where another, not quite as comfortable, nook was among the roots. He leant back, looking up at the vivid green leaves shaking in the wind. The sound of the others playing quietened as Rai focused on the soft whistle of the breeze and he closed his eyes.

"Are we forced back inside during dark hour?" a voice asked. It cut through Rai's quiet like a blade. Rai opened his eyes to see Kon having inched around beside him.

"Yes," Rai said, and closed his eyes again.

"Why?" Kon asked. Rai sighed and looked at Kon.

"Because it's dangerous," Rai said, sitting up.

"Not in the city," Kon said.

Rai shrugged. "Maut-Eln says only shady characters are

out during dark hour."

Kon thought this over. "What if I'm a shady character?"

Rai snorted. The boy was shorter than Rai and had the thin limbs of one who had to search for their next meal. "You look as threatening as a bone tree."

The thin, brittle tree could be snapped with one hand, and Rai was certain he could do the same with Kon's arms and legs.

A grin spread across Kon's face. "You aren't exactly one of the palace guard yourself," Kon said, gesturing to Rai's boyishly skinny frame.

"Not yet," Rai said.

Leaning over, Kon dipped his head. "I'm Kon."

Hesitating only a moment, Rai bowed back and said, "Rai."

"What do you do for fun around here?" Kon asked, looking around. Rai followed his gaze and noticed Zin's crew standing around, talking. Zin, however, was staring at them.

Kon kept talking, but Rai focused on Zin as he straightened and made his way over the courtyard towards them. Rai's heart stopped.

"What's this then?" Zin said as he approached.

"We are just thinking of what to do before we head in. You want to join?" Kon asked. He didn't understand. How could he? He had only been there a morning.

"You with this loner?" Zin asked, waving a hand at Rai. "Why don't you come join us? We could do with upping our numbers to help keep these Duat-damned fools in line." Zin ran his hand over the courtyard like an emperor would his kingdom.

Kon frowned, piecing together the social hierarchy in the orphanage, and that he was hanging out with lowly members. Rai said nothing but waited for Kon to go off with Zin. It was the sensible option.

After a lengthy pause, Kon said, "No, thanks."

Zin's head jerked. "No? Do you know what you're turning down? A chance to get extra food, get others to do your chores, and you're turning it down?"

"All I see is a group of lazy black sand footed fools who think they can push people around," Kon said.

Rai savoured the image of Zin's mouth falling agape in utter bewilderment. He couldn't believe anyone would talk to Zin like that. Zin was the biggest kid in the orphanage. Even the Mauts avoided him and were known to turn a blind eye to some of his antics.

Zin recomposed his face into a sneer. "You, fresh blood, are about to learn a very valuable lesson," Zin said, cracking his neck.

Rai clenched his fists. He hadn't wanted a fight, but he wasn't going to leave the new kid to deal with Zin alone.

"What are you lot doing?" Maut-Fer asked, laying a hand on Zin's shoulder. Her meaty fingers clutching knowingly tight around him. She was a big lady, and one of the few that actively tried to stop Zin.

Tension held between the bunch for a moment longer, before Zin's face softened and he said, "Just getting to know each other better, Maut-Fer." His face tightened when he turned back to Kon. "We will have to spend more time together later."

With that, Zin stalked off.

Maut-Fer gave a polite smile. "I'm glad you are getting along."

She bowed and wandered off.

"You just made an enemy today," Rai said, watching Zin join his gang, whispering to them in a huddle.

"So did he," Kon replied.

Rai had to give the kid credit. He had guts. But that was just more to spill.

Tossing and turning, Rai slept little that night worrying about facing Zin. He would wreak havoc on their lives now. And it was made worse by the fact Kon wasn't in Rai's room. Separated, they made easy targets. He rubbed his face against his soft pillow, trying to push the thoughts out of his head. They wouldn't hurt them so soon after Maut-Fer saw them arguing, he was sure of it. Despite his worries, Rai soon joined the chorus of droning snores in their shared room.

Rai felt better the following day. Rest having dulled the sharpness of fear. Whatever came they would face together, Rai thought, wandering down to the feast chamber. That was what was important.

Strutting confidently in with his breakfast, Rai eyed the room for Kon. He wasn't in yet, so Rai sat in his usual spot in the corner with his back to the wall. His stomach growled as he shovelled in his bread dipped in rich spices.

Others were seated and eating their breakfast as more filtered through. Eventually Zin and his crew came through, laughing and shoving each other around. Rai watched them with disdain as they made their way to their table.

Zin grinned at Rai.

Rai went cold.

That smug devilish grin held implications that Rai didn't want to think about. His stomach roiled.

This was a taunt.

Rai stood, throwing back his bowl. Zin's grin grew wider, and Rai darted out of the room, one of the Mauts shouting after him.

Rai tore down the corridor to one of the four boys' rooms that he knew Kon was staying in and threw back the door. It was empty. Panic had Rai twitching as he turned back out of the room. Where else could he be?

Washroom. Rai sprinted down the creaking corridors of the orphanage.

As Rai approached, he saw the orphanages artisan pushing past two Mauts who were covering their faces in shock. He was the only man working in the orphanage and spent most of his time mending the rickety building.

"What is it? Is Kon in there?" Rai asked, trying to push through, but Maut-Fer held him back.

"Stay back child, someone has fallen," Maut-Fer said.

Dread bubbled up Rai's throat. He shoved through harder and stepped into the washroom.

Lying sprawled out in a pool of blood was Kon.

The artisan covered him in a towel, and in moving him revealed a gaping wound that split the back of Kon's head. Rai felt like he was going to be sick.

"He's going to be okay," Rai mumbled as the Mauts came to his side, inspecting the gash on Kon's head.

This all felt so *familiar*.

The windows blotted out to an inky black, like it was suddenly dark hour. But wasn't it just morning? And the blood glinted a too vivid red against the grey washroom.

An eerie feeling gripped Rai.

"You did this," Maut-Fer said, not taking her eyes off Kon. "You let him brush off Zin so he could be friends with you. So selfish." Her voice was soft and haunting, not accusing, but as if she was talking about the weather.

"I... I... what?" Rai asked, stepping backwards.

"You did this," Maut-Fer said, head creaking around, her mouth drawn into a rictus grin.

"Why didn't you warn me, Rai?" Kon's head *snapped* as it spun around to stare at him. "They only hurt me because I was with you."

"I'm sorry," Rai said, walking backwards, but not seeming to get any further from their piercing eyes. "You're going to be okay. I remember you survived this."

"I can't talk or feed myself after this. All because of you," Kon said, blood running over his lips in long goopy drips.

"I'm sorry! I should have done something... I should have... I..." Rai's breath caught.

The blood pooling around Kon had reached Rai's feet and was covering his boots. Rai tried to pull them back, but blood gripped them like quicksand as it ran over his feet and up to his ankles.

Rai screamed and fell back. He yanked at his legs, trying to free them from the consuming crimson running up his calves. He kicked one leg with the other, and the blood flinched, allowing him to tear a leg free. Desperately, he battered the blood and hauled his other leg out, scrambling to his feet.

Then Rai turned and ran. Kon's blaming screams chasing him down the darkening corridor.

44

The Dusted Warren

Nya trudged along behind Kyan. They passed under an arch and into a small empty chamber. At the back of the chamber a stone hatch clung to the wall, with an iron bar protruding outward. Kyan set his book down, which he had been hugging to his chest like a mother would her child, grabbed the bar and heaved. It creaked and groaned as it slowly slid around. Kyan's arms were taut, face strained and sweat lathered.

The bar clicked vertically and Kyan stood back, breathing hard. Then with a light push, the hatch swung open into a darkened cave. Kyan laid a hand on Nya's shoulder and blew out a breath.

"You did the right thing. Rai is a good man, but he doesn't have the stomach to do what needs to be done," Kyan said.

Kyan ducked through the hatch.

If it was the right thing then why did she feel so bad? And why did Dust shy away from her?

This is how I am, Nya reminded herself, glimpses of the attic flashing red. Nya hardened herself. She had committed to this path of revenge and injustice now.

They followed the cave for a short time before they surfaced. Sunlight poured in from above giving them enough light traverse the cave floor. They clambered out onto the coarse sand, and into stifling heat of the desert.

Nya dragged herself out of the crevice in the rocks, coughing as the sand and dust caught in her throat, blinking away what got in her eyes. Kyan stood, brushing off the worst of the sand and grime, as Nya pushed to her feet. Glancing around, Nya noted they were on the other side of the high ridged rock formation that they took shelter in.

"What now? Are we going back to the cave?" Nya asked.

"No need," Kyan said. "It's well documented that the library has many exits, so I thought we would come out somewhere else." He scanned the area then nodded north-west. "We need to go that way."

Kyan carefully made his way down the screed side of the rocks. Nya squinted to the north-west, but other than another rock formation that grew some foliage she couldn't see anything. With an internal shrug, she made her way after him.

"Bom, that thing we killed…"

We didn't kill the Child of the Dark. It fled, Bom said.

470

"Do you know what it meant when it spoke of being a champion of the shadowed one?" Nya asked.

Bom was silent for a long time. Nya thought it might go back to not talking like before the library, but eventually it spoke up again.

Humans with shades are champions, Bom said.

"I don't understand," Nya said, sliding then hopping over a rock.

Neither do I. It sounded puzzled, like it thought it should know but didn't. *I just know this is true.*

Nya didn't push more. She liked that they spoke now, even if Bom was a little cold. She felt Bom bristle, forgetting it could read her thoughts. Nya thought an apology, and then focused on scaling down the side of a rock.

Kyan stood waiting and set off as soon as she caught up. They plodded through thick, soft sands with clomping footsteps, already wearied by the Sun. Nya wanted to ask where they were headed but she didn't have the energy, instead focusing on breathing and wading onward.

Eventually, they came to an outcropping of rock. A smoke stream sailed upward between its ridges before dissipating in the haze. Nya assumed it was a trick of the heat, but as they got closer, she saw two men sitting around a pot which was producing the smoke. They stood as Kyan and Nya approached and bowed their heads.

"Kyan, your mission was a success?" one asked in a soft deep voice. Both men were bald and wore the strangest clothing. It was like armour but lighter, buckles and straps held it across the front, and a hood draped across their shoulders. They wore boots that came to their knees and it was all the same dark brown colour. It looked to be far too warm for desert attire, Nya thought.

"Very much so," Kyan said, passing into the shade.

The one who spoke nodded to the other shorter man and the shorter man ran off, bounding up the outcropping with inhuman agility. Nya spun to see Kyan's reaction at the strange behaviour, but he settled down beside the pot and poured himself some coffee. He noticed Nya staring and laughed.

"It's okay," Kyan said. "Come sit. He is just running off to tell the others in the cave to come and meet us."

Warily, Nya sat beside Kyan. The remaining man said nothing as Kyan sipped his coffee and flicked through the leatherbound book. It reminded Nya of someone... Bas. These strange men with their strange mannerisms were eerily similar to Bas, the bald boy who was part of The Doomed Others.

"Are you part of the Urdahl?" Nya asked.

The man's piercing eyes landed on her. "Yes."

"Do you know a boy called Bas? Did he make it back?" Nya asked. The man peered searchingly into her eyes but didn't give any indication if he knew Bas.

"Maren isn't a big talker," Kyan said, not looking up from his book. "None of the Urdahl are, and they don't take kindly to those snooping into their ways."

"Sorry, I didn't mean to pry. I knew him," Nya said. The

man went back to staring out at the desert, but Nya could have sworn every time she wasn't looking his eyes were on her.

The Sun Eye was not long into its watch, which meant they had been in the library for a whole day and a night. Fatigue was setting in. Nya hadn't felt it with all the adrenaline pumping through her, but now the light-headedness and stinging eyes told her she needed sleep.

Jip and Pyna! I never told Kyan that they had died, Nya realised in her sleep deprived haze.

"Kyan, Jip and Pyna they…" Nya searching for the right words, memories of darkness consuming them prickling the hairs on the back of her neck.

"The Ahmune?" Kyan asked.

Nya inclined her head. And Kyan let out a breath before going back to his book. "They were good people. We must not let their sacrifice be in vain." And with that, he was scouring through that damn leatherbound book again.

"That's it?" Nya said. He cared more for that book than of his friends.

Kyan glanced up and must have seen her frustration as his lips drew to a line. "Look, Nya, they knew the risks and mission we set out for. This is bigger than any of us. If I died, I would want you to finish this. We are doing this for the future of the world, and more blood will stain the sands before this is over. Do you understand?"

"Yeah," Nya said.

She understood but didn't like it. Nya wasn't sure she

could follow through if it were Kit and Dust at risk. Ma-atan only killed the unjust, and both were the kindest beings she had ever met. *They will be fine.*

However, those like her father, who abandoned her mother, those who left her and Mother to struggle to survive, The Sand Rats that abandoned her, and those in the palace who sent her to the dark place and caused her mother's death; they all deserved the reckoning that was coming.

There was agreement and feelings of anger from Bom as Nya sat with her thoughts. It understood and fed on her emotions as she did on its. She didn't blame Bom for her mother's death, like she didn't blame a knife for those it cut. Nya had killed her Mother. She would have to live with that. But the ones who handed her a knife were going to pay.

Nya emptied her cup ruminating on dark thoughts when Kyan sprung up with a yelp. "Found it," Kyan said mouth stretched in a grin. "Ma-atan had a temple where it was said to rest on the outskirts of Asuriya."

Kyan brought the book over to Maren, pulling out a map and pointing between the two. Not being able to read was common on the streets of Yontar, but Nya felt leagues away from that world now and wished she could help.

It was well before midday when they set out, having only rested for a short time. Maren had shared some dried meat strips, which helped fight back the exhaustion.

Maren packed up the pot and put out the fire, throwing everything into a pack and slinging it over his shoulder. He then powered up the side of the outcropping with the ease of one well-travelled in the desert. Kyan and Nya tried their best to keep up, but still Maren had to regularly wait for them.

Maren brought them to a crack in the rock on the other side of the plateau. He tossed the pack in, then squeezed through, waving them through once he had landed.

"Wait, what about the rest of the Decreed?" Nya asked.

"The other Urdahl will track us. Maren has been leaving tracks for him to follow," Kyan said gesturing to a scraped footprint in the gravel. The mark was barely noticeable, but after seeing how the Urdahl moved in the desert, Nya guessed they were capable trackers.

Stepping up to the crevice and peering in, the tunnel was cramped with no room to turn if they ran into anything. *Come on Nya. After all you have been through, a small space is going to stop you?*

Nya fed her legs through the crack, pushing herself back into it with her hands. She inhaled sharply as the sides of the rock scraped along her back and sides. Turning her head sideways as it reached the crack, she dropped the rest of the way to the ground.

Nya shuffled up to let Kyan slip through, keeping a couple paces between her and Maren. As soon as Kyan landed, Maren scuttled off down the tunnel.

"Best to stick as close to him as you can. The last thing we want is to get lost down here," Kyan said.

Lost?

It wasn't long before Nya realised where the concern came from. Many other tunnels branched off, curving this way and that. Maren set a demanding pace given they couldn't stand erect and had to march on their haunches. He must have used these tunnels often to move with such ease. At some sections, Nya had to drop to her hands and knees to squeeze around a bend. The walls and floor were jagged and Nya nicked herself more than once trying to keep up, but there was a flow to them that spoke of unnatural intervention.

Nya worried it would be too dark to follow Maren, but tunnels regularly broke off and twisted up to the surface letting sunlight pour in.

Eventually, Maren took one of the smaller tunnels towards the light, and they surfaced through a slightly wider gap than they had entered.

Nya rolled her spine up to standing, and it clicked and creaked after spending so long hunched over. Kyan was arching his neck too. The only one unphased by the tunnel travel was Maren.

"The Urdahl, or The Burrowed People in the old tongue, live underground and use these tunnels between their settlements. Although I think we are on the outskirts of where they stay now. They say you can stand in some tunnels closer to their settlements," Kyan whispered to her.

"They live out here? In the middle of nowhere?" Nya asked.

Kyan nodded. "They believe hardship and struggle in this life will reward them in the afterlife."

"No, we believe hardship and struggle rewards us in this life *and* the next," Maren said, despite Kyan having whispered it.

Kyan looked chagrined for the first time since Nya met him. It was also the first time she heard him get something wrong.

They marched on under the overbearing heat of the Sun Eye. Dunes flowed around them as still waves of sand, broken by rock outcroppings small and large. Nya panted, hands pushing on her knees, as they made their way up a step-like patch of rock.

Cresting the rocky ridge, Nya gawked at her surroundings. Only a short walk across a sandy plain was the ruined capital of Asuriya. Its structures still standing tall after thousands of years of being abandoned. Rumours on how it had survived were rampant on the streets of Yontar. Nya didn't know what to believe but being so close made her feel uneasy.

"Is this safe?" she asked.

"Yes, we should be fine. We aren't getting any closer and recent reports have said others that have passed through the edges of Asuriya haven't died from the sickness," Kyan said.

"Life is returning to the places of old," Maren said, staring at it. "The signs have shown. Creatures living close are daring to enter the ruined city once more."

The hairs on Nya's arms stood on end hearing Maren's words. They sounded poetic, or even prophetic. Wildlife returning to the city was a good thing though, right? The people of Tarris hadn't reclaimed Asuriya after the calamity all those thousands of years ago because of the sickness. Anyone who had entered the city since, or even got too close, grew

477

sick and died within a couple days, making it impossible to recover anything.

Of course there were those who didn't believe in the sickness and travelled into the city in search of fortune. So a handful of relics had found their way back into Tarris through scavengers, but none were said to have survived.

Nya kept her eyes on the capital as they hiked over the rocky terrain, a rock wall on their left shielding them from the Sun Eye. As the buildings moved and shifted perspectives, Nya got her first proper glimpse of the Mad Palace, where the emperor had stayed in the old capital.

The colossal palace was said to be larger than the Thousand Floor Palace in Yontar, reaching high enough to scrape the sky. Most notably though was the huge chunk cut out the side of it, and how the debris floated, suspended in the air unconnected to anything. She had heard that it looked like an explosion frozen in time, but she had never believed it. It was too far to see much detail, but pieces of the palace *did* hang in the air around the dent in its side, unmoving.

Nya was about to ask about it when they came to the end of the rock and Maren hopped down, following a cliff side on his right.

"No wonder no one found this place," Kyan said, jumping down after him. "Most wouldn't dare get this close to Asuriya, and those who did would go into the city to loot."

They marched along hugging the cliff, another ridge raising on their left and corralling them inward. The sand here was more solid than in the open desert, making it easier to walk on. There used to be a path, Nya realised stomping and feeling the stone beneath the piled sand.

The path led them into an enclosed space, and at the back was the unmistakable entrance to a temple.

Carved into the cliff was an opening, pillars lining either side of it. As they got closer, they saw carvings of Ma-atan etched into the walls. A set of scales drawn on one pillar, with a heart depicted on one side, and a feather on the other. One of the many symbols for the Weigher of Souls.

Kyan ran his hand over the carvings. They had lost vividness over thousands of years, sand having eroded the temple walls, but it was still clear enough to make out the tapestries from times long past.

Maren stayed back, face neutral, but his distance from the temple revealed his wariness and unease.

Above the entrance, Ma-atan was carved into the stone, arms wrapping around the door, similar to the carving around the door in the Thousand Floor Palace dungeons. It had a long torso and blade-like arms, with a narrow face coming to a point. Nya had seen depictions of Ma-atan before and, although similar, this one had distinct differences. Its body looked like stacked bones sharpened at the edges and sticking out like fins. And its arms were longer than depictions she had seen before, coming all the way down to its knees.

Nya shivered afraid to take her eyes off it.

Kyan stood at the entrance, smiling.

"Are we ready to wake a god?" he asked.

45

The Many Doors Past

Rai sprinted down an expanding corridor. It lengthened even as he ran. Doors lined both sides, all different and linked to memories and places. Some little more than tarps hung over doorframes, others grand ornate brass doors with curved handles and swirling patterns.

Scents intrinsically tied to times long past hit like walls as he passed each door before petering out again. The rusty scent of blood gave way to the salty, aromatic smell of fine dining, before dissipating to the unwashed stench of sweat, all linked to key moments throughout Rai's life that flashed in his mind. He knew running was futile. This corridor had no end, but he couldn't stop. He couldn't face what the doors hid.

The stone floor swelled and crested like the ocean, making it hard to run on. The swells rose to the point where Rai was doing all he could to not be carried away by one. Rumbling rock shook the corridor and filled his ears. Rai hopped between zeniths of the flowing stone path that hurtled towards him, as they grew ever taller. Rai's throat tightened as a rise as high as the ceiling rolled towards him. There was no way over it.

Deciding between letting the oncoming swell sweep him away, Rai hesitated only a moment before crashing through the door on his right.

The door slammed shut behind him, the sound rumbling into silence. Rai lifted his head. He was in a chamber. A fireplace lay empty and cold on his left, and a long wooden table sprawling in the centre of the room marked this as a home of the powerful and wealthy. Someone sat in a chair around the table. They were nothing more than a silhouette to Rai, the window behind them blasting in light and throwing them into shadow.

Rai got to his feet, not taking his eyes from the person. Edging closer, he saw the blood at the man's feet first. Then the smell hit him, a putrid stench that made Rai recoil. He stepped back, hacking and trying to block out the smell. He remembered. Remembered killing this man.

The man's eyes snapped open, staring at Rai.

The room shook. The sound of an oncoming storm roared louder. And a wave of blood darkened the windows as it rolled into the room. Rai wasted no more time and backed through the door he had entered, as an ocean of blood crashed into the chamber. He forced the door closed and everything fell silent once more.

The door didn't take him back to the endless corridor though. An airy breeze swept through an open plan grey stoned space.

Rai stood in the war room in the Atef Palace. A stone table covered in maps of Tarris stood tall and proud in the centre of the chamber, coming to one's chest when standing beside it. A war room table wasn't one to be sat at. The empress and her advisors and generals would stand as they discussed war to respect the lives that were about to be taken. Pins stuck out from the maps marking places of importance, and pieces lay across it as a visual for the Tarrisian soldiers.

Ahead, a woman draped in a red dress stood at the balcony. The dress billowed with her black hair in the warm wind which carried her familiar scent. The red was vibrant and rich against the blue skies. Rai reached out, his stomach fluttering with a mess of emotion. She spun around, her beautiful face tear-streaked and tight with rage.

Rai let his hand fall to his side. She was breathing hard and marched towards him, then plunged a knife into his chest. Rai didn't fight it, just gasped rasping breaths and watched as her fury filled eyes faded with the world around them.

Eyes fluttering open, Rai awoke to screaming. The sky was a storm of grey clouds rolling over one another. He was in that dark place again.

Rai flipped onto his back and looked down at the hoard of husks enveloping the sky. They rained down on Sehban, his brother in arms, arms outstretched, shouting for help.

Rai knew he was going to die. He couldn't fight off all

those husks, and he had lost the rest of the Seven. But he made himself watch as the creatures ripped Sehban apart. Rai made himself remember his shrill screams and how Sehban hadn't wanted to come that day. Sehban had a family matter to attend, but Rai had asked him to come anyway. And now he was dying because of him.

Husk's heads swivelled to stare at Rai as they finished with Sehban. Their red eyes calling for blood. Rai kicked, backing away, then scrambled to his feet. He ran up the side of the black rock, across the scree, and towards a door. It stood out starkly against the otherworldly environment, but Rai had no time to think on it as he burst through, slamming it shut behind him, the husks battering against it.

Turning slowly, Rai heard whimpering. It was Larina. They were back in the cell blocks in Celabar. She held Grenin's corpse. He was beaten and bloodied, long gashes across his body, and he was missing all his fingers.

Larina looked up, eyes red and glazed. "Why did you leave us?"

Rai tried to say something but couldn't.

"They tortured him looking for you!" she screamed.

"No, this is wrong. I saved you both," Rai stammered.

"Do we look saved?!" Larina asked.

"This is wrong," Rai said, backing up into the corridor of the guards' cell block.

Rai shut his eyes. None of this was right. He tried to remember back to the last thing he knew to be true, but he couldn't.

"You left me too," Kyan said.

Rai opened his eyes to see Kyan standing atop the building in the marketplace where he had his rally. The open square was empty, aside from Rai. The sandstone buildings around him were dead; no light in the windows or faces peering from within. "Left me in that dark place," Kyan said. "Let my shade pull me down a dark path."

"I thought you had died!" Rai shouted.

Kyan held his head high, looking down his nose at Rai. Someone shoved past Rai sprinting towards Kyan. Nya. She ran for the building Kyan stood upon, tears running down her face, chased by her own shadow.

"No! Nya, wait!" Rai shouted, chasing after her, but with every step she got further away and Rai wasn't getting anywhere. Rai looked around for something, or someone, or anything that could help. Kit was walking away into one of the alleys.

"Kit! We need to go save Nya!" Rai called.

Kit turned, his face lax, the expression of one who had given up. "It's too late, Rai," Kit said. "You never cared for us."

Rai stopped running and pushing. Kit was right. He hadn't cared what happened to Nya and Kit. He had trained them so they could defend themselves, but Rai knew it wouldn't be enough. It could never have been enough. He abandoned Nya to be whisked away by Kyan and his grand ideals and left Kit to fall to the wayside. Were they going to end up like the ruined lives he had left behind the other doors?

Somewhere deep down, he knew it was yet to be decided. Yet to end in blood and tears. Yet to end as another horror locked behind a door in his mind.

No, he would not let them end up like that.

Rai broke into a run. He wasn't moving, so he ran harder.

Nya entered the building Kyan was on. He had to catch up. He had to. He pushed harder. But he still wasn't moving from the spot. He looked down and the ground moved under him, but the building grew no closer. Rai screamed and threw everything he had into bounding towards that Duat damned door.

The world around him jerked forward. He passed through the door and into a light.

Then he opened his eyes.

Rai gulped a breath of air. A high-ceilinged roof held by stone pillars filled his vision. He was in the Lost Library of Nenelan. That's right, they had been fighting that creature in the shadows, and then... Rai shot up. He was alone.

Rai? You're awake! Fax said.

"Fax, where did Kyan take Nya and Kit? We need to stop him," Rai asked, coming to his feet. He wobbled, feeling a wave of nausea.

Fax flew around him, its wings flapping. It was getting better at imitating a bird. *Nya went with Kyan, but Kit was trying to wake you. He left a short while ago to find water,* Fax said.

"Which way did he go?" Rai asked, glancing around. The jerk of his head made the library lurch and Rai thought he was going to be sick. He closed his eyes letting the nausea pass.

The library still had that eerie sound suppression, but it felt less threatening and empty now that the shadow creature had fled into its depths.

This way, Fax said, flying away from the atrium, and Rai followed.

Rai saw movement between the shelves before he heard them. Coming to the end of a row of bookshelves, Rai saw Kit with his back to him, reading a book and muttering to himself. Dust noticed Rai first and nuzzled into Kit, but he brushed her off and kept reading.

"I'm trying to figure out how to wake that Sun Eye-touched fool up Dust! I don't have time to play or—"

Rai laid a hand on Kit's shoulder and he squealed, spinning and holding the book up defensively. Then, after a moment, he peeked over the top of the tome.

"I wish you wouldn't do that," Kit said.

The book was about states of consciousness. He probably wouldn't have found a way to wake Rai in that, but the fact that he had been looking meant everything to Rai. The Kit who had given up wasn't the one he had in front of him, and Rai planned to keep it that way.

"I haven't been fair to you, Kit. I really appreciate you being here," Rai said with a bow.

Kit's face reddened as he waved the book about. "Fax something is wrong with Rai," he said.

"I'm fine. Now come on. We need to go save Nya," Rai said and walked away, Kit and Dust running to catch up.

Memories sprung from untrodden parts of Rai's mind as they walked, causing Rai to shudder and slow, but they passed after a moment. *No time for this*, Rai thought, shaking his head.

As they continued back up the library floors, the dizzy spells lessened. But the determination of breaking the curse of his past and saving Kyan and Nya remained.

They backtracked through the library, to the top floor, and through the cave towards the camp.

They've gone, Fax said, flying back from scouting ahead.

"But Kyan didn't come this way?" Kit asked, as they passed around the corner and into the massive cavern that once was alight with fires and laughter.

"Kyan must have sent word to them," Rai said, stalking onward through the space, torch held high.

"How are we going to find them now?" Kit asked.

"Come and I'll show you," Rai said.

They marched through the rest of the cave, passing extinguished fire pits, discarded crates that once held food rations and other miscellaneous belongings, indicating they left in haste. Kit wrinkled his nose as they passed the area the Decreed had used to relieve themselves at the edge of camp.

The Sun Eye's glare turned the world into a blinding white as they stepped outside.

Shielding his eyes, Rai scanned the horizon, but they had long gone. He had thought that might be the case with how cool the fire pits were. Rai veered around to the right until his aya came into view. It lay hidden in the shade, among the jagged rising hoodoo rock formations, lazily lapping water from the trough Rai had set up for it.

"Hey buddy," Rai said, running a hand through the aya's fur. The aya didn't look up. Kit snorted at the aya's lack of interest but one glance from Rai and Kit fell silent.

After swiftly packing up the trough, Rai, Kit, and Dust climbed onto the aya's platform.

"What now?" Kit asked.

Rai searched his pockets on his belt and pulled out a thin half circle dark blue gem. The gem glinted in the sunlight. Kit scrunched his eyebrows. "This is what's called lovers' rock," Rai said.

Kit gasped.

"So you've heard of it? Well, you'll know that they come in small little gems like this, and when you snap them in half, they will always point towards the other half," Rai said and placed the lover's rock on his palm. It spun and pointed the flat side, where it had been broken, northward.

"I didn't want to risk losing you or Nya, so I slipped the other halves of these two into your packs," Rai said, sliding another lover's rock from his belt. The gem turned to face Kit.

"I want to be mad, but I'm just so glad we haven't lost Nya," Kit said, with an extended exhale.

Rai whipped the reins, and the aya jerked forward, pulling them out onto the open dunes.

"Let's just hope we aren't too late," Rai whispered.

46

Silverwater Shifts

A breeze carried them into the temple. Nya tread carefully, searching the shadowed places for movement. Pillars towered at either side of them like guardians. Script etched into the pillars was surrounded by more imagery of Ma-atan. Nya walked up to one of the pillars, and a lizard Nya hadn't seen scampered upward, away from her. She traced her finger over the inset script on the stone, where faded lines all led to Ma-atan's unmistakable form.

"It was common for temples to have entry chambers depicting the deities' good deeds," Kyan said in a whisper as he stalked up the centre of the chamber, eyes narrowed on the door at the end. Maren stuck to his side, an unimpressed expression moulded onto his face. Nya brought her hand back to her side and trailed after them.

They passed through the opening at the back of the entry chamber and into the temple proper.

Stillness filled the chamber. One of untouched ages passed. It wasn't a tranquil stillness, but the unsettling still of a dark alley at night.

Nya glanced up to where the rock walls rose and opened to a crack of sky. A pool ran the length of the massive chamber floor, stagnant as a mirror reflecting the murky sky above. And seven chain links were spread out around the pool and fed into the water.

Nya peered into the pool. Her head tilted as she realised the water was silver. Or had a silver tint to it, making it more reflective than a normal pool of water. Her sharp reflection stared back. She looked tired, hair a tangle of knot work that made some tapestries look simple in design.

"I wouldn't get too close," Maren said, and Nya wrenched herself away.

"Why? What is it?"

"Ma-atan's resting place," Maren said, then walked on inspecting the murals covering the walls of the temple. Nya peered back into the silvery water but couldn't see anything other than her reflection.

Kyan had wandered off to the side where a staircase cut into the stone led up to a balcony. Nya wandered off after him, not wanting to remain beside the silverwater pool any longer.

As she crested the top step, Nya saw the balcony wrapped around the temple. Stone benches were spaced out evenly, looking onto the chamber below. Kyan ran his hand over the back of the closest bench, smiling.

"Ma-atan's temple was also known as The High Court in ancient times," Kyan said. "They brought individuals here to be Judged by Ma-atan, who would decide if they were good or evil." Kyan stepped around and eased onto the bench, as if afraid the stone would crack.

"So, this was a viewing gallery of sorts?" Nya asked and sat down beside him, trying to imagine how the temple looked thousands of years ago when it was still in use.

"Exactly," Kyan said. "Back when justice was more than twisted courts of backstabbing nobles. Justice meant something then."

"Shall we?" he asked, gesturing to the rest of the balcony.

They ambled their way around the balcony, studying the panels on the walls. The pieces were unlike anything Nya had yet seen. The sweeping lines chiselled into the stone held a beauty, and a certainty of hands well practiced. There was no scuffling around the edges or scratches.

As they wound around the balcony, it became clear that the panels were showing a story or ritual. The first panel depicted someone standing in front of a black box upon an altar. And further around showed Ma-atan rising from the pool, decorative lines all pointing to the deity as it emerged. They reached the far side of the balcony and took the other staircase down to where Maren was studying similar drawings on the walls.

The three of them crossed the chamber in silence, stalking

around the silverwater pool to the base of a raised altar where stone steps led to a dais. They stepped over small channels in the floor leading out from the dais and into the pool. Atop the platform was the undecorated black box. It had an opening at the bottom just large enough to fit a hand in.

Just like the panel carved into the mural, Nya realised.

"Maren?" Kyan flicked his head to the box. "Would you like to do the honour?"

Maren didn't hesitate and climbed the steps while Kyan watched.

"Why is Maren waking it?" Nya asked.

"It's likely it will have some form of weakening for the one who wakes the deity, much like the sandfall at the library. And the Urdahl train their pain threshold and what they can endure as part of their way of life. So it makes sense for him to do it and let me deal with Ma-atan once it has woken," Kyan said.

Maren stood in front of the box. He tried to pick it up to no avail, before bending and peering into the hole.

"What's in it?" Kyan called.

"I can't tell. It's too dark, but I think I'm supposed to put my hand in," Maren said. He exhaled and slid his hand in.

For a moment, nothing happened. Maren held a stoic grace with a hint of curiosity and concentration as he felt around inside the box.

Suddenly, Maren went rigid.

He didn't make a sound, but his body stiffened and veins bulged on his arm. Then Maren shook, his arm going pale.

Kyan opened his mouth to say something when Maren let out a bone chilling scream, causing Kyan and Nya to recoil. The big man howled and squealed like a child. Tears ran down his paling face as he tried to pry his hand free.

Movement caught Nya's eye, and she turned to see blood running down the channels and into the silver pool. Kyan saw it too, a horrified look on his face.

Eventually, Maren stopped screaming as he fell to his knees, his skin a ghostly white. He collapsed, arm coming free as he landed in a heap.

Kyan bolted up the stairs and dropped down beside him, Nya not far behind. "Maren?" Kyan asked, rolling him over. His eyes were open wide, lips blue and shivering, but he was alive.

"Is he going to be okay?" Nya asked.

"I don't know. I've never heard an Urdahl scream before," Kyan said.

Together, they led Maren down and sat him at the side of the chamber. Kyan pulled out his water-skin, holding it to Maren's lips.

What was that? Nya wondered and glanced back at the mural on the wall. The person who stood at the box had *blue* figures. But so did the handful of others at the base of the altar.

"It drained his blood," Nya whispered.

"What's that?" Kyan asked.

"I think it needs more than one person's blood too," Nya said weakly. There were six figures at the base of the altar, seven if you included the one depicted placing a hand in the box.

Just then, voices echoed from the entrance to the temple. The rest of the Decreed had caught up.

Kyan had warned each of those who volunteered, but still people stepped forward for the good of the cause. Their shrill screams made Nya cringe, and several times she had to go for a walk outside to escape their wailing.

Most of the Decreed camped outside the temple with only Kyan's trusted circle in The High Court chamber with him. The Decreed pretended not to hear the petrified screams of those who placed their hands in the box, but most couldn't help flinching and sharing concerned glances.

They had inspected each of those who volunteered after they had their blood drawn, but there was no puncture of the skin that they could make out. Many fainted and needed to be carried from the altar. But even those who didn't lose consciousness didn't speak of what they went through.

The last volunteer went up with the jittery unease of one walking to a hangman's noose. She lifted her shaking hand, pulling it back several times, before forcing it in and slamming her eyes shut. Nya stepped into the entryway chamber. She couldn't watch it again.

Nya waited until the cries had subsided before re-entering. Some of the other Decreed helped the woman, who was staring into the distance, her skin pale like the others.

Kyan passed through the makeshift medic corner, where

they had set up bedding and passed around food and water to those who were drained of blood. He wore an expression of hunger and yearning as the woman's blood ran through the channel and dripped into the silvery pool. It sent subtle ripples careening across the mirror like surface, but nothing yet stirred beneath.

No words were shared among them as they stood at the edge and the last drop of blood hit the pool. Several heartbeats and Kyan met Nya's gaze. As doubt started to itch the back of her mind, a low rumble built, shaking the chamber until it felt like an earthquake. Nya kicked away from the pool, afraid she would topple in. The silverwater trembled and convulsed like it was alive.

Then something broke its surface.

Bone-like spikes wrapped around a grey membranous head inset with two glowing red eyes. The silverwater ran off it as the god rose. Ma-atan. The Harbinger of Justice. The Weigher of Souls.

It stood, metal chains linking it to the sides of the pool. Nya had seen many depictions of Ma-atan, but the real thing made her question everything that led her here. It was terrifying. Nya could do nothing but stare. Faintly, she was aware of a few screaming and running from the chamber.

Ma-atan stood at two stories tall. How it had gotten into the temple was a mystery in itself. Its silver body was encased by spiky bone-like caging. It was long-limbed, its arms, that curved to bladed points, coming all the way to its knees with bone spikes protruding from the skin and pointing out like huge hairs.

Ma-atan took a deep breath and let out a multi-tonal roar. Everyone clasped their ears, shying away from the deafening cacophony of shrieks it produced.

Ma-atan bore down on them. Its lidless red eyes roamed the crowd, washing away the screams and stilling those who thought to run. Terror gripped Nya, not allowing her to look away.

"Ma-atan," Kyan called after clearing his throat. "We're here seeking your guidance. In the ages of your sleep, the unjust have spread like a contamination." Nya watched as the creature stared at Kyan and seemed to be listening.

"We woke you hoping you would balance the scales," Kyan said.

There was a moment of silence. Then it roared again.

"First you can cleanse our ranks, then we will go forth and cleanse the rest of Tarris," Kyan said, his voice getting louder as his confidence grew.

The silverwater still dripped from Ma-atan, filling the quiet. Those who had run for the entrance were tentatively creeping back in, and Kyan waved the Decreed closer until they stood in a loose semicircle around the pool's edge.

"Nya, would you offer yourself onto Ma-atan to be Judged first?" Kyan asked, facing her.

Nya spun, realising she stood forward from the crowd in the centre of a half circle. She gulped back her suddenly dry throat.

This was it then.

Nya knew how she would be Judged. She was born a burden, destroying the young love between her mother and father. Nya had stolen that future from her mother and had sent her into the downward spiral of her condition. Nya had nothing good to leave in the world, she had stolen and scraped by, surviving.

But she had done her best. It just wasn't enough.

Ma-atan would bring revenge and fury to the world that broke her. That was enough.

Nya stepped forward to accept her fate.

47

A Fool's Stance

Kit watched the Sun Eye as it dipped in the sky. He fiddled with the strap of his bag. *Please be okay, Nya,* he thought.

The lover's rock spun, redirecting them whenever they veered off course. Kit knew he had to trust Rai, but the last thing he wanted was to be following this rock around on the black sands of dark hour.

Dust lay sprawled, her leg hanging off the edge of the platform. Uncaring of the life-or-death situation they were in. She let out a contended mew. Kit had been convinced Dust knew what was going on when she growled at Nya for trusting Kyan, but now he wasn't so sure.

Maybe she is just conserving energy? Kit wondered. Dust started snoring.

They had reached the lost capital, Asuriya, and were skirting the edges of the ruined city. It would have been faster to cut across, through some ruins of the outer city but neither made the suggestion. Kit wasn't superstitious, but he had heard enough stories that he didn't want to risk going any closer.

A crater took a chunk out of the ancient capital further in at the Mad Palace, near the epicentre. A section of the palace had been blown apart, like the rumours said. Debris and large parts of the outer wall floated near where it had exploded. There were a lot of theories about how it came to be frozen mid-explosion. Some said Tok, the man who was said to have caused the disaster by killing a god, had held the rock there with his mind so it didn't fall and flatten him. And that he died before he could release it.

Others said the dead god caused it, as it could make anything it touched fly. Kit had seen a good number of people trying to pass rocks off as god-touched from the old capital to earn extra coin. Some going as far as to set up rigging to make it look like the rock was floating. They did not fool Kit. Others weren't as observant.

"Do you think he can do it?" Kit asked.

"Who?" Rai asked.

"Kyan, can he really wake Ma-atan?"

"If anyone can, it would be him," Rai said.

Fax flew ahead, scouting, so they didn't accidentally walk into the Decreed's camp. Except, the shade still hadn't mastered imitating a crow, kicking with its feet rather than flapping its wings.

Kit shuffled up to sit with Rai at the reins. Dust wasn't much for conversation at the moment as she snored.

"How did you know each other? And how did you both end up in the dark place?" Kit asked. He had always assumed they tossed Rai in like Nya and Kit were, but after learning that he knew Kyan, he wasn't so sure anymore.

Rai let some time pass with nothing but the soft, warm wind brushing through them under the shade of their tarp. His face was neutral, and Kit was certain he was deliberating on what to tell him. "We were part of the Seventh Sceptre," he said.

Kit burst out laughing, slapping his leg. He didn't know Rai *could* make jokes. But Kit was pleased he was finally breaking through that broody hardened exterior.

"Oh, you're serious?" Kit asked, glancing at Rai, who didn't crack a smile.

The Seventh Sceptre. Sure there were stories on the streets of the secret sect of seven assassins, but Kit hadn't thought for a second they were true. It was like saying Tok, the boy who killed a god, was seen buying milk at the market. They were phantoms to scare children, not real *people*.

Kit sat a little straighter. "Were you really?" Kit asked, and Rai nodded. "So you worked for the empress herself?"

"Yes, look I don't really want to talk about—"

They are camped up here, Fax said, flying overhead. *Outcroppings are covering them well. If you follow along the valley between the rocks, it will take you to their camp.*

"How far on foot?" Rai asked.

Half an hour if you keep the pace up, Fax said.

"Thanks Fax," Rai said. "We should stow the aya somewhere and go the rest of the way on foot."

Kit wanted to press more about the Seventh Sceptre. *There will be time later*, Kit thought. And if there wasn't, then the Seventh Sceptre would be the least of Kit's worries.

They found a section where the aya would be protected in the shade, and Rai set up a trough of water and food for it. He didn't attach the rein to anything. Kit opened his mouth to say the aya could run off, then shut it again upon realizing that Rai wasn't sure if they were going to make it back. Part of Kit thought that was sweet. Then the other, louder part, half-screamed that he was on the dying side of that equation.

Dust hopped down and stretched like she had woken from a pleasant nap, and together they moved into the valley that led to the temple of Ma-atan.

They heard the camp before they reached it. It was a subdued din compared to the ruckus they made in the cave. That worried Kit. They were a friendly cult, and their quiet couldn't mean anything good.

Hugging the rock, they snuck around until they could see the camp. It was a wide-open area, large enough to house the nearly two hundred Decreed that had set up tents and tarp shades. People passed through camp and sat around drinking and talking in low voices.

An ear rattling scream stole Kit away from watching, and he jerked back against the rock, worried they had been spotted. They listened as the sound seemed to go on forever, but eventually it subsided. "What was *that*?" Kit asked.

"It came from inside the temple," Rai whispered.

Kit poked his head around again. At the far side, pillars were carved into the rock and a tall door led into darkness. The temple of Ma-atan.

"What's the plan?" Kit asked.

Rai kept keen eyes locked on the camp. "Moving through the camp won't be too difficult. A group this large pulled together quickly means no one knows everyone. There are guards at the temple," Rai said. "People are walking in and out, but I don't think everyone will have that freedom of movement."

"Should we go back and see if there is another way in?" Kit asked.

"That could take hours, and given the screams, I think they have already initiated whatever ritual they need to do to wake the damn thing," Rai said. A shiver worked its way up Kit's spine at that.

Please be safe, Nya, Kit thought.

"Fax, think you can check the entrance out?" Rai asked. A black blur darted through the sky like a bird. Kit always wondered how shades could be so different. Fax listened to Rai, and they worked as a team, but Nya and Bom were at odds most of the time.

Fax returned and said, *Things are, for once, in our favour.*

As per Rai's recommendation, they moved separately

502

through the camp to remain inconspicuous. It was possible Kyan had people among the camp watching for the two of them, so moving individually was more nondescript.

Creeping around the rocks, Kit ducked under the tarp at the rim of the camp. Avoiding eye contact, Kit tried to walk casually, but swiftly, towards the temple. Dust wove between his legs, keeping close. He wouldn't have been able to do this back in the caves without being pulled into a circle of song and laughter. Now, though, no one even looked his way. The Decreed had a very different atmosphere since Kit was last with them.

Tarps were set up covering the camp in shade. Crates and barrels of supplies were being used as chairs for the sullen Decreed, who sat in small circles talking quietly. *They must not be staying here for long*, Kit thought. Why else would they be using the crates and not unpacking the long benches they had used in the cave?

Another scream blasted from the temple and Kit had to force himself to keep walking. He still cringed, but so did most who Kit saw. Keeping his head down, Kit reached the far side of the camp near the entrance to the temple where two guards stood watch. Rai was already talking to one of them.

Kit came up behind as if he just happened to also be entering the temple. "—and he requested to speak to me immediately," Rai was saying to a familiar face guarding the temple. Lem.

Lem was wide eyed, and not so subtly nodding along with

the lies. "Well! That all sounds right to me. Best to step aside and let these fine gentlemen inside."

"Wait! We should check with Kyan. He said no one in or out other than the inner circle," the other guard said.

Lem looked to Rai for help, and it took all of Kit's willpower not to shake his head in dismay. The man was not cut out for subterfuge.

"Surely Kyan told you I would be coming," Rai prompted.

"Yes! Kyan told me that this one and that one," Lem said pointing to Kit, "Would be coming."

The other guard didn't look convinced. "Listen, do you want to go in there and question orders when he's busy? I'm sure he would love the distraction," Lem said, raising an eyebrow.

The other guard exhaled and gestured for them to go through. Rai, Kit, and Dust hurried through before they could change their minds. Lem winked as they passed, but luckily the other guard was staring at the camp and didn't notice.

The entry chamber had a handful of the Decreed walking around the pillars, working through the script and imagery that covered them. A woman entered through the door at the back carrying a bundle of bloodied blankets. *That can't be good*, Kit thought.

Rai kept moving, passing into the next chamber. Kit jogged to catch up, slowing once he made it through. A silver pool made up the middle of the chamber, reflecting the dimming sky above. It was hypnotic, almost like a sheet of perfectly reflective silverstone.

A noise from the back of the chamber caught Kit's attention, where two men were helping a third man down from an altar. The poor guy looked like he just spent a night in the desert and was woken by being trampled by a horde of aya.

Nya stood at the base, watching with concern. Kit was about to call to her, when Rai grabbed him by the shoulder and towed him to the side of the chamber. Kit opened his mouth to complain, but one look from Rai and he closed it again. They crept up the staircase to a second level seating area that wrapped around the entire chamber. No one else was up here, so Kit exhaled and slumped against the wall, while Rai snuck up to a pillar to watch what was happening below.

"She's really going through with it," Kit said.

"She's not lost yet. I was right about it being a ritual of some kind, and by her demeanour, Nya doesn't like what's happening either," Rai said.

"That's reassuring," Kit mumbled.

"We need to figure out how to disrupt their ritual," Rai said. "They're bringing a woman to the altar."

Kit crawled over to watch as a woman stepped up to the box on the altar. Everyone in the chamber was watching as she hesitated before stabbing her arm into the hole in the box. A couple of heartbeats later and she began screaming. Kit recoiled, rolling back from the edge, but Rai stayed, watching intently. The screaming waned over time until it cut off completely. These were the guttural screams of one in agony, and they rung around his head flaring a natural instinct to run, even after she fell silent.

"They're bleeding them," Rai said.

"Huh?"

Rai gestured Kit to crawl to the edge again, where he saw a stream of blood wind its way through a channel in the floor and into the silver pool.

"We could block the channel?" Kit offered.

Then the entire temple shook.

The walls rattled, dust trickling from above. A temple that hadn't been looked upon for thousands of years now shook with the ferocity of an earthquake. And the silverwater parted.

Rai met Kit's eyes.

Ma-atan rose from the water. The silvery disproportionate body creaking as it stood. Its armoured body was something from Kit's nightmares. A creature that belonged in stories and song. A creature that shouldn't be able to be out with story and song. As if waking from their trance, screams erupted from around the chamber as people fled for the exit. The shaking settled just for Ma-atan to roar, causing everything to vibrate again before falling silent.

"We're too late," Rai whispered.

Kyan called up, asking him to bring justice to Tarris once again. Kit's heart hammered in his chest. It was like one of his nightmares of being back in the dark place come to life.

"What now?" Kit asked. "You have to have a backup plan, right?"

Rai was staring wide eyed at Ma-atan.

The god roared again.

" — can cleanse our ranks, then we will go forth and cleanse the rest of Tarris," Kyan was saying when Kit uncovered his ears.

The Decreed had started to gather at the feet of the beast like moths to firelight. Some were in awe, others were more cautious, and some looked petrified but forcing their way over anyway. Could they not see the giant, silver deity?

Dust growled at Kit's feet. "I know girl, I know," Kit said, quietly.

Nya stood ahead of the crowd at Kyan's side when he asked, "Nya would you offer yourself onto Ma-atan to be Judged first?"

Kit's heart sank, and he felt sick. He watched and waited for her to turn and run, to scream and shout, or just shake her head. Anything but what she did.

Nya stepped forward.

Kit slid down, ready to leap from the viewing balcony, his body moving before his mind could catch up, when Rai laid a hand on his shoulder. "That's a fool's thought. There's no sense in jumping down there. Stay and we can find a way to stop Ma-atan."

"There's no time," Kit said. "Besides, I find sense is best used sparingly and in small amounts anyway."

With that, Kit leapt from the ledge and into the fray.

48

Justice Catches All

The dark red slit that swam in Ma-atan's glowing eyes fixed on Nya. The Decreed fell silent as she reached the edge of the silverwater pool.

This would end the suffering. This would end the risk of her hurting others, like she had Mother. And no one else could leave her if she left first.

Thoughts fell to Kit and Dust. They would be okay. Better even. They had seen her for what she truly was. Still, it saddened Nya that the last image she had of Dust was her growling and baring her teeth. Not the feel of her fur as she nuzzled in on chilly nights, or the mew she would make to get Nya's attention.

And Mother. Nya wished she could have done more. That it hadn't ended in blood and tears, but she would be with her again soon enough.

Nya took a deep breath. The swish of the silverwater echoed around the temple as Ma-atan moved towards her. Its long-bladed arms trailing over the surface, sending out ripples across the serene plane.

Bom didn't react. Nya had expected something, anything, but it lay dormant. Perhaps it didn't understand death. It was a shade from another world, ancient and ageless from what she had gathered. Then again, did anyone understand death? The irreversible finality of it made it unknowable.

Nya closed her eyes.

A voice, a quiet voice, shouted that this was wrong.

The voice got louder until it screamed, "Nya!"

Nya's eyes shot open, and she spun to see Kit and Dust standing across the chamber from them.

They had come for her. After everything they had come for her.

They all leave in the end.

Her mother's words but it wasn't true. She had nothing to offer them but they came anyway.

A swish of air as Ma-atan drove its bladed arm for her heart. Time slowed for Nya. She felt like she stood at a precipice, wavering on the edge. Her body jolted as if she had swayed over the fall before pulling back. She wanted to live. The primal instinct ringing out like a bell breathing new life into her limbs.

Nya didn't know what was left for her in this world, but she wouldn't face it alone. And she wouldn't leave Kit and

Dust face it alone either.

If death was as unknowable as the future why wouldn't she bet on those she loved?

Bom flared with a ripple of shadow blasting out from around Nya deflecting Ma-atan's incoming attack.

"Nya?" Kyan whispered.

Nya broke into a run, shoving her way through the Decreed. Bom shot out, cracking the two men reaching for Kit across the face. She skidded to a stop beside her friends. Dust nuzzled her ankles. Kit nodded to her, a smile twisting the corner of his lips. No words passed between them. None were needed. Just having them there was enough.

Kyan ran his tongue over his teeth, then made a smacking sound. "Very well," he said, quietly. "Unchain Ma-atan. Justice catches all."

A handful of Decreed scattered around the silverwater pool.

Thump.

Rai landed in front of Nya. "Kyan, those chains are in place for a reason. Did you not see the murals? This is no temple," Rai said.

"It's a prison," Kyan replied. "Yes, I know Akarai. Humans of the past seemed to have the same weaknesses as those of today. You cannot cage justice."

Nya felt a chill. Suddenly, Nya realized that the lines on the murals she had thought were light rays actually symbolized chains. She had almost been a part of freeing this creature. It was one thing waking an ancient god from its slumber, but to free a deity their ancestors had purposefully chained and imprisoned was another.

"Kyan, don't do this," Rai said.

"I'm afraid there is no stopping what's to come," Kyan said, and fell into a fighting stance, his shade permeating outward.

Kit slid his hands in Nya's.

And chaos erupted across the chamber.

Rai and Kyan launched at each other, clashing with a burst of shadow. Their shades battering against one another. Some of the Decreed stared in awe, others backed off, unsure.

Kit turned to her. "Nya... I—"

"Kit, we need to keep them from freeing Ma-atan," Nya said, cutting him off and flicking her head at the Decreed. She didn't want to talk right now. He hesitated before nodding and sprinting to the right-hand side of the pool.

Nya bounded through the Decreed. There were two chains nearby. "Bom, do you think you—"

Without further prompting, Bom dashed to one chain, slamming against the unsuspecting Decreed attempting to pry it free.

The Decreed was too focused on unwinding the bolt that he didn't see Nya approach until her boot connected with his face. He tumbled back, eyes rolling. A fist flew at her as she turned. Nya's arm slammed up, parrying the attack, then she darted her other arm out, smacking the man across the nose.

I guess Rai's drills stuck, Nya thought in surprise as the second man tripped back. It was lucky that most of the

Decreed were followers Kyan picked up on the streets and not trained guards. She wasn't sure her weeks of training would hold up against someone who knew what they were doing.

Above them, two black blurs shot around the chamber. Rai crashed into the stone, sending pellets of rock raining down on those below. He grunted before Fax threw him back into the fight.

Ma-atan watched the two as Decreed scuttled around its feet preparing to free the deity.

Another batch of Decreed charged at the chains and Nya readied herself. Two stalked towards her, cautious after spotting their fallen comrades at her feet. They fanned out around her. Nya stepped back, her foot scraping off the edge of the silverwater pool. She had little room for fighting. A quick glance showed Bom snapping at some Decreed who were attempting to get to another chain.

The glance cost her as the first man swept in, throwing a punch. Nya's vision blurred and wavered as she toppled back over the chain at her feet. She landed hard, hitting her head on the ground.

"Stay down, girl," one said, standing over her as the other yanked at the chain.

Nya's vision steadied and she tried to push herself to her feet.

"I said stay down!" the Decreed man shouted.

"Why would they chain a god? How could chains hold a god?" Nya said, between groans.

It was the promise of taking the pain away and trusting

in a greater power that had led her down this path. But this wasn't a greater power. A greater power wouldn't be chained. A greater power *couldn't* be chained.

Kit tackled the woman trying to free the false god. The man spun, giving Nya an opening to charge him. They rolled, his heavier weight pinning her down. He forced Nya's arms out, holding them in place and grinned with satisfaction.

Nya spat in his eyes, then head butted the man on the nose with a *crack*. That one, she had learnt on the streets. Not from Rai. The man howled, letting go of her arms and grasping his nose. Nya swung her arm around, smacking him in the temple, and he collapsed to the side.

The woman had been knocked out by the time Nya turned back. However, with a creaking groan, the chain ripped from its shackle and fell into the silverwater pool with a splash.

"I'm sorry. I was too late," Kit said, as he grabbed Nya, hauling her to her feet.

Six of the seven chains were loosed.

Bom was protecting the last one, but a wall of Decreed approached, wrapping around Bom. It wouldn't be able to fend them all off. Not when she told it not to kill anyone.

"We need to defend the last chain," Nya said, her words slurring. She blinked away stars.

"You okay?" he asked.

"Yeah, I just hit my head," Nya replied.

"Maybe you should sit this out," Kit said.

"No, I'm fine. Come on," Nya said, and together they ran for their last thread of hope.

Nya battered into the first Decreed's back, throwing her weight against him. Kit punched someone and pushed past another, until they both stood between the six Decreed and the last chain. The only thing holding back an ageless deity from running rampant across Tarris.

Bom slid back into Nya's shadow and she grinned, feeling the presence and power return. Two ran at Nya. Bom darted at one like a spear, snapping their head back, while Nya stepped out of reach of a sword before sweeping back in, and kicking the Decreed in the knee. He squealed, falling. Then Bom flicked back around cracking across his face and he crumpled to the ground.

Nya spun around, narrowly ducking under a spear, thanks to a warning from Bom, who sling-shotted back and swept the woman off her feet.

Kit took a hit to the face and stumbled back. Nya flared with anger and concern, causing Bom to shoot across and spear through the responsible man's chest. He looked down, wide-eyed as blood poured from his torso. Nya's hand clasped around her mouth. She hadn't meant to kill him, but the intent she had unintentionally sent to Bom certainly felt like she had meant to. Rai had warned her shades fed off and enhanced their every thought.

Something cracked into the back of her head, and suddenly Nya was face-down on the cool ground. She tried to move, but someone was holding her.

Nya managed to turn her head and spat out a clump of blood and saliva.

Rai and Kyan fought on, throwing each other around the chamber. Another spearman forced Kit back. And ahead, a woman frantically worked the bolt free on the last chain.

Nya's breath caught.

Ma-atan watched as it fell. The clang of metal hitting stone rang out like a chime from the war bell towers. Then a roar tore through the din as Ma-atan strained against the last chain. And with a *kachunk*, it wrenched loose.

Ma-atan was free.

49

The Eye of the Victor

Unnatural speed whipped at Rai as he catapulted into Kyan, kicking him in the chest, and sending him crashing into the dais. Kyan's shade made to cut Rai down, but Fax deflected its strikes.

"Please, Kyan. Listen to reason," Rai said.

Kyan dragged himself to his feet, groaning. "Everything I do has a base of reason, Rai. Just because you don't see it does not mean it's not there. Just because you follow different reasoning, doesn't make mine wrong," he said, unsheathing his daggers.

Rai sighed and slid out his own daggers. Darkness enveloped them as their shades battled in the shadows.

Kyan lunged at Rai, lashing his blades in a precise set of movements that were adapted from an ancient style of blade work. Rai knocked away the predictable moves, but this blinded Rai with expectation, and Kyan subverted key motions at the last second, to land some blows.

Rai flipped the blade in his hand and cut the outside of Kyan's forearm. He grunted, smacking Rai's arm away and jumped back. Kyan inspected the blood running down his arm. Rai felt his own gashes running red, but he made a show of not looking at them.

Their shades radiated from them like auras.

"How can you trust that Ma-atan's sense of justice is right for Tarris now? Or that it ever was?" Rai called.

"There has to be a sense of right and wrong above everything, Rai, or the world is chaos," Kyan said, flicking his arm down, a splash of blood splattering onto the ground.

"Justice is in the eye of the victor, Kyan," Rai said.

"No, that's what victors want to believe, but they can still be wrong. They can still be Judged poorly for their choices," Kyan said.

"It's not that simple. There isn't always a right and wrong," Rai said.

"There has to be Rai." Kyan's voice trembled. "We killed so many. Woman and children. They didn't deserve to die. We listened to orders and killed whoever they pointed us at," Kyan said, his shoulders slumping.

So that's what this was about. Rai couldn't blame him. Those days haunted his nights as well. "I need to know if we were wrong for not questioning it. Should we have done more and not followed the orders blindly?"

"We did what they commanded us to do. The blood we spilled would have been drawn by our blade or another's," Rai said.

"Do you truly believe that?" Kyan asked. "I sure don't."

Kyan barrelled forward in a shadowed blur. Fax braced Rai, the impact launching them into the second level viewing gallery. They burst through a stone bench before coming to a stop. Rai coughed, waving away the dust as Kyan's shade lifted him onto the walkway.

"Don't you want to know?" Kyan asked.

"If some dusty old creature thinks what I did to survive was worthy?" Rai asked. "No, I'll continue to do what I see is right, and hope I leave this world having done more good than not."

Fax burst into a flurry of tendrils darting at Kyan. His shade threw up a swirling black wall and Fax bounced off it.

By the time Kyan brought down the wall, Rai had sprinted at him and was in reaching distance. He cracked Kyan across the face with the butt of his dagger. Kyan reacted quickly, blasting out a wave of darkness that knocked Rai back, letting him reorient.

"Doesn't it scare you?" Kyan asked and blew a clump of blood out his nose. "Being sent to one of the seven torment realms?"

"Come Duat or the peaceful reed fields of Aru, I'll be there with you, Kyan," Rai said.

"I can't keep getting up in the morning pretending we didn't slaughter all those people, Akarai," Kyan said, not meeting Rai's gaze.

A snap drew their attention as Ma-atan yanked the last chain, ripping it free.

It roared, body trembling. Rai could have sworn he saw ripples in the air caused by the creatures' shout. Rai covered his ears, but they still rung long after Ma-atan quietened.

The chamber stood still, all eyes falling on the deity. Then it drove its arm through the closest Decreed's chest and ripped out his heart. Ma-atan held the heart before popping it like soft fruit.

Screaming rang anew as the Decreed scattered like sand foxes in an alley.

"You were always the best among us. You questioned everything, and the fact that the guilt has gnawed at you speaks of your character," Rai said, eyes fixed on the devastation. "And I'm sorry I wasn't there for you. I didn't see your struggles."

Kyan stared at him for a moment before turning back to watch Ma-atan rip apart his followers. "It's killing them all," Kyan whispered. "That was Hir. I was sure he was a good man. This isn't right."

"No, it isn't," Rai said.

Kyan flinched as Ma-atan plunged his bladed arm through another of his Decreed's chests. Rai watched as his friend's face fell. With each Decreed killed, the light in his eyes dwindled. Realisation spreading like a storm. When hunting for blood, all are stained red.

Rai knew all too well, when raising a blade, even for a

noble cause, blood is spilled.

"I thought... I thought I could fix what we did," Kyan said. "All I've done is bring more to death's door. These people don't deserve this. I was a fool to think I could be deemed just. I knew the answer but didn't want to face it."

Ma-atan descended on those who put their hands in the black box. Killing each of them indiscriminately.

Kyan's face hardened. "We will be sent to the torment realms. There's no making right what we did. But I can stop this."

Kyan jumped from the ledge. His shade formed a glider, and together they swept down and grabbed one of the Decreed as Ma-atan's blade thrust into the ground.

Rai threw himself into the chamber below. Fax caught him, setting him gently on the ground before he dashed after Kyan.

Ma-atan screamed at Kyan for snatching his prey, then swept at him, sending the two hurtling across the ground.

The deity drove his bladed arm down on Kyan. Fax parried the attack as Rai slid to a stop beside Kyan and pulled him to his feet.

"We need to protect the Decreed," Kyan said. "Please Rai, help me protect them. It's my fault they're here."

Rai nodded. "Fan out. We can't cover the whole area if we are together."

They split up. Rai ran for the far side of the pool, battering away any attempt Ma-atan made on the fleeing Decreed. Fax flicked out knocking Decreed out the way of Ma-atan's strikes.

The creature screamed in frustration and swiped at Rai

sending him flying back into the wall.

Rai's vision wavered as he cracked into the stone.

The temple blurred and softened as unconsciousness threatened.

Ma-atan stabbed through more of the Decreed now that only Kyan was able to protect them. Rai hissed dragging himself to his feet.

Kyan frantically darted back and forth trying to save everyone as Ma-atan strategically chose its targets far apart from one another. He had always tried to save everyone. Rai tried to shout to Kyan and warn him that it was wearing him down. But all that came out was a hoarse mumble.

The last of the Decreed fled the temple. Finally Ma-atan was done playing with its prey and turned to Kyan, striking him with the flat of its bladed arm.

Kyan was sent rolling before coming to a stop on his back.

Rai staggered towards him.

The last light of the Sun Eye twinkled on a tear budding in Kyan's eye when Ma-atan stabbed his chest. He hadn't attempted to roll out the way. Rai stopped short, watching in horror as Ma-atan inspected his friend's heart. Rai held his breath for what felt like an age as it rolled the heart around between its fingers, then squeezed it until the heart burst.

Kyan's eyes widened as if he'd been run through with a sword, then softened to the unseeing glaze Rai was all too familiar with. Rai dropped to his knees.

He breathed hard as memories flashed in his mind. The smell of sweat and feel of the Sun at the training grounds. The glint in Kyan's eye when he finally scored a hit on Rai. Kyan slumped over dusty books and scrolls, having fallen asleep in the late hours.

Death had twisted him. Like a lone plant in the desert, Kyan had wilted. Rai should have been there. He should have been there to shield and guide him. But he had been running around Tarris playing at being a scholar.

Fax returned and fed on Rai's anger. Fed on his unfettered rage.

I should have been there.

Rai stood, shadow convulsing from him like a living aura.

Rai exhaled. He swallowed the swell of emotion roiling in his gut, leaving nothing but fury. A tear streaked down his cheek as he looked at Kyan. But that was all he allowed himself. Now was no time to grieve.

Fax readied, then tossed Rai at Ma-atan.

Hands at his side, Rai hit Ma-atan in the face, feet first, like a hammer. Then, as he fell back, Fax grabbed him again and dropped him on Ma-atan's shoulder. It turned to face them as Rai and Fax burst into an onslaught of attacks.

Ma-atan didn't show emotion, but the blows were causing pain if the growling at the back of its throat was anything to go by. Fax drove blades into its neck as Rai pulled the spikes wrapping around its face. It howled and flicked its head to the side, tossing Rai off.

He shot across the chamber, Fax sweeping in to grab him. "Thanks Fax," Rai said as they flew back at Ma-atan. On sweeping past, Rai saw his wrenching had loosened some of the spikes caging its face.

Ma-atan swiped at them, but Fax dove and arced around his swings, then hurled Rai back at its shoulder.

Fax flew around Ma-atan's head, diving in to stab and slice, distracting Ma-atan so Rai could clamber back up the rest of the way. Cresting onto the shoulder, Rai ran at its face, jumping on one of the loose spikes. It cracked and came loose.

Ma-atan let out an ear-shattering squeal that almost sent Rai spinning. Regaining his footing, Rai unsheathed his daggers and thrust into the gap.

Ma-atan screamed so hard Rai had to shield his ears in fear they would burst.

Looks like we found a weak spot, Fax said.

50

The Scream That Stilled a God

"Next time you have a bright idea like waking a sleeping god, at least tell me where you are going so I can come with backup," Kit said, pulling Nya to her feet. Her vision swam, but it was coming back slowly. Around them was a scene from the old scripts. Bodies littered the floor as a deity bore down on them.

"Don't take this the wrong way, but I'm not sure how much backup you're going to be against that," Nya said.

"Oh, I didn't mean me. He's the backup." Kit gestured to behind Nya.

Spinning around, Nya watched, mouth agape as Rai *fought* Ma-atan. He and Fax darted about its head with swift and deadly coordination. They moved as one as they shot about, constantly readjusting to whatever move Ma-atan made.

However, the damage Rai and Fax were doing seemed to annoy Ma-atan more than hurt it. They were like tiny insects buzzing around, and cutting at a god.

Nya caught a glint of steel swinging wildly at Ma-atan's side. "The chains," Nya whispered.

"What?" Kit asked.

"We need to reattach the chains," Nya said. The metal chains flopped around the floor like fish out of water, but the chamber was empty of Decreed, and those who had broken Ma-atan's bonds were no longer there to guard them.

"If we reattach the chains, we might be able to force it back into the silverwater," Nya said.

Kit squinted. "Okay, let's do it."

Nya cracked her neck, and together they sprinted across the chamber.

The temple was like a battlefield. Stray bursts of flames that Rai threw exploded around them, along with Ma-atan's wandering feet cracking and shattering the stone it stood on, throwing up pellets of rocks. They ducked under Ma-atan's swinging arm, hopped over dead bodies, and veered around Rai as Ma-atan flung him across the room. The putrid scent of death mixed with the metallic tang of pooling blood.

They reached the chains made of a metal like substance, not unlike the silverwater itself. They broke off, Nya skirting around to the furthest chain, Kit grabbing the next one down.

The chain rolled and roiled, the last link an open clasp. If she pulled that clasp back over to the ring affixed to the ground she could reattach it. Nya scooped up the end and *heaved.* Dust jumped from behind and bit the chain, hauling it in the same direction as Nya. She strained stretching it towards its mark, but it was no use.

Kit was having the same problem.

Rai and Fax flitted about around the god. She needed to indicate to Rai to bring Ma-atan further back somehow. "Bom, can you ask Rai to get Ma-atan to move closer to us?" Nya asked.

Bom shot off towards them. A moment later Ma-atan was stepping backwards, closing in on the rings. With renewed vigour, Nya yanked the chain, dragging it from the silverwater. Dust snarled, tugging at the chain too.

A little closer... There!

Nya slammed the chain link down and it connected with a satisfying *snap.*

It was a loud snap. Too loud.

Ma-atan spun, only now noticing the three of them reconnecting its bonds. It roared, and ignoring Rai, thrusted its bladed arms at Nya. She rolled to the side, feeling the whistle of the attack as it slid past her. Rai threw a plume of flame at its face that allowed Nya to get further out of reach.

Kit was still heaving his chain to the other link. It was inching closer, but Ma-atan knew what they were doing now.

Ma-atan swatted Rai and Fax, sending them flying in the opposite direction, and pivoted around to Kit.

"Kit! Run!" Nya called.

Veins popped on his forehead, his face a red, sweat matted, contortion. Ma-atan reached for Kit, giving him the slack of the chain needed to click it into place. But the win was short lived as Ma-atan rammed his hand through Kit's chest.

Nya screamed.

Ma-atan pulled Kit's pumping heart free and brought it up to its face to inspect. After a breath, Ma-atan drove the heart back into Kit and he collapsed, motionless.

Everything slowed. Nya watched, waiting to see the rise and fall of Kit's chest that would never come again. He didn't stir.

Darkness exploded from Nya as she let out a scream that stilled a god.

A storm of shadow filled the temple. A dark wind buffeted the chamber emanating from Nya. But the black wasn't coming from Bom.

She felt it now, a connection to the place with the ever-storming sky. Dark veins snaked through shadow back to the tear, back to the dark place, tying Nya to it. The dark flooded through her from that other world like she was a gateway.

Nya could *feel* what was in the shadowed wind. She could feel Rai moving towards the chains. And someone else. Lem. He was in the dark wind too, helping Rai fix the chains. Ma-atan had fallen still and made no move to stop them.

Hushed words carried on the black wind. Indistinct chatter hissing in her ear. Then something in dark saw her. Nya felt it the same way she felt Bom, a pricking at the back of her neck, a presence with its attention on her.

I see you.

The words rang in her head as a deafening whisper.

The endless tempest that threatened to consume her was coming from that voice. And now it saw her. Nya wanted to step away from it but it was all around her in the dark. She couldn't stop it. The darkness was draining everything from her.

Click. The last chain fixed back into place.

An exhaustion took over then and the black winds subsided. And everything went dark.

Rai panted, sitting at the edge of the silverwater pool. They had done it. Ma-atan was imprisoned once more.

Lem had run over to Nya and Kit. Rai should go over and check on them. Nya had fainted and Kit had his heart torn out his chest then shoved back in.

But Rai was shaken. He could still feel the power and thrumming energy that had flooded the temple from Nya. He could have sworn that something was in that black wind.

Darkness had swirled around him as they reattached the chains. Fax didn't respond to him when he was in the storm. It seemed to be in some trance that didn't cut out until Nya collapsed and the dark dissipated.

Rai looked up at Ma-atan. The Harbinger of Justice bent on one knee, head bowed. The deity hadn't tried to stop Rai or Lem as they reconnected the last of its bonds. Instead, bowing like one would to an emperor. Had it felt the presence too?

Fax had slunk back in Rai's mind and refused to produce any sort of explanation. But they had been together long enough that Rai could feel its confusion.

And its fear.

51

A New Watch

Rays of light broke through the cracks in the shutters of The Patched Cloak, creating a scattering of light beams in the common room. Dust's legs shook as she sent them out long, stretching, in a spot of Sun.

Nya leant over the bar studying Illy as she made a pot of coffee. She poured the bubbling water over the filter paper, then dumped the ground coffee beans on top, and filled the filter paper with water, letting it run through into the pot below.

"Then you just leave it to drip through," Illy said with a smile.

Nya nodded and Illy set off to make breakfast. Swivelling around in her seat, Nya spotted Kit and Wenson setting up a booth with bowls of bread and meat.

When Nya awoke in the temple, Kit had been there, seeing to her. But although he acted like nothing was wrong, and there was no mark on his chest where Ma-atan had torn into it, Kit no longer had a heartbeat.

Nya begged him to go and see a doctor, but both Kit and Rai had decided that going to a doctor would be a mistake. Tarris was a superstitious place and showing up without a heartbeat would only cause suspicion, rumour, and a mob with torches to appear at their doorstep.

Kit brushed it off claiming to be fine, and joked that some thought he never had a heart in the first place.

When Nya approached Rai, he promised to look into it, but he wasn't the same either after Kyan's death. Further closing himself off and stepping back from everyone. It wasn't long after they returned that he announced that he would be leaving.

The Sun Eye had not long begun its watch that morning. Pink and golden early morning light painted the sky in vibrant colour, and the Sun burned away any dampness from the cool night. It was the beginning of a new day.

Rai looked out across the city of Yontar atop The Patched Cloak's rooftop, and Nya stepped up to join him.

"You're leaving," Nya guessed. Rai hadn't been the same since the temple. She could see Kyan's death weighing heavily on him. He probably would have left earlier but stayed to ensure the Decreed had broken up after the death of their leaders.

He nodded. "The threat has passed. I've sent word to the

empress about Ma-atan's temple. It will be guarded now so no others can try and free it."

"And what about the," Nya searched for the right word, "You know." She had told Rai about the thing in the dark watching her. *I see you.* Its words still burned into her mind.

"I was ignorant. I thought this didn't affect anyone else. I didn't know there were more shades in Tarris. But after meeting you and Kyan," his voiced softened when he said his name, "I have to do more. I can't research this by myself. It's bigger than me and Fax."

Nya understood the feeling. She had thought she was alone, the only one with a shade. It made her not want to reach out, or say anything, in fear that she wouldn't be understood.

"Seven of us went in that day. I thought me and one other survived. But if Kyan survived, some of the rest could have too."

"You're saying there could be more highly trained killers with shades roaming around Tarris?" Nya asked.

"Possibly as many as four. I saw Sehban die, but any of the others could have made it out like I did. Kyan was young and impulsive. The others, though, were more meticulous. They could be out there doing who knows what," Rai said.

"I'm coming," Nya said.

"No. You have to look after Kit," Rai said.

Nya grimaced. Kit had survived the Judging. His skin had paled and his heart hadn't started beating again, but he was alive. For now.

"You'll be safer here," Rai said. "Stay. Live a normal life."

Nya's shadow flickered the way Rai liked to do. Rai smiled. A rare sight.

Nya no longer worried about Bom lashing out. Between Rai and Kyan's training she understood it better now and could manage the emotional fluctuations.

"As normal as one with a shade, and one who has died and come back to life can live," Rai said.

"Will you come back?" Nya asked.

"I hope so," Rai replied.

He will, even if I have to drag him here myself, Fax said, sliding out his shadow, eliciting a sigh from Rai. Nya was a bit jealous of the relationship between Rai and Fax when she and Bom were so distant. But Rai had been with Fax for five years, so maybe Bom would open up with time.

People scuttled about the city of Yontar, going about their business before the worst of the heat. Could Nya go back to living a normal life? Had she ever lived a normal life? What did a normal life look like?

Nya didn't know, but she had people at her side now. And nights can be dark when there is a promise of dawn.

Epilogue

Mirt threw back the last of his coffee. It was another late one. He was the last one in the chamber above the black tear, as he often was. Mirt leaned over a stone desk covered in scattered pages.

Pushing aside the parchment to reveal more notes, Mirt ran his tongue over his teeth.

They started calling the tear the pocket world. *A whole other world hidden within it*, Mirt thought in awe. They still had no idea where or what it really was. But the notes the recovery party retrieved held some promising research.

They had caught and dissected one of the husks, revealing that it had a similar anatomy to humans. Their ears were more complicated, leading researchers to believe they had much stronger hearing, whereas their eyes were more sensitive to light than a humans. Which made sense when they gathered in caves and dark caverns, only surfacing when they heard the promise of food. This would be helpful information for future expeditions into the pocket world.

They had found other creatures large and small there, too. New species mainly, but again, similar to some they had in Tarris. They documented all they found and had accumulated over twenty different species.

Mirt had been part of the team studying the tear from the beginning. Five and a bit years and they still understood so little. Mirt threw down his notes and sighed. He had pored over these a hundred times since their return. He was so sure they held secrets if he could just *see* them.

Bunching the papers, Mirt tapped them on the desk to straighten the edges, then piled them neatly in the corner. He patted his pockets, ensuring he had his journal and other trinkets, then made for the door. He hesitated, turning back to look at the staircase leading down. A quick glance told him the guards at the door were the night shift pair. They often changed over and didn't announce themselves or come to speak to him.

Mirt spun on his heels and headed down the steps. The descent was a lot easier than the ascent, Mirt thought, clomping down the last of the steps and into the chamber at the bottom.

The tear stared at him from the back of the room. It drank in the surrounding light. That had been one of the first things they tested before daring to get too close. Flames grew darker and desaturated the closer they were to it, but not just that, it pulled at the flames, making them bend towards it like a hungry maw.

"I'm back," Mirt said, walking up to it. The tear was comforting, a warm presence in cool, late nights. The tear had become something more to Mirt. A presence. If he was being truthful with himself, Mirt had spent more time talking to the tear than with real people over the last couple of years.

"We will be sending another research team in soon," Mirt said. "If you could grace them with safe passage, I would be grateful." He had said that with the last research team, and he heard in great detail what had happened to them, but it was worth asking again.

They left no furniture or objects in the chamber, so Mirt slid to the floor, back against the wall. He let out a contented sigh. The impenetrable blackness gave no indication of the world beyond it. Mirt didn't know anything that was that deep a black. It was mesmerising. Like looking into infinity.

"I will figure you out," Mirt said. "The others fear you, but I don't. I want to see you and all your beauty be shared with the world."

And, unlike it had ever done before, the tear spoke back.

Andrew Watson

ABOUT THE AUTHOR

Andrew Watson lives on the outskirts of Edinburgh where he rambles about made up people and places. He has a first class degree in Digital Media from Edinburgh Napier University and currently works as a freelance video editor and author. Andrew can also be found on YouTube and Instagram where he jumps around excitedly shouting about books.

Follow Andrew at:
andrew-watson.co.uk
@the_fools_tale

Printed in the USA
CPSIA information can be obtained
at www.ICGtesting.com
LVHW041739260823
756387LV00003B/487

9 781739 340018